Over the Precipice

Book 2 of the Precipice Series

Over the Precipice

Book 2 of the Precipice Series

CHARLIE MIKE ADKINS

Over the Precipice
Book 2 of the Precipice Series
by Charlie Mike Adkins

Copyright © 2025 Charlie Mike Adkins

ISBN 978-1-956904-38-3

Printed in the United States of America

Published by Blacksmith Publishing LLC
Fayetteville, North Carolina

www.BlacksmithPublishing.com

Direct inquiries and/or orders to the above web address.

Acknowledgements

Thanks to my family for your continued support and love!

On this project, the second book in the series, I collaborated with several people for their expertise, and I appreciate every one of you!

I would like to thank my dad, Emmitt Adkins, for offering his expertise on the life of the American truck driver. I suspect that many people don't realize how important truck drivers are to maintaining the American way of life. I appreciate all truck drivers, but I do have my favorite (retired) truck driver. Thanks, Dad!

My stepmother Dolores Adkins used her years of experience as an educator to step in as final editor. Her attention to detail has highlighted what a knuckle-dragger I am. I am grateful for her hours of work and her impact on the series can't be overstated.

My cousin, Kenneth Glover, helped me provide realism to the law enforcement procedures in the book. He has selflessly served his community for most of his adult life and continues to serve.

I also want to thank my brother, Matt Adkins. He's a paramedic and offered a real world look into what they face. He helped me color between the lines on what a paramedic would or wouldn't do. Matt continues to serve his community as a paramedic.

I want to thank my long-time friend and shooting buddy, Shawn Christian. He jumped in on this project, proofreading and giving me constant feedback as I was writing. I was always able to count on him for an unfiltered opinion. I think we could all use more of that in our lives.

Finally, to you, the reader. Without you, I wouldn't be able to continue doing this. I write in the genre that I enjoy. I hope the story stimulates thought. This is just a work of fiction, but there are aspects of it that I hope hit close to home. Stay safe.

Contents

Prologue x

Chapter

1 – Let's Shoot It Again 1
2 – A Completely Different Reason 11
3 – Fear Where You Live 23
4 – Hearts and Minds 41
5 – Buyin' Girl Stuff 53
6 – The Collective, Part I 67
7 – Getting Ready for a Hurricane 73
8 – Radio Check, Over 81
9 – I'm Talking to You! 93
10 – I Love Lucy 99
11 – Ambush in De Bagh Khola Pass 105
12 – The Collective, Part II 121
13 – I've Got a Bleeder 129
14 – Don't Bring a Pipe to a Gunfight 145
15 – That Looks Like a Grave 155
16 – I Need to Get Home to Edna 161
17 – Flat Screens 100% Off 171
18 – Death to America 183
19 – What Are They Planning Next? 195
20 – The Creature from Jekyll Island 207
21 – Watch Out for Deer 219
22 – The White House and Their Zionist Lapdogs ... 229
23 – I'm Rolling Heavy 233
24 – We've Got a Plan 245

25 – The Funniest Thing They'd Ever Seen 261

26 – I'm Not Stopping 271

27 – Well, That Sucked 283

28 – The Cylinder Was Empty 289

29 – Here We Go Again 305

30 – He Showed Mercy 317

31 – We're Gonna Need Another Trip 329

32 – The Nickel Tour 339

33 – Lookin' for Volunteers 351

34 – Screw This. I'm Outta Here 367

35 – Freakin' Deer 377

36 – We've Got Work to Do 387

37 – The Collective, Part III 397

38 – We're in this for the Long Haul 407

Epilogue 419

Appendix: Gear in the Precipice Series 421

PROLOGUE

Paul Michaels was a retired US Army Green Beret living with his family in rural West Virginia. During his time in the army, he had been deployed to numerous countries around the world, including several combat deployments to Afghanistan. Now, following his retirement, he was just trying to live a comfortable life on his 100-acre homestead with his wife and daughter. Paul had numerous hobbies. His wife, Sandy, had joked with him that when he left the fast-paced life of Special Forces he would need a hobby, and she had been right. A lifetime of gun collecting had provided him with the tools to continue his recreational shooting. Another hobby was reloading ammunition, which supported his other pastime. However, his most expensive 'hobby' was prepping. He enjoyed the comfortable feeling of being able to take care of himself and his family. He even coached others who were interested in being more self-sufficient.

As Paul watched the world unravel, he became more and more certain that his years of preparation and his extensive training would become crucial in the coming times. Only a few years before, he had watched the disastrous American withdrawal from Afghanistan. Now, America seemed to be inching closer and closer to getting right back into another war, potentially a world war. The American southern border was still wide open with millions of people crossing illegally into the country in the past three years. No one really knew how many illegal immigrants had made the crossing. However, the estimates ranged from seven million to eleven million, depending on which news agency was reporting on it. The exact number didn't matter to him. He saw the writing on the wall. If even a small percentage of this group had bad intentions, it could be disastrous.

With this in mind, Paul, his wife Sandy, and their sixteen-year-old daughter, McKinley, worked to prepare themselves, their home, and those they cared about for the unknown. Sandy was supportive of Paul's preparations and had come to embrace the efforts herself. Paul did his best to make things fun. He would use a camping trip to reinforce primitive skills such as gathering water or building fires. Sometimes, during hunting season, he would take his daughter along to hunt squirrels or deer. Sandy didn't participate in the hunting, but she was an artist in the kitchen and would prepare fantastic meals with the harvested game.

However, the family didn't consider wild game to be their primary plan for protein in a long-term emergency. The region around their home was teeming with game, but it was also home to a very resilient people whose culture still included hunting. In the recent decades, at the national scale, hunting was become less and less common. However, in rural Appalachia, it was just a part of life. So even though there was plenty of game, Paul also knew that nearly every home in the county had a deer rifle, and in most cases, probably several. His opinion was that the plentiful deer, squirrel, rabbit, and turkey populations would not be able to keep up with a starving population if it ever came to that. This problem would be magnified if the emergency situation also included a loss of power, and therefore refrigeration. With this in mind, he and his little family raised chickens, rabbits, and a garden.

Paul always taught others that you should prep what you eat and eat what you prep. This mindset drove what type of food they stored. When Paul helped others get into prepping, he would explain that if you never eat rice or dried beans, but those are your only food stores, you'll have a hard time transitioning to that in an emergency.

The same principle could be applied to any class of supplies. For example, he meticulously documented every battery they used in the household and that was the types of batteries he kept in storage. He would always keep a few of the other types, but he didn't maintain any significant number of those in storage. New battery technology aided in this effort, with increased advertised shelf lives as high as ten years.

When he was trying to encourage his friends and family to take precautions, he would explain that being prepared didn't mean that you thought Zombies were coming. It was simply a way of dealing with anything that interrupted your normal day to day life. For example, a power outage, an automobile accident that locked you up in traffic, or something more dramatic like the COVID scare that had swept across the globe. Of course, he also tried to prepare for more dramatic events such as an electromagnetic pulse, foreign invasion, or an economic disaster. Generally speaking, most preppers were preparing for *something*. That *something* varied from person to person. Everyone had their own opinion. Paul tried to base his ideas on his own observations of what was happening around him and on historical examples.

The United States was experiencing unprecedented inflation, so of course that became a factor in everyone's daily financial decisions. Everyone was feeling the pressure from the weakened purchasing power of the U.S. Dollar. Paul had seen other countries around the world fall into economic despair. This experience affected his opinions because he had seen it firsthand, and he viewed that as the most likely scenario he and his family would have to face.

He had also experienced a long-term power outage as the result of a dramatic ice storm. Hey had lost electrical power for eighteen days. His rural location was low on the list for the power company to get to and as a result, it had been a difficult time for the family. He had sent his wife and daughter to his parents' house in Kentucky while he stayed and took care of things on the homestead, caring for the animals and sleeping in front of the fireplace at night in a sleeping bag. That experience had prompted him to install the whole-house natural gas generator that he had been meaning to get.

His property had a natural gas right of way going through it and he received free gas, so the generator was a great fit. It was one of his most expensive preps and it had been used numerous times since installation. He had also opted for a gas stove, water heater, and furnace. The furnace still required electricity to run, but it didn't strain the generator, since it used the gas to generate heat.

He was constantly reevaluating the systems he had in place, to make them more robust and redundant. The farm had more than one source for power and water. He produced much of their own food. He had plans in place for security, communication, and even trade items. He was aware that he wasn't prepared for every situation, he was just trying to do the best he could with what he had.

This process had been going on for years, and he still had numerous ideas for improving and expanding what they had. Everything took money and he could only do it so fast. The one advantage he had was that he had started prepping over twenty years ago. However, the one prep he viewed as the most important of all was knowledge. It didn't matter if you had all the best gear and weapons in the world if you didn't practice with them and know how to use them in an emergency.

The other thing that Paul had going for him was a robust group of like-minded and capable friends.

Not only were he and his friends close, but they all shared a passion for readiness and training. They trained together, they had parties with all the families, and they all believed, really believed, that in an emergency, the best chance of survival was to pull together as a team. So that's what they did. The team would train hard, work hard and play hard. Besides Paul's range, two of the other guys had ranges on their properties, which offered more than one option for training locations.

In addition to training with firearms, they trained on patrolling, communication classes, first aid training and even surveillance techniques, which they used at work. Once Paul started working at Tri Point Solutions, he had taken the lead on running the patrolling, while James Lehmann led the comms training. Everyone on the team had a callsign that they used for radio communications when working and James's callsign was "Loki." An interesting phenomenon happened when working together and using calls signs regularly. It didn't take long before your callsign became your nickname and the guys would use the callsigns in normal conversation more often than their real names.

Paul's callsign had started off as "Doc Holiday," but had quickly gotten shortened to just "Doc." McCoy McMaster's callsign had just come naturally. Of course it was going to be "Mack." What else could it be? Mack was the co-owner of Tri Point Solutions along with Chris Wolf. Chris had formerly worked as an aeronautical engineer and had earned the callsign of "Rotor."

There were others in the group, and everyone contributed in their own way. Everyone seemed to have a bit of a specialty, and everyone, to the man, was dedicated to his teammates. It reminded Paul of his time on a Special Forces Operational Detachment Alpha, or ODA. Everyone knew his job and each one of them was good at it, despite the fact that not everyone working at TPS had been in the military.

As all this was going on, Paul, his teammates at TPS, and the rest of the country were unaware of the Hezbollah terrorists that had crossed into the country to begin preparations to attack America. A cell was operating out of Michigan and had a plan that was yet to play out. Another Iranian-sponsored terrorist organization, Hamas, had attacked Israel on October 7th of 2023 and the situation in The Middle East was getting more and more unpredictable.

The war in Ukraine continued to rage on, with the United States and other countries committing vast, seemingly unending, amounts of money and weapons to fight off the Russian invasion. However, many Americans were already growing weary of supporting the wars. The U.S. was still reeling from a disastrous end to a twenty-year war in Afghanistan, and it had left the country with no appetite for another conflict. Plus, the money was being sent with little to no apparent oversight and rumors abounded of the corrupt Ukrainian government officials enriching themselves with the money that was intended to help the country defend itself.

As if all that wasn't enough, the American President seemed to be losing touch with reality. His behavior and difficulty speaking led many people to believe that he was suffering from some sort of debilitating mental condition. Some called it dementia, others suggested Alzheimer's disease or Parkinson's. However, the White House continued to say that he was fine and as sharp as ever. The evidence indicated otherwise. Listening to the White House press secretary gave the feeling of "Don't believe your lying eyes."

Even within his own party, people began to call for the President to step down from his reelection bid. They doubted his ability to defeat Donald Trump in the upcoming election and wanted to replace him with another candidate. Some suggested the Vice President, while others began to take the approach of "Anyone but Joe." However, the public didn't know what the real plan was. They would soon find out that there were more factors involved in their future than who was running for President.

Cloaked in secrecy, a group of ultra-wealthy and influential people were vying for a power that was greater than that of the President of the United States. This group called themselves "The Collective," and rumors abounded of their existence. The term "The Deep State" had been used for years to describe the group who seemed to always stay just out of the public eye, despite the evidence of their efforts. They were imbedded in the government of the United States (and of many other countries), the U.S. Federal Reserve, the World Economic Forum, numerous national banks, the big tech industry, the pharmaceutical industry, and more. Their goal was reasonably simple: accumulate power and wealth for themselves, regardless of the damage it did to the people or the nations of the world. Their loyalty did not lie with their countries. Countries would rise and fall, but wealth and power, true power, could not be bound by national borders.

1

Let's Shoot It Again

July 13, 2024

Eastern Michigan

Zamir Syed, commander of the Hezbollah cell, closed his computer gently and leaned back in his chair. He sat in a comfortable farmhouse in eastern Michigan. The weather was mild and he had the windows open, allowing the breeze to blow through the old structure. Outside he could hear the songs of the birds as they enjoyed the weather as well. He hated to admit how much he liked this place. It was a stark contrast to the terrain and environment in his home of Lebanon. Water was plentiful here. They could drive to Lake Huron in a little more than an hour. He marveled at the enormity of the lake. It looked more like an ocean to him. Lake St. Clair was to their southeast. It was smaller, but still quite a wonder. Zamir had even organized a few trips to Lake St. Clair last summer to allow his men to swim as a reward for their dedication to their training. He was careful to send them in small groups to reduce the likelihood of drawing unwanted attention, but the men came back telling stories of how the stupid Americans paid no attention to them at all. In fact, the Americans didn't seem to pay attention to anything that was going on around them. They ran around and cooked on grills and played in boats as if they didn't have a care in the world. The message that Zamir had just received would change that.

He and his men had arrived in the United States two years ago, crossing the southern border and working their way to Michigan. This farm had already been arranged for them and he had taken advantage of their time there to prepare his unit for this day. As time had dragged on, he had sent several of his team out into the American cities to work. These men had learned more about the Americans, and brought in additional money for the mission. Zamir had learned that some cities called themselves "Sanctuary Cities." These cities protected illegal immigrants from the federal government. He couldn't imagine a city in Lebanon telling the national government that it would not obey the laws! It was unfathomable to Zamir. However, here in America, there were numerous cities that did exactly that. Lansing, Michigan was one of those cities.

Dearborn was even closer than Lansing and although it didn't have Sanctuary City status, the city didn't fully cooperate with the federal immigration enforcement policies. Zamir had seized this opportunity to send five of his men to work in Lansing and three more to work in Dearborn. They had taken various jobs such as delivery drivers, manual laborers, or food workers. As a reward for this, Zamir allowed the men to keep a small portion of their paychecks. One of the men had been working in a grocery store in Lansing for over six months. He had been particularly useful and Zamir had instructed him to be the perfect employee. Ibad Azzam started off just stocking shelves, but his performance soon allowed him to do other tasks as well. He would always show up to work fifteen minutes early. He worked diligently to perfect every task they gave him. He was helpful and courteous to everyone he interacted with. He also used the experience to improve his English. However, all of that was to facilitate his real mission.

He wrote down everything that happened in the store and took cell phone pictures and videos of as much as possible. He had documented every security camera that he could find. He knew how the inventory system worked and understood the delivery schedule. He even knew how to unlock the doors to the loading dock and back in the big trucks that made deliveries twice a week.

Ibad was thankful that he had been chosen for this mission. He had grown tired of being on the rural farm and this city life appealed to him. The five men in Lansing shared a small apartment in the city and he only returned to the farm periodically to brief Zamir. That is not to say that he had lost his focus on the bigger picture. He was ready to walk away from this job at a moment's notice as soon as Zamir said that the cell had been activated. He was about to get that call.

Ibad had just made it back to the apartment at 11:00 p.m. He had stayed through closing time, which was 10 o'clock and then finished sweeping the store before departing around 10:30. As he entered, he dropped his door key into his pocket and his phone began to ring. He pulled the phone out and looked at the screen.

"Zamir, brother. How are you?"

"As-salam alaikum," Zamir replied, using the more traditional Arabic greeting.

Ibad winced. He had grown accustomed to speaking informally with the Americans. "Wa alaikum assalaam," he said more formally. He needed to be more careful with his commander.

"Ibad, Let's have lunch tomorrow."

The words hung in the air for a moment as Ibad processed the information. It meant that Zamir wanted him back at the farm by noon tomorrow. "I understand. And my friends?" He was careful to use the phrases that they had practiced for talking on the phone.

"Yes, your friends too."

Tomorrow? He would need to wake the others to begin preparations. "Thank you. Anything else?"

"See you then." The line went dead. He slid the cell phone back into his pocket and hurried to wake the others.

The next morning, the apartment was a flurry of activity. Everyone had accumulated clothing and other items during their time in Lansing and they didn't want to leave anything behind. Bassam Khater placed their three M4 rifles in a large duffle bag that had been purchased specifically for that task. Each man carried his belongings down to the waiting vehicle. Zamir had sent them with an old Ford Explorer. It had enough seating for everyone and they were able to fit their bags in the cargo area.

At 7:20 a.m. they were pulling away from the apartment. They didn't tell anyone, and there was very little left in the apartment, nothing of which could be used to identify them. They *did* leave the partial bottle of vodka sitting on the counter. Zamir would not have approved, but he would never know.

By noon the group was back at the farm. They had stowed all their gear and everyone was gathered just inside the open door to the barn; even the two cooks were there. Mohamed Tahir, the second in command was toward the front of the group and speaking with Ahmad Abufaysal, the commander of Yellow Cell. This was the first time the entire cell had been together in one place in months and everyone was speculating on what it meant. The most common theory was that they had finally gotten the order to execute their mission. However, after two years, several of them had grown complacent and simply dismissed that as a possibility.

Suddenly the back door of the farmhouse burst open and Zamir strode out. The men fell silent. He was wearing his red Hezbollah headband. The men had only ever seen him wear that one time since they had arrived in the United States. He walked quickly, more of a march really. His face was expressionless, betraying nothing of what he had to say. Zamir walked directly up to Mohamed.

"Is everyone here?"

"Yes Commander. Everyone awaits your orders."

Zamir had a way of captivating the men. He knew the right things to do, and the right things to say to get the results that he wanted. Mohamed admired Zamir. He just wished that Zamir would trust him more. He didn't know what this meeting was about either.

When Zamir spoke, he spoke in Arabic. "My brothers!" He lifted both his arms out to his sides, hands open and palms facing up, and looked up toward the sky. "What a beautiful day that Allah has granted us!"

The men responded in agreement with several men saying "Allahu Akbar," Arabic for "Allah is great."

He slowly lowered his arms and looked at the men. He could see the anticipation on their faces. He would not give them what they wanted, not yet. "You are doing well with your training. You are staying focused on the mission and Allah is pleased."

Once again, he got a reaction from the crowd. More calls of "Allahu Akbar." More cheers.

"For years, the Americans and their allies have conducted themselves as if they owned the world. They send their troops to other countries and murder without remorse. They bomb cities and destroy villages. They steal the world's resources to feed their gluttonous population. They do this while the American people sleep here, growing fat. All the while, they claim to be the moral superiors of those they attack. They don't care about the damage they cause or the families they've torn apart. They leave nothing behind but their boot prints, death, and desolation. They think they are untouchable...safe. They think that America is a castle that they may hide in while their soldiers roam the planet, killing those who don't bow down to them. They have no idea that a great and deadly lion sleeps in their midst. They will not know until the lion has attacked and feasted on the bones of their young."

Yet more cheers. Zamir looked into the faces of the men. They were excited; Zamir had them right where he needed them. "Allah smiles on us today, for today we received our orders... to *ATTACK*!" He thrust his right fist into the air as he yelled.

The crowd began yelling and slapping each other on the back. Someone began chanting and soon the group joined in until they were like one fierce voice: "Allahu Akbar! Allahu Akbar! Allahu Akbar!"

Zamir smiled and joined them. "Allahu Akbar! Allahu Akbar!"

After nearly a minute, Zamir stopped and managed to get the group to settle down enough so he could continue. "My brothers, I tell you this: We have been tasked with a holy mission. We will strike down the infidels. We will bring fear to their homes and crush them under our boots!"

The celebration began again. Zamir allowed it to continue for a few seconds before he began again. "Tomorrow, we will conduct our final training for the mission. In the next few days, I will brief everyone on their specific missions and soon, very soon, you will finally have your chance to impose Allah's will on the infidels, and it will be a glorious day! Allahu Akbar!"

The Hezbollah fighters erupted one more time. This time, Zamir simply watched them, smiling. He did not interrupt. He knew they would eventually start to calm down. He would let them have their moment. Then he would turn them loose on America. Allahu Akbar.

That evening, he had the cooks prepare a feast for the men. He had them make traditional kibbeh, a fried croquette. In Lebanon, it was typically made with lamb or beef. They didn't have lamb, but they *did* have beef. The men were exuberant when they saw what had been prepared. They laughed and joked and enjoyed the meal, spending much more time socializing than they typically did. Zamir sat with Mohamed as they ate. The mood was infectious and even Zamir was joking around a little.

Eventually, however, Zamir decided he'd had enough. He rose from the table and spoke to Mohamed. "Let them stay and enjoy themselves as long as they want. Tomorrow, there will be no time for celebration. There will only be time for preparation."

"Of course, Zamir." Mohamed nodded his head.

Zamir nodded in return, turned, and left the room.

The next day, each of the six teams had an hour on their makeshift range to do final checks on their rifles. Each team was given some ammunition and one by one, they took turns taking their shots.

Nour Hallal had emerged as the best marksman in the group and he stayed on the range the entire day and helped the other five teams as they went through their drills.

Walid Youssef and Abu-bakr Waheed were the last team of the day. They were in Blue Cell. "Your target is at 250 meters. Do you see it?" Abu-bakr asked, looking through a set of inexpensive binoculars they had picked up at Wal-Mart.

"I see it," replied Walid.

"Get ready...fire!"

Walid's rifle was a Savage 110 chambered in .308 Winchester. The gun barked and Abu-bakr stared at the target. The round struck at the bottom of the cardboard target.

"You're low. Shoot about 20 centimeters higher.

Walid cycled the action and the rifle sounded a second time. This time the bullet struck near the center of the cardboard. There was a crude face drawn in the middle of the cardboard and the bullet punched a hole just above the left side of the mouth.

"That was a hit!" Abu-bakr cried with excitement.

Nour watched without saying anything at first. After the second shot was fired, he walked forward and spoke to the two-man team. "That was good."

The two men looked up from the ground and smiled at the praise.

Nour continued. "However, we've been training on this for nearly two years now. You should not have needed the second shot. You should already know where to aim to hit your target with the first round."

The smiles faded from the two-man team and Walid spoke up. "Nour, this scope only has..."

Nour cut him off. "Stop. Don't make excuses. When we attack, you may not have time for two shots. You *must* make every shot count. The longer you stay in your position shooting, the more likely you are to get caught. Understand this: you will have numerous missions in the coming days and if you get caught before you have accomplished all your tasks, it doesn't matter how many times you were successful, the overall mission is still a failure. *Always* try to complete the mission with the least number of shots possible." He paused and smiled slightly, in an attempt to refocus them. "I have no doubt when the time comes, you will please Allah with your actions."

The two men relaxed. "We will Nour, we will!" Abu-bakr said.

"Good. Now, once you're done, head back. I need to go speak with Mohamed."

With that statement, Nour turned and walked away, not waiting for a response.

Walid looked over at Abu-bakr. "Let's shoot it again."

2

A Completely Different Reason

July 13, 2024

Brett Hathcock's Farm, near Ashland, Kentucky

Paul Michaels and Randy "Dangle" Taylor settled in for a Saturday of shooting at their buddy's farm. Paul and "Mack" McMasters had met Brett Hathcock when they were working for the Marine Corps as contractors. Brett was still active duty at the time, but was nearing retirement. His in-laws lived on a beautiful piece of land in Kentucky, just outside Ashland, and had offered their daughter a part of the land to build a house on. He and his wife agreed and began building the house while he was still active duty. Following his retirement, they had moved into the nearly completed house as he continued to work on it to finish it up.

When he was still in the Marines, Brett was constantly asked if he was related to Carlos Hathcock, the famous U.S. Marine Sniper who had a Marine Corps record of 93 confirmed kills in Vietnam. Brett had gotten to the point that he would introduce himself as "Master Sergeant Hathcock, no relation." To say that Brett was a joker was an understatement. He was probably the funniest guy Paul had ever met. When he told Paul that he would be retiring near Ashland, less than an hour from Paul's property, they had both promised to stay in touch and they had kept that promise.

Since his retirement from the Marine Corps, Brett has signed onto Tri Point Solutions and started working security to augment his pension. His penchant for making jokes had quickly earned him the callsign of "Joker".

The terrain on Joker's property was dramatically different than the rugged hills at Paul's place. Despite being less than 50 miles apart, the terrain here was gentle rolling hills. This had helped to facilitate building a long-distance range across his father-in-law's pasture. From a shooting bench beside the barn, the farthest target was at 875 meters. It wasn't extreme, but it was definitely farther than Paul could set up on his own property. Paul's longest shot was right at 600 meters and the only way he was able to set up that shooting lane was by shooting from the ridge across two hollers into the side of a large spur. This had required cutting down numerous trees to clear the lane and it had taken him several days to complete.

Paul and Dangle had arrived an hour earlier, checked in with Joker at the house and then headed out to adjust the steel targets and set up some paper targets. As they were setting out their gear, Joker pulled up in a John Deere Mule side by side.

"All right boys, you're safe. The Marines are here now."

Paul laughed. "Yeah, now that SF has secured the area."

Joker turned off the Mule. "SF? What is that, Security Forces or something?"

Paul just rolled his eyes.

"What are we shootin' today boys?" Joker asked, rubbing his hands together and looking at the guns on the long table.

Paul answered first. "I have my .300 WinMag and my almost-an-M24." Paul had guns similar to the army issued sniper rifles he had used during his time in Special Forces. In the gun world, a "clone" was an exact copy of a military firearm, down to every detail, and that was usually very expensive to do. Some collectors liked to do that, but Paul wasn't concerned with exact copies. His rifles were similar to the military rifles and might pass as a clone to the casual observer. However, he wasn't trying to mimic every detail, he just wanted a rifle that felt familiar to him, like the ones Uncle Sam had loaned him. He wasn't concerned with authenticity to the original, just performance in the form of accuracy and reliability.

He still referred to his 300 WinMag as his "Mark 13". The action was correct and the Accuracy International chassis was correct, but the real Mk13 had an unusual tapered barrel to facilitate the issued suppressor. Paul's rifle had a more traditional full profile barrel with a Surefire SOCOM Suppressor-Ready Muzzle Brake for his SOCOM 300 SPS suppressor. The one thing that *was* the same was the accuracy. His rifle was just as accurate as the one he had used in the army. It was an impressive rifle and he loved shooting it. He maintained a meticulous log book of his shots and round count. One of the disadvantages of the .300 WinMag cartridge was that it burned up barrels faster than most other cartridges. He needed to replace the barrel about every 1,000 to 1,200 rounds. Paul was on his second barrel.

The other rifle he had with him was a Remington 700 set up similarly to the army issued M24 sniper rifle. He had the same Leupold scope that the army used, however his rifle was a short action. The M24 was a long action. His rifle was actually closer to the Marine Corps' M40 short action Remington 700, but he couldn't bring himself to call it an M40. He had painted the rifle in a very acceptable copy of the new army camouflage pattern and had mounted the same type of Harris bipod he had used in Special Forces. He had a couple other rifles set up for long range shooting, but they were still at home in a gun safe.

"I have my Six Five Creed," Dangle said. Dangle had bought the Ruger American Predator from Paul. Paul had gotten it in a trade and didn't really want to get into 6.5 Creedmoor, so he had decided to sell it. Dangle didn't have a long-range rifle at the time, but wanted one. It just worked out. "How about you? What ya got?"

Joker was pulling a large plastic gun case from the side by side. "I have my Bergara chambered in *I'm gonna beat your ass*," he replied, strait faced.

"Paul's still shooting old Remingtons from the last century," he continued. "Welcome to the future, boys."

"Oh, here we go. Let the trash talking begin," Paul said, shaking his head. "Where's your 30-06?"

"I'm letting that ol' girl take a break today. I need to gather some more data on this one. I've only shot it a handful of times, but so far, I'm loving this rifle. It's a freakin' tack-driver."

"I'm sure it's a nice rifle, but you still gotta do your part. Can you even handle that thing with only nine fingers?" Paul asked, pulling out a twenty-round box of the big .300 WinMag cartridges from his range bag and placing it on the table.

Dangle looked up at the statement and before Joker could respond, he asked, "Nine fingers? You only have nine fingers?"

Joker held his left hand up, with his fingers open and extended, revealing that half of his left middle finger was missing.

"Holy crap! What happened?"

"I had a flashbang with a faulty fuse go off in my hand. Peeled the end of my finger like a banana."

Dangle was shocked. "Was this in combat?"

"Hell no, it was a training iteration down at LaJeune. They rushed me over to the Naval Hospital. I looked like I had survived a freakin' cartoon bomb. My face was all covered in soot. All the hair on my face was singed, and I walk in the door of the hospital holding my hand up in the air with this bloody bandage wrapped around my finger." Joker was acting out the story as he described it.

Paul and Dangle were now laughing at his description, picturing the old cartoons with the bombs that inevitably left some character with a burned face and smoking hair.

Joker kept going. "So here I am, walking past all these moms with their kids in there for the freakin' sniffles or whatever and I look over and I see these kids looking at my bloody hand with horror on their faces. So, I just said the first thing that came to mind: *'Don't pick your nose kids, or the boogers will bite your finger off!'*"

By this point, Paul and Dangle were rolling with laughter. Trying to catch his breath, Paul said, "*That* was the first thing to come to mind?"

Joker was laughing too at this point. "Well, you hafta understand. My grandfather lost his finger to a shotgun accident as a kid and I used to always hear that from him growing up. So, when I lost *my* finger, I guess my brain just took me back to that."

Paul was still laughing as he pulled a handkerchief from the cargo pocket on his tactical pants, and lifted his sunglasses to wipe at his eyes. He was laughing so hard, his eyes were watering. "I guess that's one way to bond with your grandfather, blowing your finger off!"

"Yeah, well, you gotta do what you gotta do," Joker replied as he sat his range bag next to the gun case. He then opened the case and removed a Bergara Divide with a camouflaged stock. "Okay, what's first, Long Range Larry?"

Paul didn't react to the jab. "We have paper targets set up at 100 meters to confirm zero. The targets have one-inch squares, so essentially one minute of angle from here. I figured we'd confirm zero before we stretch our legs."

The three men settled in, side by side on the table, everyone donning hearing protection. At this close range, all their scopes had sufficient magnification that they didn't require a spotting scope to see where they were hitting. There were three targets set up and each target had four squares on the paper. They all took their time and shot at their own pace.

"Everybody good?" Paul asked, once the shooting had stopped. "Y'all wanna go down and look at the targets, or do you have everything you need?"

"I'm good," Joker answered, "but you both already knew that."

"I think I want to make a slight adjustment," Dangle said. "Will you take a look at mine and tell me what you think?"

Paul looked through his scope at Dangle's target. He had a good group with all the rounds in a tight triangle, but they were off to the right side of the square. He made adjustments on the scope. "Try that. Send three more."

Dangle shot a few more rounds and then paused as he inspected his work.

"What do you think?" Paul asked.

"I think I'm good."

"All right, first, let's reset your turrets and then we'll get at it," Paul said, making the adjustments to the scope. "If you want to go first, I'll spot for you." He got up and walked behind Dangle, grabbing his spotting scope that was mounted on a tall tripod, allowing him to see over Dangle's shoulder. "Do you want to dial elevation or hold?"

"Oh, I'm not ready to hold yet, let's dial it," Dangle responded. He was new to long range shooting, but was adapting to it very quickly. He was very experienced with a pistol and carbine and those skills were transferring nicely to this shooting style.

"Okay, no problem. Do you see the silhouette target at the wood line on the right at the top of the first rise?"

Dangle was looking over the top of his scope. "I see it."

"Do you want me to tell you how far it is with the rangefinder, or do you want to practice your range finding with your scope?" Paul asked, picking up the laser range finder.

Dangle looked to his left at Joker who was looking back at him. "Well, what's it gonna be?" Joker asked. "Do you want the short cut, or do you want to do the work like a man?"

Dangle shook his head. "You're both jerks. Fine! I'll range it." He looked through his scope again. "It looks like..."

Paul interrupted. "Is your scope at maximum magnification?"

Dangle raised his head and looked at the magnification dial on his scope. "Yep." He returned to looking through the glass again. He reached up and adjusted the parallax knob without taking his eye off the target. "I have...I'm gonna say...two point one. No, two point two mils top to bottom."

Paul sat back down beside Dangle and slid his notebook and a pencil in front of him. "Okay, here's the formula. We know that the steel target you're looking at is twelve inches wide and twenty-four inches tall. So, plug in twenty-four here and your mil measurement of 2.2 here." Paul motioned to the formula written in the notebook.

(Height of target (in inches) x 25.4) / Size (in Mils) = Range in meters

"This is bull," Dangle said. "I told my teacher in high school that I was never going to need algebra." He had a disgusted look on his face.

"Tactical math," Paul responded with a grin.

"Well, I can tell you what I'm not doing: I'm not doing that with the pencil." Dangle pulled out his phone, opened the calculator app, and began typing in the numbers. "Okay, so 24 times 25.4 is 609.6. My measurement in mils is 2.2, so 609.6 divided by 2.2 is 277 and some change. So, 277 meters." He looked up from his phone at Paul who was looking through the laser range finder.

"You got it!" Dangle could hear the approval in Paul's voice. "Good job! The range finder says 290 meters. That's close enough for government work."

Joker couldn't pass up the opportunity. "Oh! Good enough for government work? That means it'll barely work on its best day and catastrophically fail when you need it most!"

Dange and Paul both started laughing.

"Anyhow, as I was saying, now we're going to look at your ballistic chart and see what we need to dial on your elevation turret for 300m," Paul coached, still laughing at Joker's joke.

"I've got that," Dangle said, executing a few swipes on his phone and opening up his Ballistic Computer app. "Oh, that's not much of an adjustment." He looked up at his elevation turret and made the adjustment.

"By the way," Paul said. "There's an app for doing that distance calculation too."

Dangle glared at him. "And you waited until I was done to say that?"

"Well, we need to know how to do all this without our phones. That's why I print off my ballistic charts and keep them with my rifles. I printed yours for you too, remember?"

"Yeah, I've got it, but my phone is faster. What's the app for calculating the distance?"

"There's more than one, but I use iMilDotCalc." He turned his phone around to show him the app. "Right here you select what the unit of measurement is for the target. I have mine set to inches. You enter in your Mil measurement here and hit the Compute button. Let's do your target." He started typing into the phone. "Twenty-four inches and you measured 2.2 Mils. Calculate. 277.09 meters."

Dangle pointed at the phone. "See! I was right. It's 277 meters, not 290!"

"The calculation is only as good as the data you put in. Your measurement of 2.2 Mils might have been a little bit off. Let's see what 2.1 Mils says." Paul made the adjustment on the app. "290.29 meters."

"Crap!" Dangle exclaimed. "I almost said that!"

"Yeah, but look. This target is pretty big and it's a short range shot. Two hundred seventy-seven meters versus two hundred ninety meters is not going to make a difference. It's still minute-of-bad-guy. Now when we start pushing out to greater distances, or smaller targets, that's a different answer."

Dangle looked over at Paul. "Minute-of-bad-guy?"

"Yeah," Paul answered. "You know, minute-of-angle is about an inch at a hundred. Well, minute-of-bad-guy means it may not be within an inch, but it's close enough to hit a bad guy." Paul was smiling as he explained the slang.

"Oh, I get it. I like that. I'm using that. Speaking of bad guys. We knew the measurement of the target here. What about in combat, what did you do there?" Dangle asked.

"Actually, in combat, I usually *did* have a laser range finder. However, if I didn't, I could still do what you just did. You can get the Mil measurement of the distance across the bad guy's shoulders, then use eighteen inches as a generic measurement. Obviously not everyone's shoulders are the same width, but a good generic number to use is eighteen inches. To cut out the step of changing that into centimeters, I just used forty-six centimeters as a generic number. That's essentially eighteen inches. That made the calculations faster. I would just divide forty-six by the number of Mils and move the decimal point one place to the right. That gives you the distance in meters."

Joker was getting fed up with all this. "Are we going to shoot, or just give math lessons all day?"

"All right, all right. Dangle, you ready?"

"Yep." He settled in behind his gun. He had a sand sock under the rear of the stock and used it to help adjust his rifle.

Paul had moved back to the spotting scope. "Okay, the range is hot."

Boom! Joker's rifle went off.

Ding! The steel target rang as his bullet struck it.

Dangle jumped and looked over his left at Joker. "What the hell, dude?"

Paul was laughing.

"While you two were over there dreaming about your high school math teachers, I was actually getting ready to shoot. Now hurry up, let's shoot." Joker cycled the action on his rifle as he spoke.

"Well, to be fair, I *did* say the range was hot," Paul added, still chuckling.

Dangle shook his head as he settled back in behind his rifle.

Paul looked through the spotting scope again and then spoke up. "No wind. Hold center."

Boom! Dangle's rifle sounded and he was rewarded by the sound of the steel ringing as his bullet found the target. "That's what I'm talking about!" Dangle said as he sat up.

"Impact. Dead center," Paul responded, still looking through the spotting scope.

This is how it went for the next couple of hours. Just three friends enjoying a nice day at the range. The weather was good and the jokes were non-stop. Everyone was talking trash, laughing, and just generally having a good time. They had no way of knowing that 350 miles to their north, another group of men was practicing with their rifles too, but for a completely different reason.

3

Fear Where You Live

Five Days later, July 18th 2024

Western New York State

Simon Walker woke to the sound of the alarm on his cellphone. He had chosen an especially annoying alarm that he couldn't just ignore. Now he was regretting that decision. Maybe tomorrow he would wake up to chirping birds or a carefully chosen song that gradually got louder and louder until it pulled him from his slumber, refreshed and in a good mood. He threw back the covers and sat up, stretching before reaching for the screeching phone. With a quick tap, he silenced it and looked at the time. He had done the calculations before he went to sleep, but now, with a foggy brain, he tried to check his math from last night. *Let's see, I need to be out of service for ten hours...so I can log back in...let's see...* He lightly shook his head as if trying to loosen the cobwebs. *Forty-five minutes. That's it, forty-five minutes. Plenty of time.*

He leaned forward toward the cab and tossed the phone onto the passenger of his Volvo long haul sleeper semi. The truck was comfortable. He had spent the money for a good mattress for the sleeper and he was happy he had. "That's money well spent right there," he had told his wife at the time.

He was correct. The mattress was the perfect mix of soft and support. Match that up with good sheets, a nice comforter and the perfect pillow, and that made for a great night's rest while he was on the road. He had to be off the clock or "out of service" for ten hours anyhow, so why not try to get at least eight solid hours of sleep? A good sleeping setup was the perfect tool for the job.

He rotated around and dropped his feet off the edge of the mattress, stopping to stretch again. He recalled a self-help guru on satellite talk radio one time asking, "What motivates you to get out of bed in the morning?"

Simon knew what his answer was: his bladder. He reached over and retrieved the clothes that he had carefully stashed the night before. He always staged his things the same way every night. A place for everything and everything in its place. The sleeper was comfortable, but let's be real here, this wasn't a full-blown camper. There was only so much space and it needed to be neat and organized or things could get out of control very quickly. He had seen truckers over the years that kept the inside of their trucks in a constant state of chaos and confusion. That wasn't the way for Simon. No sir, his truck was tidy. He arranged his clothes so that the first thing he needed was always on top. In the warmer weather, he didn't like sleeping in socks, but he liked to put them on first, so they were on top. He grabbed them and started his morning ritual.

Less than five minutes later, he was standing outside his truck with his thermos in his hand. He locked the door and headed into the Flying J Travel Center off Interstate 90 in western New York State. First things first, the bathroom. Then to the coffee station. A man needed to have his priorities. Now the question was: did he want breakfast now, or just a snack. He pulled his phone from his belt and glanced down at the time again. Yep, breakfast.

Twenty minutes later, with his bladder empty and his belly full, Simon headed back out to the truck. Before he could begin his work day, he needed to sign in on his electronic log book. He wasn't even supposed to do his pre-trip inspection unless he was logged in. He unlocked the door and climbed up into the cab, retrieving his tablet. He opened the app, logging in and officially started his day before firing up the big machine. New York limits the amount of time you can let your truck idle, but that wasn't a factor for his pre-trip. In the old days, truckers would let their trucks idle all night to run the heater or air conditioner, depending on the weather. Nowadays, however, that was a good way to get a knock on your door and a ticket in the middle of the night. His truck had an auxiliary generator that he could use that didn't violate the state laws. His brother had once told him: "If you ever have any question on how to do your job, don't worry. The government is sure to tell you how to do it."

Simon reached down and turned on the lights and the four-way flashers, then climbed out of the truck. He needed to check every light to make sure nothing had gone out since his last check. Any light that was out, even aftermarket lights, put you at risk for a ticket. Simon's truck only had the factory installed lights, no auxiliary lighting or aftermarket lights. Even a non-critical light that you added could warrant a stop by the Department of Transportation if a bulb went out. He didn't want the headache and the factory lights on the Volvo worked just fine.

He was a creature of habit. Simon considered that a good thing when it came to his pre-trip inspection. Do it the same every time and you won't miss anything. He checked his tires first. As he got back to the drive tires, he visibly inspected the brake shoes. At the back of the trailer, he checked the lights. His four-way flashers utilized the brake lights. That was beneficial because he could check his brake lights by himself, without needing someone else to hit the brakes in the truck.

Once he made it back to the front of the truck, he raised the hood. At the front of the truck, he went through his mental checklist: pitman arm, drag link, he continued down the list checking each item as he had done countless times before. Belts were next. Everything was good so far. Time to check the load.

He walked back to check the load of lumber on his flatbed. Simon was an owner-operator -- he not only owned the truck, but the trailer as well. He knew that trailer inside and out. On the way, he stopped at his tool compartment and grabbed his ratchet bar, using it to check the tension on the straps. He also paused to listen for any sign of air leaks -- nothing. Satisfied that everything was in order, he completed his three hundred sixty degree walk around, and headed back toward the cab. After stowing his ratchet bar, he climbed back into the truck.

Sitting down in the driver's seat, it was time for coffee. He grabbed his recently filled thermos and poured a cup of coffee into his travel mug. He blew on the coffee a couple of times before risking a quick sip. It would need a minute. He sat it in the cup holder and retrieved his phone. He opened the Apple Maps app to check traffic conditions. He scrolled down his intended route, checking the first hundred miles or so, and nodded a slight nod of approval when he saw no indications of a problem. He glanced down at the gauges to see if the air pressure had built up yet. It looked good. He snapped the phone into the holder on the dash.

He retrieved the coffee; it had been sixty seconds or so since his last attempt, maybe it was ready. A tentative sip proved that it was not. He didn't have the lid on the travel mug yet, since he was trying to let it cool a little, so he was careful as he replaced it in the cup holder. Time to do the final check of air pressure. He turned off the engine. Simon then pressed the brake pedal firmly to the floor, watching for the initial drop to be indicated on the gauge. *Check*. He continued to hold the brake pedal down as he watched the gauge for any additional movement that would indicate an air leak. Nothing.

This day was starting off great. He felt good. The weather was perfect and the traffic looked like it was cooperating...so far. He snapped the lid onto the travel mug and restarted then engine. It was time to get moving. He pushed on the clutch. Truck drivers were starting to drive trucks with automatic transmissions. Not Simon Walker. He was old school. He wanted the control of the manual transmission. For Simon, big trucks were *supposed* to have manual transmissions. That's just how it was meant to be. He slipped the truck into gear and began easing out on the clutch. He didn't touch the fuel pedal. He didn't need to. The truck started rolling forward. He made his way across the parking area to the exit and turned left onto 77. A few seconds later, he was merging onto Interstate 90. He glanced down at the cup of coffee again, deciding to give it another minute rather than risk scalding himself.

A while later, the coffee cup was empty as he merged onto Interstate 86. Simon liked this stretch of road. This was a beautiful area. Over the last several years he had driven this interstate countless times. He knew the turns, where the best truck stops were, and where he was most likely to encounter traffic. It was comfortable and familiar. He was settled into his seat and was listening to satellite radio when the phone rang. He glanced over at it in the dash mounted holder. It was his wife. Simon reached over and swiped to answer it, tapping the icon for the speaker phone. "Hi Honey," he said, returning both hands to the wheel.

"Hey, I was just calling to see if you're still on schedule to be home tomorrow."

"Yeah, so far everything looks good. Why?"

"*Weeell*," she said, dragging out the word, "my sister asked if we would like to come over for dinner."

"Hmm," he replied. "Now that I think about it, I may be late."

"Oh, shut up. It's not that bad. Where are you now?"

He glanced over at the green sign announcing the upcoming Exit 23 for US Route 219 and the towns of Limestone, NY and Bradford, Pennsylvania. "I'm on I-86 near..."

The windshield exploded, showering him with glass. He felt like someone had just hit him in the chest with a sledge hammer. The bullet entered his chest just above and left of his heart. As he reflexively reached up with his right hand, the truck veered to the left, striking a Chevy Cruze that was passing him in the left lane, pushing the car into the concrete highway divider. The driver of the little car slammed on the brakes, leaving behind a scar on both the asphalt and the concrete barrier. Simon tried to reach for the steering wheel, but his left arm wouldn't react. He managed to grab the wheel with his right hand as he hammered the brake and the clutch simultaneously. The truck veered back to the right as the heavily laden trailer pushed forward, releasing the pinned Chevy. Physics dictated the resulting jackknife. The truck was approaching the bridge over the Allegheny River, completely out of control as the sides of Simon's vision began to grow dark. His hand slipped from the wheel as he started to slip into unconsciousness.

As the trailer pushed forward, the truck rotated to the right until the driver's door was facing forward. Both his feet slipped off the pedals as his body lost the ability to transmit signals to his limbs. Smoke rolled from the drive tires as they were pushed sideways on the asphalt. The left side of the front bumper impacted the guard rail prior to the bridge. The resulting force against the big truck slowed the forward momentum of the tractor as it violently scraped its way down the guard rail in a shower of sparks. The tractor trailer finally skidded to a halt, blocking both lanes.

The driver of the Chevy Cruze managed to get the little car stopped only a few yards from the back of the trailer, despite getting hit in the face by his airbag. Unfortunately, the woman driving the old Chevy Suburban behind him didn't see it coming. She was reading a funny text from her daughter when she heard the crash in front of her. By the time she looked up and realized what was happening, it was too late. Just as she hit her brakes, she slammed into the little car at nearly 70 miles per hour, shoving it forward and sandwiching it between her vehicle and the rear of the trailer. The man in the Chevy Cruze did not survive this second impact. Had the woman been driving a newer vehicle, perhaps the anti-collision features could have prevented her from hitting him, perhaps not. However, the impact of her large heavy vehicle with the smaller car ruptured its nearly full fuel tank and gasoline began spilling out onto the road, slowly spreading into an ever-widening puddle on the highway.

The drivers in several cars behind the wreck immediately slammed on their brakes, reacting to the crash. The car immediately behind the Suburban came to a halt about fifty feet from it, the antilock brakes preventing it from skidding. A man burst from the passenger side door, telling his wife, who was driving, to stay in the car with the kids. The man ran to the driver's door of the old Suburban and reached for the door handle just as something ignited the gasoline. The explosion threw the good Samaritan backwards toward the concrete divider. When he impacted the divider, his legs struck the concrete, but his upper body was above it. His momentum carried him over the divider in an airborne somersault and a passing car in the other lane struck him while he was still in the air. The man's wife screamed in horror as she watched her husband die right in front of her. As the man bounced off the windshield of the car in the other lane, the driver's reaction resulted in a four-car pileup on that side of the interstate as well.

As all this was happening, Simon Walker succumbed to the gunshot wound. The only merciful part of this scene was that Simon didn't have to endure the pain of being cooked alive, as the fire would eventually spread to his truck and engulf the cab. From the time he was shot, until the time he died, only nine seconds had passed. Somehow, through all this, Simon's phone had managed to stay in its holder. Had Simon been alive he would have heard his wife screaming his name.

Wooded area between Interstate 86 and North Parkside Drive

Fifteen minutes earlier

Walid Youssef and Abu-bakr Waheed parked their car on the shoulder of North Parkside drive, a small road that ran right beside Interstate 86. They checked to make sure there were no other cars on the road and slipped out of the vehicle, moving northeast into the trees. Walid carried his Ruger American bolt action. Abu-bakr carried one of the American

M4 rifles. He was only to use that if they were discovered and were forced to fight. They only had to move about fifty meters and they set up in the spot they had identified the day before. Zamir had dictated this specific location for their attack, but he had also told them to check it and make sure that what he had seen on his maps and online was accurate. It was. Zamir had sent out scouts to check many of the shooting positions in the last several months, but this was one of the locations they had not gotten to.

The side of the road was slightly elevated and gave a clear line of site up Interstate 86. Between them and the road was a small dirt track that led down to the river. *Most likely for fishing access*, Abu-baker had thought, when he saw it. Walid wanted his shot to be no more than 200 meters because he was nervous about missing. This site was ideal. From their position they could see the back of a large road sign at 150 meters. The plan was to shoot as the truck reached the sign. This position also allowed him to lay behind the trunk of a large tree with the rifle between the tree and the road, aiding in their concealment. They both wore camouflage clothing, but Zamir had assured them that it wasn't even necessary as people driving down the interstate would not be looking into the woods.

Their instructions were clear and simple. They were to wait, undetected in this position until 1:00 pm. After that, they were to shoot the first truck driver they saw, regardless of what type of trailer he was pulling. Then they would immediately escape the area along a planned and practiced route. The final part of the instructions was not to be taken alive.

Mohamed had brought up the point that it would be better to shoot tanker trucks. However, Zamir was firm in his response. "We'll shoot at the appointed time, regardless of the type of truck. We want to induce fear in all the drivers, not just those driving tankers. Besides that, we wouldn't know if the liquid being carried was flammable or not, or if it would even ignite. Besides that, waiting for a tanker introduces uncertainty into the timeline. No, America relies on these trucks for everything they use in their day to day lives. The roads are constantly full of these trucks. The shooters will take the first truck that they see after the appointed time and that is not open to discussion."

As he settled into his shooting position, Walid tossed some sticks and a rock out of the way to make it more comfortable in the prone position. He placed a small throw pillow in front of him and carefully lay the rifle on the pillow. He settled into his position and looked through the scope. It was now 12:55. He was breathing so hard that as he looked through the scope, he could see it rising and falling with his breaths. He needed to calm down and settle his nerves. Even at 150 meters, he knew that he could miss. He closed his eyes and concentrated on his breathing. Slowly inhale, slowly exhale, slowly inhale, slowly exhale. He opened his eyes and lowered his face back to the rifle again, peering through the optic. That was better. It wasn't perfect, but it was better.

"Two minutes," Abu-bakr said.

"Two minutes," Walid replied. He began looking over the scope as far as he could see down the road, looking for the big eighteen wheelers.

"One minute."

"One minute," he acknowledged. He saw the truck. It was a silver-colored truck pulling a loaded trailer. He couldn't tell what was on the trailer yet. It was still a long distance away, but not for long.

"Time."

This time Walid did not give a verbal response. He lowered his face back to the scope. The truck was still too far away. He watched it as it grew closer to the sign.

Abu-bakr raised his cell phone and pressed record on the video recorder. He quietly mouthed the words: *Allahu Akbar, Allahu Akbar, Allahu Akbar.* He didn't give any more time updates. He didn't want to create stress that might cause Walid to rush the shot. It was now 1:01 pm. He saw Walid shift slightly as he adjusted his point of aim. *Allahu Akbar, Allahu Akbar.*

Boom! Abu-bakr reflexively jumped even though he knew the shot was coming. He saw Walid's body react to the recoil. He looked down at the phone to ensure that he kept everything in the video. He saw the big truck swerve one way and then the other before it seems to fold in half, dragging down the guardrail until it finally screeched to a halt. He wasn't sure how long the whole event had taken, but he suddenly realized it was time to go. He said *Allahu Akbar* one more time, making sure that he said it loud so that it would be on the video then he stopped the recording. He looked down at Walid who was transfixed by the scene playing out in front of them. He grabbed him by the arm and pulled. He spoke in Arabic to Walid. "Walid, we need to go. Now!"

When Walid looked up at him, his eyes were wide. "What?"

"It's time to go. We have to go."

Suddenly, Walid was able to refocus. He jumped to his feet, bringing the rifle with him. He reached down and snatched up the little pillow and both men turned and ran through the trees toward the waiting car. They stopped at the edge of the road to make sure no other cars were visible. Walid's heart was beating so hard, he was certain that Abu-bakr could hear it. They didn't see any cars, so they rushed the last few steps to the vehicle. Walid opened the back door and laid the rifle on the blanket waiting on the back seat. Abu-bakr handed him the M4. He laid it in the blanket with the Savage and wrapped the blanket around them both before closing the door and running around to jump into the passenger seat. Abu-bakr already had the car started as Walid accidentally slammed his door with more force than necessary.

Abu-bakr took a deep breath and shifted the car into drive before slowly pulling out and heading south along the road. He continued for about two miles until he came to the turn off to Irvine Mills Road. He used his turn signal as he turned left in a controlled manner. He continued down Irvine Mills, crossing over Tunungwant Creek and a set of railroad track. He stopped at the red light, engaged his right turn-signal and waited. Neither man spoke. He could hear Walid breathing heavily. He thought he heard an explosion in the direction of the attack. He looked over at his passenger. "How are you, Walid?"

Walid looked to his left, made eye contact with Abu-bakr and broke out into a broad, toothy smile. Abu-bakr began to smile as well. He glanced up at the light. It was still red, but no traffic was coming from his left so he pulled out onto 219 toward Limestone and accelerated up to the speed limit, but not over it. After a moment Walid finally spoke. "Did you see it? Did you see what I did? One shot, just like Nour said!"

"I saw it brother. Allah is pleased." Abu-bakr glanced to his left and saw a large blue and white billboard advertising the

University of Pittsburgh. The sign had the slogan "Love where you learn" emblazoned on the left side. He smiled to himself. That was the old America, he thought. The new America will be "Fear where you live."

They had a week to get set up for the next attack. They were to take a circuitous route to central Maine. Their next attack would be on Interstate 95, north of Bangor, next Friday at 11:25 a.m. The other five teams would be executing their attacks all over the country at the same times. They wanted to leave no doubt that these were organized attacks on America's homeland. If the attacks weren't happening at the same time, people might claim that they were random acts of violence, but using this method, there was no denying that America was under siege.

Today, in addition to their attack, the other five teams were hitting targets in California, Colorado, Iowa, Oklahoma, and Alabama. Next week when they were attacking in Maine, the other teams would be attacking in Illinois, Minnesota, Florida, Arkansas, and Idaho. The message was designed to tell the Americans that no state was safe, no truck driver was safe. The ultimate goal was to stop the big trucks from driving.

At 1:55, Abu-bakr pulled over into the parking lot of a gas station. He didn't need gas yet, but he needed to send a message at 2:00. He leaned over and pulled a notebook out of the glove compartment and opened it up, studying the page. Then he set the notebook in his lap and pulled out his phone. He typed the message: "I picked up the bread and at least two cans of beans. I'll be home soon." He looked at the message and back at the notebook again, making sure the code was correct, he looked at the clock on his phone and waited until it changed to 2:00. He hit the SEND button.

Over the Precipice

East Michigan

Same Day, Same Time

Zamir was looking at his phone, waiting for the message. His phone chirped and he touched the bubble, opening the message. A smile crept across his face.

"What does it say, Zamir?" Mohamed asked, leaning forward in his chair, his face expectant.

"It is from Walid and Abu-bakr. They successfully executed their mission. At least two additional cars crashed and they are on their way to the next location."

The information was not exactly correct, because from their vantage point, the two-man team did not realize that four more cars had crashed. They had suspected it from the sound, but couldn't confirm it. Zamir would learn the exact numbers from the news reports later.

"Are they the last ones to report in?"

"They are. We had six attacks, five crashes. Faheem missed the driver, but shattered the windshield. The driver managed to get the truck stopped on the side of the road without crashing. I still consider that a success. That driver will tell the story of how he narrowly escaped with his life and he never saw the attack coming. His story may even strengthen our message by striking fear into the hearts of the other infidel drivers."

Zamir felt vindicated. He had been preparing for this moment for years and now his time had come. Eventually, this mission would eclipse even the attacks in Israel by Hamas because this mission was against the United States, the great, *untouchable* United States. They were starting to appear to be less untouchable. It had been nearly twenty-three years since this country had felt fear. He was blessed to be the one to bring it back.

Mohamed interrupted his thoughts. "Were any of the trucks tankers?"

Zamir scowled back at Mohamed. He held the look until he saw Mohamed react from the discomfort of the situation and look down at his hands. "Yes, Mohamed. One of the trucks was a tanker."

Mohamed looked back up with anticipation on his face. "And? Did it explode?"

Zamir furrowed his brow as he responded sardonically. "No, Mohamed. It didn't explode."

"So, it wasn't fuel?"

Zamir sighed before responding. He was tiring of Mohamed revisiting this obsession with shooting at tanker trucks. "Actually, yes, Mohamed. It was a gasoline tanker. The truck even turned over onto its side, but the tank didn't rupture. Apparently, those tanks are very strong."

"Oh," Mohamed replied weakly, looking down at his hands again. "I was hoping..."

Zamir shot up to his feet, leaning forward and putting a finger in Mohamed's face. "I know what you were hoping," Zamir spat. "You were hoping that one of them would shoot a tanker truck, the tank would explode in a gloriously destructive way, and you could reiterate your opinion that we should only shoot tanker trucks." Zamir spoke rapidly in a mocking tone. "You wanted to throw that in my face and tell me that it proved your point that we should be shooting tankers! You will learn your place! *I* am the commander of this mission! *I* will make the decisions, and *my* decisions are final! Do you understand?!"

Mohamed's shoulders shrank under the verbal assault and he meekly shook his head in acknowledgement.

"That's not good enough, look at me like a man!" Zamir screamed.

Mohamed looked up, but his posture remained that of beaten dog. "I understand, Zamir," he finally said.

"You understand *what*, Mohamed?"

Mohamed tried to salvage what little bit of self-respect he had left. He sat up straighter and looked Zamir in the eye. "Commander, I understand that I am your subordinate and I will obey your orders. Your orders will be followed and I won't question them." He did his best to not sound like a scolded child as he spoke, although he was unable to pull that off.

Zamir sat back down and began to calm himself down. He realized that he was breathing hard and he concentrated on getting it back to normal.

He stared at Mohamed for a moment longer and then spoke in a normal tone as if the outburst hadn't even happened. "As I was saying, all the teams have now reported in. This is a glorious day." He looked down at his phone, leaning forward as he read the messages again.

Mohamed took a breath and slowly released it before speaking. "How long do you think it will be before we start seeing results?" His voice still sounded weak, as if he were afraid to speak.

Zamir leaned back in his chair and looked over at Mohamed. "That depends. First, we'll have to see how quickly the truck drivers react and secondly, we'll need to see the reaction of the American public. By next week, I suspect that we'll start seeing the beginning of the effects. However, it could be sooner. Americans are weak and unaccustomed to fear. That could potentially lead to faster results." He reached for his chai and took a tentative sip, testing the temperature.

Mohamed observed Zamir, astonished at how calm he was. He glanced down at his own chai. He could see the steam rising from the cup and chose to leave it for another couple minutes. "Zamir, I trust in the plan, but what do we do if our mission does not get the desired results?"

Zamir did not move the cup from his mouth, but simply looked over the cup at Mohamed and then took another sip before calmly placing it on the table. One side of his mouth began to curl upward into a slight smile. "Mohamed. This mission will be successful. This is merely the first phase."

Mohamed was shocked. What else had Zamir kept from him? "What? What do you mean the first phase? What is the next phase?"

Zamir leaned back in his chair again and simply looked at Mohamed for a long moment before finally responding. "Mohamed, as you just stated, I am the commander of this mission. It is my decision what information I share with you and when I share it. However, now that we have begun Phase One, it *is* time to explain the rest of the mission."

Over the Precipice

4

Hearts and Minds

July 18, 2024

Paul and Sandy's Farm

"Okay ladies, I call the next drill *Hearts and Minds*," Paul said to his wife and daughter, smiling as he said it.

"Why do you call it that?" Sandy asked, tucking a strand of her brown hair up under her ball cap.

McKinley already knew the answer and just rolled her eyes, as teenagers do. "You don't wanna know, Mom."

Paul continued as if McKinley hadn't said anything. "Well, Honey, I'm glad you asked. We're going to start from the holster and when the timer goes off, you'll draw your pistol and engage the seven-meter paper target with two rounds to the chest, followed by one to the head." He paused. "*Hearts and minds.*" He was still smiling.

Sandy just looked at him for a second. "You're a dork."

Paul laughed out loud. "That's funny right there. I don't care who ya are!"

This elicited a slight giggle from McKinley.

"Okay, I'll demonstrate first." He handed the shot timer to McKinley and stepped up to the seven-meter line.

"Eyes and ears," Paul said as he grabbed the electronic hearing protection that was draped around his neck and placed them in his ears.

The two women pulled on their electronic earmuffs and turned them on. Everyone was already wearing safety-rated sunglasses.

Once she was sure that she had her earmuffs adjusted the way she wanted them, McKinley looked over at her dad. "Shooter ready?"

"Ready," Paul responded as he adjusted his feet, placing his left foot slightly forward of his right.

Beep. The shot timer announced that the time has started.

Paul drew his pistol and fired three shots in slow and even succession before returning his pistol to the holster.

"Five point one two," McKinley called out.

They all looked at the target. The target was shaped like a silhouette with a section in the center of the chest that was a lighter color. Centered in the middle of this lighter section was a small number 10. There were two holes, nearly touching, just to the right of the number. There was one additional hole in the middle of the nose.

"Two to the heart and one to the mind," Paul said and turned to look at the women.

"This is a fun drill and it works on a few different things. First, there's a smooth draw from the holster. Y'all are running your Smith & Wessons, so as soon as you clear the holster, defeat your safety, engage the chest twice, transition to the head for the single shot, reengage your safety, and reholster. Any questions?"

Sandy spoke up. "Do we have to go that slow?"

This elicited another giggle from McKinley.

"Well, no. But for now, just go as fast as you can get your shots on target." Paul turned to face the target again.

"Let me try it one more time." He looked over at his daughter and motioned toward the shot timer in her hand.

"Shooter ready?" she asked.

He turned to face the target and simply gave a nod.

Three seconds later, the shot timer sounded off.

Paul instantly drew and fired three rapid shots before smoothly replacing the pistol into his holster in a quick, smooth movement. He turned to face the women. Both of them were looking at the display on the shot timer.

Sandy looked up. "Okay, point taken. One point five four."

McKinley looked downrange at the target. "Your shots weren't as tight, but they were all still inside the lines of the chest and head."

"Go as fast as you can go, and still be on target. Speed doesn't matter without accuracy. Start out slow and as you get more comfortable, keep pushing yourself and speed will come naturally."

McKinley had been shooting regularly with Paul, and when it was her turn to shoot, the practice was apparent. Sandy didn't shoot as often. She was still comfortable with the drill, but she wasn't as fast or as accurate as McKinley.

Paul was having the time of his life. He loved to shoot and he loved to spend time with "his girls," as he called them. Today he was getting to do both.

They shot the pistols for a while and tried a few different drills, focusing on the basics, but still trying to push themselves to be faster and more accurate. However, after about forty-five minutes, Sandy spoke up. "I want to take a break from the pistols. Did you bring the rifle I like?"

"I sure did. It's right there," replied Paul, motioning toward the shooting bench, where several gun cases lay. A range bag sat on the table with the gun cases. He pulled the hearing protection from his ears and let them hang around his neck.

"Let's head over there and we'll break out the rifles," he said as he started toward the bench.

Paul had driven one of the side-by-sides up and set up the range prior to Sandy and McKinley's arrival. He had set up the paper targets and placed several rifles on the shooting bench. Sandy's favorite rifle was one of Paul's Ruger 10/22s. She referred to it as *her gun*. He had several of the Rugers, in various configurations. However, her favorite was a simple carbine with a wooden stock and a traditional three to nine power rimfire scope. It wasn't fancy, but it was accurate and reliable, and she liked it. Paul had replaced the factory barrel with a threaded barrel that facilitated the attachment of his .22 suppressor.

Years ago, when Paul decided that he wanted to get a suppressor, a teammate had told him to get one for his .22 first. This friend had several and had offered his advice. "I shoot my .22 suppressor more than all my others combined," the friend had told him.

Paul hadn't listened to him. Paul had a 5.56 suppressor at work, so that's what he bought first. He added a .30 caliber Surefire later, then the .22 and a .45 caliber. His latest acquisition had been a SilencerCo Spectre 9 for his 9mm guns. Now, he said he was done buying them, but he had said that before.

However, his friend had been right. Paul shot his Dead Air Mask .22 Caliber suppressor more than any other he had. The bottom line was that .22 was fun and inexpensive to shoot and he had several .22s with threaded barrels. He just moved the little lightweight suppressor from gun to gun. It was great fun. With supersonic ammunition, it wasn't silent, but it was quiet enough that he didn't need to use hearing protection. Subsonic ammunition was a different story. They were completely silent. The problem with the subsonic rimfire ammunition was that some of it didn't always cycle semi-automatic guns. However, Paul had discovered that CCI made an ammunition called "Standard Velocity." The manufacturer's claimed speed was 1,070 feet per second, which was just a little below the speed of sound, and therefore subsonic. It ran great in Paul's semiautomatic platforms and he now bought it by the case.

Paul also had a couple of bolt action .22 rifles with threaded barrels. One of them was a Ruger Precision Rifle Rimfire. It was set up like a long-range rifle and he used it as a low recoil, short range trainer for the girls. The other was a beautiful takedown model by Tactical Solutions called the Owyhee. They both functioned just fine with either subsonic or supersonic ammunition since the shooter would manually cycle the bolt after every shot.

A year earlier, Paul's cousin David had called him from the sporting goods store at the mall because they were clearing their inventory. The store had made a new policy that they would no longer sell guns as a protest against gun violence. "Paul, you need to get up here. They are selling these Tactical Solutions Owyhees for five hundred dollars on clearance. They're normally over a thousand!"

Paul had driven up to the mall and met his cousin. The store had two of the guns left. David had already bought one of them; Paul bought the other. That gun now sat on the table with a Leupold scope on it, awaiting its turn.

Paul pulled the Ruger 10/22 from the case and sat it on the table, as Sandy took a seat on the bench. He reached into his range bag and came out with three loaded ten-round rotary magazines for the gun and one fifteen-round magazine, placing them next to the rifle. "Do you want to start off on paper, or go straight to the steel?" he asked Sandy.

"Oh, I've had enough of the paper targets, let's ring some bells," she replied.

"I love it when you talk sexy like that," Paul replied with a wink at his wife.

McKinley reacted almost immediately. "You two are gross. Quit it!"

Paul turned to look at his daughter. "You *do* know how you were made, right?"

McKinley put both her index fingers in her ears and pinched her eyes shut. "I'm not listening! La la la la la la la."

Paul and Sandy both burst into laughter.

Sandy lightly slapped her husband on the hip with the back of her hand. "You quit picking on our baby!" she said before turning to McKinley and tapping her on the leg.

McKinley kept her fingers in her ears but opened her eyes and looked at her mother.

Sandy motioned for McKinley to pull her fingers out of her ears. McKinley cautiously complied.

"He's done. You can relax," she said.

McKinley looked back over at her father again. He was pulling another rifle out of the case, still smiling. She just shook her head and looked back at her mother. "I don't need you two to scar me, you know," she said, her expression serious.

Sandy chuckled again as she responded. "Okay, okay. We certainly wouldn't want to *scar* you."

McKinley huffed as she reached for one of the gun cases that she recognized and began unzipping it. She pulled out a POF USA Rebel, chambered in .22LR. She pulled open the Velcro flaps of the magazine pouches on the outside of the case and removed two Ruger BX-25 magazines. This little gun used the same Ruger magazines as the 10/22. She sat one of the mags on the table and reached for the box of CCI ammunition to begin loading the other.

Paul was screwing the suppressor onto the 10/22 for Sandy. He sat the rifle back down on the table in front of his wife and stood behind her. "Do you want a bag to shoot from?" he asked.

"No, I'm good," she replied, grabbing a ten-round magazine and seating it. She pulled the charging handle to the rear and released it, then settled into her shooting position.

"Going hot!" Sandy announced. She had both her elbows on the table and was looking through the scope. Her right index finger moved up to the safety and disengaged it with a quick push and a barely audible *click*. Her hearing protection was on the table beside her elbow.

Click. The little Ruger made no more sound than an air rifle. As the bullet found its mark on the steel, they all heard an unimpressive ding. Sandy looked up at Paul. "Was that a hit?"

"That was a hit. It's just not very loud with .22," he replied.

"Hmm," Sandy said as she settled back in behind the rifle.

"I guess it's been a little while since I shot. I was expecting that to be louder."

"If you really want to ring it, once you're done with the .22, we can launch some three hundred Blackout or five-five-six," Paul replied.

"We'll see. I like this gun. It doesn't kick," she replied before sending another couple of muffled shots downrange eliciting two more subdued reports from the steel target. She was shooting the standard velocity CCI ammo, so the shots were essentially silent.

Once Sandy was ready to take a break, Paul moved the suppressor over to the Rebel. The suppressor was hot, but not so hot that Paul couldn't handle it by putting on his Mechanix tactical gloves. The Rebel was McKinley's favorite .22 to shoot.

Paul had made some adjustments to the little gun. He had removed the factory barrel shroud, providing access to the threaded barrel. He also installed a better trigger, which was a dramatic improvement over the heavy factory trigger. That was a cool aspect of the Rebel. Even though it was a .22 long rifle, the trigger group was compatible with standard AR-15 triggers. Paul had taken advantage of that fact to put a wonderful Hyperfire trigger in the little gun. Finally, he had added a Vortex red dot optic and a sling to make it comfortable to use and carry.

McKinley practiced from several different shooting positions, while her mother reloaded magazines for her as Paul coached. She preferred the larger fifteen round and twenty-five round Ruger magazines. That was a great feature of this gun. Paul considered the fact that it used the same magazines as Sandy's Ruger 10/22 a big win from the preparedness standpoint. Magazine compatibility reduced the logistical requirements for him and would allow Sandy and McKinley to share magazines.

Paul had bought a Ruger American bolt action rifle in 5.56mm for the same reason -- it used standard AR-15 magazines. When he bought it, he had taken it over to Dangle's house after getting it set up with a scope, suppressor compatible muzzle device, and sling.

"Whatcha got there?" Dangle had said as Paul pulled the gun out of his truck. Before Paul could respond, Dangle's dog, Tripwire came bolting out of the house and ran full speed, straight at Paul.

Paul stopped to greet the dog and pet her before responding to Dangle.

"I got that Ruger five-five-six I was telling you about."

Dangle stepped off his porch, walking toward Paul, meeting him halfway with his hand out. "Well, let's see it."

Paul opened the bolt and handed the rifle to Dangle, who felt the weight of it before turning to the side and throwing it up to his shoulder, looking through the scope toward the woods. "I like it man. It's a lot like my 6.5, but it's smaller. It feels light. That's not a very fancy scope, though," he said, trying to get a rise out of Paul.

"Yeah, I got that gun for one specific reason," Paul began. "Let's say that the flag goes up and I need to loan a gun to someone to help defend against the bad guys. Well, if that guy is not well trained or disciplined or if he just freaks out, he might not be able to maintain trigger discipline with an AR-15. If he's using this gun, he won't have a choice. It's a bolt action, but I can still pass him one of my AR mags for it," Paul said, accepting the gun back from Dangle.

"Yeah, that's not a bad idea," Dangle said, looking down at the gun.

"But seriously, you love your fancy scopes. That one looks pretty basic." He motioned toward Paul's rifle with his chin as he spoke.

"The same idea. If I'm handing it to someone who is less experienced, a simple duplex reticle is easy to understand. Plus, this thing isn't designed for long range shooting. It's just a straight forward gun with a straight forward scope. This is a three to nine by forty scope. That's a super common setup that many people are already familiar with. If I'm buying a rifle, literally to be a spare, I don't want to spend a bunch on it. These are pretty cheap," Paul concluded.

"So, are we gonna shoot that thing, or what?" Dangle asked.

That Ruger five-five-six was now on the table, next to another bolt action rifle, Paul's Remington Model Seven chambered in .300 Blackout. After the girls had shot for a while with their

.22s, Paul pulled out the .300. "How about a little bigger round?" he asked.

Sandy didn't recognize the rifle. Many of Paul's guns looked the same to her. "I don't want to shoot anything that's going to kick the crap out of me," she said, looking at the compact rifle.

"Don't worry, I wouldn't do that to you. This one doesn't kick much more than your .22. It's a three hundred Blackout," he explained as he attached the .30 caliber suppressor.

"Yeeeah," she drug the word out. "That doesn't mean anything to me."

"It means it doesn't kick. And if we shoot the subsonic ammo, it's super quiet." He pulled out a box of 220 grain subsonic ammunition and began loading the internal magazine.

"Check this out," he said. He cycled the bolt, chambering a round and threw the rifle up to his shoulder. He sighted in on the hundred-meter target and squeezed off a round. It was nearly as quiet at the .22, however, the resulting gong on the target was significantly louder.

"That's what I remember!" Sandy said, pointing at the target.

Paul smiled. What a great day this was turning out to be.

5

Buyin' Girl Stuff

July 18, 2024

Paul and Sandy's Farm

Paul Michaels and his family returned to their house after a great day at the range. The weather had been nice, and everyone had generally enjoyed themselves. Paul started gathering up the guns and other gear from the bed of the side-by-side.

"I'm going to get started on dinner," Sandy announced as she walked through the front door.

McKinley started toward the door as well.

"Hey, not so fast. Grab some stuff and help me carry it inside," Paul said to McKinley.

"So close," she replied before turning back to the side-by-side.

After a couple of trips, the two of them had carried everything in and Paul started sorting through it. "After dinner, you can help me clean guns," he announced to McKinley.

She just rolled her eyes. "Yay," she responded unenthusiastically.

Paul heard his phone ding. He sat the gun case in his hand down and retrieved his phone. He started reading. "Honey, don't bother with dinner," he said without looking up.

Sandy looked over from the kitchen. "What?"

"We need to run to town. We can pick up something to eat while we're there. Grab your purse, and keys. We're taking both vehicles," he said, still looking down at his phone.

"What are you talking about?" she asked.

Paul looked up. "McKinley, grab your purse too. Let's go. Now. We're going now," he said forcefully.

"What is it?" Sandy asked again, concern creeping into her voice.

"Come on, something has happened and we need to get ahead of this," he said, grabbing Sandy's keys off the key rack and holding them out to her.

McKinley looked at her mother, confusion on her face.

Paul was losing patience. "Come on. I'll explain everything in a minute, but stop what you're doing and let's go."

Sandy grabbed her purse, which was hanging on the back of a kitchen chair by its strap. McKinley disappeared into her room, reemerging with a wallet in her hand.

Paul ushered them out the door and they all started down the sidewalk toward the driveway.

"Okay ladies, here's the deal. There's been a coordinated terrorist attack on the U.S. and there's going to be reaction. I don't know what kind of reaction yet, but..."

McKinley stopped walking. "Wait! What? What kind of terrorist attack?"

Paul reached out took her by the elbow, nudging her toward the vehicles. "I don't want to waste time on this right now because I doubt anyone is reacting yet, and I want to beat them to the punch. You ride with your mother and when we get going down the road, I'll call you and explain everything as we drive, but right now, just get in and follow me. I'll call you in a minute."

With that, Paul turned, got in his truck, closed the door, and started the engine. Then he thought of something. He jumped back out of his truck and opened the garage door. He quickly disappeared inside and reemerged carrying four empty military fuel cans. He sat them in the bed of his truck and returned to the garage, retrieving three empty yellow cans for diesel. One last trip provided three traditional red gas cans. He jumped back in the truck and hit the button to close the garage door. He glanced over at Sandy and McKinley who were both watching him, wide eyed.

He pulled his earbuds out of his pocket and quickly tucked them into his ears. He didn't have the feature on his older truck that allowed him to use his phone through the speakers of the vehicle like Sandy had on her new Durango. He looked over at them again and motioned for them to follow him as he slipped the old truck into drive. As he reached the end of the long driveway and turned out onto the paved road, he glanced back at them in his mirror. He could see Sandy's dark brown hair behind the steering wheel and McKinley's bright red hair on the passenger side. He was careful to drive at a normal speed and fought the urge to drive faster than normal.

Dang, he thought. *We should have brought McKinley's car too so we could have filled it up with gas while we were out. That's okay, I'll get it later.*

They all knew where the dead spots in the cell coverage were and he waited until he was nearly to Route 10 where he knew he would have reception, then he glanced down at his phone and hit the speed dial button to call his wife. The phone picked up immediately. McKinley spoke first.

"Dad, seriously, what's going on?"

"Okay girls, here's the deal. There were a bunch of shootings all around the country today, all at the same time. I just skimmed the article, by my Signal thread with my buddies had like fifty messages and I had twelve missed calls while we were at the range. They attacked tractor trailers all over the place. I don't know what kind of reaction we're going to see, but there's gonna be one."

"So why do we need to run off to town like it's an emergency?" It was Sandy's voice this time.

"We don't know how people are going to react. So, we are going to grab some supplies in a calm and collected manner before people make a run on the stores."

"You really think that will happen?" It was Sandy's voice again.

"I don't know, but we're already pretty well stocked at the house, so we're just going to grab a few extras to help cover us in case people start losing their minds." His voice was calm. McKinley started to calm down from the scare that he had given them by rushing them out the door.

"Ok, Dad, so where are we going?"

"I have the supply list in my phone. We're stopping at the pharmacy first, then the farm supply store. After that, we'll grab some drive through, then hit Walmart. We'll stop by the gas station on the way back so we can fill up both vehicles and the fuel cans. I brought all the empty ones."

Paul had built a fuel shed because he didn't want to store fuel in his garage or barn. He used the small concrete block structure to store gasoline, diesel, propane, Coleman fuel, and kerosene a safe distance from any other structure. He also kept spare oil and other fluids for conducting maintenance on his various machines and equipment.

McKinley spoke up again. "Dad, I thought you always said that we should avoid panic buying."

His response was calm. "That's right Honey. That's why we aren't going to run out and try to clean the store out of everything they have. I have an organized list. The things on the list are supplies that we were already going to be getting in the next couple of months anyhow, with a few exceptions. We're just moving the timeline up. On that note, try to keep to the list. If you see something else that you think we should have, we'll evaluate it. Regardless, we're going to get what we need to round out our supplies. One family's list isn't going to impede the community's ability to buy what they need. Besides, I doubt there will be an immediate impact. The stores will likely keep getting shipments, at least at first. If things go sideways, it's probably not going to be today, so our shopping today shouldn't have any impact on the big picture."

He paused and waited for a response.

After a moment, McKinley finally responded. "Yeah, I guess that makes sense." Apparently, she had taken the time to evaluate his assessment before answering.

"Ok, listen girls. I need to hang up so I can make a couple more calls. I'll talk to you when we stop at the pharmacy, okay?"

Sandy and McKinley both acknowledged and they hung up. Paul had a few minutes before they got to the pharmacy and wanted to take advantage of the time while he had cell coverage. When you live in rural West Virginia, you quickly figure out that there are areas where you don't have cell phone reception.

His first call was to his parents. Paul's father answered, then Paul added Scott with a conference call so the three men were on the phone at the same time. Scott picked up on the first ring.

"Hello? Paul? I called you earlier. What the hell's going on?"

"Hey brother. I have Dad on the phone with us."

"Hi Dad," Scott responded.

"I'm here boys. I can hear you both. Alright, Paul, like Scott just asked, what in the world is going on?"

"I haven't had time to do the research yet. I'm actually behind the eight ball on this because me and the girls were up at the range and I didn't have my phone with me. I'm going to dive into it as quick as I can, but here's what I have so far. There were several simultaneous attacks on truck drivers in different parts of the country."

Scott cut in. "We know that man, but what do you think this all means for us?"

"That's why I'm calling. Obviously, all these attacks were the work of a single, coordinated group. They hit at more or less the same time at numerous locations, even in different time zones, so they're definitely organized. I suspect in the first few hours here, some people will be in denial and they'll try to downplay it or they'll just bury their heads in the sand and try to get on with their lives because they think it won't affect them." Paul glanced over at the clock on the dash, mentally calculating how long he had left before he got to the pharmacy.

"I haven't even turned on the radio yet, but I'm sure every news station in the world right now has their own expert talking heads telling everyone what to think. We can get to that later. I only have a few minutes right now because I'm making a supply run. As soon as we hang up, I want you two to do the same thing. Look at your supplies. If there is something you can get locally that you haven't gotten around to picking up yet, go ahead and get it. Think about the perishables. Milk doesn't last long, so if you don't already have it, pick up some powdered milk, things like that."

Scott jumped in again. "Where are you headed now? The gun store?"

"No. You've seen my ammo supply. I'm good on that, and I'm definitely not going to spend money on another gun right now. I'm grabbing feed for the animals and some general supplies from Walmart. When you go out, stay calm and stay alert. People probably haven't started panicking yet and when they do, it will most likely be in the urban areas, not in the country. Of the three of us, Scott you're the one most likely to see craziness first because you're closer to a city than either of us. Just do a supply run when you get off work, then get back home. Speaking of that, Scott, it may get crazy for you at work too, so..."

Scott cut in. "Yeah, my boss already told us to expect it."

"That makes sense. Some people won't even react, but others may go nuts. Just concentrate on keeping yourselves safe. Do a critical evaluation of your supplies and try to get what you need. If nothing happens, then it will be no big deal. You'll just have some extra supplies. However, if things go south, you'll be glad you did it."

This time it was Charles who spoke up. "Boys, your mama and I are fine. I'll ask her what she needs and we can run to the store, but you two just keep yourselves safe. Maybe this will blow over soon."

"Maybe Dad, but for the time being let's assume the worst and hope for the best."

Paul took the turn onto Route 60 in Barboursville and glanced in his rear-view mirror, checking to make sure Sandy and McKinley were still behind him. They were, although another car had managed to get between them. "Okay guys, I gotta go. I'm almost to the pharmacy. I'll check in with you later. For now, just take care of yourselves and get what you need."

The stop at the pharmacy didn't take long as Paul always kept a robust store of first aid supplies and medications. However, he did grab an extra supply of over-the-counter medications that he knew his family used, plus a couple of bottles of multivitamins and other supplements. As he headed to the checkout counter, he walked past the first-aid section. He knew he was well stocked, but he couldn't resist and he paused long enough to grab a few extra items such as triple-antibiotic ointment, ACE bandages, alcohol wipes, medical tape, and some various sizes of sterile gauze. As he loaded his haul onto the checkout belt, he expected a question from the young lady ringing everything up. However, she didn't seem to notice anything out of the ordinary and told him to have a good day as he went out the door.

As Paul left the pharmacy, he made a quick call to Dangle to make sure he knew what was going on and then to Mack.

"Mack, I'm driving right now. Can you post to the group chat and make sure everyone is aware of the situation?"

"Yeah man. Everyone knows. Haven't you looked at the chat?"

"Sorry, I've busy taking care of things with my family. I'll reach out in a little while, okay?" Paul glanced at the clock on the dash again, trying to assess how long it would be before he got home. "I'm not sure how long it's going to take, but I'll check in later."

"All right buddy," Mack replied. "We'll talk later. Keep your powder dry."

"Always," Paul replied and the two men hung up as Paul turned into the parking lot of the farming supply store.

This stop netted several fifty-pound bags of chicken food, rabbit food, and a few other items. All this went into the bed of the truck. Next, as promised, they ran through a drive thru and then it was on to Walmart.

As Paul walked into Walmart with his family, he was scanning the crowd, looking for any indication of concern, panic, or threats. Everything appeared normal. Sandy and McKinley noticed the same thing.

"Dad?" McKinley asked.

"Yeah, Baby?"

"Nothing seems any different than normal," she said as she scanned from left to right.

"That's a good thing. We're trying to get ahead of things. Hopefully, I'm wrong and this will all be for nothing. But if I'm right, we'll be glad we did this," he replied.

"Okay," Sandy cut in. She and McKinley were both pushing a shopping cart. Paul had his own. "How do we do this?"

He stopped and faced his girls. "First things first. You two go to the pharmacy section and I want you to get six months' worth of everything you two need," he said deadpan.

"Wait," McKinley shot back. "What do you mean by everything we need?"

Paul didn't hesitate. "Feminine hygiene, shower stuff -- whatever you have in the bathroom that you need on a day-to-day or month-to-month basis. Estimate how much you use in a month and buy six times that."

"Seriously, Dad?"

"Look. I pay attention to how many boxes of tampons we have in the supply closet, just like I track the toilet paper, paper towels, and other stuff. However, I don't actually know how much you use in a month. I just put it on the grocery list when I see us get down to a certain point, so I know how many boxes of everything we have. However, I hadn't gotten around to calculating how fast you go through it. You should be able to think about it and at least get close. Take one of the carts, get everything you can think of that you need. Notice that I said things you need, not things you want. Don't worry about body wash or shampoo. We have at least a year's worth of that. If anyone makes a comment, just laugh it off and don't acknowledge anything about an emergency or anything like that. Just keep moving and get it done. Once you have a full cart, go ahead and check out and take it out to the Durango then come back inside. Text me when you're back."

Neither of them said anything. They just stood there looking at him.

Finally, Paul spoke. "Do you understand?"

"Okay," said Sandy with a sigh. "What are you doing?"

"I'm grabbing a few things from the camping section, then I'm getting extra bags for the vacuum sealer, Ziplocs, paper plates, paper towels, and some other disposable items. That should fill my cart up." He looked down at the list on his phone, then continued. "After that, I have additional items on the list for when I come back for the second round. Just act like it's any other day at the store. We don't want to draw any attention to ourselves. I have the other key to the Durango, so we can work independently for this part. By the time we both are going for our second trip, we can link up and hit the food section together. Got it?"

Sandy spoke up again. "I can't help but feel like maybe we're overreacting."

"We may be," responded Paul. "However, what does it hurt? If nothing happens, we don't buy tampons for a while. So what? Now let's get moving." With that, he put his hands back on his shopping cart and headed down the aisle toward the camping section.

Sandy turned toward McKinley. "Okay, I guess we're buying girl stuff." She used air quotes as she said "girl stuff."

McKinley responded with a slight giggle. "I guess we are." They both pushed their carts in the direction of the pharmacy.

A half hour later, Paul had already loaded his first purchase into the SUV and was grabbing batteries from the stand-alone battery station. He knew he had a sufficient supply at home. He always kept a lot on hand. However, now he felt the need to add to his supply. He selected some AA, AAA , CR123, and CR2032 batteries that he knew some of his optics used. As he was dropping the last of them in his cart. He did a mental calculation of the cost. *Dang, batteries are expensive.* He felt his phone vibrate. He pulled it out and looked down at the screen.

We're back inside. Now what?

He didn't bother texting back. He just dialed Sandy. She picked up immediately.

"Hello?"

"Hey, meet me over behind the checkout area. I'm getting batteries."

Two minutes later, they were all together again and heading toward the back of the store. Sandy and McKinley were pushing empty carts as Paul looked at the list on his phone. "Okay, according to my inventory, we have four bottles of bleach at the house."

Sandy looked up as she tried to picture the shelf over the washing machine. "That sounds right."

"We're going over to the cleaning section to grab some more bleach, Clorox wipes, and other cleaning supplies first."

"We need more than four bottles?" McKinley asked.

"I've talked to you about all the things bleach can be used for. Plus, it will keep and we can even use it as a trade item if it ever came down to it."

McKinley grinned at the suggestion. "How much for that bacon, Mister?" She then answered herself in a mock exaggerated country accent. "How about a pint jar of bleach?"

This elicited a chuckle from Sandy.

Paul grinned too, but replied more seriously. "I hope it doesn't get to that, but either way, I'd like to make sure we have a good supply."

This is how it went for the next hour or so. Paul went over his lists and added items where he thought they could benefit from additional inventory. They ended up adding hygiene supplies, cleaning supplies, more food items, the batteries he had selected, and even some socks for McKinley.

When they got home, everyone pitched in to empty the vehicles of the supplies. As they put things away, Paul added them to his lists, keeping up the inventory of what they had. Finally, he flopped down on the couch, exhausted. He glanced across the room at the pile of gear from the range earlier.

Crap. He still needed to clean the guns. Maybe he could still rope McKinley into helping. Or *maybe* it could wait until tomorrow. He pulled out his phone to check his messages again and sighed at the number of them. It looked as if nearly everyone he knew had texted him. He was going to advise everyone to prepare for the possibility that these attacks might lead to further problems—and things could always get worse. Paul was right on both counts.

Over the Precipice

6

The Collective, Part I

July 18, 2024

The chairman spoke first at the unscheduled meeting. "Thank you for taking time from your busy schedules. You all know that I don't like unscheduled meetings, but I felt that this was an appropriate time to call one.

Several of the other ten people on the screen nodded, while a couple responded with subdued answers indicating that it was fine.

"Considering the recent events of the attacks in the U.S., I'm sure that some of you may be wondering if some members of The Collective were aware of the plan, and you were excluded. I want to immediately put those concerns to rest. I can assure that we were not aware of the plans to launch terror attacks on U.S. soil. If we decide to move that direction in the future, everyone on this call will be included in that discussion."

Several silhouettes on the screen could be seen nodding.

"Of course, we *did* facilitate the entry of millions of undocumented migrants across an unsecured border over the last few years. So, while we didn't specifically participate in the planning of these terror attacks, we did facilitate the conditions to allow them, and I for one, was assuming it was only a matter of time," the chairman continued.

"Now, before I continue, would anyone else like to add anything?" He paused to allow the others to speak up.

The tech CEO spoke up first. The screen said "—Del Mar—" under his silhouette. "My first impression is that these attacks didn't go far enough," he began. "And, from the reports that I've seen, none of the attackers were killed or captured, so do we have any way to find out if they intend to continue, and what is their end goal?"

The chairman fielded the question. "I've reached out to our Iranian friends, but they are not sharing anything yet. I assured them that if they wanted to maintain the flow of money, they will need to include us in future plans."

"And how was that received?" asked the woman in Washington, D.C.

"They claimed that the cells in the United States were given some freedom to decide when and where to attack. They claimed that they didn't know the attacks were going to happen either."

"Do you believe that nonsense?" It was Del Mar again.

"No. That was a blatant lie. I suspect they're claiming ignorance in an effort to keep us in the dark. I know how that regime operates and there is no way they would give that much latitude to a subordinate commander." The Chairman maintained his cool demeanor as he spoke.

"I know everyone on this call is aware that we paved the way for Joe to cut a deal with Iran last September to free up six billion dollars for them. We all also know what they immediately did with that money, since one month later Hamas attacked Isreal. That money allowed them to finalize the planning for that attack and very likely facilitated these attacks on the United States as well."

The Chairman placed his hand on his computer mouse and clicked 'Send' on a prepared email.

"I've just sent a file to your secure email accounts with everything we know right now about these attacks. Obviously, there's information in that file that has not been made public yet; some of it will never be released to the public. As our informants in the various agencies continue to obtain information, I'll share anything pertinent with the group. I'll give you some time to review the information and we'll discuss it at our next scheduled meeting."

Thirty minutes later, The Chairman left his secure communication room and walked to his home library. He nodded to William, a member of his protection detail as he passed him. "William."

The man nodded back with a simple response. "Sir."

William looked like the stereotypical bodyguard. He was a muscled six-foot-tall white man with a military haircut, cauliflower ears, and a suit that was tailored to allow the concealment of a handgun and radio. The dark gray suit, thin black tie, and pressed shirt radiated professionalism as he stood in the hallway outside the library with his hands clasped loosely in front of him.

The Chairman had a rule that he didn't want to hear the security radios, so William also had a Bluetooth earpiece linked to the radio. The old days of the discreet earpiece wire coming out of the collar were long gone.

The Chairman paused in the doorway and turned to William.

"I don't want to be disturbed."

The big man turned and reached for the door as The Chairman crossed the room toward the majestic desk, the centerpiece of the room.

"Of course, sir."

He closed the door and resumed his position beside it.

The Chairman settled into the upholstered chair and opened his laptop. After meeting all the security requirements, he initiated a video call to the CEO at Steel Global Group. The call connected almost immediately.

"Hello, sir. What can I do for you today?" Archibald "Archie" Newsome answered in a pleasant voice, as one did when talking to a valued client.

The Chairman did not bother with formalities; he got straight to business. "Is everything prepared?"

"Yessir. Everything is prepared in accordance with our agreements."

"And the additional locations?" The Chairman asked.

"Yessir, we finished with the last of the new locations over a week ago." Archie replied, sounding very pleased with himself.

"What about the communication project?"

Archie deliberately made the effort to maintain the same tone to the response. "That has proven quite difficult. However, I anticipate success on that project in the near future."

The Chairman instantly saw through the nebulous language. "The near future is not an answer. When will the project be complete?"

"My team feels that six weeks is a realistic number."

The Chairman forced himself not to yell as he felt his blood pressure rising at the answer. "Six weeks?! It was supposed to be done a month ago, and now you're saying you need another six weeks?!"

"Well, there are logistical challenges due to the terrain. Plus, we're using a small crew to keep the signature low. This is a very specialized crew of highly trained individuals. I'm sure you understand. We only hire the best."

The Chairman flexed his jaw. "How much?"

"Sir?"

"How much is it going to cost us to speed up the process. I want it complete in three weeks." The Chairman was furious.

"Oh, well, I mean, I could potentially add another specialty crew, but I'd probably have to bring them in from Switzerland, so it's probably not really feasible."

"How...much?" The Chairman enunciated each word through gritted teeth.

"Well, sir, if you insist, I could probably get the other crew. Of course, I'll likely have to pull them off another job, so I would say another..." He paused as if he were calculating, although The Chairman knew that he wasn't. "...six hundred thousand would probably do it."

The line was briefly silent as the Chairman took a breath. "Five hundred thousand and I won't..." He stopped himself. He wanted to say, 'five hundred thousand and I won't kill your family. Instead, he said "...and I won't treat this as a breach of contract.

Archie smiled. "I think that's an acceptable compromise Mr. Pres...um, I mean, sir. I'll have it done. We at Steel Global genuinely appreciate your business. Is there anything else I can help you with today?"

There was no response.

"Hello?" Archie looked down at his phone. The Chairman had hung up.

Archie chuckled lightly. "Pleasure doing business with you."

7

Getting Ready for a Hurricane

July 18, 2024

Charles and Edna's Farm

Charles walked back to the house after talking to his sons. He had been out in the barn working on one of his numerous projects when Paul called earlier. As he entered the house, he didn't see Edna, so he called her name.

"I'm in here," she called back. She was in their bedroom, folding clothes on the bed. "What's up?" she asked, as she shook out a t-shirt and laid it on the bed to begin folding it as he entered the bedroom.

"I just hung up with Paul and Scott. Did you have the television on while I was outside?"

"No, I've been working on laundry for a little while and just getting some things done around the house." She finished folding the t-shirt and placed it on a stack of others. "Why do you ask?"

"Apparently, there were some shootings around the country and Paul seems pretty sure that it's terrorism."

Her hand shot up and covered her mouth. "Oh no. How bad is it?"

"I don't really know yet, but Paul really feels like we should go ahead and stock up on anything we might need in the immediate future. You know, just to be safe." His expression was solemn and he intentionally kept his tone calm and even in an attempt to prevent his wife from being too alarmed.

"Well, what do you think?" She dropped her hand back to her side.

"I don't really know what to think. I need to check the news, but Paul and Scott seemed to be in agreement that we should go ahead and get anything we think we might need, so I'm going to take their advice. Do you want to go with me?"

"I guess I can do that. Just let me finish folding this load of laundry and we'll take off. Give me about five minutes." She grabbed the next item from the laundry basket.

Charles took a step toward his wife and gave her a quick kiss on the cheek. "That'll be fine, Dear. I'll just wash up while you finish here." He headed for the bathroom to wash the grime of his project off his hands.

Forty-five minutes later, they were at Walmart. Charles was leaning on the partially filled shopping cart in front of the dairy cooler. As she turned around with two pounds of butter, Edna suddenly noticed her neighbor, Jenny.

"Well, hello Jenny. How are you?" she said with a warm smile.

Jenny had a bewildered look on her face for just a moment as her brain placed where she knew this woman from. "Oh! Hi Miss Edna. I'm fine. How are y'all doin'?"

"We're okay. We're just picking up a few things. Did you hear? There's been some kind of shooting." Edna leaned in and lowered her voice conspiratorially.

"Um, I heard something, but I don't know anything about it," she replied softly.

"Oh, Jenny, what happened to your lip? You have a cut there," Edna said, noticing an injury on the left side of Jenny's mouth.

She covered her mouth with a cupped hand. "Oh, yeah, I tripped. I'm clumsy sometimes."

Billy walked up as the two were talking. He dropped a six pack of beer into the cart beside Jenny. "Hurry up Jenny, we ain't got time to be hangin' out in Walmart all day. I got crap to do," he said without acknowledging Charles or Edna. Edna noticed Jenny startle slightly as the beer landed in the cart.

"Billy, you remember our neighbors, don't you?" Jenny said, sounding uncomfortable.

He looked up and made eye contact with Charles. "Oh, yeah. What was your name again?"

Charles didn't offer his hand. "Charles," he replied.

"Oh yeah, Charles." He looked over at Edna. "Betty, right?"

Charles interrupted before Edna could answer. "My wife's name is Edna."

"Yeah, yeah. I knew it was something like that." He looked down at the cart that Charles was still leaning on.

"Damn, y'all getting ready for a hurricane or somethin'?"

"No. Haven't you heard? There's…"

Charles cut Edna off. "No. No. We're just doing some grocery shopping. It was good seeing you kids, but we don't want to keep you. I know you're in a hurry. Take care."

He looked over at Edna. "Come on Honey, we still need to grab a couple of things." He nodded his head toward the direction of the breakfast meats.

"Um, okay." Edna looked back at Jenny.

"You take care of that sweet cat. We'll see you later, Jenny."

"Bye, Miss Edna."

As Charles pushed the cart away, he glanced into Billy and Jenny's cart. He noted that it only had some cereal, milk, ramen, and beer in it. He kept walking.

Billy watched as the older couple walked away. He turned to Jenny. "What were you yappin' with them about?"

"Nothin' Billy. She just said hi to me."

He didn't acknowledge her response, but motioned toward the departing couple. "What the hell do those two need with all that food? Did you see all that?"

"You heard him. They're just doing their shopping. They probably only get to the store once a month. You know how old people are." Her voice was soft as she spoke.

"Yeah," he said, looking down the aisle at them. Charles was pushing the cart and Edna had her hand tucked around Charles' left arm. "Old, *rich* people."

Later that evening, Charles and Edna had the groceries put away and had settled onto the couch to watch the news and try to figure out what was going on with these attacks. They checked a few stations before settling on one of the major news networks. There was a panel of two men and a woman sitting around a table, already in the middle of a conversation.

The woman was speaking. She was an attractive black woman wearing a perfectly tailored red suit that accentuated her trim physique beautifully. She brushed her long black hair away from face as she spoke. "That may be so, Colin, but we have no evidence at this point that this was foreign actors. This could just as easily be right-wing gun nuts trying to create problems for this administration ahead of November's election. And let's be honest here: the rise in Christian Nationalism has been directly tied to the increase in hate crimes in America. Their complete intolerance of modern society has encouraged violence for years."

One of the men interrupted her. He was bald with a very neatly trimmed goatee. He also wore a stylish, perfectly tailored suit. "Now Abby, let's not jump to conclusions. We don't know..."

She cut him off before he could finish his statement. "I'm not saying that's what this is, Victor. I'm just saying that it wouldn't surprise me if that's what it turns out to be. I know the FBI and Homeland Security are acknowledging that it's a terrorist attack. I just won't be shocked if tomorrow they reclassify this as domestic terrorism."

Now it was Colin's turn. "We should really show some restraint before making any predictions. There are numerous locations involved; countless law enforcement agencies are cooperating to investigate each site. I'm sure as more details emerge in the coming days, we'll be able to draw a much better picture of the situation.

"I agree," began Victor. "I don't think..."

Abby cut him off again "Victor, you're a gay man! The white Christian Nationalist movement has shown no tolerance for you. How can you sit there and defend them?" Her voice had climbed an octave.

"I'm not defending anyone! I'm just not accusing anyone yet either. Look, I've seen my fair share of discrimination. Yes, I'm gay. *And* I'm black. I've lived with discrimination my whole life..."

Charles reached over and plucked the remote control from Edna's hand. "Let's find a different channel." He looked down at the remote and found the right button to cycle through the channels, finally settling on another news broadcast. This one had a fifty-something white man in the field. His graying hair was in slight disarray from the wind. A chaotic scene was visible in the background. Numerous law enforcement vehicles were visible with blue lights flashing. The reporter was looking directly into the camera.

"The California Highway Patrol has established a corridor around the crash site as emergency crews work to empty the tanker of all fuel. Again, we want to reiterate that no fuel leak has been reported, but an official from the Federal Motor Carrier Safety Administration stated that all the fuel must be pumped out of the overturned tank before they can continue with recovery operations. Unfortunately, the driver, Antonio Mendez, was pronounced dead at the scene. You can see here," the reporter motioned to his left. The camera panned to the indicated direction. "An impromptu vigil has sprung up for Mr. Mendez. He lived only seven miles from the crash site with his wife and three children. The community has shown an overwhelming amount of..."

Charles started searching through the channels again for another station, stopping on another discussion in a studio. A lone anchor sat behind a desk. The screen was split and the other side had the words "On the phone with Geraldine

Wilkerson, Department of Homeland Security." Below the words was a photo of a woman of about sixty wearing a conservative white blouse and smiling for the camera.

The woman's words were slightly distorted as they often are when a phone call is broadcast through the television. "Our official statement remains unchanged. First and foremost, we ask that the American people do not panic. Everyone should continue on with their day-to-day life. The threat has passed and we're working around the clock to bring those responsible for these reprehensible attacks to justice. Homeland is leveraging numerous state and federal agencies to keep our citizens safe. This includes the FBI, FEMA, US Marshalls and BATFE."

Charles turned to Edna. "Did she say FEMA? Why would FEMA possibly be involved in this?"

Edna wasn't concerned. "Oh, Honey, we don't really know how these things work. I'm sure they're just trying to help."

He turned back toward the television as the bodiless voice continued to explain how everything was under control. "I guess."

8

Radio Check, Over

July 19, 2024

Paul and Sandy's Farm

Paul's phone rang and he looked down at the screen. It was Mack.

"What's up Mack?"

"Hey buddy. Did you get everything squared away yesterday?"

"Yeah, for the most part, but everything still seems pretty calm. Maybe it was an overreaction," Paul answered.

"Maybe," Mack began. "However, others are taking notice too. We got several calls this morning for security work. Are you good to go on the schedule?"

"Probably. How soon are we talking?"

"First shift is tonight, starting at 1800, but I wouldn't need you until tomorrow morning, 0600 in Winchester. Can you do it?"

Paul considered this for a moment. He would be over two hours from his home. However, he hadn't seen any indication that that things were deteriorating. "Normal pay?" Paul asked.

"Yeah, same as the Louisville job. You'll be a site lead. Normal shifts, twelve on twelve off. We have a room onsite where you can sleep if you just want to stay there since you have more of a drive than some of the other guys."

"What are we guarding?"

"Some big industrial supply warehouse company. I just sent the info to your phone. They deal with logistics. Apparently, one of the trucks that got hit was somehow affiliated with this company, so their corporate bigwigs are reacting by adding armed security. They're worried about liability if they don't. They have some unarmed rent-a-cops onsite, but now they want *actual* security. The rent-a-cops will still be doing their thing, checking access badges and handling freight coming in, that kind of thing, so we'll communicate with them, but the physical security duties will be on us."

Paul's phone buzzed in his hand and he looked down at it, reading the information. "Corporate Drive? Yeah, that sounds like a good place for a warehouse. Okay, I'm in. Can you send me the roster?"

"You got it buddy. Let me know if you need anything."

"Standard loadout?" Paul asked.

"Yeah, they want us to be low vis with the ability to ramp up, so dress for concealed carry. Keep your AR and armor and all that in the truck and ready to go. I already added the packing list to the Signal chat. We have the new radios we're trying out, but go ahead and bring your regular one too in case we have any issues with the new ones. Loki is still working out the bugs."

"You got it man. If I think of any questions, I'll send you a message."

"Sounds good. Talk to you later," Mack said, wrapping up the conversation.

"Later."

The two hung up.

Paul clicked the blue and white icon on his phone for the Signal app and saw the packing list:

Dress for concealed carry/collared shirt

Pistol/spare mags
Radio/spare battery/charger
Rifle/mags
Plate Carrier
Concealed armor-optional
Night vision
IFAK
Flashlight

We'll have the company first aid bag onsite, plus the regular supplies that we normally have. If you're going to stay onsite, bring a cot or whatever you want to sleep on. There is no laundry, so bring plenty of clothes. There's a bunch of food places nearby, plus there's a break room with snack machines and coffee. Shifts are 0600-1800 and 1800-0600.

As Paul read the message, he was already developing a plan for additional gear. He always traveled with his get home bag in his truck, plus he was going to take a couple of five-gallon fuel cans, food, and of course his suppressed AR-15. His truck also had a toolbox in the bed that was stocked with tools and various emergency gear. He scrolled down to the next message:

Schedule:
Night shift is 1800-0600
Day shift is 0600-1800

We're starting tonight:
Night shift: Irish & Pikey

Day shift: Doc & Loki
Night shift: Irish & Pikey

Day shift: Doc & Loki
Night shift: Irish & Buck

I'll post more of the schedule after I iron it out. The first contract is for seven days, so we have at least that much work. Text me if you have any days that you're not available. More to follow.

Paul needed to talk to Sandy to let her know what was going on. He found her in the living room watching TV.

"Hey, you got a sec?"

She paused the sitcom. "Yeah, what's up?"

"Mack just called. We got a security gig."

"That didn't take long. Where is it?"

"Winchester. It's about two and half hours from here. Are you good with me taking off for a few days?"

She didn't hesitate. "Yeah. We still have to keep the lights on. Besides, I don't think this whole situation is going to be that big of a deal."

"I'm still undecided. We need to work under the assumption that it could get ugly at any moment. You have the emergency plan. It's in my office. If I need to head home, I will. For the time being, we just live our lives, but we need to be ready to react to whatever happens," he said.

"I know the plan. Go. Make money. Protect things. That's what you do," she added playfully.

"All right. I'm going to go to bed early. I need to leave here at three o'clock tomorrow morning."

She chuckled. "Better you than me."

"All right," he said. "I'm going to go get my gear ready."

The next morning, he pulled into the jobsite at five thirty and met up with Irish and Pikey.

"What's up guys? How'd it go last night?" he said as a greeting.

Pikey spoke up. "All quiet on the Western Front. It's pretty straight forward. Come on, I'll give you the nickel tour."

Alex Murray, callsign "Pikey," was clearly of Scottish descent. His fair skin was the subject of countless jokes. Paul had once told him that he wasn't white, he was translucent. He was married with a young daughter, and was a reliable teammate. Pikey was the kind of guy who was easy to be around. He was always quick with a joke and smile. He could perfectly mimic a Scottish accent, which Paul thought was hilarious. It was even funnier when he was around Tony "Irish" Quinn who could do an Irish accent equally well. The two would sometimes argue back and forth in their respective accents, entertaining anyone who was close enough to hear.

Pikey led the way around the facility giving Paul the ins and out of the jobsite. As they were talking, they saw Loki arrive and start talking with Irish, who was undoubtedly doing the same thing.

"That's the rear gate," Pikey said, motioning to a large gate toward the back of the spacious parking lot. "You'll get trucks coming in back there at all hours. The Alpha Security guys will take care of checking their paperwork, but we've been providing overwatch when it happens because they leave the gate open while they're doing their thing. It might not be as big a deal for you on day shift, but for us, we were a little more concerned. You can't see what's back there during the night. We've already identified the need for additional lighting to the client. We'll see what happens. Probably nothing."

They continued to walk around the back of the building.

"Over here is one of the weak points we've identified. You can see that tree over there with limbs hanging over the fence. Someone could easily climb that tree, use the limb to clear the fence, and then drop inside. Plus, there are no cameras covering that area. We've been keeping an eye on it. That's in the report too. We've asked that they get a tree service in here to cut the limb off. Like I said before. We'll see what happens." He started walking again.

"Let me show you all the access points to the building." He continued around the complex, briefing Paul on their duties and responsibilities for the next ten minutes, before leading him inside and doing the same thing for the interior of the building.

"We both spent a couple of hours each last night just walking around and getting familiar with the place, looking for security concerns. Everything is in the duty log. I'm sure y'all will find even more in the daylight. You got any questions?" Pikey's voice betrayed his fatigue from working the night shift.

"Nah man, I got it. Go get you some rest. Are you going home?"

"Oh yeah. I'm only about forty-five minutes from the house. I'm gonna go crash hard. I'll see you in twelve hours," he said.

"Sounds good, brother. Do I need that badge?"

"Oh yeah," Pikey said, pulling a lanyard from around his neck. "Here ya go. This badge will open any room in the building. They gave us full access."

"Thanks man."

"You know it," Pikey replied wearily.

After Irish and Pikey left, Paul and Loki spent the first part of their shift familiarizing themselves with the facility and establishing their routine. Mack had dropped off a black Tri Point Solutions Suburban for the jobsite. They both stashed their gear in the vehicle. It was parked beside the building in a way that would not block the natural flow of traffic through the parking lot and it was quickly accessible if they needed to get to their gear.

Tri Point did not provide gear or weapons. Everyone had to have their own stuff. As a result, everyone's gear was different. Much of it was similar, but not exactly the same. However, there were a few requirements. The pistols were limited to 9mm or .45 ACP. Rifles had to be 5.56mm AR variants.

The two men finished their reconnaissance and walked back toward the Suburban.

"Hey Doc, you running your CZ tonight?" Loki asked.

"Yeah." He lifted his shirt tail to briefly expose his P10C. "How about you? What do you have?"

Loki was wearing a light windbreaker. He pulled it open to reveal a Smith & Wesson M&P 9mm Shield. "I have my Smith. It's easier to conceal."

"Yeah, I get that. What rifle did you bring?"

"I'll show you what I have." Loki opened the back of the big SUV with the key fob.

Once it was open the two men did a quick comparison of gear so they would know everything that was onsite. Both of them had AR-15 pistols with ten and a half inch barrels and mounted infrared lasers. They also had similar plate carrier setups. The plate carriers had magazine pouches for additional AR-15 magazines plus a radio pouch. Each man had his own version of an Individual First Aid Kit, or IFAK, which included a tourniquet.

Loki had a PVS-14-night vision monocular, while Paul had a set of PVS-15 night vision goggles, which covered both eyes. After comparing notes and finalizing their plan for the night, they settled into the front seat of the vehicle for a few minutes before they needed to do their next round. Loki was in the passenger seat and grabbed the clipboard to log their activity.

Paul reached over from the driver's seat and turned on the radio, tuning it to a news station.

"...as grocery stores around the country are reporting higher than normal sales. The Albertsons in Bakersfield, California reported their highest single day of sales on record. However, despite the higher demand, most major retailers are reporting that they do not anticipate the surge outpacing their supply.

Online suppliers are also reporting an uptick in orders. Once again, there are no indications of shortages."

The broadcast continued. "On a related note, gun stores around the country are also reporting increased sales of both firearms and ammunition. A spokesperson for a major gun store in Raleigh, North Carolina spoke to us earlier today."

A different voice came over the radio. "Yeah, we stayed busy all day. It was mostly handgun and ammunition sales, although we also had a bunch of people interested in MSRs."

A reporter's voice responded. "MSRs? And what is that?"

"Oh," the man responded. "That's a Modern Sporting Rifle, like an AR-15."

The reporter again: "You mean assault rifles?"

"No. These are all semi-automatics, so they aren't assault rifles."

"But doesn't AR *literally* stand for Assault Rifle?" the reporter asked.

The man chuckled. "No. That's a common misconception. It's Armalite Rifle. You see..."

Paul spoke up. "I can't believe people are still recycling that."

Loki looked up from the clipboard. "What?"

"The reporter. He...never mind. Do you have the log updated?" Paul reached over and turned the radio down until it was barely discernable.

"Yeah. I got everything. What was up with the radio?" Loki asked as he tossed the clipboard up onto the dashboard. "I wasn't listening."

"Oh, they were just saying that people hit the grocery stores and gun stores hard today," Paul replied, lowering his window to let in some fresh air.

"Well, that was predictable. Did they say anything about the banks?" He lowered his window too.

"Not in that report, but it wouldn't surprise me if that's next. We'll see. I'm still hopeful that this is going to blow over."

Loki looked over at him. "Is that what you think is going to happen?"

"I mean, potentially. It was certainly a disruption, but from what I'm seeing so far, it's not that big of a deal in the grand scheme of things. Of course, the families that just lost their husbands or fathers wouldn't see it that way, but on the national scale, it's not that dramatic. It's certainly no 9/11," Paul said flatly.

"Yeah, I guess we'll see soon enough."

"Yes. Yes, we will. Don't get me wrong, I still plussed up my supplies, but if I thought the sky was falling, I wouldn't be pulling security in Kentucky. I'd be at home protecting my family and homestead."

"Fair enough. Obviously, I'm here too, so that tells you that I'm in the same boat. But I don't know. I just can't put my finger on it. Something doesn't feel right." Loki pulled his phone out and read a text message.

Paul continued. "I definitely agree with that. It's hard to believe that they haven't caught anyone yet." He motioned toward Loki's phone with his chin. "Is everything okay?"

"Yeah. It's my wife. She's just checking in. I heard that they found shell casings at more than one site, though. Maybe they'll pull some prints off them."

Paul looked over at him. "I hadn't heard that. Where did you hear that?"

"It was in a news report earlier. I heard it on the way here."

"Did they give any additional information?" Paul asked, turning slightly to face Loki.

"No. They just called them shell casings from a high-powered rifle."

"Well, that could be anything. Plus, the freakin' news calls all kinds of things a *high-powered rifle*." He used air quotes as he said *high-powered rifle*.

He continued. "I heard them report on a raid on someone's house one time, where some three-letter agency found an *arsenal* of seven guns and over a thousand rounds of ammunition and they acted like they'd discovered a freakin' nuclear bomb." He used the air quotes a second time as he said *arsenal*.

Loki laughed. "Yeah. Seven guns. *Scary*. Hell, I have three with me."

"Three? What else do you have?" Paul asked.

"I have my Shield on my ankle," he said with a grin.

"Well played sir. Well played." Paul was smiling now too.

Loki stared at him for a moment. "Well?"

"Well, what?" Paul asked, suppressing a smile.

"Well, what else do you have?"

"Okay, you got me. I have my P10S as a backup. What can I say? I'm a sucker for magazine compatibility."

"You and those CZs man," Loki said, shaking his head with a grin. He glanced down at his watch and got serious again. "It's about time for a perimeter check."

"Okay. Let's do a radio check. I'll take the first patrol," Paul said, pulling out his radio and opening the door.

He closed the door and took several steps away from the vehicle.

"Loki, Loki, this is Doc. Radio check. Over." Paul watched through the windshield as Loki raised the radio.

"Doc, this is Loki. Lima Charlie. Over."

"Loki, Doc. Same. Out." Paul walked back over to the open window of the vehicle.

"Sounds good. I'll check in when I get to the rear gate."

"Cool," Loki responded. "I'll be here."

Paul walked off and disappeared behind the massive structure.

9

I'm Talking to You!

July 21, 2024, 10:00 a.m. Eastern Standard Time

Winchester, Kentucky

Paul started his shift at 6:00 a.m., just as he had for the last three days. He had already conducted the handover brief and was now four hours into his twelve-hour shift. He was working with Pikey today. Loki had the day off. So far, this job had been easy money. The only drama in the last few days had been a couple of teenagers who had parked by the back gate to smoke pot. Irish and Bill "Buck" Wagner had run them off as soon as they sat down on their tailgate. Buck was the youngest person working for Tri Point and Mack had started calling him "Young Buck." It didn't take long before that got shortened to "Buck" and became his callsign.

After this shift, Paul was going to drive home for a three-day break. For the time being, he just needed some coffee, so he headed into the building and struck a direct route to the breakroom. As Paul neared the door, he heard the television going. It was on a news channel and they were discussing the upcoming presidential election. Paul glanced up at the screen and then turned toward the coffee station.

As he pressed start on the Keurig coffee maker, the announcer launched into the next story.

"New reports are coming in about various trucking organizations demanding protection. Joining us now from New York is Vincent Capitani. Vinny, what are you hearing out there?"

The screen changed to show a short reporter with dark hair and a prominent nose. He spoke with a notable New York accent.

"That's right, Cliff. Several organizations representing American truckers have spoken up about concern for the safety of their members. Law Enforcement has yet to make a single arrest following last week's widespread attack on our nation's number one delivery system for nearly everything we need in our daily lives. A recent report from the Bureau of Transportation Statics shows that approximately three quarters of everything we buy, eat, or use in the United States arrives by tractor trailer. Representatives from the American Trucking Association, the Truckload Carriers Association, the National Association of Small Trucking Companies, and more have released a public statement. We have a clip of that statement."

Once again, the screen changed. This time it was a small conference room. An overweight man stood behind a wooden podium with several flags flanking a United States flag in the background. Several men and one woman sat in chairs neatly arranged in front of the flags. The man in front was balding with a ring of white hair encircling his shiny head. The glare of the lights off the man's head was the first thing Paul noticed. The clip began in the middle of the man's prepared speech. His name was displayed on the bottom of the screen. *Stanley Ray Morris, President, American Trucker Association.*

"I know that the FBI has stated that they believe the threat has passed. However, our collective organizations," he paused to motion to the group of people seated behind him, "have no reason to believe that's true. The FBI has called it a terrorist attack and we believe that part's true. However, the terrorists are still out there. How are we supposed to sleep at night sending our dedicated drivers out into what could become a combat zone at any moment?"

Stanley paused as the group behind him offered a polite applause. Additional applause could be heard from somewhere in the room that was not visible on the screen.

"I'll tell you this right now! Law Enforcement had better start showing results, or you're gonna see more people decide that this would be a great time for a vacation! We've seen an eight percent increase in drivers turning down loads. Now this is not our organizations directing this. It's drivers making this decision on their own. I'm talking company drivers and owner-operators alike. This is just truckers; husbands and wives making a decision that they need to be safe. Safe for their families. All of our organizations make this public statement right now. We will not penalize any driver for taking a leave of absence in the interest of their own safety."

He pointed directly at the camera as he continued.

"I'm talking to you, Mr. FBI Director! Get out there and do your damn job!"

Paul turned and walked out of the breakroom with his coffee. *Well, this is getting interesting.*

Paul walked across the parking lot to the Suburban. Pikey was standing outside the Suburban, beside the driver's door, looking down at the clipboard as Paul walked up. The driver's window was down and the radio was on.

The man on the radio was stressing the importance of staying calm.

> "The most important thing to remember is there is no need to panic. The shortages in the grocery stores will be short-lived. The Federal Emergency Management Agency has asked that citizens not panic buy and please just purchase what you need. They have stressed that widespread panic buying could create artificial shortages, such as the now reported shortage of toilet paper in some areas."

Pikey looked up. "What's up, buddy?"

"I hear there's a new shortage of TP," Paul said with a grin.

"Yeah, just like COVID all over again. People love their toilet paper. That's apparently the new currency."

Paul chuckled. "Yeah, how much for a Big Mac? That'll be two and half rolls. Please pull around to the first window."

Now it was Pikey's turn to laugh.

"I did buy a few extra things right after the attack, but there were no shortages yet. Plus, I was already stocked up pretty well, so it wasn't that dramatic," Paul said, more seriously.

"Yeah, same here. Nothing major. I picked up another case of powdered milk. My kid loves her cereal in the morning. It's not like we can stock up on milk, but if we mix up some powdered milk and pour it over cereal, I think we can sneak it past her."

He turned and gently tossed the clipboard into the front seat. "Did you hear about the riots?"

"What?" Paul said, raising his eyebrows at the news.

"Yeah, Chicago, San Francisco, and Detroit. I think that's it. Of course, the riots were just a cover for the real purpose."

"Let me guess," began Paul. "Looting?"

"You guessed it. Guess what the number one thing being stolen is?"

Paul thought for a second, then smiled. "Toilet paper?"

Pikey chuckled. "No, but that was a good guess." He paused for effect. "Flat screen TVs!"

Both men burst out in laughter, then Paul was the first to speak. "Hey man, don't judge! People need new TVs to make up for the lack of toilet paper!"

"Oh yeah, definitely. There was a shoe store in Detroit that got raided. I saw the video. They busted out the glass doors and were carrying out stacks of shoe boxes. One guy even showed up with a shopping cart and brought it in with him! It was a madhouse. Freakin' people, man. Freakin' people."

He was shaking his head. "In Chicago, a mob attacked a police car and set it on fire."

Paul was incredulous. "And what exactly are they protesting? Why are they attacking the police?"

"Who knows man. Some people are just looking for a reason to be assholes. Apparently, a terrorist attack is as good a reason as any."

Paul shook his head slightly as he considered the statement. "Apparently. Is that it? Three cities?"

"So far. At least that's the only ones I've heard of. I just saw it on X when you went in to get coffee."

They stood there for a moment, contemplating, Paul sipping his coffee.

Pikey broke the silence. "You still going home tonight?"

"Yeah, I'm going to take a few days off, then I'll get back into the rotation."

"Cool. Say hi to the fam for me," Pikey said genuinely.

"Yeah man, you know it."

10

I Love Lucy

July 21, 2024

Paul and Sandy's Farm

Paul arrived home to a full house. McKinley had friends over. He walked through the door wearing his tactical pack with his gear in it and carrying his rifle case by the handle.

"Honey, I'm home from the club!" He was attempting a Puerto Rican accent. This was a joke that he had with his wife referencing an episode of the old TV show, *I Love Lucy*.

"Hey babe, I'm in here," Sandy responded from somewhere in the house.

He headed to his office and dropped off the gear, returning to the living room as Sandy entered and gave him a quick kiss.

"How was work?"

"It was fine. How were things here?" he asked.

"As per SOP," she replied.

He grinned. He loved it when she used military jargon.

"Good. What's up with all the teenagers?"

"Well, McKinley wanted to have friends over. I didn't think you'd mind," she said.

"No, I don't care. What are they doing in there?" He could hear voices from the large utility room.

"She shared some freeze-dried Skittles with them, so they asked if they could see the freeze dryer," she responded, motioning toward the utility room with her head.

Paul headed toward the voices. As he got close to the room, he could hear McKinley.

"Yeah, the food stays good for twenty-five years. My dad has like a hundred years of food saved up," she was announcing as he walked into the room.

"McKinley!"

She stopped and turned toward him.

"Dad! You're home!" She started across the room to give him a hug.

He accepted her in an embrace and whispered in her ear.

"Can I talk to you for a sec? Out here?" He motioned toward the living room.

McKinley turned to the two girls and one boy still inspecting the large machine setting on the industrial cart.

"Hey guys, give me a sec."

Only one of the girls responded. She was a small girl, just over five feet with short blonde hair.

She responded with a simple "Kay."

Paul led McKinley out of the room.

"What did I tell you about talking about our preps?" Paul asked in a low voice as soon as they were far enough out of the room that he was sure the other kids wouldn't hear him.

McKinley stared back at him blankly for a moment before responding.

"Dad, it's just Abbie and Ellie."

Paul didn't share the same nonchalant attitude.

"First of all, it's not just Abbie and Ellie. Who's the boy?" he said with gravity in his voice.

"Oh," McKinley began. "That's just Noah. He's Ellie's brother. He's harmless."

Paul didn't respond to that statement.

"Secondly, I don't care who they are. You know the rules. We don't tell people about what we have."

"Daaad," she drug out the word. "You tell people all the time. You're always talking about prepping with *your* friends."

"That's not at all the same. The people that *I* talk to are a trusted group of like-minded people, and they're all preppers too. We're working together to build a group of people to support each other in an emergency. That," he pointed in the general direction of the utility room, "is a group of kids who don't need to know what we have." He was concentrating on maintaining an even tone without raising his voice. However, he was legitimately angry.

"Seriously Dad, they're my friends. They aren't going to try to break in and steal your stuff. I just don't see what the big deal is."

Paul took a deep breath before continuing. "Get your friends out of the utility room and don't say anything else about our preps. Things are getting dicey out there and I don't need a bunch of kids showing up asking for handouts." He stared directly into her eyes, his face serious.

She crossed her arms over her chest.

"Am I perfectly clear?"

She dropped her arms in a dramatic show of defeat.

"Fine Dad. *Sorry*."

She turned and stalked off, back to her friends.

Paul heard her as she reentered the utility room.

"Come on guys. Let's go to my room. I want to put some music on. If you want anything to drink, grab it from the fridge there. We have *everything*."

Paul sighed again in exasperation before turning and heading back to his office. He went in and closed the door behind him. *First things first*, he thought and worked the combination on his gun safe. He opened his backpack and gun bag, retrieving his night vision and AR-15. He turned to the safe and carefully returned them to their designated spots, leaving the door open on the safe. Next, he pulled out his dirty clothes bag from his pack and zipped the bag back up before stashing it in the closet. He still wore his pistol. He never took that off, not even at home.

Paul's phone chirped and he grabbed it, opening the Signal app to see the message. It was from Mack.

> Biden just dropped out of the race

Paul quickly responded.

> That was not completely unexpected. However, the primaries are done. I wonder what they're going to do about that?

The phone chimed again.

> They've already announced that Harris is going to take his place.

Paul thought for a moment before answering.

> Hmm. Well, this is getting interesting.

He put his phone away and went over to his work bench. He had a gun in the vice that he'd been working on for his cousin, David. David had picked up a new Armalite AR-10 chambered in .308 and Paul was mounting the scope for him. Anyone could mount a scope, but Paul had a tool that made it easier to ensure the scope was mounted perfectly level, so he had offered to mount the scope for David. David was happy to accept the help. He clamped the adjustable barrel clamp level on the barrel and placed the reference level on the top rail of the upper receiver. He then used the dial on the gun vice to adjust the gun until it was perfectly level. Once he had the gun where he wanted it, he dialed in the adjustable level on the barrel clamp level until it matched the smaller one.

Now all he had to do was place the smaller level on the top adjustment turret of the scope and carefully turn the scope in the rings until it was level too. Finally, he used his Fat Wrench torque wrench to tighten the scope ring screws to the correct torque setting. This could be a little tricky because tightening one side could actually move the scope, so he was careful to tighten one side a little, then the other side and keep doing this until he had everything tightened down and the torque wrench clicked. He finished off by going around all eight screws and checking them with the torque wrench one last time while watching the level very closely to ensure there was no movement.

Perfect, he thought.

Paul removed the levels and placed them back in the case. He then removed the big rifle from the vice and threw it up to his shoulder, peering out the window through the scope. It looked right. The eye relief was correct and didn't cause any scope shadow.

Perfect, he thought to himself a second time.

He carried the gun over to the gun safe and placed it in the front rifle position across from his AR-15 before closing the door and locking the big safe. He returned to the bench and replaced the torque wrench in its case before placing the tools back on the shelf over the bench.

Music was coming from McKinley's room. She was playing a remake of *Tennessee Whiskey*. He grinned. He liked this version. Humming along, he left the room and closed the door behind him. He needed to go check the news.

11

Ambush in De Bagh Khola Pass

July 21, 2024

Later that Night

Paul walked outside to get some fresh air. He had finished watching the news and was thinking about the recent attacks. He walked over to his firepit and settled into one of the chairs facing the fire ring. He would have loved to have been sitting around a campfire, but he didn't feel like lighting a fire in this heat. Instead, he settled in with a beer and leaned back in the dark. Even though it was still warm out, compared to the heat earlier, it felt pretty good. He took a sip and placed the bottle in the cup holder. Leaning back, he closed his eyes. Something had been niggling at the back of his head about these attacks. He couldn't help but think about the way most of the attacks had been initiated in Afghanistan. He wasn't asleep, but rather drifting off in thought. His mind drifted back to his second tour in Afghanistan...

It was 2007, Firebase Lane, in southeastern Afghanistan. The team had planned a mission to a local village to deliver medical supplies and offer free medical care, provided by the team's two medics. This type of mission was called a MEDCAP, short for Medical Civil Action Program. Many people in Afghanistan had never seen a real doctor and to them, an 18 Delta Special Forces Medical Sergeant would be the most highly trained medical professional they had ever encountered. The mission had two primary goals. First, it was exactly what it appeared to be on the surface: a medical outreach meant to spread the word that the Americans were there to help and meant no harm to the people who were not members of the Taliban. Secondly, it was an opportunity to talk to the locals and gather intelligence from those who were willing to talk.

The village was located through a mountain pass and during the planning, the team tried to find an alternate route back. However, after careful analysis of the map, they determined that they would be required to cross the mountains through the same pass on the return trip. This violated the standard security protocol, but there was no way around it, so they decided to go ahead with the mission and attempt to mitigate the risk with a heightened security posture near the pass.

During infiltration, they drove through the village of De Bagh Khola right before the pass. The mountains loomed over the left side of the trucks. The village was to their right and beyond that, the dry riverbed of the Arghandab River. The river would swell with water during the winter months, but at this time it was completely dry.

They slowly rolled down the dirt road. Typically, in this scenario, the children of the village would come out and beg for food. This village was an anomaly. No adults acknowledged them as they drove by, and no children were even visible. The captain spoke up over the radio.

"All, this is Alpha. Stay sharp. This is looking weird. Over."

Paul acknowledged from Truck Two, followed by the Team Sergeant in truck three.

Trucks One and Three had an M2 .50 Caliber Machine gun mounted to the turret. The second truck had a MK19 40mm automatic grenade launcher, commonly called the Mark Nineteen. Additionally, each truck had one man sitting in a chair mounted in the bed of the truck manning an M240 Machine Gun, facing backwards on a pedestal mount. This position was called the tail gunner. The trucks were modified HMMWVs called Ground Mobility Vehicle. However, the Special Forces teams just called them GMVs.

The GMVs were exclusively used by Special Forces and were designed to provide the twelve men with as much firepower as possible. In addition to the main gun in the turret and the M240 Machine Gun mounted over the tailgate, the front passenger had the smaller M249 Machine Gun mounted on a swing arm outside his door that could be quickly deployed when additional firepower was needed. In addition to all the guns, an AT-4 84mm Anti-tank rocket was mounted in a quick release mount on the roof of the truck, directly above the driver's door. Of course, every man still had his primary weapon, usually an M4 Carbine, and a sidearm, which at the time was a Beretta M9 pistol.

Paul didn't carry his M4 as his primary rifle. He preferred to carry a MK12 SPR. The Mark Twelve Special Purpose Rifle was a specialty rifle built on the M16 platform. It was considered a shorter-range sniper rifle with a twenty-inch stainless steel barrel, Leupold scope, bipod, and improved trigger. It was chambered in 5.56mm NATO, like the M4s, although it typically used a heavier seventy-seven grain bullet. Paul carried the specialty MK262 seventy-seven grain ammunition in his magazines. However, in a pinch if he ran out of ammunition in a firefight, and someone passed him one of their magazines, he could also fire the lighter M855 green tip sixty-two grain ammunition used in his teammates' M4 rifles. Firing the different ammunition would affect his zero, especially at longer ranges, but if you ever run out of ammunition in a firefight, that's a small price to pay.

To guard against this, Paul's standard loadout was a double thirty round magazine in the gun, plus nine magazines in pouches on his plate carrier, giving him a total of eleven magazines, or three hundred thirty rounds. In each of the trucks, the team had ammunition cans filled with loaded magazines. Paul had included an additional can in his truck with the his ammunition.

On the day of the MEDCAP, Paul was traveling in the second truck, his MK12 was resting between his knees. As they exited De Bagh Khola, the road followed the natural lay of the land, turning north and into a mountain pass with high ground on both sides. This was the area identified during planning as the most dangerous part of the route. Everyone was on high alert. The gunners trained their guns on the ridges as the drivers scanned the road in front of them looking for any anomalies in the sand that could indicate the presence of a mine or Improvised Explosive Device. The drive through the pass only took about five minutes and the back side of the mountain opened into a wider valley that led west, in the direction of the target village.

After nearly two hours of driving, Paul and his team finally arrived in the village without incident. As the crow flies, the village was only about five kilometers from the Firebase. However, traveling in the mountainous environment turned the trip into a thirteen-kilometer movement, or about eight miles. The slow rate of travel, along with several security halts had resulted in the team only covering about five miles an hour. They arrived at the village at about nine in the morning.

The team conducted a meeting with the elder men in the village. This type of an interaction was known as a Key Leader Engagement, or KLE. They explained to the old men what they were there to do, and the men smiled and emphatically accepted the team's offer. Numerous intelligence reports had identified this area as a likely route for the Taliban when moving north or south through this region. That had led to the selection of this village for the MEDCAP.

The team set up the medical site in an old, unused compound that had been identified by the village elders. The team arrayed the vehicles around the site, utilizing the main guns on the GMVs to provide overwatch. Two more men positioned themselves on foot to watch the crowd and scan for closer threats. Paul was on the high ground with the MK12, positioning himself to see east and west down the middle of the village, ready to react to threats. He had Mario, one of the 18 Echo Communication Sergeants with him, helping him scan the area and keeping them closely connected to the team via radio.

Additionally, two members of the team with an interpreter screened the people as they showed up, describing an incredibly diverse number of ailments. The screeners were also trying to identify anyone they thought could be a potential source of additional information. When they identified those people, they went to a different, private area for "special medical evaluation." The idea behind this was to isolate them and question them where no others could hear them, encouraging them to speak more freely and offering additional rewards beyond the free medical care such as food or cash. It seldom worked because the locals were either supporters of the Taliban or they were too scared of the Taliban to risk saying anything. Occasionally though, someone would share useful information.

Only men and children came to the MEDCAP. The women were forbidden to speak with Americans. The Afghan men would prefer to let their wives die rather than allow a male American "doctor" to see them. However, the men would bring their children, including the little girls. One man showed up with an infant, no more than six months old. The child had been born with a terrible disfigurement. Her right leg was only about half the length of her left, normally formed leg. He asked the medic if he could fix the child's leg. The medic looked at the little child and explained that there was likely no way to fix the child's leg, not even with surgery.

Through the interpreter, the man responded. "You Americans say you're here to help, but when we ask for help, you say you can't. Is there nothing you can do for her?"

The medic, Peter, was quick on his feet. He immediately turned to his bag and pulled out a bottle of children's chewable vitamins.

"This is vitamins. She's too young to chew them up, but you can dissolve them in her milk, and they will help the other aspects of her health."

The man's attitude instantly changed.

"Maybe they will help her leg grow too!"

Peter maintained his composure.

"They do help with bone health."

The man grabbed Peter's hand and shook it emphatically.

"Thank you. Thank you. Insha' Allah" (If God wills it).

Peter looked at the interpreter.

"Does he understand that vitamins will not make her leg grow?"

The interpreter, Baray, slowly shook his head.

"Sir, he believes that if Allah wants the medicine to work, the medicine will work."

"Well, just to be clear Baray, the medicine is not going to work on *that* problem."

"Yes sir. I know."

Many of the problems *were* treatable. One man had severe flaking of the skin on his head. Peter identified the condition as a bad case of dandruff. He gave the man a bottle of Head & Shoulders shampoo and described how to use it. He also explained to him that he could purchase a similar product locally to continue the treatment.

A man brought in a young boy with some road rash from falling in some rocks. Peter was able to clean the wound out, treat it with an antibiotic ointment and bandage it. He sent the tube of antibiotics with the man and another set of dressings to replace the ones he had applied.

After four hours, the team had seen nearly every child and most of the men in the village. At the very least, every child had gotten some vitamins. It was time to speak to the village elders again before departing. The captain took the time to thank the men for agreeing to allow the team to help. The eldest man in the village asked the captain when the team would be able to return to do this again. As was the plan, the captain gave a vague answer and didn't commit to anything.

There were two reasons for this. He didn't want to make a promise that he couldn't keep, but more importantly, he would never provide them with the team's traveling schedule that could be shared with the Taliban, facilitating an attack. Finally, at two in the afternoon, everyone loaded up and began the trip back to the firebase.

As the team approached the mountain pass prior to De Bagh Khola, the captain queued his radio.

"All, this is Alpha. We're going to stop just prior to entering the pass and conduct a security halt. I want to assess the situation before we continue. Over."

Both trucks confirmed they understood.

A few minutes later, at the mouth of the pass, the first truck pulled to the right and faced the high ground on that side. Paul's truck turned left and faced the high ground on that side. The trail truck stopped in the middle of the dirt road, the gun facing toward the rear. The gunner was watching for threats following them, but also scanning to his sides.

Paul stepped out of his truck with his MK12 hanging loose in his hands. He tossed the sling over his neck and looked over toward truck one. He saw the front right door open, and the captain step out.

Without warning, an explosion sounded from the high ground in front of the captain's truck as an RPG was fired at the stationary vehicle. Paul watched in horror as the truck seemingly disappeared in the explosion of the impact. He pressed the button on his radio and spoke loudly, but clearly.

"Contact right! Cap's down!"

Paul's gunner immediately turned the turret to face the threat and began raining forty-millimeter grenades on the area where the signature from the RPG could still be seen. The trail truck joined in the fight as well with the fifty-caliber heavy machine gun.

The Team Sergeant's voice came over the radio.

"I'm calling it in." As all this was going on, the Team Sergeant calmly stayed in his seat, calling the SOTF, the Special Operations Task Force, reporting the TIC, or Troops in Contact.

Various enemy guns joined the fight. It was a mixture of machine guns and AK-47s. They didn't have the angle they wanted because the team had stopped prior the best ambush position, but they were still within range and the bullets began impacting the ground near the team. Paul heard a couple of bullets strike the armor plate in front of the MK19. The gunner flinched, but didn't stop shooting.

The driver of Paul's truck, Mario, jumped out of the GMV and ripped the AT-4 from the roof of the vehicle. He ran out in front of the truck about twenty yards and threw the weapon up on his shoulder as he dropped to one knee. He reached up with his right hand and cocked the weapon. He paused and glanced behind him to ensure no one was in the backblast area of the weapon.

"Backblast area clear!" he yelled. Sighting in on a group of muzzle flashes, he pushed the trigger with his thumb. *Click.* Nothing. He looked at the large green tube for a second as his brain tried to process what had just happened.

"Misfire!"

He re-cocked it and resighted on his target. A burst of bullets struck the ground to his left. He pressed the trigger a second time. *Click.*

"Misfire!"

He jumped back up to his feet, keeping the tube pointed in the general direction of the enemy as he turned and began running back toward Paul. Paul took off running toward him.

"Did you pull the pin?" he yelled.

"What!?" screamed Mario, his face red and covered in sweat.

"Nothing. Give it to me!"

Mario did as he was told, practically throwing the AT-4 to Paul as he ran by, continuing to the relative safety behind the GMV.

Paul ran a few more yards, looking at the back of the AT-4 as he ran. He saw it. The little silver safety pin was still in place at the back of the rocket. In his haste to get the rocket into the fight, Mario had forgotten to pull the safely pin.

Paul quickly snatched it out and dropped to a knee. He heard a machine gun open up and saw a spray of sand in front of him about twenty-five yards and slightly to his right. They were trying to figure out the range.

The thump-thump-thump of the MK19 stopped as the gunner paused to reload another belt of grenades. The fifty-caliber machine gun on vehicle three picked up the rate of fire as the other man reloaded. Everyone but the Team Sergeant was out of their trucks and returning fire. There was nothing for cover besides the trucks themselves. There was nowhere to go and they couldn't leave. They weren't leaving the men in Truck One. They were going to fight in place until they could get everyone out.

Paul re-cocked the weapon, sighted on the muzzle flashes of the machine gun, pushed the safety lever to the side, and pushed the trigger with his thumb. Boom! The rocket launched out of the tube and struck the side of the mountain just below the ridge.

That's when Paul realized he didn't have his helmet on. The backblast of the rocket blew his ballcap forward onto his forehead. The only reason it didn't blow it off was because he had his Peltor earmuff style hearing protection over the hat. He had taken his helmet off earlier and forgotten about it. Luckily, he had his Peltors on because they not only provided hearing protection, but they were also plugged into his MBITR Radio and he could hear the other team members communicating. In this case, they also kept him from losing his hat.

Paul heard someone on the radio as he jumped to his feet and ran back toward his GMV.

"That knocked out one of the guns! Shift fire to the others!"

Paul had the expended AT-4 tube under his right arm and was pinning his MK12 against his body with his left hand as he ran. He made eye contact with Mario and Mario waved for him to run behind him as he provided covering fire. Paul followed the guidance and ran behind the GMV. He paused and threw the empty AT-4 into the back of the truck, taking care not to hit the tailgunner who was putting down sustained fire with the M240. The AT-4 is a single use weapon and can't be reloaded. However, soldiers are taught to always take the tube with you if possible, to prevent the enemy from getting it and repurposing it.

The radio came to life again. It was the Team Sergeant.

"CAS in inbound! Seventeen minutes!

The call to the SOTF had resulted in them sending Close Air Support, or CAS, but *seventeen* minutes! That's a long time in this situation.

Paul leaned through the open driver door and grabbed his helmet off the radio. He squatted down and quickly removed his hat, threw it into the truck, and donned the ballistic helmet.

Mario looked over at him.

"I forgot the fuckin' safety pin, didn't I?

"Don't worry about," Paul yelled back. "We got this."

He turned and ran hunched over at the waist to the rear of the truck and dropped to the ground. He rolled onto his side and extended the bipod legs on his rifle, then rolled back onto his belly to peer through the scope.

No spotter, no range finder, just a rifle. The range finder is *right there*, inside the truck.

Screw it, identify a target. They aren't that far.

He raised his head slightly and looked over the scope. The rear bumper was in the way. He repositioned.

There. Now I can see.

He scanned the hillside, looking for movement. He saw it in some boulders all the way at the top of the hill. He remembered concentrating on this area during mission planning. He had taken the time to measure the distance to the ridgeline since that's where the attacks typically initiated from. He knew that the generic answer was just over 300 meters. He looked up at the ridge. That looked right. He glanced at the inside of the open scope cover at his data.

300m 1.8 mil

350m 2.6 mil

Okay, I'm not dialing that. Let's hold 2.2 mils high.

He didn't detect any side wind. He held to the right of the large boulder where he had seen the movement a moment ago and lined up the two-mil hashmark on the location. Nothing. He didn't see anyone. He fought the urge to lift his head and look around. Then he saw it. Just a flash of movement, but there was definitely someone behind that rock. He concentrated on his breathing. He could see the reticle in the scope moving up and down and realized that he was still breathing hard.

Control yourself.

He took a deep breath and refocused on the spot where he had seen the movement. Then he saw it. A man with an AK leaned out from behind the rock, shooting toward the rear truck, the Team Sergeant's truck.

2.2 mil.

Crack!

Paul's rifle barked and he temporarily lost sight of the target during the mild recoil. However, he regained the target just in time to see the man hit the ground. His head and torso were visible on the ground sticking out from behind the boulder. The AK47 was on the ground in front of the fallen man.

Gotcha!

He started to reposition to get a better view and look for more targets when he heard another heavy machine gun open up beside him. It took him a minute to understand what he was hearing.

That's Cap's truck.

Paul looked over toward Truck One. The dust was settling down now and he could clearly see the truck. It appeared to be fine!

He ducked behind the rear wheel and reached for his push to talk button.

"Alpha, Alpha, this is Whiskey, Over."

Nothing.

"Alpha, Alpha, this is Whiskey, Over."

After another second the captain's voice came over the radio.

"Whiskey, this is Alpha."

Paul heard him cough into the radio before continuing.

"We're back in the fight!"

What the hell? He had been looking right at the truck when it was hit! This didn't make sense.

Who cares? They're good!

"Alpha, Zulu is on the horn with SOTF. Do you have casualties? Over."

"Negative Whiskey. We're good. We're up."

Paul was trying to make sense of it, but now was not the time. Now it was time to shoot. There was probably fifteen minutes before CAS would arrive. However, the addition of another heavy machine gun and another M240 to the fight seemed to have slowed the incoming fire.

"Alpha, this is Whiskey. Do you want to relocate? Over."

"Negative Whiskey, we've got their heads down. Just got an update from SOTF. They redirected an A-10, seven minutes out. Over."

Seven minutes? That's more like it!

Paul crawled forward to get the angle on the guys to the left.

"Copy. Seven minutes."

The earlier RPG had struck the ground just in front of the passenger side headlight. The resulting blast had completely engulfed the truck with smoke and dust from the explosion. From Paul's perspective, the truck had simply disappeared and, in his head, been destroyed. The captain had been standing behind the open door, which had flown back and hit him, knocking him to the ground, stunned but uninjured.

It had taken them a couple of minutes to regain their senses and allow the dust to settle so that the gunner could see to return fire.

Paul saw a man with an AK jump up and run along the ridge, trying to get closer to them. Most of the ambushing force was farther into the pass and this guy was attempting to improve his angle on the team.

Paul tracked him as he ran. He was still pretty far out for a shot with the SPR. He glanced up at his data again.

600m 8.9mil

A round skipped off a rock to his front and he heard it as it zipped overhead nearby.

The captain's voice came back over the radio.

"All, birds are three minutes out…"

"Dad?"

Paul opened his eyes. He was home, sitting in front of his fire pit. He spun around to see a flashlight bouncing across the yard toward him.

"I'm over here, Babe."

"Whatcha doin' out here?" McKinley asked playfully.

"Oh, you know. Just enjoying the night air," he responded. He felt like he could almost smell the powdery desert dust mixed with the smell of gunpowder.

"You've been out here for a few minutes. I was wondering if you were lighting a fire."

"Nah, I thought about it, but it's still a little warm for that," he said, turning in his seat to face her.

"Dad! It's never too warm for a fire. If you build one, I'll hang out with you."

Paul could tell she was smiling.

"You know, maybe a small fire would be nice. Give me a minute. I'll grab some wood from the woodshed."

12

The Collective, Part II

July 22, 2024

There were more people on this call than his last one. This meeting included the primary members as well as numerous secondary, less influential, meaning less important, members. One of those was the newly accepted Representative Adam Schiff of California. Nancy was not thrilled about it, but she had been outvoted, despite being a senior member.

The Chairman began the meeting.

"Thank you all for attending. I would like to take this opportunity to welcome our newest member from Maryland. I assume you've been briefed on the protocol?"

Adam Schiff's screen had the word "Potomac" under his blacked-out silhouette. He responded as Nancy had directed him.

"Yes, Mr. Chairman."

"Good," responded the Chairman. "Then we'll continue."

Adam Schiff was serving as a Representative from California. He claimed the six hundred fifty square foot condo in Burbank as his primary residence to escape the $7,000 taxes in California and to establish his residence there. However, he considered his three thousand, four hundred twenty square foot home in Potomac, Maryland to be his home.

His three-word response followed the protocol Representative Pelosi had explained to him. As a new junior member, his job was to shut up, listen, and learn. It didn't matter if he had something he considered useful to add to the conversation.

She had been very direct in her instructions, despite being inebriated when she explained the rules.

"Just sit there and keep your damn mouth shut. You're still on probation, and you will be until you're not. Don't open your mouth unless you're asked a question. Am I clear?"

Nancy was legitimately pissed over his acceptance into the formal inner circle of The Collective. The masses of The Collective didn't even know they were a part of it. They were simply pawns carrying out the wishes of the formal members. The inner circle used them to accomplish tasks and support their efforts. For decades, the term "Useful Idiots" had been used to describe these individuals who supported a cause without fully understanding who or what they were supporting. The Collective never used this phrase; however, they certainly took advantage of the principle.

Nancy had considered Adam to be just one more useful idiot. However, over the last few years, he had gained a significant amount of influence and that damned Soros had put his name up for a vote. His acceptance had passed...barely. Soros probably did it just to spite her.

The Chairman continued.

"As you all know, our efforts to remove Mr. Biden from the ticket have finally been successful. This is a direct reflection of my efforts as well as numerous other members. Nancy was notably influential in conversations with Joe and Jill."

Nancy's cheeks flushed at the rare praise from the former president.

"We have decided to have Vice President Harris take Joe's place as the Democratic Presidential nominee for November."

No one spoke, despite the fact that nearly half of the people on the call were not in favor of the selection.

"Let me put your concerns to rest. We are well aware of her low approval rating. However, over the next few days, our operatives in the media will eliminate all negative reporting and lift her up as the best possible choice for the next president of the United States. They will completely ignore her earlier incompetence and paint her as a strong independent thinker with outstanding leadership skills and an impressive resume of leadership and tough decision making."

The woman in Washington spoke up.

"How are we supposed to overcome the fact that she can't even answer a question. She's a legitimate imbecile. I would have been a better choice."

The Chairman answered immediately as if he had anticipated the question and had a prepared response.

"I agree that you are a better choice for president. However, you've already lost a presidential bid and to be frank, you're not popular with the American people. We all appreciate your efforts and contributions, but we had to go with the more viable candidate and right now, that's Kamala Harris."

Washington didn't respond.

"I can assure all of you that Ms. Harris will become very popular, very quickly. You have all received your instructions to reach out to both traditional and non-traditional donors. We'll have plenty of money to push her candidacy across the finish line."

The member from New York City responded.

"I assume we have our safeguards in place."

"Yes, of course. We're concentrating our efforts in the swing states. Our 'non-partisan' supporters will be mailing numerous mail-in ballots to the areas that are most likely to vote Democrat. Additionally, we are working to ensure that non-citizens votes will be counted since they are obviously most likely to vote in our favor. Additionally, just like the last election, we have plenty of counterfeit ballots prepared to bump us across the finish line in the event of a close race."

Germany responded to this statement.

"The Republicans are pushing for voting integrity measures that will prevent that from working. What assurances do we have that they will not be able to stop our efforts?"

The Chairman paused before he responded. He appeared to be looking down at something. He was looking at his notes.

"In the last election, we were able to add millions of votes for Joe and no one batted an eye. If we could make the American people believe that an extra fifteen million people came out to vote for Biden, we'll just have to do the same for Harris."

The German was not convinced.

"What if these efforts are stopped? What if the Republicans are able to neutralize our efforts? They may have learned from the last election. The election deniers are already very vocal and they've pointed out the inconsistencies. I thought it was too obvious at the time. I didn't believe that the public would accept the claim that Joe got more votes than any presidential candidate in history, even more than you." He took a breath. "By a long shot."

The Chairman did not immediately respond, so the German continued.

"Every one of our efforts have fallen short so far. We've even weaponized the Department of Justice against him and his popularity has grown. Tell me, Mr. Chairman, why is she our best choice and how are we going to defeat this popular movement to maintain a fair election?"

Everyone on the call detected the condescension in his tone, including the Chairman.

"That was a two-part question, and they're both valid questions. First, let me tell you why she is our best option. She is aware of us and she understands our power and influence. She also wants to be accepted into the inner circle. She feels that if she can secure the office, she'll be useful and influential enough to be a part of this group. Quite frankly, she's correct in that assumption. Clearly, we, as a group, are more powerful than the President of the United States. However, we need to control the presidency to be in the best position to advance our agenda. She knows that if she's sitting in the Oval Office, we'll have no choice but to bring her in.

"I ask that you look at it from my perspective. We know that she's not very intelligent. She can't respond to questions. She doesn't understand domestic or international policies. I get that. However, she's easy to control. She does what I tell her. You've heard me make the statement before that I would like to have a mouthpiece in place to be the face of the Presidency while I was making all the decisions from the protection of anonymity. She will provide us with that opportunity. She is legitimately incapable of complex thought. She *needs* someone else to make decisions for her and tell her what to do. If we are able to install her in the White House, we'll have the perfect puppet to do *our* will. Joe typically did what he was told. However, he would still go against our guidance sometimes when he felt his idea or vision was better. It was arrogance on his part. We won't have that problem with her since she has no vision. She just wants the power."

Numerous silhouettes could be seen nodding in agreement. Adam observed the others nodding, so he nodded as well, trying to fit in.

"I haven't forgotten the second part of your question. You asked how we are going to defeat Donald Trump's popularity. That's an easier answer. We control the news. We are going to paint her as the only possible choice. The moral choice. The choice of women, minorities, and freedom. Our messaging will paint Trump as a totalitarian, a Nazi, literally Hitler. We're going to pull out all the stops and throw all of our resources into this election. We will not lose."

Switzerland spoke for the first time in the meeting.

"And if we fail? If he still wins?"

The Chairman sighed audibly. He was tired of being grilled.

"If Trump is able to somehow win, we'll play obstructionist politics, just like we have in the past. We'll hinder every move, every cabinet appointment, contradict every statement he makes. I don't think this is going to be necessary, but if he wins and survives long enough to take office, we'll make sure that his efforts are thwarted at every juncture."

This time it is was Del Mar that spoke.

"And these terrorist attacks? How do they play into this?"

"That's a more complex problem. Initially, I thought there was a possibility that we could use the attacks to postpone or cancel the election. Now, I don't think that's a realistic option. The conspiracies would fly that we orchestrated the attacks just for that reason. However, we're already working with Federal law enforcement to insinuate that right-wing Trump supporters are behind the attacks."

The woman in Washington scoffed.

"We already know that this was an Iranian-backed attack. What happens when that comes out to the public? We all know it's going to happen sooner or later."

"Yes, it will," The Chairman answered. His response was cool.

"The FBI is going to insinuate that the right-wing extremists facilitated the attack in order to undermine the current administration. Reports will indicate a month's long investigation showing that these Trump supporters were able to overlook their racist xenophobia in order to undermine Biden and ultimately Harris."

The German was not convinced. His accent sounded stronger when he was angry.

"That sounds like a fantasy. If I were an average citizen, I wouldn't believe that."

The Chairman felt like he was defending himself from a multifaceted attack. His normally measured presentation cracked slightly as he began to get frustrated by the group pessimism.

"Look, we have to work with the hand we were dealt! We will work every angle to win the election. If we fail, we'll regroup and undermine Trump, and if I have my way, we'll put a bullet in his head...and we won't miss again."

Everyone in the group remained silent. Adam didn't know what to think of all this. This was not what he was expecting. He wasn't exactly sure *what* he was expecting, but it certainly wasn't this.

The Chairman regained his composure and took control of the conversation again. He cleared his throat before speaking.

"Everything this group has voted to support is in place. We have people who have registered as Republicans so they can be the 'Republican' poll watchers. We have counterfeiters producing ballots. As I mentioned before, we are producing tens of thousands of additional mail-in ballots. And let's not forget that we can still create chaos with protests, riots, and violent mobs. We'll defeat Donald Trump, at the polls or through other means. We *will* win. Period. We'll shove our agenda through with the help of Hollywood, the media, and our zealots. This is going to happen. Trump's vision for the future is *not* an option. If we need to break the peoples' backs to get our way, that's acceptable. America will fall at our feet or it will simply fall. At this point, I'm okay with either one."

13

I've Got a Bleeder

Nour Hallal and Ahmad Abufaysal slowed as they approached their designated location on Old Malad Highway, about thirteen miles north of Malad City, Idaho. They pulled off the main road in front of a gate leading to a private road. Ahmad quickly jumped out, bolt cutters in his hand, and cut the lock on the gate. It was a traditional cattle gate with two signs on it. The top sign identified a Transmission Line Right of Way on the property. They had studied this area for days and were already aware of the powerlines to the east. They weren't concerned about that. The lower sign identified the location as private property. They weren't concerned about that either.

He unthreaded the chain and pushed the gate open, allowing Nour to drive through. As soon as Nour passed him, Ahmad reclosed the gate and draped the chain over it to make sure it would stay closed before turning and running the short distance to where Nour was parking the vehicle out of view behind a stand of trees. He took the time to turn the car around and back it into the hidden parking spot behind the trees. Off to their right side, the ground climbed sharply to the southwest to several large monolithic stones protruding from the hillside. That was their shooting position.

The sight overlooked Interstate Fifteen from an elevated position and offered a clear shot at the roadway. They would be targeting the southbound lane and using the Old Malad Highway to escape to the north. Both men surged with confidence, still riding a high from last week's successful attack in Colorado.

Nour opened the trunk and handed the M4 rifle to Ahmad before retrieving the Winchester 30-06 bolt action for himself. He already had the internal magazine loaded, so he paused and ran the bolt, chambering a round and placing the safety in the *SAFE* position. He heard Amad chamber a round in the M4 as well. Holding the rifle in one hand, he closed the trunk and they turned together to climb the short distance to the rocks.

Neither man spoke as they climbed the hill. Even though it wasn't very far, the terrain was steep and the dirt crumbled as they walked, forcing them to work harder to maintain their footing. By the time they settled into the shooting position, both men were breathing hard. Ahmad was wearing a small pack. He unslung it and removed two bottles of water, handing one to Nour. They both took the time to get a drink. Ahmad twisted the cap back on his bottle, dropped it in the pack, and withdrew a small camouflage range finder they had purchased at Wal-Mart. He held it to his eye and looked out at the interstate. He spoke in Arabic as he pointed across the road.

"If you engage there, that will be one hundred fifty meters."

He moved his arm to the right a little.

"Right there is two hundred. It's a little farther, but you'll have a better angle on the driver."

Nour reached into the open pack and retrieved a towel that they had stolen from a hotel. It was rolled up and wrapped in duct tape. He lay the towel on the rock in front of him and carefully placed the wooden stock on the towel before peering through the scope.

"I see the spot you're talking about. I agree. The two-hundred-meter shot is the better choice. I can make that."

He left the rifle in place, but raised his head up slightly to look over the scope. Glancing down the road, he saw a tractor trailer approaching in the south-bound lane. He returned his eye to the scope and tracked the big truck as it got closer. As it reached the point identified as the two-hundred-meter spot, he quietly mouthed the word *bang*.

"Yes, yes. That's a good angle. I'll take that shot."

"Good," said Ahmad, looking down at his watch. "We have a half hour before we will shoot. Practice your shot as much as you need, but rest your eyes for the last ten minutes. I'll keep track of the time for you."

Nour just nodded and returned to looking through the scope.

At that moment, one mile north of their location, two men were finalizing their preparations for a day on the water at Devil Creek Reservoir.

Brad Baxter was doing a final check of the trailer that held his bass boat. Rich Webster was using a small ratchet strap to secure a cooler in the boat. Climbing down, Rich brushed his hands off and walked up behind Brad, inspecting his work.

"Are you *ever* gonna finish that?" he said with a smile.

"Shut up," Brad shot back. "It's done. Is the beer secure?"

"Of course, we don't want a party foul on the way to the lake."

"Okay," Brad continued. "Let's get the rest of the stuff from your truck moved over here and get on the road."

"Yeah, man." Rich turned and headed back to his truck to grab the last of his things.

A few minutes later, they turned left onto Old Malad Highway and headed south toward the Reservoir. It was a nice, clear day. Both men had their windows down and were enjoying the breeze as they paralleled Interstate Fifteen on the east side. They were talking trash about who was going to outfish who when a rifle shot rang out.

"What the hell?" asked Brad. "Did you hear that? That sounded like a shot, and close!"

Then they heard the crash. The sound of crushing metal, car horns, and skidding tires was unmistakable.

"Holy crap!" Rich yelled, leaning out the window and looking down the road.

"I see it! Keep going! It's just up ahead, over on the interstate!"

As they pulled up nearly adjacent to the crash, Brad started slowing down to get a better look.

"Dude! That's an eighteen-wheeler!"

Suddenly, the realization hit him as if someone had yelled it in his face. It had been all over the news for a week. Someone has been shooting tractor trailer drivers. He stopped the truck, slammed it into park, and jumped out. Slamming the door, he ran around to the front of the truck and looked up at the crash that was barely visible from this angle. The interstate was at a higher elevation, but the truck had hit the middle divider and from what he could see, it appeared to be resting against it, smoke and steam rising from the hood.

He heard voices behind him and spun around. Two men were running down the hill. Both had rifles in their hands. One man ran behind a clump of trees, but the other turned and ran straight toward him. Brad made eye contact with the approaching man a split second before the man raised a rifle and fired two shots at him while running. They were wild, unaimed shots that went high. Brad ducked instinctively and ran to the opposite side of the truck.

Rick was outside the truck, standing in the open passenger door.

"What the hell, man?!"

The man with the rifle snatched the gate open and stood in the opening, taking careful aim at the truck that was now only about twenty-five yards away. Ahmad rotated the selector switch from semi to three-round-burst and unleashed a hail of gunfire at the truck. The bullets punched through the sheet metal of the driver's door, passed through the cab, and two of the three rounds struck Rich in the gut. He fell backward into the shallow ditch behind him, grasping his belly and shrieking in pain.

As soon as the shooting stopped, Brad peeked over the hood and saw that the man was looking back toward an approaching car. Brad ran around the open passenger door, passing by the feet of his fallen friend and dove across the seat, ripping open the center console and grasping the Glock he carried there. Sliding back out of the truck, he snatched the pistol out of the holster and dropped the holster to the ground. He quickly racked the slide, chambering a round, then looked over at this friend, who was writhing on the ground.

"Hang in there, Rich! I'll get these terrorist bastards!"

With that, he ducked low and sprinted around to the back of the truck, slipping between the tailgate and the boat, just as the little car came bouncing up onto the pavement and veered right. He raised the Glock in both hands, arms locked, and opened fire. The rounds slammed into the windshield, every round creating a spiderweb effect on impact. The car jerked right, tires tearing into the grass, skidding dangerously close to the slope beside the road. For a second, it looked like they were going over—but the driver yanked the wheel and wrestled it back onto the pavement as Brad kept firing.

Boom, boom, boom.

He followed the car with his pistol as it passed him, pulling the trigger as fast as he could. As the car passed him, he saw the rear driver's side window explode. He continued shooting.

Boom, boom, boom.

The car kept moving. Brad swept to the left and inadvertently put two rounds through the hull of his boat – though he didn't realize he had done it. The car disappeared from his sight as it passed behind the boat and accelerated away from him. Brad hopped over the trailer tongue so he could see the car again. He took careful aim at the rear windshield of the care and pulled the trigger again. Nothing happened. He looked down at the pistol in his hand and the slide was locked to the rear. *That was fifteen rounds already?*

Rich's groans pulled him back into the moment. Brad glanced up at the car speeding away in the distance, then turned back to look toward his friend. He couldn't see him from this side of the truck. He jumped back over the trailer tongue and returned to his friend. He tossed the empty gun into the cab and dropped to his knees beside Rich.

"Rich! Rich! Are you okay?!"

"No, I'm not okay, dumbass! I've been shot!"

"Hold on buddy, I'm calling 911!"

Brad pulled his phone from the clip on his belt and called 911 as he ran back toward the boat. With the phone in one hand, he used his other hand to climb up in the boat, scrambling toward the small white first aid kit that was held in place against the hull with a Velcro strap. He reached for the strap just as the operator answered."

"911, what is your emergency?"

"My friend's been shot! Send an ambulance right now!"

He pulled the first aid kit from the bracket and turned back toward the side of the boat. He had the phone held to his ear with his right hand and the first aid kit in his left. He jumped back out of boat, stumbling forward as he landed. He threw his hands out in front of him to catch himself and both the first aid kit and phone hit the asphalt. The phone went sliding into the grass beside the road, but the first aid kit popped open from the impact, spilling its contents all over the road and into the grass.

"Damn it!" he cried as he chased the phone.

"Sir?" the operator was saying.

"I'm here, I just dropped the phone! I'm here! Send help! I saw the terrorists! They shot a truck and then my buddy!" He was shrieking into the phone.

"Sir, I need you to calm down so I can understand you. I see that your location is on Old Malad Highway north of Malad City, is that right?"

"What? Oh, uh, yeah. How'd you know that?" His voice was high and rapid.

"Sir, I can see your GPS location. Emergency personnel have been dispatched to your location. Is your friend alert?"

Brad looked at Rich who was still grasping his belly, curled up in the fetal position. Then he looked back toward the first aid supplies strewn around the ground. He took a step toward Rich and then paused, looking back toward the supplies. *What do I do? I don't know what to do!*

"Sir! Sir! Can you hear me?"

"I have a first aid kit, but I dropped it. I...I...I don't know what to do!"

"Sir, I need you to take a breath and listen to me."

Brad felt like his heart was going to burst from his chest. Everything was happening so fast. The sides of his vision began to get dark. He squeezed his eyes closed, shook his head, and took a deep breath. He opened his eyes. He was okay. *Rich! He had to check on Rich!*

"Sir, can you hear me?"

Brad turned and ran back to Rich's side, dropping to his knees beside his friend a second time.

"I can hear you. He's shot in the stomach. What do I do?"

"Sir, is your friend conscious?"

"Yes, yes, he's awake! There's blood all over his shirt! It's on the ground!"

Brad's brain registered a sound. What is that? He looked up. He saw a police car racing up the road toward him. It was moving fast!

"I see the police, but I need an ambulance!"

He jumped up, waving his hands and jumping up and down as if the deputy could somehow miss him with his truck partially blocking the small road. He dropped back down to his knees beside Rich, not even aware that he had dropped the phone on the ground beside him. He put his hands on his friend. His left hand was on Rich's side and his right hand was on his shoulder.

"Hang on buddy! They're almost here. Can you hear them? They're almost here!"

As Brad looked down the road at the approaching police car, he realized that he wasn't just hearing one siren. He heard all kinds of sirens. He looked up the hill toward the interstate and he understood. There were a several various emergency vehicles on the interstate too. They were everywhere. When he returned his focus to the police car in front of him, he was surprised to see that it was already stopped, a single man jumping out. *When did that get there? Where was the ambulance? Shouldn't they be sending an ambulance?* He was having trouble processing the scene.

The Sheriff's Deputy drew his service pistol as he exited the vehicle.

Deputy Avery Wilcox had his gun trained on Brad. Brad didn't understand why a policeman would be pointing his gun at him.

Deputy Wilcox immediately began barking commands. "Show me your hands!"

"I'm not the bad guy!" Brad still couldn't process what was going on. "My friend's been shot! We need an ambulance!"

"Show me your hands right now!" The deputy was laser focused. He was speaking loudly and clearly as he closed the distance to the men on the ground.

Brad was dumbfounded. "You don't understand! My friend needs an ambulance. He's been shot!"

"I understand. An ambulance is on the way, now show me your hands and stand up!"

Brad didn't move. He looked down at Rich who was still groaning. With a start, Brad realized that his left hand was in Rich's blood. He held it up in front of his face, his eyes fixed on the dark liquid now staining his hand.

"Now!" the deputy yelled forcefully.

"Now? Now what?" Brad couldn't understand what was happening. *Why was this cop treating him like he was the bad guy here?*

"Show me your hands now!" the deputy repeated.

Slowly, Brad complied. He raised both his hands to shoulder height, but his eyes stayed fixed on the blood on his left hand.

"Now, stand up and step around your friend."

Brad rocked back on his feet and managed to stand up without using his hands to push off the ground. He looked down at his stricken friend as he stepped around him.

"Keep your hands in the air and turn around."

Again, Brad complied, but he couldn't be silent.

"You don't understand, officer. The terrorists shot my friend!"

"Ok, if you do what I say, we're going to talk about it, but right now, I need you to interlace your fingers behind your head and walk backwards toward me."

"Ok," responded Brad. "But you need to help my friend." He put his hands behind his head as instructed. He could feel the wetness of the blood on his fingers. He took a step backwards, tentatively feeling the ground with his foot before committing to the movement.

"We're going to help your friend. Are you injured?" Deputy Wilcox asked.

"What? No. No, I'm not hurt, but my friend is bleeding. He's been shot in the stomach!"

Another siren sounded as it came up the road toward them.

Deputy Wilcox kept his issued Glock 17 on Brad with his right hand as he used his left hand to pull out a set of handcuffs from a pouch on his duty belt.

"Keep walking toward my voice."

In a swift, practiced movement, the deputy holstered his firearm, and grasped Brad's wrist pulling it behind him and applying the first cuff. Without hesitation, he repeated the motion with the other side, effectively cuffing Brad and taking control of him. Deputy Wilcox glanced over at the form of the man on the ground. He could see the blood on the man. He had to move quickly. He pulled Brad backwards the few steps to the patrol car.

Deputy Wilcox began performing an expedited pat down of the man.

"Do you have any weapons on you?"

"No. I had a pistol, but it's in the truck."

As he quickly checked the man, the deputy slapped the man's right pants pocket and felt something solid. He looked down to see a small pocket knife clip visible on the man's front right pants pocket. He pulled the knife out and stuffed it in his back pocket. He then retrieved the man's wallet from his right back pocket and stuffed that in his own pocket as well.

"You had a knife."

"Oh. Yeah, I have a pocket knife. I thought you meant a gun. My gun's in the truck."

"Do you have any other knives, needles, sharp objects, or other weapons on you of any kind? Anything that can hurt me."

"Um, no. I just had the one knife."

The deputy opened the back door.

"I need you to take a seat so I can help your friend," he said as he stuffed the handcuffed man into the back seat and closed the door.

Brad was incredulous. *What's going on here? Why am I being treated like a criminal?* He sat on the front of the seat looking out the window. The cuffs felt unnecessarily tight.

Deputy Wilcox redrew his sidearm and reassessed the situation. The truck was not quite in the middle of the narrow road. The driver's door was closed, but the front passenger door was open. The wounded man lay in the grass outside the open door; his head angled downhill on the mild slope. *Were there threats?* He didn't know. He registered the sound of the additional emergency vehicles on the interstate nearby but stayed focused on the situation in front of him.

He began closing the distance, circling wide around the fallen man, looking toward the open door of the truck, and keeping the fallen man between himself and the vehicle. He had his pistol presented in front of him in a well-practiced two hand grip. As he made it far enough to see around the door, he saw the other pistol laying in the seat, but couldn't see anyone in the truck. The truck was a four-door, but the back door was closed and he couldn't tell if there was a potential threat in the back seat. He needed to check it, so he continued past the fallen man, glancing down at him, assessing if he was a potential threat. He decided that the unknown, uncleared back seat was the first priority. He approached the door and snatched it open, keeping his weapon trained on the space. It was empty, so he slammed the door and looked toward the rear of the vehicle. There was a boat on a trailer.

The deputy backed up to gain some distance and remained facing the vehicle, careful not to put his back to the man on the ground. With the wounded man to his right, he walked sideways back to the boat, quickly closing the distance and peering over the edge to make sure there was no one hiding in the boat. It was clear, so he returned his attention to the man who was still groaning and writhing in the grass.

He closed the distance to the casualty and dropped to a knee. He needed to make sure there were no weapons. He holstered his sidearm and looked down at the man, noting the blood. *Damn! I don't have any gloves!* He reached up and pressed the button on his radio, calling dispatch.

The dispatch operator responded.

"Hey dispatch, can you put a rush on the bus? I've got a bleeder."

The dispatch operator responded again, indicating that she understood.

"Hey buddy, do you have any weapons on you or anything that can hurt me?"

The man responded through gritted teeth.

"No. No. I need help."

Deputy Wilcox glanced up as the ambulance arrived, pulling up behind the parked cruiser. Both vehicles still had their emergency lights going. Two paramedics appeared from the ambulance and quickly approached the scene. One of them had an aid bag thrown over one shoulder.

The deputy spoke to the man again.

"Who shot you? Did the other man that was with you shoot you?"

"What?!" the man forced out. "No! There were terrorists! The terrorists shot me." He strained as he tried to speak.

A freckle faced paramedic in his mid-twenties dropped to the ground beside the man and began to assess the casualty. He spoke to the deputy without looking up at him.

"Hey Wilcox, what do we got?"

The deputy stepped back to give the men some room.

"Gunshot to the abdomen. That's all I know."

"Okay, got it. Thanks."

Brad continued to observe from the back seat of the cruiser. When he saw the paramedics drop to the ground beside his friend he collapsed back into the seat with relief. *Click click.* As he sat back against the handcuffs, they tightened up more on his wrists.

"Ow!" he cried out, instinctively jerking forward away from the seat.

In his haste to get Brad into the cruiser, Deputy Wilcox had not taken the time to double lock the handcuffs, which would have prevented them from tightening up more.

Brad saw the deputy walking back toward him.

"Hey!" Brad called out to the deputy. "Hey! These cuffs are too tight! Hey!"

The deputy walked right past the cruiser toward the ambulance.

"Hey!" Brad called again, trying to get the deputy's attention. The deputy gave no indication that he heard him.

Deputy Wilcox walked around to the passenger side of the ambulance to the personnel door and pulled the door open. Attached to the inside of the door were pouches for rubber gloves. He surveyed the selection. He needed a set of large gloves. The XL pouch was full, the medium pouch was nearly empty and the small pouch was full. The pouch marked Large was completely empty.

"Of course," he muttered under his breath, withdrawing two gloves from the XL collection and closing the door. He turned and started back toward the casualty, pulling the gloves on.

By the time he made it back to the scene, the paramedics had cut most of Rich's clothes off with trauma shears and were finalizing their assessment, already treating the wounds. Two bullets had passed through the man so he had entry and exit wounds to deal with. Deputy Wilcox walked straight over to the pile of blood-soaked clothes and started digging through them until he found what he was looking for; the man's wallet. He opened the wallet and checked the driver's license.

Richard Webster, Chubbuck, Idaho

This guy's not far from home. He pulled out the other man's wallet and examined the name and address. *This guy just lives up the road. What the hell happened here?* He looked up the hill at the chaos on the interstate as he stashed the two wallets back in his pockets again.

He walked back around the truck, stopping in the middle of the road. He looked around the site, taking in everything, noting several nine-millimeter shell casings in the road. He then turned his attention to the truck and the multiple small caliber bullet holes in it, all on the driver's side. He then looked back in the direction that the rounds must have been fired from, noting the open gate and fresh tire marks where someone had obviously spun their tires. Maybe this *was* another terrorist attack. It was time to go talk to this guy in the back seat. But first, he needed to call this in.

14

Don't Bring a Pipe to a Gunfight

Later that same day

Near Mink Creek, Idaho

Ahmad coughed violently, spraying blood onto the dashboard. The bullet had punctured his lung and lodged against his spine. His breathing was labored between the coughing fits. Nour looked over at his wounded teammate and frowned. He knew that he needed a doctor. He also knew that he wasn't going to take him to a hospital. He returned his attention to the road. He was concentrating on staying just under the speed limit, so as not to attract attention, but he knew that the car would attract attention even without speeding due to the bullet holes. He needed to find a place to hide until it got dark.

After leaving the shootout on Old Malad Highway, he had followed it north until it intersected with U.S. 91. He then turned south on U.S. 91 and drove through a very rural area, only passing a few vehicles. U.S. 91 eventually changed to Route 36, where he was now. It had taken him an hour of nerve-rattling driving to get here. He gripped the steering wheel so tightly that his knuckles were white and his hands were aching. He had to lean a little to see through an undamaged portion of the windshield. One of the bullets had narrowly missed him, punching a neat hole in the seat about an inch and a half from his right arm. Ahmad had not been so lucky.

Nour eyed every dirt road that he passed, looking for one that didn't look heavily used. The area around U.S. 91 had been flat agricultural lowland, but now the terrain was changing and the hills seemed to be getting bigger the further he drove. He spied a dirt road coming up on the right side just as a white pickup truck with large tool boxes mounted in the back and some kind of logo on the door passed him, going in the opposite direction. He saw the guy in the passenger seat pointing at his car through the windshield as they passed by.

Nour looked up at the rear-view mirror and saw the brake lights illuminate on the truck. He made a decision. As soon as he came to the dirt road, he stomped the brakes, cranked the wheel to the right, and left the pavement. He drove as quickly as he could, leaving a huge plume of dirt in his wake as he tried to put distance between himself and the curious men in the truck. The road narrowed immediately. It was a forestry road and his car was not well suited to the road, but he pushed on.

Behind him, the father and son team that formed Jackson Plumbing was turning onto the road. The reports of the attack were all over the radio and Brad Baxter had been able to provide a vehicular description to the authorities. There were numerous other attacks today too, but the man on the radio didn't have any details yet.

The men in the truck were Ian "Jack" Jackson and his son, Ian Junior. Junior had seen the vehicle and pointed it out to his father. There wasn't much of a discussion before they decided to chase down the car.

"Go ahead and call 911, son. Tell them where we are and tell them that we're going to keep the car in sight until the cavalry arrives," the elder Jackson ordered.

Junior was looking down at his phone.

"No service, Dad. Just keep going. The service through here is spotty. As soon as I get some bars, I'll call."

The older man just grunted and turned onto the dirt road where the dust had yet to settle.

"Where the hell do they think they're going? Do you know where this road goes?" he asked.

"No," his son replied. "I've never gone down this road. It looks like some kind of service road."

"Yeah, ya think?" the older man grunted back as they bounced through a pothole.

As they drove, they were confident that they were still on the trail because they could see dust in the air. They drove for a couple of minutes before the older man spoke again.

"How about now, you got service?"

"No. Still nothing."

Jack frowned but kept driving.

After a few minutes, Junior nearly jumped from his seat as he saw the car stopped up ahead.

"There it is!" he screeched. "There it is." He was pointing frantically at the little car visible up ahead.

"I see it son, I'm not blind. Calm down."

The older man let off the gas and let the truck drift to a stop about fifty yards behind the car. It appeared to be leaning slightly to the left. The trees crowded in on both sides and after a few yards, sloped uphill in both directions.

"What are you doing, Dad? Let's go. Get up there, we're going to make a citizen's arrest!"

His dad didn't respond. He just leaned forward against the steering wheel and stared at the car, one hand absently stroking the graying beard on his chin.

"Dad? Did you hear me?"

"Hush up, Junior. I'm trying to figure this out. And how exactly do you plan on making a citizen's arrest? Do you have your gun with you?"

"Well, no. But I'll grab a length of pipe out of the back. And we have zip-ties. We can tie them up and take them to the police station."

The older man continued to study the situation, then shifted the truck into park.

"I don't know. I don't like it," he said.

"What's not to like, Dad? We'll be heroes!"

His dad grunted again, still skeptical of the situation.

"Come on, Dad! We can do this!" The excitement in his voice was aggravating the young man's father.

"Okay. We'll do this, but you do *exactly* as I say. You hear me?"

"Yessir!" he said, opening the door and jumping out.

"Hold on, hold on. Go around to the tool box and get us a couple of lengths of pipe and a handful of zip-ties."

"Yeah!" the young man exclaimed as he closed his door and bolted for the back of the truck.

The older man killed the engine and exited the truck, but stood behind the open door, leaning into the open window, still observing the car. He hadn't seen any movement, and he couldn't tell if there was anyone in the car. They had seen what appeared to be two people through the shattered windshield when they passed them earlier. But now he couldn't see into the car. The rear windshield was intact, and completely coated in a thick layer of dust.

His son rounded the tailgate with two pieces of metal pipe. One was about a foot long and the other was closer to two feet long. A half dozen zip-ties were sticking out of his pants pocket.

"I'm ready. Here." He extended the shorter of the two pieces of scrap pipe that had been cut on their last job.

"Fine." Jack said, accepting the pipe and gently closing his door, despite the fact that his son had just slammed the passenger door. "Check your phone again. Do you have service?"

"Dad!"

"Do it." Jack said stoically.

Junior tucked his pipe under his arm and dug his phone out again. He stared at the screen for a few long seconds.

"Well?"

"No, nothing." He slipped the phone back into his pocket again. "Come on, let's get 'em!"

His father drew in a deep breath and let it out in a long exhale. "Ok. Here's the deal. I'm going to go around the driver side and you'll approach on the passenger side. Stay a little way from the car, near the trees. Don't move too fast. Don't get ahead of me. Do you understand?"

"I got it." He started to take a step.

"Stop," Jack commanded.

Junior froze and looked back at his dad.

"I'm not done. Don't get ahead of me and don't go all the way to the front. Stop as soon as you can see them. Then we'll step up to the doors at the same time. Got it?"

"I got it, I got it. Come on," he answered impatiently.

Jack sighed. "Ok. Let's go."

Junior immediately took off, walking faster than his father, excited for the hunt.

Jack snapped his fingers and Junior looked back at him. Jack pointed to the ground adjacent to himself and offered a harsh look at his son.

Junior nodded his understanding and waited until his father was beside him before continuing at his father's pace.

They both instinctively began trying to walk quietly as they would when hunting, despite the fact that anyone in the area would have known they were there. As they neared the back of the car, they both pushed outward, putting a little more distance between themselves and the sides of the trunk. Jack motioned to Junior to go slow. Junior nodded his understanding silently. Junior spotted a head in the passenger seat. He looked over at his father and did his best to mimic what he had seen in military movies. He put two fingers to his eyes and then pointed to the front seat. After that he held up his pointer finger trying to convey that he could see one of them.

Jack nodded in acknowledgement. From his angle, he still couldn't quite see into the driver seat. However, he could see the front tire. It was in a deep rut, the frame of the car resting solidly on the firm surface of the hard packed dirt road. When he looked back up at Junior, he was holding one finger in the air, then two. *Crap he was counting down.* Then he raised the third finger and jumped to the side of the passenger door, the pipe held back like a baseball player about to swing for the fence. He froze.

Jack quickly closed the last couple of steps to the driver's door and peered into the car. The driver seat was empty. Jack looked up at his son who was slowly lowering the pipe.

"He's...he's...dead."

"What?" Jack asked and squatted down to look through the driver's window at the passenger seat. There was a man slumped against his seat belt. He *did* look dead. His shirt was covered in blood and he wasn't moving.

"Well, crap," Jack muttered under his breath. "Hold on, son. I'll come over there."

He walked around the front of the car, glancing down to see that the front plastic bumper cover was also contacting the dirt road. *That explains why they stopped.*

Jack rounded the passenger side and joined his son at the door, staring at the unmoving body.

"Do you think we should check for a pulse?" Junior asked, his voice suddenly sounding much less confident.

"No, I don't think we should touch anything. I think we should get out of here and drive until we get cell service and then we can guide the cops up in here so they can take control of this."

"Yeah, Dad. I think you're right. Let's get out of here." They both took a couple tentative steps back toward their truck, still looking at the bloody figure in the car. Almost simultaneously, they both turned to go back, Junior in the lead.

He took one step and then suddenly stopped. Jack nearly ran into him.

"What are you doing?"

Junior didn't answer. He was just looking back toward the truck. Jack stepped to the side to see what his son was looking at. Fifteen yards away, a man stood in the road. He had a military-style rifle to his shoulder and it was pointed right at Junior.

Jack spoke first. "Sir? Sir, there's no need for..."

Crack!

Junior instantly crumpled and fell against the rear quarter panel of the car, sliding down and coming to rest in a pile, unmoving.

"NOOOO," Jack screamed and fell to his knees, reaching for his son. Junior's eyes were open and not blinking. Jack grasped at his son's bloody shirt and pulled him toward himself, then slowly lowered his torso to the ground. His legs were bent under him at an odd angle.

"No, no, no! Junior!" Jack sobbed. "No!"

Jack heard the crunch of a boot in the dirt and looked up. His eyes filling with tears. The man was now only a two or three step away.

"What have you done?!" Jack screeched.

The man didn't hesitate as he raised the rifle and shot Jack in the head.

154

15

That Looks Like a Grave

Later that same day

Little America, Wyoming

Nour pulled into the Travel Center in Little America, Wyoming. The Chevy pickup truck was roomy and comfortable. It had plenty of room for the gear that he had transferred from his stranded car. It had also been nearly full of gas when he confiscated it from the two men he had murdered in Idaho.

Nour stopped in front of the green and white gas pumps and got out. He was dressed in a clean shirt and jeans, since his other clothes had blood on them. He had donned a red and white Coca-Cola ball cap and sunglasses. He left the glasses on as he entered.

He avoided eye contact with the few people near the front of the store and headed for the bathroom. After relieving himself, he took extra time to wash his hands and arms, all the way up to his elbow. After drying his hands, he headed to the automotive cleaning section where he found a bucket and grabbed it. This Travel Center catered to RVs, which were common in the area. He found a set of sheets labeled "4 Piece RV Sheet Set" and dropped them into the bucket. Then he added a four-pack of washcloths, two towels, a bar of soap, and a bottle of Fabuloso Multi-Purpose Cleaner.

In the camping section, he found a medium sized shovel and a hank of paracord. He carried his haul up to the counter and set the bucket in front of the attendant. Without speaking, he turned to the stack of bottled water on display and added a case to the counter. The attendant scanned everything without a word until he announced the total. Nour added thirty dollars for gas and collected his purchase.

He walked back out to the truck and dropped the tailgate before placing the items next to the bundled blue tarp in the bed. He closed the tailgate and after he was fueled up, he pulled into the spacious parking lot and parked facing east, away from the setting sun. He pulled out his phone, turned it on, and opened Google Maps. He examined the desert on the other side of I-80, directly south of the Travel Center and made his decision.

He dropped the phone into his lap and opened up the center console to retrieve his notebook. After checking the codewords, he wrote down the encoded message, then double checked it. He picked the phone back up and entered in the message. He paused with his finger above the send icon. With a sigh, he sent the message, and waited.

Two minutes later, he received the response. He copied it into the notebook, then powered down the phone. He decoded the message. As he read the words, his face flushed with frustration. He hurled the notebook against the passenger side window and pounded the steering wheel with his fist.

A surge of emotion hit him – raw and overwhelming. He was frustrated and disappointed, but most of all, he was angry. He wished he could turn around and find those two guys with the boat on their truck and kill them -- slowly and painfully. He wished Ahmad would have killed them when he had the chance. He wished...he wished...

It didn't matter. He still had work to do.

He took a deep breath, regained his composure, and started the truck. He turned out of the parking lot and passed under I-80 just as the sun disappeared below the horizon. He switched the lights on and followed the dirt road into the desert until he reached the area he had identified earlier on the phone. He turned off the road and drove slowly out into the desert, carefully avoiding anything that could potentially get him stuck. He kept driving, getting some distance from the road to reduce the likelihood that anyone would discover what he had done.

He exited the truck and collected the shovel. He realized that he didn't know which way to position the grave. He had to turn the phone back on and use Google earth to determine which direction faced Mecca. Finally, he was able to begin. He was surprised at how difficult it was to dig, but after several hours, and numerous water breaks, he had created a man-sized hole with the spoil deposited on both sides.

Next, he retrieved the bucket, cleaner, soap, towels, and washcloths, placing them on the ground a few feet from the hole. With a sigh, he pulled on the blue tarp until he could wrestle the body of his fallen teammate onto the ground near the supplies. He opened the tarp and carefully undressed Ahmad's body. He poured a few bottles of water over the body and then several more into the bucket and scented it with a splash of the cleaner. He used the washcloths, soap, and water to meticulously clean his friend's remains. He paused several times to inspect his work with a shielded flashlight. After cleaning the front of the body, he replaced the water in the bucket and rolled the body onto the clean towels, being careful not to get any more blood on the body from the tarp.

He repeated the ritual of cleaning his friend's body, ensuring that he was as clean as possible. He even took the time to clean under his fingernails. Finally, he spread the sheet on the ground and carefully transferred the body onto it. He gathered the sheet around him and used the paracord to bind it in at the head and feet, in accordance with Islamic law.

He squatted down and scooped up his comrade, wavering briefly before continuing to the prepared grave. Carefully, he placed the body at the edge of the hole before climbing in. He respectfully positioned the wrapped corpse in the grave, then climbed back out.

Refilling the hole was significantly easier than digging it. It was also faster. He stood back and reviewed his work. Once again, he used the flashlight, shielding it with his hand to reduce the signature. The dirt was mounded.

That looks like a grave, but I know it's going to settle. It's going to have to work. He hoped that the grave was far enough from the dirt path.

Nour took the time to pack up and wrap everything in the tarp before placing it all in the bed of the truck. He retrieved Ahmad's prayer mat from the cab. Removing his shoes, he stepped onto the mat and prayed, facing Mecca. Once his prayer was complete, he put his shoes back on and rolled the mat up, placing it by the grave. He looked around and found a couple large rocks and used them to pin the mat in place. He turned to go, then stopped.

No. That's a bad idea. That will draw attention to this place. He removed the rocks and tucked the mat under his arm as he returned to the truck.

As he placed his hand on the door handle, a wave of grief hit him, and he froze. He closed his eyes and took several deep breaths. He looked back toward the grave for a long moment.

Finally, he climbed back into the truck and turned toward the interstate. He would follow the instructions in the message: *Avoid the interstates and return to Michigan.*

16

I Need to Get Home to Edna

July 27, 2024

Charles and Edna's Farm

Charles entered the house after feeding the animals. He heard the news playing on the television in the living room and called his wife's name.

"Edna? Honey?"

"I'm in the living room," she called back.

"Okay. I'll be right there."

He went to the kitchen sink, washed his hands, and poured himself a jar of sweet tea. As he walked into the living room, he was dragging the jar across his forehead.

"It's already hot out there and it's not even nine a.m. What's going on with the news?" he asked, plopping down in his easy chair.

"Well," Edna began. "you know there was another round of attacks yesterday."

"Yep," he replied, taking a sip of his tea. "Nothing close to here though, right?"

"No, there were six more attacks, but Arkansas was the closest."

"Well, at least there's that."

Edna abruptly grabbed the remote and muted the television, then turned toward Charles, her face tense with stress.

"It doesn't matter," she said. "People are going crazy all over the place."

"What do you mean?"

She pointed at the television, a slight tremble visible in her outstretched finger. "Look at that!"

The screen showed a video that must have been taken the night before -- it was dark, with numerous fires visible. A caption indicated that it was in Baltimore. Along the bottom of the screen, city names scrolled across in a banner:

> Atlanta, GA; Baltimore, MD; Chicago, IL; Detroit, MI; Fayetteville, NC; Houston, TX; Los Angeles, CA; Louisville, KY; Minneapolis, MN; New York, NY; Philadelphia, PA; Portland, OR; Seattle, WA; San Diego, CA; San Francisco, CA; St. Louis, MO; Washington, DC

"Do you see that? That's all the cities with rioting and looting right now. Louisville is on that list! Louisville! And they're not even talking about the all the places where people are clearing out the grocery stores! That's essentially everywhere, probably even here! The man on the news was telling everyone to stay calm, but that's just making it worse!"

"Maybe it's not as bad as it seems. The news always plays everything up," Charles responded, but he didn't sound like he believed it.

"No. This is just what Paul warned us about. We need to take another look at our stuff and if we need anything, we need to get it *now*."

Charles wasn't used to seeing his wife stressed. She dealt with things as they came, but she was clearly shaken. *I need to calm her down.*

"Honey, it's okay. We have what we need. But if it will make you feel better, go ahead and take a look again. I'll run into town and get you whatever you need."

She stood up. "I'm gonna do exactly that. I'm getting the list that Paul made us and going over it again." She took off for the kitchen pantry where she had the list in a cabinet drawer. She took the list and sat down at the kitchen table with a notepad.

Charles returned his attention to the television and turned the sound back on. The news anchor was reporting that truck drivers all across the nation were refusing to drive. Larger cities were reporting nearly empty shelves in the grocery stores. The big box stores were reporting record sales as everyone tried to get what they needed before it was unavailable.

Charles thought about the people living in small apartments in the big cities. It was unlikely that they would have had the space to store food even if they wanted to. *How many of those people live day to day on take out and delivery?* As if the news anchor had heard his thoughts, the story changed to show restaurants displaying "Closed" signs in the middle of the day. One sign read "Closed--Out of food." *I bet that's an effort to keep people from trying to break in and steal food,* he thought. *The trucks just stopped running and they are already out of food? How is that even possible?*

Charles heard Edna rummaging through a drawer in the kitchen.

He returned his attention to the television and checked another news channel. The screen showed a picture of dozens of fuel tankers sitting in a lot somewhere in Texas.

> "...with no drivers to move the fuel, the tankers you see behind me will not be delivered. Gas stations depend on regular deliveries to keep the fuel flowing to our vehicles. Sources tell us that some stations normally get deliveries every few days, whereas other locations with larger tanks may go as long as a month before refilling. Of course, this is affected by the amount of demand and during times of higher fuel consumption, these delivery dates are often adjusted to meet consumer needs. As Americans, we are accustomed to a constantly available supply of gasoline and diesel. If fuel distribution companies are unable to get the fuel deliveries moving again, very soon, that may no longer be the case."

Great. Now there's going to be a run on gas, he thought. *When I run into town, I'll go ahead and top off the tank.*

The news anchor made a few more comments about the fuel before moving on to the next story.

> "In California today, a Brinks armored vehicle was attacked with rifle and pistol fire in San Francisco. The attack happened just four miles from the home of the Representative Nancy Pelosi. The San Franciso Police Department reports that there were no injuries and the armored vehicle was able to escape with minimal damage. Brinks has issued the following statement:

The words appeared on the screen as the news anchor read the announcement.

"Criminal elements attempted to intercept a Brinks Security armored transport today. Our highly trained and professional security agents successfully extracted themselves from the attack with no loss of life or cargo. We assure all Brinks clients that you can count on us for the same quality and security that you have become accustomed to, and we expect no interruption of service. Thank you."

Charles shook his head. *The world's gone crazy.*

Edna walked back into the living room.

"Here ya go. You were right, we don't need much, but I'd feel better if you got this." She held a piece of paper out for him.

Charles stood up, accepting the list. He glanced down at it.

He mumbled as he read the list.

"All-purpose flour, milk, powdered milk, laundry detergent..." He continued to move his lips silently as he read over the short list.

"This doesn't look too bad. It shouldn't take long." He walked to the sink and deposited his empty tea jar, then started toward the door.

"Okay, be careful," she called to him as he went out the door.

Twenty minutes later, Charles was pulling up to the intersection of Route 32 and Route 23. Walmart and Tractor Supply were to the right; the Exxon station was a mile and a half to his left. He immediately knew something was different -- he couldn't recall ever seeing the traffic this heavy. He sat at the intersection for a couple of minutes, waiting for a break in the vehicles so he could turn left.

A couple minutes later, he finally made it to the intersection of U.S. Route 23 and Old U.S. 23, turning right toward the entrance. The Exxon station was a bit of a landmark in the area. It was built to resemble a small castle and looked like it would be more at home in Disney World than in rural Kentucky.

The station had ten lanes for gas, consisting of five double-sided pumps. Every lane had at least six vehicles backed up, waiting. It was a mess -- clearly beyond the intended capacity of the parking lot.

As he turned into the parking lot, Charles stopped and analyzed the scene for a moment. It was chaos. At the other end of the parking lot, two drivers were outside their vehicles yelling at one another. It looked as if one of them might have backed into the other.

Somewhere behind him, someone tapped their horn, and Charles looked up at his rearview mirror to see that more cars were trying to enter and he was blocking them. He pulled over to the side of the parking lot to allow them to pass him.

He looked over toward the ornate building and saw there was even a line waiting to get into the store. Charles glanced down at his own fuel gauge.

Three quarters of a tank. I think I'll go on to Walmart. I don't want anything to do with this mess.

It took some careful maneuvering, but he made it back onto Old U.S. 23 and pulled up to the light to turn south, back toward Walmart. Normally, it would have been about a three-minute drive from here. That was not going to be the case this time. He felt the frustration rising as he waited through the second cycle of lights at the intersection and still hadn't made it back out onto Route 23. He took a deep breath and reminded himself to be patient. It's fine. *Everything will be fine.*

Back at home, Charles' cell phone rang on the kitchen table where he had accidentally left it. Edna picked it up and looked at the screen. It was Paul. She answered.

"Hey, Honey," she said as a greeting.

"Oh, hey Mama."

"Your dad forgot his phone, that's why I'm answering it."

There was a short pause. "What do you mean, he forgot his phone? Where is he?"

"I asked him to run into town and pick up a few things," she replied cheerfully, as if it were any normal day.

"Mom! That's why I was calling you. I was going to tell y'all not to go anywhere." The frustration was apparent in his voice.

"Oh, it's fine Honey. We're just getting a few last-minute items. I was looking over the list you gave me again and I was thinking that..."

Paul interrupted her. "Mama. Mama."

She stopped talking.

"It's going to get dangerous out there. Have you seen the news today?"

"Well, yes, but the nearest rioting is in Louisville. That's a bit of a drive from here. I seriously doubt Louisa is dangerous."

She heard her son let out a huff.

"I don't think you understand. The worst stuff is in the cities, sure. But that doesn't mean that people in the country won't panic too. We've talked about this. Most people don't keep more than a few days' worth of supplies on hand at any given time. I get it that you feel safe, and that's good. No, that's great, but we need to be realists here. I need to call Scott. When Dad gets back, tell him not to go anywhere else and call me to let me know he made it home safe. Okay?"

Her chest tightened as the anxiety she'd tried to suppress came rushing back. "Okay, Paul. I'll have him call you."

"Thanks Mama. I love you."

"I love you more."

"We'll talk soon. Bye."

"Okay, bye," she said as the call ended.

This was about the time that Charles realized he didn't have his phone. He was going to call Edna and tell her that this was going to take longer than anticipated.

"Dang it!" he said, as the realization hit him that he couldn't call her.

The traffic started moving and he refocused on the road, finally making it back onto the main road and turning toward Walmart. A few minutes later, he turned off Route 23 onto Blair's Way, which led to the Walmart entrance. He was greeted by another chaotic scene. The parking lot was full and additional cars were parked in the grass around the parking lot. Multiple vehicles choked the lanes between the parked cars. Charles observed two Lawrence County Sherrif's

Department patrol cars with their lights on in the parking lot as well.

I'm not doing this, he thought. Unfortunately, there was no reasonable way to get turned around and he was stuck in the backed-up traffic trying to get into the parking lot. He shifted the truck into park and rolled the window down, leaning out slightly to try to see around the green Nissan Cube in front of him. *Who would buy something like that? He thought. That has to be one of the ugliest...*

Boom, boom!

Two gunshots rang out. Charles flinched instinctively and pulled himself back into the truck. He saw the reverse lights on the car in front of him illuminate -- it started backing toward him. He looked in the rearview mirror to see if he could give it some space. He couldn't. The car behind him was right on his bumper.

Charles hit the horn just as the little car impacted his front bumper. The driver pulled forward and barely cleared the car ahead of her as she turned left. Charles watched as the car lost traction while the woman tried to accelerate.

"What in the world are you doing, lady!" he yelled out the window as he saw the woman's face come into view.

Charles could see the panic on her face as she wrestled with the wheel, trying to bring the car under control while keeping the accelerator pinned to the floor. The rear end of the car came sliding around just as she neared the line of cars behind him. Charles turned in his seat just in time to see her slide sideways into a pickup truck several places behind Charles in line and come to a stop with an audible crunch. Several other drivers were now blaring their horns at the lady. Charles could hear yelling through his open window.

Okay, this is getting out of hand, he thought to himself. He made a snap decision. He turned the wheel slightly to the left and took advantage of the space created by the woman's departure. He shifted the truck back into *Drive* and eased forward, following the line in the grass created by the panicked woman. The difference was that Charles drove calmly and carefully across the flat grass toward Route 23. He didn't try to return to the entrance road, but rather angled directly toward the main road.

Several other drivers saw him and followed suit, but Charles reached the main road first. He glanced quickly to his left to make sure there was room and immediately entered the road, accelerating hard to get up to the same speed as the approaching cars. He stayed in the right-hand lane and put his right turn signal on. In less than a minute, he was taking the off-ramp back onto Route 32 and turning toward home.

I think we have enough flour. I need to get home to Edna.

17

Flat Screens 100% Off

July 28th, 2024

Tri Point Solutions Conference Room

The Tri Point Solutions team had all been called in with the exception of Buck and Irish who were on shift in Winchester. The conference room was not fancy, but it did have two nice wooden tables put together end to end in the middle and surrounded by simple padded chairs. The end wall displayed 3'x5' American flag and various plaques and framed photos lined the sides of the room. A small table was positioned by the door with a Keurig coffeemaker, an open box of coffee pods, and a case of bottled water.

"All right guys, grab your coffee if you want it and have a seat," Mack began. Chris "Rotor" Wolf was seated beside him with an open laptop in front of him.

Pikey was the last to sit down, opening an energy drink. "No coffee for me," he said with a smile.

Mack just shook his head. "Thanks for coming in guys. I know a couple of you were on shift last night, but we felt like we needed to get everyone in the same room to make sure the whole team is up to speed on what we know. I'll make sure that Irish and Buck get all the information as well. Rotor's been working on an intel brief for what we know so far and we'd like to get some feedback from the group, so feel free to speak up if you have something that will be of use."

Rotor motioned to the large flat screen mounted on the wall at the end of the conference table, opposite from the flag. He clicked something on his computer and the screen lit up with the Tri Point Solutions logo. Beneath the logo it said:

S2/Intel Brief
28 JUL 24

Everyone turned in their seats to look at the screen as Rotor continued.

"I've organized everything into a timeline." He clicked his mouse and the screen changed to the next slide. "Each event will have a corresponding date beside it for reference. I just have the major events that are pertinent to our job and ultimately to our families as well. The timeline starts with eighteen July, the day of the first attacks."

He continued. "The same day, we saw an unorganized and localized response to each of the attack sites. These included Alabama, California, Colorado, Iowa, and New York. By the following day, we saw the feds starting to get organized -- FBI, Homeland, U.S. Marshals, and FEMA started mobilizing. Initially, there wasn't much of a reaction from the civilian population as everyone just tried to figure out what was going on. We did see some individual states mobilize their state police to increase their presence along the interstates, but obviously, that didn't have an impact. We'll come back to that point.

"We saw a mild reaction from various transport organizations. Obviously, we picked up the gig in Winchester as a direct result of this and we're working through some more requests right now. Moving on; here we are on the twenty first and we saw some scattered rioting. I assess this as just opportunists taking advantage of the situation to act like savages and steal other people's stuff. If we look at the locations..." He changed the slide to show a map of the continental United States. A few red dots were displayed showing the location of the events. "We see that it's the usual actors, Chicago, Detroit, Frisco, etc., nothing that's of concern to us."

Joker jumped in with a quick comment. "Today only! Flat screens, a hundred percent off."

Rotor didn't acknowledge the joke. "Now, compare that to this one."

The screen changed again.

There was an audible reaction from the group as they looked at the map of the country with red dots seemingly on every major metropolitan area and smaller dots all around the country in nearly every state.

"FEMA has created a new website for tracking this event. I pulled this image off that website about an hour ago. It's pretty clear that the panic is spreading. The red dots indicate looting or rioting. Not every state has it, but it's pretty damn close. Looks like West Virginia is still holding out, Doc." He dipped his chin at Paul, using his callsign.

Paul grinned. "Well, to be fair, we don't really have enough people in Best Virginia to riot."

Loki looked over at Paul. "Doc, did you just say *Best* Virginia?"

Paul was still grinning. "I said what I said."

Rotor continued. "Well, no looting, but this next slide overlays incidents where law enforcement responded to incidents believed to be related to supply chain concerns."

Click.

The screen changed again. The red dots were still there, but yellow dots were added. *A lot* of yellow dots.

"As you can see Doc, neither Kentucky nor West Virginia escaped this one. In fact, all forty-eight continental states, plus Alaska have reported incidents. These are mostly places where people were fighting over stuff at grocery stores, big box stores, gas stations, that kind of thing. Hawaii had some notable increases in sales, but they're the only ones with no major incidents as of this morning. Of course, they're half a world away."

He continued. "One of the immediate impacts we've seen is the cost of fuel. Gas is now pushing five dollars a gallon around here. It's worse in other places. I saw on the news that it's over ten dollars a gallon in California. I've been doing some analysis and following some online reports. I expect it to continue climbing. If you have the room to add more fuel to your fuel storage, I recommend you do it now before it gets any higher."

Everyone was serious again. They had all topped off their spare fuel tanks last week, although the amount of storage varied from person to person.

Rotor continued. "In response to the latest attacks, countless agencies are flooding the interstates with law enforcement, both marked and unmarked. Additionally, I'm sure you've all seen the advertised hotlines and online reporting portal for tips. The FBI is supposedly manning both of those, but we all know how efficient they are."

This elicited a collective chuckle.

"Now back to the timeline," Rotor continued. "Twenty Six July, second wave of attacks. I know this is common knowledge by now, but these were in Maine, Minnesota, Florida, Arkansas and Idaho. Of course, the one in Idaho is the one that resulted in a shootout with a couple of private citizens that stumbled on the bad guys just as they launched their attack."

Pikey spoke up. "Huh, will you look at that? An armed private citizen was able to fight a terrorist."

Loki responded with a smile. "Yeah. We should make a constitutional amendment guaranteeing the right of people to have and carry guns. Oh, wait..."

Rotor waited for the chatter to die down and then began again. He wasn't amused by the antics. "As I was saying, one civilian was wounded and the bad guys got away. This morning, an Idaho Game Warden found their getaway vehicle. It was full of blood. The investigation is ongoing, but the FBI CSI took control of the site. Nothing has been released yet, and I'm not holding my breath. The one thing that they *are* reporting is that they found two additional dead at the scene. It looks like they killed a father and son and took their truck. They have an APB out on the missing truck, a 2019 Chevy Silverado four-wheel drive work truck. It should be pretty easy to find. It has a Plumbing company logo on it.

"Additionally, citizens in Florida reported a blue Ford Explorer fleeing the scene, but nothing has come from that one yet. That was just west of Tallahassee where the interstate runs through a Wildlife Management Area."

Rotor changed the slide again to one with bullet comments on it. "What we do know is every attack has taken place on an interstate. So far, they've only targeted tractor trailers. No specific type of tractor trailer has been singled out. They've hit everything from empty flatbeds to fully loaded tankers. All the attacks happened at roughly the same time, regardless of time zone, and in every case, they appear to have planned the attack at a location with an escape route· that was *not* the interstate."

Paul spoke up. "They're trying to make sure everyone knows it's a coordinated attack."

"Exactly," Rotor responded, pointing at Paul as he said it.

Paul continued. "Well, if we look at the seven-step terrorist planning cycle, that could potentially be supporting the final step, escape and exploitation. No one has taken credit for this yet. Typically speaking, terrorists want to advertise their work. They want to publicly announce '*we did this and this is why*'. The coordinated aspect of the attacks leaves no doubt that one organization executed all the attacks. Now we'll have to wait and see who speaks up."

Dangle spoke up for the first time in the meeting. "The seven-step what?"

Paul turned to face him. "The seven-step terrorist planning cycle. It's essentially a blueprint for how terrorists typically prepare for and execute an attack. I've talked to Mack and Rotor about this a few times."

Mack answered. "Yeah. Doc, why don't you give the room a quick rundown of it."

"Sure," Paul began. "I can't remember it all word for word. It was part of a course we did in Special Forces. But the bottom line is that the first few steps revolve around target identification and planning. Then," he paused as he thought, "step five is rehearsals and step six is the execution of the attack. The seventh and final step is escape and exploitation, as I mentioned a second ago. The exploitation part is essentially when the bad guys take credit for what they've done and why they did it. We haven't seen that yet, which leads me to think the attack isn't over."

Rotor was jotting something down on a notepad beside his computer.

Mack took over again. "Thanks, Doc. I tend to agree, so we're gonna work under the assumption that more attacks are coming. We've had two sets of attacks and there could potentially be a third one coming, so act like it. This is *not* the time to relax. This is the time for increased vigilance, at work and at home. These first two waves have certainly been successful in inciting terror in the public, and we've all seen how people can act when they're panicked."

"Oh yeah," Joker responded.

Mack clapped his hands together. "Okay, that wraps up the intel update portion of the meeting. Anyone have anything to add before we move on to Operations?"

Paul answered. "I heard a discussion on the radio that they are considering postponing or suspending the election in November. Have you seen anything about that?"

Rotor leaned back in his chair, no longer using the notes on his computer. "From what I've seen so far, it's been bounced around, but most indicators are that they are going to continue, but they may be putting out enhanced security measures around polling sites."

Paul responded with a simple. "Okay. Thanks."

"Anyone else have anything?" Mack asked.

Loki spoke up. "Yeah, with the increased security posture, will there be any adjustment to the rules of engagement on the job site?"

Rotor sat his pen down and reached for the mouse as Mack fielded the question. "Actually, yes. We're covering that part next. Effective immediately, these are the increased measures we'll be incorporating into our sites."

The screen showed a list of the updates.

"All company vehicles will be maintained above three quarters of a tank. Our client has onsite fuel tanks for both diesel and gasoline and we've negotiated arrangements to keep our onsite vehicle topped off. Now, with that being said, that doesn't help us getting back and forth to work. Most of us live pretty close, but Joker, Dangle, and Doc, y'all are a little further away and fuel could potentially become a problem for you."

"We'll talk offline after this to see if you want to stay on the standard schedule for this job, work a reduced schedule, or just bow out of this one. Either way, we should be good."

Joker, Dangle, and Paul nodded in acknowledgement.

"Additionally, we're putting one of the satellite phones at the site. Rotor or I will have one of the other one so that leaves us one spare. Right now, I'm leaning toward sending it home with Joker or Doc since they're the farthest away and if comms go down, I'd like to be able to reach out to y'all." He looked over at the two of them.

Joker responded first.

"I'm down, but do you have any smaller phones I can try first and work my way up to the Sat Phone? That thing is huge and

I don't think I'll be able to stuff it into my prison pocket right off the bat."

Mack just shook his head as everyone else in the room cracked up at Joker living up to his callsign.

"Okay, well, Dangle, I know you're working on your Ham setup right now, so I'd say it makes the most sense for Doc to maintain it. You good with that, Doc?"

"Yeah man, of course. Whatever you need," Paul responded. "Plus, Dangle's not that far from me, so in an emergency, I could run over to his house to pass information. For that matter, Joker's not that much farther."

Mack nodded. "Sounds good. Now back to Loki's question about the ROE. Yes, there will be an adjustment. We are also adding the bear spray foggers to the site and two of the X26 Tasers. We've discussed the gate situation at the site with the client and the gate guard will advise us when they need to open the gate so we can provide additional security if required. When there are no vehicles entering or exiting, the gates will remain closed and locked. If anyone is trying to breach the gate, the Standard Operating Procedures remain in place. Call the sheriff and if necessary, start off with the bear spray. Save the tasers for self-defense if anyone manages to breach the fence. Standard self-defense protocols are in place for the use of deadly force. We all know the headache that comes with that, so let's maintain our professionalism out there. Call it in, deescalate, defend. Any questions on that part?"

Rotor spoke again. "We'll keep putting out the schedule several days in advance in case we have any interruption to cellular or internet, so everyone should know when they're working."

Mack spoke up again. "No real change to the personal packing list. We already have armor, night vision and rifles on the list. However, if you want to plus your kit up, feel free. I'm adding a little more food, water, and some extra clothing to my vehicle. Plus, some camping gear, just in case."

No one spoke, but everyone nodded their agreement.

"All right guys. If no one has anything else to add, that's it for the meeting. Joker, Doc, Dangle, hold back and we can talk about the schedule."

The three of them stayed in their seats as the room slowly emptied.

Mack and Rotor both stayed seated as well.

"Okay guys, what are you thinking?"

Joker responded first. "For the time being, can you put me on a reduced schedule for a couple weeks and we'll see how things look?"

"Yeah, man," Mack responded as Rotor made a note.

He turned toward Paul and Dangle. "What do you guys think?"

"I don't know, but if we keep working, could you put us on the same schedule so we could use one vehicle to come down," Paul said.

"Yeah, I'd be okay with that, but could you wait a few days before putting me on the schedule. I need to get some stuff ironed out," Dangle said. He looked over at Paul.

"Can I still leave Tripwire at your place, even if you and I are on the same shift?"

"Oh, yeah. No problem. Sandy won't mind. Plus, my dog is always happy to see Tripwire."

"Cool." Dangle looked back to Mack. "Let me iron out the details and I'll give you a call."

"You good with that Doc?" he asked.

Paul nodded. "Yeah, I can use a few days to work around the farm anyhow."

Rotor closed the laptop and stood up. "Good deal. I'm going for some coffee. Anyone else?"

Everyone else followed his lead.

As they headed out the door, Dangle said "I would love some coffee in my whiskey."

Mack looked over at him. "Dangle! It's ten thirty in the morning!"

Dangle didn't even look back at him. "Fine! Bailey's it is."

18

Death To America

July 30, 2024

Eastern Michigan

Nour made it back to the camp. It had taken him several days to work his way back to Michigan. Immediately after burying his friend in the desert, he had ditched the stolen truck and stole another vehicle, a white Toyota Celica. It was reasonably easy. He found a house where there were no lights on and broke in. The keys were hanging on a key rack by the garage door.

He drove on back roads for two hours before pulling into a Walmart parking lot. He drove slowly around the parking lot, looking for another white Celica. He didn't find one, so he got back on the road and drove until he saw another full parking lot. This one was a grocery store. He repeated the exercise and near the middle of the parking lot, he found what he was looking for. It wasn't the same year model, but it was close. He pulled out his small toolkit and quickly exchanged the license plates before getting back on the road.

The idea was that when the owner of the stolen car reported it missing, the cops would be looking for a white Celica with that license plate, and not this one. Most people didn't inspect their license plates and with any luck, it would be a while before it was discovered. He had already decided that if there was an opportunity to exchange the plates a second time with another white Celica, he would, although he wasn't going to make a specific effort to find one.

It had worked. He had traveled mostly at night and used the daylight hours to keep the car hidden in inconspicuous locations. Avoiding interstates, it had been a slow and meticulous trip, using paper maps for navigation.

Nour walked out of the makeshift barracks after stowing his gear. The Celica was parked in front of the barn with various other vehicles. He headed over to the main house to meet Zamir. Glancing down at his watch, he suddenly felt completely exhausted. It had been a long few days. Walking up to the door, he knocked three times and waited.

"Enter!" It was Zamir.

Nour walked into the house and moved to the large dining room. As Nour entered the room, Zamir stood up and embraced him, speaking to him in their native tongue.

"Nour, brother. How are you?" He pushed Nour back by the shoulders and then reached out and took Nour's hand in both of his own.

"Commander. I'm fine. I apologize for my failure. I gave Ahmad a proper burial in the desert." He braced for the inevitable reprimand.

Zamir showed no sign of grief. "Failure? You succeeded. Ahmad succeeded! He died a martyr's death! A warrior's death in service to Allah. That is nothing to mourn, we will celebrate his life, not dwell on his death."

Nour felt a tentative wave of relief wash over him.

Zamir motioned for Nour to take a seat then sat down across from him. "Our mission has been an overwhelming success. America is spiraling into panic. Nearly everyone has made it back. We're still waiting for Omer and Bassam to return from Florida, but other than them, everyone is here. I have a call later today with Commander Ebrahim to discuss the details and tell him of our success."

One of the cooks entered and placed a cup of chai in front of each of the men without saying a word and then slipped back out of the room as quietly as he had entered.

"I've already debriefed the other teams. Now, tell me everything."

Nour couldn't recall his commander ever being so informal with him. His entire demeanor was different. He was relaxed. He almost seemed...happy? *Was that it? Was he happy?*

Nour reacted to the mood. He felt himself starting to relax too. He started his story from the time they left and concluded it with arriving back here a few minutes ago. Zamir didn't interrupt him at all. He just encouraged him to tell the story, taking notes as he listened. He smiled when Nour told of the two attacks and looked serious when he described the shootout. When Nour finally finished the story, he dropped back into his chair, mentally spent. He had barely slept the last couple of days.

Zamir tossed the pen onto the table and picked up his cup, finishing off the chai.

"You did well, Nour. Allah is pleased with you. You honored us and more importantly, you honored Allah. When I speak with Command Ebrahim later today, I will tell him of your bravery."

Nour didn't feel brave. He still felt as if he had partially failed, even though he knew that everyone in this camp, himself included, was fully prepared to die for this cause.

Zamir waited patiently as Nour finished his second cup of chai before excusing him.

"Nour, I know you must be exhausted from your travels. Go. Go sleep. The cooks will prepare you a meal when you want it. I have no other requirements for you today. We have a long day tomorrow, so I want you to rest."

Nour got up, thanked Zamir again for the chai and departed, closing the door gently as he exited.

As he walked back to the barracks, it felt surreal to be back here again. He hadn't been gone very long, but it felt like it had been months. Once he made it back to his bunk, he sat down and removed his shoes. He lay back on the bed and fell into a deep sleep almost immediately.

Two hours later
In the farmhouse

Zamir watched the clock on the computer, waiting until it was time for his meeting with his commander back in Lebanon via secure video chat. When the time finally came, he stared at the computer screen and waited for the call to come in. Fifteen seconds later, it did. He clicked the icon to connect the call.

"Commander Assaf, As-salam alaikum," he said, speaking in Arabic and using his commander's formal title. He and his men would often refer to him as Commander Ebrahim, but this was not the time.

186

"Commander Syed, Wa alaikum assalaam," he replied, using his formal title in return. "I've been following the progress of you and your cells. I'm pleased to see the success. The planning and training have paid off."

"Thank you, Commander." Zamir smiled at the praise. "I can't express to you how much my men and I are honored to have been selected to lead the attack to crush the American devils."

"Yes, yes. Have all your men returned?"

"No, Commander," Zamir replied. "I'm still waiting on one team, but I expect them soon. They are avoiding major roads, and they have a long way to drive, so the return trip will be slow."

The commander slowly nodded his head without expression. "I see. And you've debriefed the remainder of the team?"

"Yes. I'm preparing my report, and I'll be sending that to you on the secure email. However, the simple answer is that the men performed as they were trained."

This statement was intended to shine the light of success on himself as the commander, without overtly asking for praise.

"I understand that one of our men was martyred?" Assaf stated it as a question.

"Yes, Commander. Ahmad Abufaysal was killed as they escaped. Nour Hallal was able to bury him in accordance with our laws."

Zamir watched the screen closely for a reaction from Assaf. He stroked his chin absently and looked away from the screen as he appeared to be assessing the statement.

Assaf returned his gaze to the camera. "We've chosen the right team to prepare the enemy for our attack."

Zamir stared at the screen for a moment, processing the statement. *What did he say? Prepare the enemy for the attack?*

"I'm sorry, Commander. I don't know what you mean. As you know, we've already begun the attack. The Americans are cowering."

Commander Assaf smiled a knowing smile. Zamir did not. He sat, stone-faced, staring at the image on the computer.

"Zamir, you have done well, but this was merely a supporting element of the main attack. I didn't want to burden you with this knowledge, as I feared it might distract you from the importance of your mission. Understand, just because you aren't the main element of the attack, it doesn't lessen the value of your efforts."

The words stung Zamir as if he had been slapped in the face. The irony was lost on him that he had withheld information from Mohamed, his second in command, while his own commander was simultaneously withholding information from him. He felt the blood rush to his face and had to make a conscious effort to prevent the insult from broadcasting in his expression.

With effort to maintain a cool demeanor, he calmly responded. "Of course, Commander. I am here to serve. We are honored to be a supporting effort that will glorify Allah with our actions."

That was the right answer. Zamir knew it, even though it was not what he was feeling. He was insulted. He had been misled to believe that he *was* the main attack, not *supporting* the main attack. He cleared his throat as he struggled to maintain his composure. Then he continued.

"Commander, what do you require of us?"

Commander Assaf smiled again. He knew that Zamir was angry, or at the very least, upset. However, he wasn't showing it. Good. He had set the stage for his manipulation. He had just knocked Zamir down a notch, now he would pull him back in, give him a new purpose, and renew his sense of urgency.

"Zamir, its true that your efforts were not the primary blow that's meant to cripple our enemy. However, your first phase set the stage and your next phase is a component of the main attack that will bring a weakened America to its knees."

He paused as he let that information work on Zamir's mind. He saw Zamir lean forward toward the screen. *It was working.*

"The next phase is a cyberattack that will target America's infrastructure, specifically, the electrical grid, water treatment facilities, and their emergency reporting infrastructure, the 911 service."

Zamir was shocked. Not only was he unaware that this was part of the plan, he didn't think they even had the capabilities for such an attack. "Sir, I thought we had been unsuccessful in our cyberattack tests."

"That's true. However, we have some capable...friends who have been more successful. They've been working with our teams in Iran and will be leading that aspect of the mission. They've been conducting test runs for several years to probe for weaknesses and are now positioned to launch the attacks.

We've been waiting for them to be ready before we launched your attacks on the supply system."

Zamir listened intently, but didn't speak.

"Once we launch the cyberattack, the Americans will immediately begin working to fix everything. This is when your team will execute the next step."

Zamir continued to maintain his silence, but he felt his heart rate increase.

"Following the initial attack, while the power is down, your team will begin your second phase, the targeted sabotage. However, we have numerous other teams who will be joining you and conducting sabotage in other parts of the country at the same time. You will be limited to one area. Collectively, you will *all* ensure that the recovery efforts are unsuccessful."

Zamir didn't quite know how to react to this news. He had known his team would be conducting sabotage missions. He had informed Mohamed of that fact a week and a half earlier. However, he had been led to believe that his team's sabotage missions were the main attack. The cyberattack and the other terror cells were new information.

"Commander. We're honored to be entrusted with this task. I have worked on recommended infrastructure targets. I have included explosives training to keep the men's skills sharp. My thoughts are that we concentrate on substations and natural gas pipelines that feed power plants. I've identified several in various..."

Commander Assaf held up his hand to silence Zamir. Zamir obeyed and leaned back against his chair.

"Muhammed Bari and his team have been working on that for over three years now. They've had significant..." He paused as if trying to decide how to word this correctly. "They've had significant assistance from outside of our organization. The planning is done. You'll need to study the plan and execute it on the timeline that will be provide. Muhammed Bari will send everything to you via secure email. You'll have all the information you need this afternoon."

He continued. "The dictated timing is important because this will be followed up with an additional cyberattack on air travel, cellular carriers, and the banking system. Apparently, the electrical grid and cellular carriers were exceptionally easy to compromise."

Zamir's analytical mind was sprinting, trying to keep up with all the new information. Suddenly, he saw a flaw in the plan.

"Commander, if the power is down, then the internet may be interrupted. How would we be able to complete the second cyberattack on the cellular networks, banks, and...what was the other one?" he asked.

"Air travel," Commander Assaf said, grinning. "Don't worry about that. Believe me when I say that everything has been taken care of. It's truly shocking how many enemies America has. We have many experts from around the world who are working together on this. You're not going to think of anything that hasn't already been analyzed and reanalyzed a dozen times."

Zamir understood the implied statement. *Stop asking questions.* He considered the implications of the revelation. *There are multiple countries involved. I wonder who the others are. Russia? China? North Korea? Maybe Turkey? But they're members of both NATO and the UN. Surely not. Well, maybe. Yemen? Venezuela? Maybe.* His mind whirled with the possibilities. *Oh, Syria? I'd forgotten about them. I know Afghanistan has helped us. Do they even have the ability to do more than just provide weapons?*

Assaf interrupted Zamir's thoughts as he continued. "One challenge we had initially been unable to overcome is that many of these systems have redundancies and they are decentralized, especially the 911 service. It's scattered throughout the country and required some time for our allies to develop a sufficient method to target all the major systems at the same time." He paused as he appeared to reconsider the statement. "More or less at the same time."

"I understand, Commander." Zamir's looked away from the screen momentarily as his brain processed the new information. "You said that my team is one of several? How many teams do we have?"

"I'm not going to share that with you Zamir because it is unimportant to your mission."

"Of course, Commander. Forgive me."

Assaf didn't acknowledge the request. "Do you remember how easy it was to enter the United States?"

Zamir had thought about that often. "Of course, Commander. They have essentially no national defenses for their homeland. In fact, in most cases, they were facilitating the unregulated entry of foreigners."

"Exactly. We used that to our advantage. In numerous cases the government even provided the transportation. It was as if they were intentionally facilitating the invasion of their own country. America is complicit in its own demise. They deserve what they get. We needed to act while they were weak, and they are weaker now than at any time in recent history. The world is laughing at them. They claim that the greatest threat to their national security is climate change!" Commander Assaf chuckled. "Climate change! Can you believe that? They are inviting their enemies into their homes while fighting the weather!"

Zamir smiled politely.

Commander Assaf composed himself and continued. "As I was saying, I'm not going to tell you how many teams we have in the United States, but I'll share with you that we have more than enough to accomplish our mission. I wanted to make you aware of the other teams so when you saw the other attacks, you'd know it was all part of the plan. Additionally, when you see your targets, you'll see they are all in one region of the country. I wanted you to understand why. You're responsible for the targets in one area, while other teams will take care of their own areas. You'll have no knowledge of what they're doing, and they won't know what you're doing. This method will prevent the type of long-distance movements that were necessary during the attacks on the trucks."

"May I ask why we didn't use the other cells as part of the attacks on the trucks? We could have had a greater affect."

"That's a fair question. I didn't want to use more than one team in the event that any of your men were compromised. If you had failed, I had a secondary team prepared to take over and accomplish the task."

Commander Assaf didn't wait for a response to his answer. "Now, I know you insisted on bringing blasting caps with you, for the second phase, and I allowed that. They will prove to be useful. However, I knew at the time we already had assets in place to get you the supplies you would need. We have loyal believers who have spent many years working their way into positions to gain access to explosives in construction and mining companies. We also have teams that are experienced in created improvised explosives. There are others of course. We have workers in airports, cell phone companies, and various other locations who will be called upon to provide additional support in lesser ways."

Zamir was at a loss for words. He just sat, staring at his commander, waiting for him to continue.

"It's a somewhat unlikely group of several nationalities, including non-Muslims. However, we have been able to form an alliance for a common goal. We must stop the reign of terror and oppression being forced on the world by the United States."

Zamir didn't care. He was ecstatic that he was to be included on this next phase.

"They are our allies," he replied. "I'm happy to have allies in this war, Commander. Death to America."

Commander Assaf smiled as he responded. "Yes Zamir. Death to America."

19

What Are They Planning Next?

August 1, 2024

Paul and Sandy's Farm

Paul had made a friend several years ago at a nearby gun show. It turned out that Tom Wallace lived just over a mile from Paul's farm on his own family farm. His parents lived next door to him on the same property. A third, smaller, house sat empty next to them. It had been their starter home before building their current one. Over the last few years, Tom had become a trusted friend. Additionally, Sandy and Tom's wife Cheryl, got along great.

Tom and Cheryl raised chickens and a small garden. Like Paul, Tom was a dedicated prepper. This had been a major factor fostering their friendship. As part of his prepping, Tom liked to preserve what he grew. He was also quite the fisherman and enjoyed hunting. Unlike many parts of the country, hunting was still quite common in southwestern West Virginia. The local schools even closed for the first week of deer season because of the low attendance. It just so happened that in West Virginia, rifle season opened the Monday before Thanksgiving, so it worked out. They would close school for the entire week, calling it "Fall Break," rather than the more obvious choice of "Hunting Break."

Paul and Tom had enjoyed many conversations over the years about the need for self-reliance. They often shared ideas and helped each other with projects. Tom had a strong respect for the military and enjoyed talking with Paul about his time in the service. Tom's son had joined the West Virginia National Guard and worked out of the armory in Parkersburg.

The two men made plans to support each other in the event of an emergency and had even worked out a communication plan using their BaoFeng radios. They had experimented with the little radios and found that even though the advertised range of the radios was much farther, they couldn't talk to each other from their homes, likely because of the mountainous terrain between them. However, if they both went to the high ground between the two homes, the radios could connect.

Paul suggested a workaround.

"If we know we are going to need to communicate, we can put two more radios on the ridge between us to act as a retrans site."

Tom was intrigued. "How would that work?"

"Well, we'll need to do a test to see if it'll work in this terrain, but in theory we can set up a retransmission site between us. Then, as long as both our radios can hit the retrans site, it will act as a relay between the two. It will essentially leap frog the transmission," Paul explained.

"Oh, that's pretty cool. Do you know how to do it?"

"Yes, I've done it. It sometimes reduces the clarity of the transmission, but it'll work in a pinch."

Paul elaborated. "When I did it last time, it was in an urban environment and the retrans site was on top of a building. I ran an extension cord up to the radios to keep them charged so I could leave them turned on the entire time we needed them. For this situation, we'd have to look at something different. I wouldn't want to leave them up there all the time. I'd just want to put them in place when we decide we need them. Then, we'd have to figure out a way to keep them charged."

He paused as he considered the problem. "We could potentially put one of my Goal Zero solar panels up there to keep them charging as long as the sun is out."

"Do you think it would provide enough power to keep them running?" Tom asked.

"I guess it would depend on how much we're transmitting and how much sun we were getting. However, those oversized BTECH batteries I have are pretty good so I think it would probably work. We could go up every few days and check on them, but yeah. I think it'll work."

"BTECH batteries?" Tom asked.

"Oh yeah. It's an American company that specializes in Baofeng radios. They're out in...North..no..South Dakota, I think. I always get my Baofeng stuff through them. They're legit."

Tom was excited about the idea. "This is cool, we need to try this. How many radios do you have?"

"I have three of the UV-5Rs. They are older five-watt radios. When they came out with the new eight-watt radios, I bought four of those, so I have a total of seven."

"Seven?! You have seven radios?" Tom asked, his eyebrows raised.

"Well, I kind of retired the five-watt radios, so I typically only use the eight-watt versions. Luckily, the new ones use the same batteries, so I use the old batteries with them too. Oh, and I have a few of those cheap Walmart-Special FRS radios too. I don't really count those, although I'd be happy to have them if they were the only thing available. Which ones do you have?"

Tom thought about it. "I just have two. As far as I know, mine are just five-watts."

"We can try it with those, but you should consider getting the stronger ones. My eight-watt radios are called the BF-F8HP, although they have an even newer version of it now. I think it's called the PRO. I can't remember exactly; I'd have to look it up on their website."

 Paul had suggested that Tom come up with a callsign so they weren't using their names over the radio. Tom didn't hesitate.

"Copperhead," he had said.

"Copperhead? Why Copperhead?"

"Because Copperheads are not aggressive as long as you don't mess with them, but if you mess with them, they'll fight."

"All right, Copperhead it is. My callsign at work is Doc Holiday, but it got shortened to Doc, so when we're using the radios, just use that," Paul replied.

"Okay, Doc," Tom said with a grin. "But if we're using the radios, anyone in the area with a radio can hear us, right?"

"Well, yes, assuming they are in range and monitoring the same frequency or have a scanner," Paul answered. "However, we're pretty remote out here and we can come up with code words if we think it's a concern."

That conversation had been three years ago and the two had tested the system several times. They had needed to try three different retrans sites before they found one that worked well, but now they had it figured out. They had also learned they needed to use the eight-watt radios to be consistently reliable. As a result, Tom had bought a couple of the newer radios. Finally, they developed a few code words, and a method for transmitting numbers securely.

Now that there was an actual emergency situation in the country, Paul was glad they hadn't waited to try to work it out. Trying to get radios delivered now would probably be next to impossible.

Paul had invited Tom over to the house to meet with him and his former teammate, John "Miner" Adams. John had been in Special Forces with Paul and, after getting out of the Army, had done some overseas security work for the government. After a couple of years of that, he had decided to use his G.I. Bill to go to gunsmithing school. He now lived just outside Chillicothe, Ohio. He had a small gunsmithing business and still did a little stateside contracting for the Army from time to time. John had gotten the callsign of "Miner" when doing security overseas and the nickname had stuck with him.

Miner was already at Paul's house when Tom arrived. Miner's German Shepherd was sprawled out on the floor and jumped up when Tom knocked on the door. Paul was already opening the door because the motion detector had alerted him of Tom's arrival. Paul's dog, Kimber, was by his side. She greeted Tom and was rewarded with a quick scratch on the back.

"Miner, I'm sure you remember Tom, right?" Paul asked.

He stood up, extending his hand. "Oh yeah, how have you been?"

"Good, man. Good. Although I've been dealing with the craziness just like everyone else." Tom shook Miner's proffered hand. The two dogs padded off toward the living room to play.

"Yeah," Miner replied. "When Paul asked if we could get together today, I told him he'd better have the good bourbon if I was going to burn the fuel to come down here."

Paul tapped the bottle of Jefferson's Reserve on the bar. "And I obliged."

Miner picked up his glass and held it up in front of him. "Yes, yes he did." He took a sip. "Unfortunately, Tom, I think we're out."

Tom let out a laugh. "I don't think so." He walked over to the bar, grabbed a glass, and went to the freezer for some ice.

Sandy appeared from the bedroom, walking toward the front door. "Hey, now you boys play nice in here," she said with a smile.

"You heading outside?" Paul asked.

"Yeah. Me and McKinley will be out in the garden. If you boys need anything, well, take care of it yourself. Don't bother us."

The three men all burst into laughter.

"Yes ma'am," said Tom, still laughing.

"Come on Mic!" Sandy called.

McKinley came out of her bedroom and the two of them disappeared out the door.

"I appreciate y'all coming," Paul began.

"Especially me," Miner interjected with a smile.

Paul rolled his eyes. "Yes, Miner. Especially you. I got it, gas is expensive."

Before Paul could continue, Tom looked over at Miner. "Are you at least staying the night down here?"

"Oh yeah," Miner said. "I'm planning on enjoying Paul's whiskey, so I'm definitely spending the night."

Paul's dog, Kimber, walked up and laid her head on Miner's leg.

"Hey, pup. I didn't see you come back in here." He gave her some scratches behind the ears.

"Dogs know dog people. What she doesn't know is that she's going to have another playmate soon," Paul said.

"You talking about Dangle's dog?" Miner asked, scratching the dog's head.

"Yeah, he should be here anytime."

"Dang, it's gonna be a freakin' zoo in here," Tom said. He had his own dogs, but they were at home with Cheryl.

As if on cue, they heard the motion detector announce the arrival of another vehicle.

A few minutes later, all four men were settled in around the table and Paul was finally able to get to the point of the meeting. The three dogs were now wrestling and playing in the living room floor.

"I've talked to each of you independently, so everyone already knows what this is about. As you know, I'm part of a robust Mutual Assistance Group with the guys that I work with down in Kentucky. Unfortunately, all of them except Joker are a three-hour drive from here. Because of that, Dangle,

Copperhead, and I have our own plans for supporting each other around here. Plus, I have my parents and a cousin not too far from here. I consider them to be part of this as well, but it's pretty informal."

Paul looked over at Miner. "You and I have had numerous discussions about it, but we've never really included you in the planning because you live farther away. However, to be fair, it takes me about the same time to drive to my parents' house as it does to get to your place. Anyhow, considering everything that's going on, I think we need to take a hard look at our plans and figure out a way to bring you into the fold, if we can figure out a way to make it work."

Paul paused and waited for Miner to respond.

He took another sip of his drink as he considered the statement.

"With the gasoline situation, I'm just not sure how feasible it is. Don't get me wrong, I'd love to be a member of a practicing MAG, but I just don't know if it's realistic at this point."

Tom leaned forward. "Well, what about this. How about we establish this as your fallback position and if it ever comes to that, we can at least have a plan in place for you and your family."

Miner grinned. "Oh, that was already my plan. If I ever got blown out of my place, this is the most logical place to go."

Paul interjected. "Yeah, we've talked about it, but there's no real plan in place. I have some space here, but we might have to get creative with the living arrangements."

Miner leaned back in his chair. "Well, if it ever came to that, and I'm not saying it will, but if it ever did, I'd do my best to pull my RV down. I have a pretty decent fifth wheel that could act as our housing. I'd load it down with supplies and bring everything with me. I have my guns, ammo, food, and miscellaneous other supplies. Now, once I got here, we'd have to figure out someplace to store everything so we could have the space inside the RV for living, but I'm sure we could iron that out."

Paul nodded. "Yeah, if nothing else, we could store your stuff in my shop."

Tom spoke up at this statement. "I have room at my place too. I'm not far from here."

"Cool," Miner said. "I doubt I'd ever actually bug out, but it's good to know that I have options."

Paul changed the subject. "Alright, another thing I wanted to bring up is that I've been working with Dangle on long range shooting. We've shot a few times here on my range and we've gone down to Joker's place and shot there." He motioned toward Tom. "Tom is also interested in it. I thought it might be a good idea for you two to link up and start shooting together. Ya'll could work as sniper team if we ever needed it. I'll continue to help you train, of course."

Tom looked back at Paul. "That sounds great, but I figured if we ever needed anything like that, you'd be taking care of it."

"Well, yes, if I can. But if I needed to be doing something else, or if we needed two teams, it would be good to have some redundancy."

Tom addressed Dangle. "What do you think? We live close enough that it would be pretty easy to get together to do some shooting."

Dangle's face flushed a little red. "Well, I don't know if I'm ready to do any sniping, but yes, I'm interested in getting better. I'm game."

"Okay," Paul said, slapping his hands lightly on the table. "It's decided. We'll start training together."

Paul's phone chimed on the table in front of him. He glanced down at the screen. "Mack just sent me a message." He paused for a moment as he read.

Check out this link. We'll see how this plays out

 The message had a link to a news article. Paul tapped the link, and read the first few lines of the article.

"What is it?" Dangle asked.

"Apparently, the army is offering to provide military trucks to haul critical supplies to areas of the country that are struggling because civilian trucking has been reduced by over ninety percent."

Miner chuckled. "That's going to be like trying to fill a swimming pool with an eye dropper. That's not going to be nearly enough."

Paul continued to scan down the article. "Yeah, they didn't quite put it that way, but they acknowledged as much and said that cargo will be prioritized to support medical needs and food supply, followed by fuel and other needs deemed critical by local and federal agencies. Whatever that is."

As Paul continued to read, the phone chimed again. It was another message from Mack.

Turn on the news right now

"Uh-oh," said Paul, sliding his chair back to stand up.

"What is it?" Tom asked, reacting by standing up too.

"Mack says to turn on the news. Something's going on." Paul walked into the living room and found the remote. He turned on the television and found one of the twenty-four-hour news stations.

The scene that appeared on the screen was chaotic. Numerous emergency vehicles were visible with flashing lights, the most prominent being a black armored vehicle with the word "SWAT" on the side in bold white letters.

The reporter was not visible, but was speaking over the video.

> "...playing out on U.S. Route 41 just outside of Murfreesboro, Tennessee. This is following a shootout between law enforcement and two men in a blue 2012 Ford Explorer. Reports are spotty right now, but so far what we have is that the confrontation began when a Rutherford County Sherriff's Deputy, Shawn David Wilson, pulled the Explorer over. At this time, we don't know why Deputy Wilson pulled over the vehicle, however, at some point during the traffic stop, gunfire erupted. A nearby Tennessee State Trooper and the Murfreesboro Police Department responded to the call for help."

The other three men joined Paul in the living room and were now standing around the TV.

> "During the incident, Deputy Wilson was wounded and unfortunately, we've received word from the Tristar Centennial Medical Center in Nashville that he has died from his wounds. State Trooper Wendell James Barlow was also wounded with non-life-threatening injuries. He's expected to make a full

recovery." Pictures flashed up on the screen of the two men.

Dangle spoke up. "I saw an article that said a Ford Explorer was seen leaving the scene of the attack in Florida."

"Yeah, I saw that too," added Tom. "I wonder if this is the same guys."

The reporter continued.

> "We're a few minutes away from a press conference with the Tennessee State Police and the Tennessee Bureau of Investigation. However, eye witnesses have reported that at least two people in the Ford Explorer were killed during the exchange of gunfire with law enforcement."

Paul raised his cellphone and dialed Mack, putting it on speakerphone. Mack answered after two rings.

"Hey, Doc. You watchin' this?"

"Yeah. I have you on speakerphone with Dangle and two of my other buddies," Paul answered.

"Cool. Yeah, we've been watching it. We're thinking this might be one of the shooting teams," Mack replied.

"We were just talking about the same thing. The first thing I'm wondering about is that if these were the guys in Florida, and now they're in Tennessee, where were they going?" Paul said.

"That *is* the question, isn't it?"

"Yep," replied Paul. "Where were they going, and what are they planning next?"

20

The Creature from Jekyll Island

August 3, 2024

Paul and Sandy's Farm

Paul and Dangle had decided to take on more shifts in Winchester. Tri Point Solutions was suddenly in very high demand and Mack had called them asking if they could cover shifts.

"We're able to offer an improved pay scale due to the demand," Mack said on the phone.

"What are we talking here?" Paul asked.

"An extra twenty-five an hour for shift leaders and an extra twenty an hour for everyone else," Mack answered.

Paul raised his eyebrows. "How are you doing that?"

"Here's the thing man," Mack continued. "We are fielding ten to fifteen calls a day asking for armed security. We already renewed the contract in Winchester at a rate that will support it, so we're going to meet our obligation there. Oh, and they also agreed to top off the fuel of anyone who drove in to cover a shift. Apparently, they have a pretty significant underground storage tank and security is very important to them."

"Okay. Have you talked to Dangle yet?" Paul asked.

"Yeah. He said he's down if you are."

Paul thought about this for a moment. Things had continued to deteriorate around the country since the last terror attack. However, the area around his home was essentially calm. He hadn't heard of anything significant that had concerned him.

"I'll doublecheck with Sandy to make sure she's comfortable with it, but I'll tentatively say yes. When would you need us?"

"Day shift, starting tomorrow morning."

"Okay, so you need an answer right away. I'll let you know within the hour, but I think it will be fine."

"Good deal," Mack said. "We're going to cover some other new contracts too. I've called up some of our guys who were in reserve. They were happy to take the job because a lot of businesses are closing their doors and they need work."

Paul thought about that for a second. "Who'd you get?"

"We got Woody and Farmer right now, plus I'm checking with a couple of other guys." He used the callsigns for Spence Woodbury and Jeff Southard.

"Oh man. It would be great to see those guys. I haven't seen them in a while," Paul replied.

"Unfortunately, you still won't. We're putting them on the new jobs. You'll still be on the Winchester job since it's the closest one to your house."

"That makes sense. The less driving, the better. I heard on the radio that gas has gone up to twenty dollars a gallon in most places. It's over forty in California. I haven't been off my mountaintop in a few days, so I haven't seen it for myself," Paul added.

Mack sighed. "I can confirm it. It's eighteen to twenty a gallon around here. That's why we negotiated for the fuel to continue the contract in Winchester."

"Hey, I have a question for you," Paul said suddenly.

"Whatcha got, man?"

"How about an ounce of silver per hour instead of the extra twenty-five dollars?"

Mack couldn't tell if he was joking or not. "Silver is up to forty dollars an ounce right now, so hell no." He chuckled a little as he said it.

Paul immediately countered. "Okay. Okay. Let's see. An extra twenty-five an hour comes out to three hundred per shift. Silver's forty dollars an ounce. That's seven and a half ounces. How about seven ounces a day and I work at the regular rate?"

Mack laughed out loud this time. "Oh! You're serious. Let me check with Rotor and see what we have. I know we have a significant stash of the Mutiny Metals one-ounce and two-ounce rounds, plus I know there are tubes full of the one-ounce Indian Head rounds in the safe. I'll double-check, but we could probably do that."

"All right, so for four days of work, it would be regular pay plus twenty-eight ounces of silver. If you can't do it, cool. I'll still do the work. However, I know when you bought the silver, you paid a helluva lot less than forty dollars an ounce for it."

Mack laughed again. "Leave it to Doc to start negotiating when I offer more money. I'll let you know."

"Fair enough. Well brother. I'm going to go talk to Sandy. I'll shoot you a message on Signal after I talk to her," Paul said, wrapping up the conversation.

"Sounds good, buddy. See ya."

With that, the two men signed off. A few minutes later, Paul confirmed that he would be there in the morning for the 6:00 a.m. shift change and he would pick Dangle up on the way.

Mack immediately responded.

> *I talked to Rotor. He asked if you want your entire paycheck in silver this week*

Paul smiled as he read the message.

> *If y'all are serious, yes.*

Mack answered.

> *All right. Done.*

Paul was surprised they had agreed to the offer. However, he had also see inside the safe at the TPS office and he knew what they had.

> *Cool. Thanks. I'll be there.*

"When will you be home?" Sandy asked. She was in the kitchen preparing lunch.

"I'm going to work tomorrow through Wednesday, then I'll drive home after my shift on Wednesday. So, four days total," he answered. He was judging her response.

She was slicing a tomato from the garden for BLT sandwiches. She continued without looking up at him.

"Are you sure you're okay with that?" Paul asked, concerned that she was scared.

She sighed, then answered. "Normally, I don't mind, but I'd be lying if I said I wasn't a little nervous this time."

"I don't have to go."

"No, I don't want you to cancel. You already told them you would be there." She finished with the tomato and moved to a loaf of bread that she had baked earlier. She selected a different knife and began cutting the bread for the sandwiches.

"I'll call Tom and make sure he's available if you need anything."

"Yes, please do that. I want a refresher on your radios too, in case we have any problems with the phones." Her tone was even and measured.

"Okay. I'll call him right now."

"Thanks. Lunch will be ready in five."

Paul moved to her and hugged her from behind, tapping her on the cheek with a light kiss, then walked away to call Tom.

"What's up brother?" It was Tom's most common way of answering the phone when Paul called.

"Hey man. I have to head out of town for work for four days, starting in the morning. Would you be able to keep an eye on things for me?"

"Of course, man. They have us working from home right now anyhow. You know, with the cost of gas and all. I don't normally do that, but I guess that's the world we live in, right?" Tom sounded upbeat.

"Yeah. I guess so. I'm going to run up to the ridge after lunch and put the retrans box in place. I'll call you for a radio check, let's say…two o'clock?"

"Sounds good. I'll have my radio on," Tom replied.

"Thanks man. I really appreciate it."

"No sweat, brother," Tom said. "I got your back."

"I know, and I appreciate it."

"What time are you taking off?" Tom asked.

"I'm going to head out super early in the morning. I have to pick up Dangle first and then be in Winchester by 5:30. I'll be home Wednesday night."

"Okay. I gotcha. Should be no problem. Tell Sandy to call anytime. I'll keep the radio by the bed at night too."

"That's perfect," Paul responded.

"Hey, have you been watching the news today?" Tom asked.

"I actually haven't. I've been working on some projects around here. Why what's up?" Paul asked, concern creeping into his voice.

"Dang, man, a lot. First of all, there's been a run on banks. Apparently, everybody's trying to get their money out in cash. Banks all over the place are closing their doors saying they don't have any more money. There's a crapload of people protesting all over the place, demanding their money."

"Holy crap," Paul responded. "No, I didn't even know that, although to be honest, I was expecting it."

"Yeah, apparently, the banks don't keep anywhere close to the amount of money that is deposited," Tom said.

"I know, it's because they practice fractional banking. They loan out most of the deposited money, working under the assumption that everyone is not going to ask for their money back all at once. I'm telling you every person in the country should be required to read *The Creature from Jekyll Island.* People wouldn't trust their banks *or* their government nearly as much. Of course, I'd say right now, trust is way down on both of them."

"Definitely! I recommend that book to everyone. Anyhow, people are pissed. I wouldn't want to be a banker right now. There are picket lines in front of some of the bank presidents' homes!"

"Yeah, I get it. People develop this trust for banks, but banks are less concerned with their customers than they are for the profit margin. That's the cost of doing business with banks. They're a business. They're trying to make a profit any way possible," Paul said.

What he didn't say was that he took a portion of every paycheck and drew it out in cash, storing it in his safe. It was essentially his savings account. It didn't earn interest, but it was worth the tradeoff for the security. Savings account interest rates were so low now, it didn't make much of a difference. Plus, he had heard rumors of the government tracking personal finances. He didn't know if that was actually true, but if it was, drawing out small amounts at a time shouldn't garner any attention. This was in addition to his quarterly purchase of silver. Once or twice a year, he tried to buy a little gold, but that didn't always work out financially, so he only had a few pieces. The last time he bought gold; he bought a half ounce for just over twelve hundred dollars. Gold was now over three thousand dollars an ounce.

"That's not all," Tom continued. "There are some truckers who have gone back to work. Some of them are driving in freakin' bullet-proof vests!"

"Seriously?" Paul asked, incredulous. Then he thought about it. "Well, to be fair, they gotta work. What better time to renegotiate the cost of delivering a load? I bet they're making a killing."

"Oh, I have no doubt. It's not enough, though. The news said the number of trucks now working is only twenty to twenty-five percent what it was before the attacks started. The big shipping companies are saying they'll continue to work, but with limited availability and at an increased cost. Even Amazon has suspended the free delivery and they won't guarantee when it will get to you!"

"Really?! I guess it makes sense though. If you can't get the drivers to carry the goods, how are you going to guarantee delivery, and if it's costing them an arm and a leg to get drivers, they aren't going to absorb that cost. They'll pass it on to the consumer."

"Yep," Tom answered. "If you don't want to pay the delivery fee, I guess you don't really need it."

"This is crazy, man," Paul said, trying to think of the repercussions of the situation. "I'll tell you what's probably going to happen if it hasn't already," Paul offered.

"What's that?"

"I bet perishables like milk, eggs, and bread are going to be among the first things to disappear from the shelves."

"Are you kidding, man? That stuff's *been* gone. Now they're struggling to even keep canned goods in the stores," Tom said.

"If that's the case, think about what that's doing to the farmers that're out there producing that stuff. For that matter, every company in the country that's producing goods," Paul added, shaking his head, thinking about the second and third-order effects of an eighty percent reduction of shipping capacity in a country the size of the U.S. "The economic impact of this is going to be staggering. In fact, I'd be willing to bet that it's already been catastrophic for some of the smaller companies."

Tom's voice rose an octave as he responded. "Oh, Dude! I saw an article this morning about that. They don't even know how to calculate how much money has been lost at this point."

The line when silent for a moment as the two men let that statement hang in the air. Finally, Paul spoke up again, returning to the original point of the call.

"Well, I gotta get going. I'm going to head up the hill to put the retrans site in place. I'll call you for the radio check."

"Fourteen hundred hours," Tom said, using the military time format to indicate 2:00 p.m.

"Yessir." Paul grinned at his civilian friend using military time correctly. Tom enjoyed learning military related skills that could be useful. He also liked the novelty of using the military time format. He used it when talking to his active-duty son too.

A little while later, Paul arrived at the retrans site in his side by side. He had constructed a retrans module, as he called it, by putting two of the radios in a waterproof box with a Baofeng Repeater Interface. He had drilled holes in the box for the antenna cables and an incoming power cable. He then used silicone sealant to keep everything waterproof and protected. He ran the antenna cables to a couple of nearby trees and attached the antennas in the trees to get a little extra elevation. Finally, he positioned his large Goal Zero solar panel facing south and secured it with tent stakes before plugging the power cables from the box into it.

Paul had taken the time to write out a set of instructions for setting the system up; that paper was also inside the box, taped to the lid inside a waterproof sandwich bag. After he completed the installation, he inspected it to make sure everything was right. Finally, he walked back over to the side by side and retrieved another radio. Checking the time, he keyed the radio. "Copperhead, Copperhead, this is Doc. Radio check. Over."

The response was prompt. "Doc, this is Copperhead. I have you Lima Charlie. How me? Over."

"Copperhead, this is Doc. Lima Charlie. I'm gonna do another radio check when I get back to the house. Over."

"Good copy, Doc," came Tom's reply.

"Doc out."

After completing the radio check, Paul reached into the back of the side by side and pulled out a two-foot square of camouflage netting cut from an old hunting blind. This was his private property and no one should be in the area. However, if anyone was trespassing, he hoped that it would make the box less likely to be discovered. He had no way of camouflaging the solar panel without impeding its ability to work, but its position on the south facing slope was offset from the deer path on the ridge and that was going to have to suffice.

He reviewed his work one last time and got back in the side by side to return home. He would conduct the additional radio check when he got home and then finish his preparations for work. Tomorrow was going to be an early day.

21

Watch Out for Deer

August 7, 2024

Eastern Michigan

The last few days had been a flurry of activity for Zamir and his men at their training location in Eastern Michigan. Commander Assaf had only given them two weeks to study the targets and get everyone in place to execute their missions. Zamir was barely sleeping. He had been driving the men so they would be refreshed on numerous tasks, quizzing them on routes and contingencies. They rehearsed over and over.

A week ago, they had met with their support teams to pick up the materials they would need to conduct the next phase of their mission. The packet sent by Muhammed Bari and the planning team had provided detailed instructions on how to pick up vehicles, weapons, and explosives in Dearborn. Zamir had gone himself to link up with the team in a warehouse on the east side of the city. They drove past the location first, looking for a green sign on the door that said *Employees Only*. The sign would only be in place if everything was safe.

"I see the sign," Haig El Knoury said as he slowly drove past the entrance.

"Yes, Haig. I see it too. Drive around the block and then pull in. As you pull in, go to the left side of the building. They should be expecting us. There will be an open garage door to pull inside."

Haig did as he was told. As they pull around the left side of the building, a garage door was opening and Haig carefully eased the Toyota pickup truck inside. Someone closed the door behind them. The inside of the building was well lit. It wasn't a very large warehouse, but there was enough room for several vehicles to be parked against the back wall to Zamir's left. The plain concrete floor was dirty and stained and as Zamir looked around, taking in the scene, he saw men all around the open space. Everyone's attention was on them. Zamir suddenly became aware that his mouth was dry.

"Turn the engine off," he said, being careful not to let his voice betray his anxiety. He opened the passenger door and, as he was getting out of the vehicle, he saw a man approaching him, walking so fast he looked as if he was about to break into a run. Zamir could feel his heart racing. Suddenly, relief washed over him as he recognized the man's smiling face.

Hassan Reza threw his arms open. Zamir hadn't seen him in over two years. *Has it been two years? Yes, over two years.*

"Brother Zamir! It is so wonderful to see you!"

Zamir allowed the man to embrace him as the other three men exited the pickup truck.

"It's good to see you too, Hassan," Zamir said, extracting himself from the man's embrace.

"Come, come, we have much to discuss. I have so much to tell you," Hassan added enthusiastically, motioning to a folding table with several folding chairs haphazardly placed around it on the other side of the room.

Another man approached as well and corralled the others away to an unseen part of the warehouse. Zamir recognized that man too, but could not recall his name. He was part of the support cell they had met in Texas soon after crossing the border. *The cook? I think that was the cook.*

Zamir allowed Hassan to lead him to the table and within a minute, a man arrived, providing them both with chai.

Hassan rubbed his hands together in anticipation of the conversation. He was an excitable fellow and his childlike energy was annoying to Zamir. However, Zamir could not deny the effectiveness of his efforts. He had successfully facilitated their arrival two years ago and now he was here again, providing them with the necessities they needed for their next phase.

"You obviously received your instructions from Muhammed Bari. I was so excited when I got the word that you would be here soon to meet with me. I had everything in place before you began your attacks. We didn't want to move anything after the attacks had begun and Muhammed wanted everything staged close to you to reduce the amount of movement."

He rattled on, barely seeming to breath as he spoke rapid fire at Zamir.

"We've been so busy since I last saw you. I'm supporting another team too and I had to deliver what they needed. This is so exciting! I just can't tell you how honored I am. I sent my assistant, Asim, to meet with the other team because I wanted to meet with you personally. You know I've always looked up to you, right?"

He didn't wait for a response.

"Of course you know that. Of course you do. Everyone looks up to you. You commanded the first attacks on the American homeland! You're a hero, you know!"

Zamir was tiring of this babble, although he *did* like being called a hero. *He was a hero, wasn't he?*

Zamir placed a hand on Hassan's shoulder, causing him to stop talking.

"Hassan, I'm very happy to see you too."

Zamir knew how to manipulate Hassan. "The only reason we've been so successful is because of the incredible support that you've provided. I look forward to speaking with Commander Assaf so the I may tell him about your good work. Would that be okay with you? Would it be okay if I share that?"

Hassan's entire face seemed to light up. His eyes widened and he looked like he was about to jump from his seat and celebrate.

"Oh! Of course, of course," Hassan replied, speaking just a little too fast. "You're too kind, Zamir. You're a hero! Did I tell you that? You're a hero!"

Zamir closed his eyes and nodded slighting a few times. "Thank you, Hassan, but we do this for the glory of Allah. I'm sure that Allah is pleased with your work as well. Can you show me what you've prepared for us?"

Hassan beamed. He motioned to the papers spread across the table. "Oh, yes. Of course, of course." He motioned to the papers on the table. "Okay, so I have the same packets that you have. Each of these is one of the locations that your team will be responsible for. It's a mix of several different types of targets because they wanted to keep you in one area."

"I know about that," Zamir said.

"Oh, of course you do." He side stepped so he could reach the open map on the table. "So, you already know that your area will be here." He used his finger to draw a circle on the map.

"It's essentially Michigan, Indiana, Ohio, most of Kentucky, part of West Virginia and the western part of Pennsylvania. This area is rich in coal and natural gas and has numerous lucrative targets." He looked up at Zamir with a smile. "Wait until you see what I have for you. You're going to love it."

The time since that meeting with Hassan had been more than hectic. It had nearly been an impossible task. However, as Zamir looked at the plan on the dining room table of the farmhouse, he was finally starting to feel as if it could be done.

He glanced down at his watch. It was August 7. Everyone would be leaving tomorrow. The attack was scheduled for August 10, and he had no time to waste. Everyone would be leaving except for the cooks. They would stay back to maintain the farm until they were needed for something else. Mohamed, his second in command would be leading one of the larger missions and Zamir would be leading the mission he considered to be the most important -- an attack on the John E. Amos Power Plant in Winfield, West Virginia.

The plant was one of the largest coal burning plants in the country, although that wasn't the only reason it was selected. The planning cell in Iran had determined that it was one of the most easily accessed power plants in the region. The plan was to target power generation all over the country. In

Zamir's area, the John E. Amos Power Plant was the one they determined was the most attractive target based on their capabilities and weapons. It produced nearly three thousand megawatts, transmitting electricity to countless locations in the region. Also, it maintained a gargantuan coal yard with well over one and a half million tons of coal in it.

There were other reasons he had chosen to lead the attack on the plant himself. First, Ahmad Abufaysal had been the Yellow Cell leader and had been killed. The attack would take an entire cell to accomplish. They needed a leader. However, the most influential reason was that Zamir had assessed the power plant as the most impressive of the targets and he wanted the glory of leading that mission personally. He would never say that out loud. He would never admit to seeking admiration or praise, yet he secretly craved it. He needed it. It was one thing to say that one of his elements had conducted the mission successfully. It was something completely different to say that he had taken it upon himself to lead the men into battle, emerging victorious.

Zamir walked to the kitchen. Both cooks were in there working.

"I'll be at my table. Bring me some chai," he ordered.

"Yes, Commander. Right away."

He returned to his table and reached for the packet of papers. He had printed off everything Muhammed Bari had sent him. He shuffled to the last page and withdrew it, dropping everything else back onto the table. He read over the page again for what seemed like the tenth time. It may have *been* the tenth time, he'd lost count.

> All attacks must be executed at 4:30 a.m. Eastern Time. If you do not coordinate the times, an early

attack could cause an increase in security at other locations, leading to mission failure. You will not fail. If you must martyr yourself, Allah will be pleased and you will be rewarded in Jannah.

For those who are not martyred, the mission is not over. You will continue to sow terror in the hearts of the godless. Go into the population, kill the people. Take what you need from the non-believers and use it to continue your fight. Kill them in the streets. Seek them out in their homes and kill them in their beds. Use whatever methods you must, but never stop. The United States will be a defenseless lamb that you must slaughter. Feast on the spoils and bring praise to the name of Allah.

Zamir gently lay the paper back on the table and stared across the room at the window. He didn't acknowledge the cook as he carefully placed the chai in front of him and retreated back out of the room. The young man knew not to disturb his commander when he was working.

Zamir's mind was racing. He thought about the van outside that he would be using to get to the power plant. He thought about the tools which had been provided by Hassan and his team. He leaned forward, changing his focus to the map on the table. He found the power plant, identified by a red circle. Tracing the road going south from the plant, he read the names of the towns; Poca, Nitro, Saint Albans. He followed the road until it intersected with Route 60, the road he intended to use to escape the area heading west and looked at the names of those towns; Hurricane, Culloden, Milton, Barboursville, Huntington, Kenova. That took him to the second red circle: the Catlettsburg Refinery. It was a huge refinery just across the state line in Kentucky. There was also a small airport only a couple of miles from there. This would be a good area to conduct his guerilla warfare. Huntington was a medium sized city with people to kill. Charleston was bigger, but it was too close to the John Amos Power Plant. His instructions were to leave the area after the attack. The Catlettsburg Refinery was just a bonus. It was not on his list of targets from Muhammed Bari, but Zamir thought it should have been.

A smile crept up one side of his mouth. *They didn't tell me to destroy it, but they didn't say not to.* The map showed train tracks all around the area. He followed the lines with his finger. *If they are turning me loose to destroy America, I'm going to destroy train tracks too. I'm going to destroy everything.* The grin expanded to a full-blown smile. *I think this will be fun.*

Later that night

Catlettsburg, Ky

Paul and Dangle had finished their four days of work and were heading home on Interstate 64. Just after they passed the Catlettsburg Refinery on their right, the interstate crossed over the Big Sandy River, the boundary between Kentucky and West Virginia. Paul's headlights illuminated the sign over the road:

Paul smiled. "I'll tell ya Dangle. No matter how many times I drive under that sign, it still makes me feel good to be home."

Dangle smiled back. "Yeah, I may not have been born here, but I feel the same way."

They continued in silence for the next few minutes. Paul was mentally counting down the miles to the exit. He needed to take Exit 8 to take Dangle home first before going home. Glancing over at the clock he did some quick math estimating what time he would be home. He grabbed his phone and held it up to his face to unlock the screen, then held the phone out to Dangle.

"Hey, can you dial Sandy's number and put it on speaker?"

"Sure," Dangle replied as he followed the instructions.

A moment later Sandy's voice came on the line.

"Hello?"

"Hey, Babe. You're on speaker phone, so don't say anything you don't want to be public."

Paul heard her scoff. "Okay. Hi, Dangle."

"Hiii, Saaaandy," he replied in a sing-song voice.

Paul continued. "We just crossed the state line. I'm going to drop Dangle off, then I'll be heading home. I should be there in a couple of hours."

"Okay, be careful. Watch out for deer."

Paul smiled. "I love you too."

After Paul had dropped Dangle off and helped him unload his gear, he was pulling back out onto Route 37, heading home. His mind drifted to his bag tucked safely in the back seat with a box of silver in it. When Pikey had met him at the worksite to relieve him this evening, he had passed Paul the small, heavy box.

"Mack said to give you this," Pikey said, presenting the box. It was taped up and had the word *Doc* scrawled on it in black marker.

"Thanks, brother," Paul answered, accepting the box.

"What is that, ammo? It's heavy."

"Nah, I took payment for this week in silver," Paul said, smiling.

"What? We can do that?"

"I don't know. You'll have to do your own negotiations."

"Damn! I wish I'd thought of that," Pikey shot back.

"Well, it's not too late. Mack didn't say it was a secret."

Paul's attention was pulled to the side of the road where he saw movement. He let off the gas and watched as two deer looked up at him, seemingly unperturbed as he passed within a few yards of them grazing in someone's front yard.

"I wonder if people have started shooting them yet?" he thought. "If they haven't, I bet they will soon."

22

The White House and Their Zionist Lapdogs

August 9, 2024

Near Beirut, Lebanon

Muhammed Bari woke early. He barely slept last night. He skipped breakfast; he was too anxious to eat. Instead, he showed up in the command center at 5:45 a.m. Today was the day. It had finally arrived. The timeline for the attack had been the subject of many discussions over the last couple years. There were several people who wanted to wait for October 7 to coincide with the Hamas attack on Isreal. Others had advocated for September 11. Still others preferred to attack on December 25. However, in the end, the decision had been made that the attack would proceed as soon as the hackers had finalized their preparation. Muhammed still remembered when the decision was made.

"We don't want to use a date to drive our actions. Any date we choose will be the date that is seared into the memory of every American for generations," Hossein al-Nada, the commander of the Iranian-led cyber team had stated. Essentially, the attack would take place as soon as possible.

As the multi-national team made progress on the various aspects of the plan, Hossein had been constantly involved, keeping his commander up to date on challenges, progress, and ultimately, a proposed timeline.

It was mid-June, 2024 when the team of hackers finally announced they were ready for execution. The Hezbollah leadership made a rare trip to Iran for a secure meeting in a mountain bunker complex just outside Tehran to finalize the attack. Ebrahim Assaf and Muhammed Bari were among those who made the journey.

As the group assembled in the large underground room, the buzz of lights was a constant annoyance to Ebrahim. The room smelled musty and there were too many people. The air was not circulating and it was getting hot. Ebrahim was annoyed with the situation. As he was about to complain to Muhammed, the men at the front of the room stood up and a distinguished looking man with a short white beard walked in dressed in the uniform of the Islamic Revolutionary Guard. He wore the rank of Major General. Ebrahim recognized him from pictures, but had never seen the Commander-In-Chief in person.

The room was completely silent as he took his place behind a small, minimalistic podium. "Welcome. Please take a seat."

Not everyone had chairs, but those who did, sat down. The General placed some papers on the little podium and withdrew a set of reading glasses from his uniform breast pocket. He began in a measured, even tone.

"Five years ago, I made a statement to the world. I stated that we have plans to take down the White House and their Zionist lapdogs. I boldly announced to the world that we will not just fight in one spot. I said we would fight them on the global level. I have never backed down from that position. Today's assembly is proof of my resolve, the resolve of everyone in this room, and that of our brave jihadists already fighting in the United States."

This last statement was met with nods and some appreciative mutterings around the room.

"The United States wishes to destroy the entire Islamic world. They are not just the enemy of Iran. They are the enemy of every Muslim, every Muslim nation. They must be stopped. If we do not stop them, then who will?" He raised one fist into the air. "WHO?!" He was beginning to speak louder, pulling the room into his orbit.

Ebrahim was captivated. He had forgotten about the heat in the room. He no longer noticed the stench of too many bodies in a confined space. He was mesmerized by this man.

"Our fight has already begun. We started it in Israel and now we have taken the fight to the United States. They think it is over. They think these small tactical events are the extent of our efforts but they're wrong. These are but pieces of a puzzle. A puzzle that, when completed, will achieve victory on a strategic level, a global level." His voice was getting louder still, his tone more fierce.

"Today I tell you that we have chosen a date for the attack. I will tell you this: soon, very soon, we will bring America to her knees. She will beg for mercy, but there will be none! Western civilization is characterized by cruelty and the projection of war on the world. Now they will experience the same cruelty as we deliver war to their doorsteps!"

This statement elicited a cheer from the crowd. Ebrahim saw a man in front of him slap the man next to him on the back in celebration.

"I've said before that the attacks of September 11, 2001 divided the history of the world into two parts: before September the eleventh and after it. Now, after nearly twenty-three years, we will eclipse the efforts of those martyrs. Compared to our next attack, September the eleventh will be little more than a battle. NO! A skirmish! We will weaken them until they tear themselves apart. We will expose them for the filth they are, and cleanse the earth with their blood!"

Ebrahim had listened to that speech only a month ago. He now knew the date of the attack. It would be today, August the ninth at noon in Lebanon. That would be 5:00 a.m. on the east coast of the United States and 2:00 a.m. on the west coast. The Americans would wake up to a world of darkness. He looked down at his watch. Three hours to go.

23

I'm Rolling Heavy

Three hours later

Paul and Sandy's Farm

Paul didn't know why he woke up, but he did. He glanced over at his phone on the night stand. It was just after 5:00 in the morning. He stretched and rotated around to sit on the side of the bed. As he stood up to go to the bathroom, several joints popped and clicked, a result of over two decades of physically abusing himself in the Army.

After relieving himself, he was washing his hand when he suddenly realized that he heard the low hum of the generator running. It was programmed to kick on automatically if the power stayed out for more than ten seconds. *Was that what woke me up?* He wasn't sure, but he decided he was just going to stay up, so he headed over to the closet to collect his clothes for the day. After dressing, he returned to his nightstand to retrieve his watch, flashlight, and pistol. He left the bedroom and quietly closed the door, careful not to disturb Sandy.

He racked the slide on the pistol, slid it into his leather holster, and headed for the kitchen to make a cup of coffee. Kimber greeted him, stretching.

"Hey girl. Good morning to you too."

She yawned in response. He finished making his coffee and headed to the living room, cup in hand, and Kimber close on his heels. He settled onto the couch with his cup and grabbed the remote to check the news. Kimber sat down in front of him, staring at him.

"What?" he asked.

She trotted to the front door and down, looking back at him.

"Fine," he said, placing his coffee and the remote on the end table and getting back up to let her outside. He held his hand up toward her, showing her his palm.

"Wait," he ordered.

He opened both the main door and the storm door then looked back at her.

She was watching him intently.

"Okay."

She bolted out the door. He watched her for a moment as she ran into the dark yard to take care of her morning ritual. He controlled the storm door, closing it quietly. He knew if he just let it go, it would slam, potentially waking Sandy or McKinley.

Before he sat down, he looked at the remote on the end table and changed his mind. He knew whatever he saw on the morning news was going to be more doom and gloom. He turned and followed Kimber outside, pulling his flashlight from his pocket as he went out the door.

Paul had so many flashlights that Sandy had jokingly accused him of collecting them. His current every day carry, or EDC, was a rechargeable Baton 3 Pro made by Olight. He had been looking at their Arkfeld Ultra, but hadn't pulled the trigger on it. The Arkfeld was a cool idea, specifically designed for EDC. It was flat and therefore less obtrusive than the more traditionally shaped Baton he was carrying. It was more expensive and he had been dragging his feet on spending the money.

Paul fed the rabbits, goats, and chickens and collected the eggs in a basket they kept in the coop for that purpose. He also checked on the garden, stopping to select a green pepper that was calling his name. He was imagining an omelet later with green pepper, tomato, ham, and onion.

He returned to the porch and placed the basket of eggs there with the pepper on top. *I might as well finish the rest of my chores before it gets hot,* he thought to himself.

By the time he went back inside, it was daylight and his flashlight was stashed back in his pocket. Kimber followed him in and settled onto the floor in the living room. He returned to the kitchen and made another cup of coffee, before returning to the couch. The first channel he checked was Fox News. The bottom of the screen displayed a red banner with bold white letters stating: ***Breaking News: National Power Outage.***

Paul bolted forward in his seat. He nearly spilled his coffee. Kimber jumped up, reacting to her master's movement. He stared at the screen. Three people, two men and a woman, were positioned behind a large news desk with the FOX logo emblazoned across the front of it. Each of them had a coffee cup sitting on the desk in front of them, displaying the same logo.

The woman, an attractive blonde in a revealing white blouse was talking.

"...are coming in from around the country. Even here in the studio, we're running on backup generator power."

A *man with a full head of sandy blonde hair took over.*

"Initial reports are that this is a result of a multi-faceted cyberattack. Officials from the Cybersecurity and Infrastructure Security Agency have scheduled a press conference today at nine o'clock eastern time. We're hoping they'll be able to shed some light on what the problem is and how long it will be until we can get the lights back on."

The other man, a black man with a neatly trimmed beard and tailored suit spoke next.

"Now, Peter am I understanding this correctly? This was a two phased attack. The first part of the attack targeted 911 services in most major metropolitan areas across the country and at the same time, something happened in water treatment facilities? Then a few minutes later, the national electrical grid was targeted. Is that right?"

"That's how we understand it right now. I think the authorities are still trying to iron this out, but whoever did this, this is not a rogue group like those who shut down the gas pipeline on the east coast a few years ago. No, this is a state actor," the first man answered.

The woman again:

"I know several congressmen have been complaining about the vulnerability of our power grid for some time now. Haven't efforts been made to harden our defenses? I mean the whole country is not on just one grid. There are numerous interconnected grids, but any of them should be able to function if the others shut down, right?"

The black man fielded her question.

"I'm not exactly sure how that works. We've reached out to Fox News contributor, Morgan Murray. He'll be on later this morning to explain this better for us. He's a consultant for the federal government and author of the highly acclaimed book: *House of Cards; The Fragile American Power Grid.*"

Paul looked down at his phone. It appeared to be working, but his phone only worked through the Wi-Fi from the Satellite Internet service. He didn't have cell coverage at his house -- there were no towers close enough. As long as he had power in his house, he should have a working cell phone. He opened his contacts and started to call Mack, but he paused with his finger hovering over the call icon. *Nope. Mama and Dad.* He scrolled up to his parent's home number and hit the call button. He muted the television as the phone rang. It appeared to be working.

"Hello?" His father's voice was groggy. He had obviously woken him up.

"Dad, it's Paul."

"Son? It's early. Is everything all right?"

"No, Dad, it's not. The power's out!" Paul said quickly.

"Oh, son, why are you calling about that? It happens all the time. I'm sure it will be back on in a few hours."

"No, Dad, that's not what I meant. The power is out in the whole country! It was some type of massive coordinated cyberattack. They hit the water treatment plants too."

Charles sat up in the bed. "What? How can they do that?"

"I don't know, I just know it was a cyberattack. I don't know how they did it," Paul answered. He heard the stress in his own voice.

"You mean it was a computer virus? They can do that with a computer virus?"

"I'm sure it was more complex than just a virus, but yeah, that's the idea," Paul said.

Paul heard his mother's voice. "Charles, what's wrong?"

Paul could tell his father was holding the phone away from his mouth as he answered. "It's Paul, Honey. He said there's a computer virus or something. I'm sure it's no big deal. Go back to sleep. I'll tell you about it later."

Charles returned the phone to his mouth. "Okay, son, I'm back. Now about this power outage, as I was saying, I'm sure they'll have it figured out in no time."

"Dad! I need you to listen to me. This is not a standard outage. You need to get up and tend to your things. Don't just fire up your generator and leave it running. You'll need to conserve your gas. I'll come down and help you later today, okay?"

"Oh, Paul, I think that's a bit of an overreaction, don't you? You shouldn't use the gas. It's expensive right now," Charles responded, dismissing the suggestion.

"No, Dad, I don't think it's an overreaction. I'll see you this afternoon."

"Okay. I don't think it's necessary, but if it will make you feel better, fine," Charles said, now fully awake.

"Yes, it will make me feel better. Tell Mama I love her."

"I will son. Bye."

"Bye, Dad."

Paul hung up the phone frustrated. It was still early, so he was going to get things organized around here, make sure that Sandy knew what was going on, and head out right after lunch. He checked his messages. Nothing yet from the guys. They probably weren't up yet or they were having connectivity issues, so he posted a quick message to make sure everyone knew what was going on, assuming the message went through. He then checked one of his favorite online news sites.

"Nation reeling from massive cyberattack. Where is the government?"

Nope.

"Major carriers struggling to maintain cellular communications"

Yep. Let's try that one. Paul clicked on the article and quickly scanned it. Cellular carriers were using generators and mobile towers around metropolitan areas to keep the service functioning. *That was interesting. Those generators will quickly become targets.*

He clicked back out of the article and looked for another.

"America under attack. Is this an act of war?"

Of course it's an act of war, jackass. The question is: Who did it?

He continued down the site checking a couple more articles, trying to gain as much information as possible. Then the site stopped responding. He closed the app, reopened it, and tried again. Nothing. It wasn't reacting. Frustrated, he put his phone away and decided to wake up Sandy to let her know what was going on. He checked his watch. *She'll have to get over it. I'm waking her up.*

Paul went to the kitchen and made his wife a cup of coffee, careful to add the amount of cream and sugar she liked, then went to the bedroom. "Hey Babe," he said, trying not to startle her.

She stirred and opened her eyes. "What are you doing?" she asked.

"Here, I brought you coffee. I need you to wake up. Things have gotten worse."

She sat up, looking concerned, but reaching for the coffee. She took a sip before responding. "Okay, let's have it." Her voice betrayed her annoyance at being awakened.

Paul sat down on the edge of the bed. "I don't have all the information yet, but my best guess is that the whole country just got hit with a massive cyberattack. They disabled the 911 service, then attacked a bunch of water treatment facilities before taking down the electrical grid for the entire country." He paused. "Or something like that. I'm not sure of the details yet."

She stopped as she was about to take a sip and glanced through the open bedroom door at the light on in the other room. "So, we're on generator power right now?"

"Yep. I'll monitor it. If my suspicions are correct, I'm going to be doing a lot of oil changes on the generator because I don't expect the power to be back on any time soon."

She carefully placed the coffee cup on the nightstand and turned back to face her husband, now clearly concerned. "Okay, now I understand why you woke me up. What's our next move?"

"First things first, we need to get things set up here in case the gas stops flowing for any reason and we lose the generator. Secondly, we need…"

"Wait, wait," she interrupted. "The gas can stop flowing, and we'd lose power?"

"Well, I mean it's possible. I haven't seen anything that would indicate there's problem with natural gas yet, but we need to be prepared for that."

She looked off in the distance. "All that food in the freezers…"

"Yes, that would be one of *many* concerns."

"But I thought we were getting our gas from the well right over the ridge," she said, concerned.

"We are. Like I said, I don't think it's a concern anytime soon. However, I want to go ahead and have all of our redundant systems prepared in case we need them. Plus, this afternoon I need to run down to Mom and Dad's. They aren't taking this seriously. I need to go down and check on them," Paul said. "Speaking of which, I think you should call your dad and check on him too. The power is out everywhere, so I'm sure he's in the dark right now."

"The phones are working?" she asked.

"Well, somewhat. Ours is working because we have StarLink. I called Dad on their house phone and that worked. Your dad only uses a cell phone, so I don't know if it'll work or not. Give it a try and if you can't get through, text him. If the coverage is spotty, he should get the message the next time his phone connects to the network."

"Oh my gosh. This is unbelievable. The whole country?"

"I don't know about Alaska, and I would guess that Hawaii is okay, but yes, the whole continental United States."

She absently put her hand over her mouth. Paul gave her time to process, not saying anything else to her. "Okay," she said, suddenly sounding more resolute. "We'll deal with it. We have plans in place, I guess now we'll see how well they work."

Paul offered a weak smile. "Yes ma'am. I guess we will." He stood up. "I'll let you finish your caffeine, but I'm gonna go get started on things and then I'm going to pack for the trip to Mom and Dad's."

She stopped him, concern returning to her voice. "Pack? How long do you plan on being gone?"

"Oh, I'll be back today, but I'm rolling heavy. I don't know what to expect out there."

"Are you going by yourself?"

"I'll try to get ahold of Dangle and see if he wants to go with me. If I can't get through to him, I may just take 37 and stop by his house on the way. That actually might be the better route anyhow. I could avoid the interstate that way."

She considered this answer. "Okay. Okay. I'll be out in a minute."

Paul walked to his office and entered the combination into his main gun safe. He opened the door and appraised the collection. *Yep*, he thought to himself. *I'm rolling heavy.*

24

We've Got a Plan

August 9, 12:30 p.m.

Paul and Sandy's Farm

Paul decided to take the Durango rather than his pickup truck because it got better fuel economy. Plus, it had plenty of room for gear. He took his favorite AR-15, his body armor, an aid bag, spare socks, and of course his get home bag that went with him everywhere. He also took his night vision and his helmet so he could mount the night vision if he needed to use it. He always carried his pistol and a spare mag, but today he had opted for the double mag carrier so he had two spare mags, plus one on his plate carrier.

He had tried to call Dangle before leaving the house and didn't get through, so he was just going to drive there and talk to him in person. Paul made his way out to Route 10 and turned south. He only passed one car before reaching Branchland Lumber and turning onto Four Mile Creek Road. He looked at the lumber and hardware store. It was dark and the parking lot was empty. *Well, that was predictable.* He continued to navigate the country roads through the mountains, emerging on Route 37 and after fifty minutes of driving, he arrived at Dangle's house. He pulled right up to the house and tapped the horn to make sure Dangle knew he was there. He was exiting the vehicle just as Dangle came out the door. Tripwire bolted past Dangle and ran up to Paul, not a care in the world.

"Hey, crazy," he said to the dog as she got to him, bending to roughly pet her. She was as happy as she could be.

"What's up, Dangle?" Paul said to Dangle as a greeting.

"Well, the power's out, phones are out. You know, another day at the office." He offered the joke, but he wasn't smiling.

"Have you been able to get any news?" Paul asked.

"No, I was about to fire up the generator for the fridge and to get my internet back up, but I haven't done it yet."

"So, you don't know what's going on?"

"I mean, I know the power's out."

"Oh, brother, it's so much more. The power is out coast to coast."

"What?!" Dangle exclaimed.

"Yeah man. It's looking like a terror attack. Listen, I have to go check on my parents. I was going to ask if you wanted to go with me. I'll help you get your generator moved and set up, and fill you in on what I know, but after that, I gotta to go."

Dangle thought about it for a few seconds. "It's already getting warm. I probably need to run the generator for a couple hours anyhow to keep the fridge and freezer cold. I'll go with you. We can fire it up and I'll just let it run while we're gone. You can fill me in on what's going on while we're driving. What is it, a little over an hour from here?"

"Yeah, but I don't know exactly how long we'll be gone," Paul answered.

"It'll be fine. Come on, give me a hand."

Thirty minutes later, they were driving on Route 37 toward the town of Wayne. Dangle's gear was now sitting next to Paul's on the folded down back seats. Paul tried to recount everything he had learned so far. Then they turned on the satellite radio and got some more news. By checking a few different stations, they were able to paint a pretty good picture of what was going on.

Dangle turned the radio down so that he could talk. "Alright. So now, what's your take?"

"What do you mean?" Paul asked.

"I mean how bad is this? Are they going to be able to get the power back on soon? And what about the damage done to the water treatment plants? You heard the news, apparently whatever they did, they managed to create some kind of overload. There's physical damage to the plants."

Paul kept his eyes on the winding road. He was silent for a moment, thinking. "Best guess?" he asked.

"Yeah, of course. Best guess. I know you don't know for sure, but what do you think?"

Paul sighed. "I'm sure they are working to fix whatever damage was done. I just have no way of knowing how much damage was done, so I don't know how long it will take. The interruption of the trucking has already done immeasurable damage to the country's economy. This will shut down everything, exacerbating that situation. Finally, I think people are going to start losing their minds pretty soon and then anything's on the table."

"Wow, don't sugar coat it man," Dangle said.

Paul drove up onto the bridge crossing the Big Sandy River from Fort Gay, West Virginia to Louisa, Kentucky. The bridge was unique. It was T-shaped. It had a ninety-degree intersection in the middle of it. Dangle looked out the window. "Wow, the drought is having an effect on the river. The Big Sandy is super low."

Paul couldn't see the water level from his side of the vehicle. "Well, it's not very deep to begin with."

"Yeah," Dangle said. "I think I saw the bottom right there."

"Wow, that *is* low."

"Anyhow, back on subject. You think it's gonna get bad quick?" Dangle asked.

"Brother, I'll bet it's bad all over the place right now. There were already riots and looting before the power went out. It's going to do nothing but get worse, and eventually, it's going to spread to the country. We feel insulated in West Virginia because the craziness of the big cities doesn't usually trickle down to us, but I don't know how long that's going to last."

Paul's phone chimed. "Hey! I have service. I'm going to check on Joker while I can." He pulled his phone out and used the voice command to call Joker.

Dangle's phone starting dinging too as his messages came in. He pulled it out and started checking them.

Paul's phone was connected to the vehicle via Bluetooth, so the ringing sound came through the vehicle speakers. After two rings, Joker answered.

"Hello?"

"Hey, Joker. I'm just calling to check on you. I didn't know if you'd have service or not."

"Hey, Doc. Well, we didn't earlier, but it came back online a little while ago. I guess they got the towers up on generators or something. This is some kind of crazy, huh?"

"Yeah man. Are y'all good?"

"Oh, yeah. We're settled in. My in-laws are next door and they have a generator going. If we need to, we'll move some stuff over there. We'll probably sleep over there tonight too so it's not so damn hot. The only other thing I'm worried about right now..."

Paul waited for him to finish. Nothing. "Joker?" Nothing. "Crap, we just lost him." Paul looked up at the CarPlay screen and hit redial. It didn't connect.

"Dang it!" Dangle said suddenly. "I just lost signal too."

"Did you get anything good from your messages?" Paul asked him.

"My parents and siblings are okay, so that's a relief. I tried to open a message from my little brother, but it didn't work."

They were passing Yatesville Lake on their right side. "We can try again when we come back through here, maybe it'll work."

"Yeah, maybe."

Paul could tell he was annoyed, so he just turned the radio back up.

Twenty minutes later, they pulled off Route 201 and then turned into the driveway. Paul could see his dad's old truck sitting in the driveway by the door. Everything looked normal. He parked behind his dad's truck and jumped out, and headed straight for the door, not waiting on Dangle. As he approached the door, he heard the hum of his father's gasoline generator. Without knocking, he walked into the kitchen. His mother was coming out of the pantry.

"I figured that was you pulling up. How was the drive?"

Paul crossed the room and embraced his mother.

"Oh!" she said, not expecting the hug.

As he released her, she asked, "Are you okay, Honey?"

Paul took a deep breath of relief. "Yes Mama. I'm fine. What about y'all?"

"Oh, we're right as rain. We've been without power before. That's the cost of living in the country, isn't it?" She smiled at him and then stepped away from the door as Jenny came out of the pantry behind her.

"You remember our neighbor, Jenny, don't you honey?"

Paul looked at the box in Jenny's arms. Jenny returned his gaze sheepishly.

"What's going on here?" Paul asked.

"Oh, I'm just being neighborly," Edna said. "Miss Jenny here is low on food, so I'm helping them out until things get back to normal."

"I see," Paul said. "I didn't realize you had company. I didn't see a car outside."

Jenny looked up at him. "Oh, um, yeah, with gas prices like they are, I just walked over. It's only a couple hundred yards." She looked back at Edna.

"Um, Miss Edna, we really appreciate you helping us out. If we can do anything to repay you, please just let us know." Jenny's voice was soft and almost apologetic.

Edna patted her on the shoulder. "Don't you think anything of it, Dear. I'm happy to help. Paul," she said, turning toward her son, "will you get the door for Jenny?"

"Yes ma'am," Paul replied respectfully to his mother. He moved back to the door and held it open for the young woman.

Jenny stopped in the doorway and looked back. "Thanks again, Miss Edna," she said, then turned and disappeared out the door, jars lightly clinking in the box with each step.

"She's such a sweet young thing, don't you think, Paul?"

"I actually do, Mama. It's not her that I have a problem with. It's that husband of hers. I don't like him."

"Oh, Paul, you worry too much. Now, why was it you felt the need to drive down here when gas is so expensive?"

Paul realized that Dangle hadn't followed him in. "Just a sec, Mama." He walked back to the door and glanced out. He saw Jenny walking away down the driveway and looked back toward the barn to see Dangle talking with his father. He ducked back inside.

"Mama, I don't think y'all realize how serious this situation is. I tried to explain it to Dad this morning, but he didn't seem like he was hearing me. Maybe he just wasn't awake enough yet."

"No, he was awake. We talked after you hung up. We just don't think it's as big of a deal as you do. We've been here for a lot of years. Do you know how many power outages we've had?"

Paul pulled out a chair. "Here, Mama why don't you sit with me."

"Okaaay," she said, sitting down in the chair.

Paul pulled out the adjacent chair, turned it to face her, and sat down. He reached out and took both her hands in his. "Mama, do you trust me?" His face was serious and he was looking straight into her eyes.

"Of course I do, you know that."

"You started storing food and preparing for emergencies based on my recommendations, right?"

"Yes. You know we did," she answered tentatively.

"You trusted me enough to do that then. I need you to trust me now when I say this is not just a power outage. Okay?"

She looked down at their intertwined hands and stayed silent for a moment before replying, more serious now. "Okay. Tell me what we need to do."

Dangle and Charles walked through the door. Paul released his mother's hands and stood up. His father approached and the two men shook hands.

"Hey, Dad. Did Dangle bring you up to speed on everything that's going on?"

"Yes, he did. I guess I didn't realize how serious things were. I've been trying to do my best around here like I normally do in a power outage, but it sounds like I'm going to have to step up my game if it's going to be that long."

Paul didn't immediately respond. He was thinking. He stepped back so he could face both his parents at once. "I think y'all should come to my farm," he suddenly blurted out.

Charles and Edna both immediately began protesting.

"There's no way we can do that. I need to be here to take care of the farm, the animals," Charles said.

"We'll take the animals with us. I have rabbits, you can bring yours. I can expand my rabbit hutch. I have plenty of room in my hen house for more chickens. It's not even close to full."

"That's the least of the problems," his father continued. "I'm about to bring in the harvest. If I abandon my fields now, we'll lose a year's worth of crops."

"Dad, you aren't going to be able to sell your crops this year! Sure, you could harvest your personal stuff, but what good is that if you aren't safe?"

Edna spoke up, using a calm voice. "Honey, be reasonable. There's no way we can leave our home."

Paul didn't know what to do. "Okay. How about this: How about y'all come up for a week to see if things calm down. If the power comes back on, I'll run you right home. How about that?"

"Even that's tough," Charles began. I feed the animals every day, and with this drought, I've been monitoring the fields constantly to make sure they have enough water."

Paul sighed. "Okay, how about four days? You can give the animals enough food for that long and give the crops extra water before you leave. They'll make it that long."

Charles seemed to be considering it. "Three days. Things should blow over by then and I'll be worried about the fields even doing that."

Paul was going to take what he could get. "Deal. How long until you can be ready?"

"Slow down, slow down. We'll need some time to get everything set up and pack. There's no way we can go today. Besides, I got a call from Scott earlier. He's heading this way."

That changes the equation. If Scott's here, he could help keep an eye on things. "When's he getting here?" Paul asked, evaluating the situation.

"He's leaving Sunday morning. He should be here that evening," Charles replied.

Paul turned and paced across the kitchen, thinking. "Today's Friday, so you'd be alone tomorrow and then he'd be here the next day," he said, more to himself than to anyone else.

"Let's see if his phone is working. I want to talk to him." Paul pulled his phone out and looked at it. No service. "Is your land line still working?"

"It was earlier today. That's how he called us," Edna answered.

Paul walked over to the kitchen phone and plucked the receiver off the wall. He got a dial tone. Looking down at his phone, he retrieved Scott's number and dialed on the land line. It started ringing. "It's ringing," he announced to the room.

Paul looked back and saw Dangle looking out the window of the door. *He's pulling security. Good.*

"Hello?" It was Scott.

"Scott! It's Paul."

"What are you doing at Mom and Dad's?" he asked, surprise in his voice.

"I came down to check on them and I think they should come up and stay with me." He looked over at his parents who were looking back at him. "You know, for a few days."

"Well, I'm heading up there in a couple days. Things are getting kinda crazy down here. I told my boss I was taking my vacation time. He said I couldn't. I had to make him understand that it was happening, so he might as well approve it. He got the message, but asked if I'd work through tomorrow. I figured it was a fair compromise. Plus, I still gotta pack up."

"Well, you obviously still have cell service. What about everything else?"

"I have cell service *now*. It's been coming and going. I guess you know the power's out. We have a boil-water notice, but it's still flowing, for now at least. The stores are pretty much picked clean and its crazy in the city. But I'm good at the house. I'm charging my phone in my Jeep or in the ambulance at work. I'm good for another day. I'm working twelve hours tomorrow, then I'll get a good night's rest and punch out early Sunday."

Paul wanted to tell him to screw working another day and jump on the road now, but he knew Scott wouldn't do it. "Okay man. Listen, when you get here, if we can't communicate, just dig in and I'll be back in a few days to get everyone. Let's say...Tuesday. I need to give Dad some time to get the farm set up so he can be gone for a few days. I know I don't need to tell you, but this is serious. It's already dangerous out there and it's going to get worse."

In typical brother fashion, Scott took a swipe at Paul. "Oh, it's okay for you to drive to Kentucky, you're a Green Beret, but I need to be extra careful, right?"

Normally, Paul would have joked along with his brother, but not today. "Scott, I'm serious. Don't take this drive lightly."

"Okay man, I got it. I'll see you soon."

"Wait. Do you have enough gas?" Paul asked.

"I said I got it covered, man. I'll see you soon."

"Yeah, see you Tuesday."

Paul hung up the phone, but continued facing the wall, collecting his thoughts. After a moment, he turned to face his parents and Dangle.

"Okay Dad, you win." He sighed. He was worried for his parents, but he was trying to figure out what the right answer was here. "Scott will be here the day after tomorrow. So tonight, and tomorrow night, you need to be extra vigilant. I want you to put a pistol on and keep it on you at all times. Don't leave the house for anything. You need to turn that generator off and conserve your fuel. You should be good just running the generator for a couple of hours at a time. You'll have to figure it out, but two hours running should buy you somewhere between eight and twelve hours before things start melting, depending on how well your fridge and deep freeze are insulated. Of course, the more you open the doors, the shorter that time gets."

"I know how to do it son. Like I said before, we know how to handle a power outage," Charles said.

Paul was apprehensive. He didn't want to leave, but he also knew that he had to get home to his wife and daughter. "Let's go ahead and get you outfitted with your gun before I leave. I'd like you to have a pistol on your belt and have a rifle outside of the safe and loaded."

"Oh, that shouldn't be..."

Paul cut him off. "Dad, will you just do this for me, please?"

Edna stepped in to mediate again. "Charles, Honey. What's it going to hurt?"

"Okay, okay. I'll do it right now." He left the kitchen, heading toward the bedroom.

Paul turned to his mother. "Mama, I know you want to help out that girl next door, but in the future, I really don't think you should show anyone what's in the pantry, especially considering the current situation."

"I won't. I'll be careful."

"And pay attention to what's going on around the property. If anything feels off, you and Dad need to retreat to the house and protect yourselves, understand?"

"Paul, we understand. It's fine. Scott will be here before you know it."

Charles walked back into the room. He had his .38 revolver in a cheap nylon holster on his belt. He carried his shotgun in one hand and a box of shotgun shells in the other. He sat down at the table and loaded the gun, shoving in shells until it wouldn't hold any more.

"There we go." He stood up and started to place the shotgun just inside the door of the pantry.

"Dad, you didn't put one in the chamber."

"Oh, I don't like to do that if it's going to be sitting out like this."

Paul took a breath. "If you need it, I mean really need it, the time it takes you to rack it could mean the difference between life and death. Will you please just rack it and put it on safe?"

Charles mumbled something that Paul couldn't hear as he hoisted the shotgun, cycled the slide, and checked the safety. "There. Are you happy now?"

"Actually, you can put another one in the tube now."

Charles glared at him.

Paul recognized that his father was getting frustrated with him too, but he still plucked one more shotgun shell from the open box and slid it into the shotgun before double checking the safety and placing the gun just inside the pantry.

"Thanks, Dad. Hopefully you'll never need it, but better safe than sorry."

Paul saw Dangle look at his watch. "You thinking about your generator?"

"Yeah. It's fine, but it's been running for a while now and we'll still need another hour to get there."

"Okay," Paul said. He turned to his father and extended his hand. Charles took it and they shook hands briefly. Paul looked his father in the eye. "I love you, Dad. I just want you to be safe."

Charles' expression softened. "I know. We'll be fine. We'll see you in a few days."

"Yessir." He turned to his mother who was still seated at the kitchen table. He leaned down and hugged her. "You keep that one in line, Mama," he said motioning back toward his father.

She giggled. "I always do."

Charles scoffed.

Paul turned toward the door. "I'll bring my truck when I come back down so if you need some overflow for your stuff, we'll have it. And your land line seems to be fine, so you call me if you need anything, okay?"

"Okay, son. Get moving. Go take care of that wife of yours and our grandbaby," Edna said.

Dangle said goodbye to them too and waved as he walked out the door. Paul followed him, pausing to lock the door before pulling it closed.

Paul closed the door on the Durango and pushed the start button. The Hemi roared to life. He spun the vehicle around and paused before pulling back out onto the road.

Dangle looked over at him. "Don't worry brother. We've got a plan."

"Yeah," Paul said. "We've got a plan."

Over the Precipice

25

The Funniest Thing They'd Ever Seen

August 10, 2:30 a.m.

Putnam County, West Virginia

Zamir had conducted a reorganization in preparation for this phase. He had lost two men in Tennessee plus Ahmad in Idaho. Zamir decided he would take the remaining four men of Yellow Cell with him to hit the power plant. The other eight men would separate into four two-man teams to hit the smaller infrastructure targets, which were electrical substations and a natural gas pipeline. Each of the two-man teams had two targets that they were to hit before regrouping. After they regrouped, they would form two four-man teams to conduct guerrilla warfare against the public.

One of the four-man teams would go to southeastern Indiana. The other would terrorize western Pennsylvania, while he and his team would concentrate on western West Virginia and maybe even eastern Kentucky. If he hadn't sustained casualties, he would have had enough men to send another group back to Michigan.

He and his team had arrived on the evening of the eighth and had spent the time since then conducting reconnaissance and confirming that everything was the way it was laid out in the target packet. Luckily, there was high ground west of the plant with a powerline right of way that offered a clear view of the facility. They would have preferred to be right across the road, but they had discovered a group of houses there and they didn't want to be challenged. Instead, they chose to hide in the woods, working in shifts while always keeping at least two men hiding in the van nearby.

With so little traffic on the road, Zamir had elected to only do one drive by recon in the van. They couldn't afford to draw attention to themselves by driving past the plant numerous times. Not to mention, they were getting low on gas and Zamir wanted to save enough for the escape after the attack.

At 2:30 a.m. all five men met at the truck for their final preparations. They checked their weapons and explosives one last time. Nour and Faheem opened their backpacks to do another check of their items. Everything was prepared, so they took some time to pray.

After their prayer, Zamir called the men back together at the van. He checked the time. It was almost 4:15 a.m. -- time to go. The plan was to breach the front gate at exactly 4:30. Fahad Hijazi and Bilal Din would go with Zamir to destroy the turbines and generators. Nour and Faheem would split off for their own part of the mission.

Zamir picked up his U.S. Army issue M4 carbine and checked the chamber for the third time. It was still loaded. "It's time," he said to his cell. Bilal was in the driver's seat. Everyone else was in the back with their packs already on and their rifles slung. Hassan had provided them with additional semiautomatic rifles. They would leave their two bolt action rifles in the van during the assault. Zamir also carried a pistol, a Turkish made gun called a Zigana F.

Zamir checked the time again. "Let's go, Bilal."

Bilal didn't say anything. He just shifted the van into drive and pulled out. He drove out to Winfield Road and turned south. As he approached the entrance to the plant, he passed under an overpass. He felt like he could hear his own heart beating. He sucked in a breath and slowly released it as he approached the gate. A uniformed man stepped out of a guard shack. Bilal hit the gas, aiming for one of the low motorized gates. The guard jumped back out of the way as the van crashed through the gate with the sound of metal on metal. Bilal slammed on the brakes. The back door opened and two quick shots from Zamir put the guard on the ground.

Bilal was already out of the van, running around to the now open side door. Fahad was holding Bilal's backpack out to him. Bilal quickly donned the backpack and then accepted his AK-47 from Fahad. Without a word, Zamir, Fahad and Bilal dashed toward the building. Zamir had studied the route over and over. He didn't need the map or notes anymore. He ran straight to the door they planned to use for access to the structure. Fahad was right on his heels. As they arrived at the door, Zamir pointed to it and called out "This one!"

Fahad stepped up with his Halligan tool. He quickly made entry and the three men continued. On the south side of the facility, Nour and Faheem ran toward the coal pile, negotiating another gate and running across a set of railroad tracks.

Most people don't realize how difficult it can be to get coal to start burning. The coal burning plants would pulverize it to make it more combustible. However, that's not to say you can't ignite coal if you have the right tools. Nour and Faheem had the right tools. Nour stopped at the bottom of the coal pile and clicked on his headlamp. Faheem continued to run.

Nour pushed forward and climbed onto the coal pile, his feet sinking in, and coal sliding down as he pushed forward. After several seconds, he crested the side and found the coal to be firm where they had been using coal dozers to move it. He ran toward the center of the pile. The dark coal seemed to absorb the light from his headlamp and he stumbled twice but managed to stay on his feet. When he judged that he had run about one hundred fifty meters, he stopped and dropped to his knees, placing his rifle on the coal. He slipped one arm out of his backpack and slung it around in front of him. He withdrew the explosive device provide by Hassan back in Michigan.

Nour pulled the protective sheath from the rod protruding below the explosives and forced the rod down into the pile of coal. He opened the cover of the electronic switch and flipped the switch, confirming that the timer started. It was designed to continue, even if someone discovered it and turned the toggle switch back off. He retrieved his rifle and pack and turned to run back the way he came. After fifty yards, he dropped to his knees again and pulled out the thermite incendiary device, placing it on the coal. This device had an identical looking switch. He repeated the process and armed the device. He noted the time.

The two devices were synced. The explosive had been selected carefully because different explosives explode at different rates. Hassan's team had chosen an explosive with a low Relative Explosive Factor. This low R.E. Factor would cause the explosives to act with more of a pushing effect, rather than a cutting effect. This explosive push would create a giant cloud of airborne coal and coal particles. A second and a half later, the thermite would launch a fireball into the mixture, igniting the coal and coal dust with a devastating effect. The thermite pack would continue to burn at four thousand degrees Fahrenheit, further ensuring the coal pile would ignite.

Faheem was emplacing an identical setup on the other side of the coal pile. Those timers were synchronized with these, providing redundancy to the system. Nour scrambled down the side of the coal pile and worked his way back to the van. His next job was to provide security until Zamir's team returned from placing the shaped charged on the turbines and generators. The shaped charges didn't actually contain much explosives. It wasn't the size of the explosion that would do the damage, it was the shape. Shaped charges, when used with the appropriate amount of standoff would focus the explosive power into a superheated jet, cutting through anything in its way. Zamir, Fahad, and Bilal had been practicing the emplacement for a week. They only had to do enough damage to the internal workings of the turbines and generators that the machines would not be able to be repaired. If they were turning when the shaped charges went off, they would likely tear themselves apart in a spectacularly violent way.

As Nour arrived back at the van, he heard gunfire from the building and instinctively turned toward the sound. He wanted to run in and provide additional firepower, but he knew better than to do that. His job was to stay here and deal with anyone who showed up. He walked over to the fallen guard and shined his light in his face. He saw his eyelids close tighter in response to the light. *He's not dead yet.*

Nour pointed his rifle at the man's head, but paused. He looked over at the mangled gate they had driven through. It had short, decorative points sticking out the top of it. It was now in a crumped heap beside the guard. *I have a better idea.* He rolled the guard over onto his belly. The guard offered a weak groan of complaint. Heaving, he pulled the nearly unconscious man over to the gate by his shirt.

More gunshots from inside. Nour glanced in that direction and then returned his attention to the man. He stepped over the man and now stood over his back, one foot by each elbow. The man's face was pressed into the pavement. Nour reached down and grasped the man's collar with both hands and pulled up and forward, draping him over the twisted metal so that two of the points were pressing against the man's throat. The man reacted to the pressure as the sharp barbs poked as the tender flesh of his neck. With one swift movement, Nour raised his foot and drove his boot down hard onto the back of the man's neck, driving the spikes through the flesh, one of them coming to rest against the front of his spine. The man spasmed for about a second and then lay still.

As Nour heard footfalls running toward him, he grabbed at the rifle dangling by its sling and turned toward the approaching person.

"Nour! It's me!" called Faheem. Nour lowered the gun, looked down at the man once more and walked casually toward Faheem.

"Did you have any problems?" Nour asked.

"No. Everything worked as they said it would. After I armed the explosives…"

They both turned toward the sound of more people approaching.

"Hey!" a man called. He was wearing a hardhat and Nour's headlamp reflected off the stripes on his clothing. A second man was right behind him. They were both running toward Nour and Faheem.

Without a word, Nour and Faheem raised their rifles and fired multiple times. The two men crumpled, their momentum carrying them forward. Faheem distinctly heard the sound of one of the hardhats striking the pavement. He smiled as he saw it slide a few feet in their direction before stopping upside down and rocking back and forth a few times.

Nour turned to Faheem. "You watch that way, I'll watch this way. Zamir should be coming from that direction. Make sure you know what you're shooting at before you pull the trigger. We don't want to shoot our guys."

Faheem nodded and moved to the corner of an open framework that housed stairs.

More gunfire from inside. Nour looked down at his watch. *They should be here by now.*

He saw movement in the direction where Zamir should be coming from. *There he is! Finally!*

He raised his arm over his head to make sure Zamir saw him.

"Hey! What the hell's going on?"

That's not Zamir!

Nour turned slowly and started walking toward the man. His headlamp was intentionally pointed in the man's face. The man raised his hand to shield his eyes, but it didn't help.

"Hey man! How about you get that light outta my face?" The man had a gruff voice. He was accustomed to telling people what to do.

Nour closed the last few feet to the approaching figure and turned the light off. The man stopped, trying to see, but he still couldn't. Nour lowered the rifle and jammed the barrel into the man's belly. He doubled over the rifle and Nour pulled the trigger, blowing him off the muzzle. He landed on his back, with a satisfying thump. He grasped at his ruined abdomen. Nour smiled.

Faheem's voice cut through the night. "Do you need help over there, Nour?"

"No! Watch your area!" Nour calmly turned his light back on, pointing it in the man's face again. He was writhing and groaning on the ground.

Nour heard him try to speak, but it was barely discernable. "You...shot...me..."

Nour dropped the rifle, letting it hang by the sling and withdrew his fixed blade knife from his belt. He knelt beside the man and placed the point of the knife on the side of the man's throat, the sharpened side of the blade was facing forward. He drew back his other hand and struck the pommel of the knife, driving it through the man's throat. The point didn't quite make it out the other side. The man instinctively grasped at the blade as Nour pulled it forward with a sawing motion, cutting the man's jugular, esophagus and trachea before ripping out the front of his neck. The man clutched at the gaping wound for about a second before he fell silent and stopped moving. Nour calmly wiped the blade on the man's pantleg since his shirt was now covered in blood. He stood up and placed the knife back in its sheath, taking the time to snap the keeper around the handle.

His brain registered footsteps running toward him. He turned, grabbing his rifle again.

"Let's go!" It was Zamir's voice.

Nour didn't wait, he turned and ran toward the van. "Faheem, go to the van!"

The five men piled back into the van. Balil was in the driver's seat again. He quickly turned the van around and drove through the open hole they had created. As they turned left onto Winfield Road, they heard the report of the shaped charges going off. It was impossible to distinguish the individual charges because they had been synchronized, just like the charges in the coal pile.

Zamir looked at the clock on the dashboard. "Keep going! Faster!"

Balil accelerated. Two minutes later, as they were passing under Interstate 64, the dark sky behind them seemed to turn briefly to daylight. Zamir was turned in his seat looking back, expecting it. The flash was immediately followed by a thunderous roar as the sound reached them.

Balil, however, was not prepared. He reflexively ducked and swerved. The right front fender struck the concrete barrier that was in place due to ongoing construction. The men in the back were thrown to the side of the van. Balil stomped the brakes as he pulled the wheel back to the left, away from the point of impact. The van's tire screeched in protest. He let off the brake as he turned the wheel back to the right and drove off the left side of the road. The shoulder was unusually wide here. Various construction materials were staged in the grass next to the shoulder.

Thump. Thump. Thump.

Balil plowed down several road cones as he reentered the road way. The van settled back onto its suspension and Balil adjusted the steering to get back into the southbound lane. He eased back onto the accelerator as he regained control of the vehicle. He was gripping the steering wheel with all his strength. As quickly as it had begun, it was over.

Balil glanced over at Zamir in the passenger seat as he tried to regain control of his breathing. He returned his attention to the empty road in front of them. His heart was thumping even harder than it had been earlier, at the beginning of the attack.

Slowly, a smile spread across Zamir's face. Then he chuckled. Then, without warning, he burst into laughter. "Ha! You should have seen your face!" he said, pointing at Balil, and still laughing.

Balil started to relax. Then he started to smile. Zamir was laughing uproariously at this point. Balil then broke out laughing. The remaining three men didn't know what to think of this at first, then one by one, they started laughing as well. They thought this was the funniest thing they'd ever seen.

26

I'm Not Stopping

August 11, 6:07 a.m.

Home of Benjamin Tuffin, CEO of JP Morgan Chase Bank

There was a light knock on the bedroom door. Benjamin "Ben" Tuffin opened his eyes. *What in the world?* Ben got out of the bed, glancing over at his wife. She wasn't moving. Ben retrieved a bathrobe and walked across the cavernous bedroom to the door. He opened it slightly, allowing a beam of light to spill into the room. He leaned his head into the opening and before the man standing in the hallway could speak, Ben launched into a verbal assault.

"Have you lost your mind? Since when is it okay to come to my bedroom? You're done here, Franklin. You'll be on the street by lunch!"

"Sir, if I may?" the head butler asked.

"What?!" Ben said, trying to scream and whisper at the same time.

"Sir, my apologies, but there is a group of men downstairs from your office and I felt it was urgent enough that you would prefer that I disturb you," the man said in a measured, professional tone.

Ben just glared at the man. Finally, he glanced back at his sleeping wife and then stuck his head back through the partially opened door. "Fine! I'll be down in a minute."

Ten minutes later, Ben was dressed and walking down the huge, curving stairway to the library. He stopped before walking into the room and took a breath before walking in. Three men were standing in front of his imported Italian wood desk that had been hand carved nearly a century earlier. They didn't look like they had good news.

Ben was known for being cool under pressure. There was a reason that his salary last year was thirty-six million dollars, and it wasn't because he was rash.

"Gentlemen, I'm going to work under the assumption that there's a good reason you're standing in my library at six o'clock in the morning." His voice was calm, but there was a hint of a threat in the tone. He walked past the three men and settled onto his elegant overstuffed chair behind the desk. The desk had been ridiculously expensive, but he needed it to complete the feel for the room. All told, he had spent over $230,000 on the furnishing for this room, $787,000 if you counted the artwork, but he had finally gotten it the way he liked it. Leaning back, he put his hands together in front of his chest.

Walter McAbee looked nervously to the other men for support. He didn't receive any.

"Well, Walt? Spit it out. What is it that brings you into my home to drag me out of my own bed?"

"Um, sir. There's been a breach," Walter clearly was worried that the messenger might be the one punished for the news.

Ben didn't show any reaction. "Explain *breach*," he commanded calmly.

"Sir, this morning, um, this morning everything...well, everything crashed. I mean everything. It began with millions of dollars in unauthorized transfers being initiated. Then, before we could get it under control, it started deleting customer data and..." He looked over at the two men with him, who said nothing. "...and we couldn't stop it. It's gone sir. It's all gone. The backups, everything."

Ben sat up and pulled a small yellow notepad over in front of him. Retrieving a beautiful black and gold pen with his name engraved on it, he looked like he was about to write something on the pad. The pen just hovered over the paper for a moment. Then he placed it down gently beside the pad. "And how, exactly, did they get past our firewalls, our security protocols?" he asked, still sounding completely calm.

"Well, sir, um, it seems to have initiated from *inside* our system. It was already there. Cybersecurity thinks that it was uploaded the same day of the cyberattack on the power grid, the ninth. Then, for some reason, it sat dormant until today. We don't have the details yet sir. Our best people are working on it right now."

"How did this happen? Was the power even on to allow this 'breach' to take place?"

"We were operating on backup power. The best we can tell, the worm was designed to execute at 5:23 this morning. However, even if the power had not been on, it appears that it would have happened as soon as the power did come back on." He swallowed hard. "Sir."

Ben nodded his head slowly, digesting the information. "What's the damage?"

"Sir?"

"What's the damage? How much did they get?" His eyes drilled into Walter's, causing Walter to look down.

"We don't know yet." Walt stared at his own shoes.

"What's your best estimate?"

Walt again looked at his companions who remained stoic. He returned his gaze to the CEO. "Sir...billions."

Similar conversations were happening all over the country at the same time. What the banks, airlines, and cellular carriers were learning was that they had been infiltrated on August ninth when the power was still on and the internet was still working correctly. The hackers had emplaced the cyber version of a time bomb moments before attacking the power grid. That bomb had gone off this morning at 5:23. Money was stolen. Data was erased. Servers destroyed themselves. And America fell farther into the abyss.

The Iranian regime had more than one international partner. Each partner was responsible for a different portion of the assault on America, based on their capabilities. The Iranians had the brute force portion of the plan. They would conduct the attacks on the trucks, power plants and other infrastructure. The responsibility for the cyberattack had fallen to the Chinese contingent.

The Chinese believed they were destined to rule the world – not merely hoped or assumed, but knew it. They saw America as nothing more than a means to an end. Most westerners struggle to comprehend the Chinese culture, and the Chinese Communist Party was more than willing to exploit that. In their view it was a patriotic duty to take advantage of anyone who was not Chinese. If a Chinese company did honest and transparent business with a foreign entity, it would be seen as unpatriotic. Cheating, lying, and even stealing from foreigners was not only acceptable – it was expected.

Imagine this: An American company hires a Chinese manufacturer to produce a product designed in the U.S. The first batch arrives perfect—exactly to specification. Pleased, the American company places another order. Gradually, the Chinese company begins cutting corners. They might substitute a slightly lighter fabric or a lower-grade steel. The differences would be subtle at first, barely noticeable. But once those shortcuts became the new standard, they'd push them further—again and again—while continuing to charge the same price. If confronted, they would deny any wrongdoing or blame it on a manufacturing error. But in the end, they had successfully deceived the Americans—and in their eyes, fulfilled their patriotic duty.

The Chinese Communist Party had spent years—and untold sums of money—developing ways to cheat and steal from the United States. So, when the opportunity arose to deliver a decisive blow, the Chinese government didn't hesitate. They were more than willing to cooperate with the Iranians if it served their national agenda—and that's exactly what they did.

For years, they had been probing various aspects of American infrastructure, quietly identifying weaknesses and vulnerabilities. Now, the time had come to put that knowledge to use.

Not every attack was successful, but enough of them were to achieve their objective. They had siphoned billions in wealth from unsuspecting Americans. And while they assumed they would eventually be identified as the culprits behind the cyberattacks, they weren't concerned. By then, it would be too late.

Of course, the average American had no way of knowing this. They weren't worried about their billions of dollars, shareholders, or even their 401(k)s. They weren't thinking about how they were going to retreat to their vacation home in the islands or fuel up their luxury yachts. They were worried about bare pantries or the food in the refrigerator spoiling. They feared violence, theft, and the inability to call for help. And at that moment, in South Carolina, Scott Michaels was worried about getting home to his parents.

Scott carried the last of his things out to his Jeep Cherokee. The first thing he had loaded had been the remaining food in the house. He had two coolers, filled with food and ice. He had been able to get ice from work and he used it to pack his refrigerated items into three coolers in his home. The last few days, he had been cooking on his grill in the back yard and had reduced the food enough that he now only needed two of the three coolers. He had a few boxes with his canned good and other dry food such as cereal, instant potatoes, and ramen.

As a paramedic, he had built himself a nice aid bag with medical supplies and a small gym bag of additional first aid items. Those were safely packed behind the food. The Jeep also had bags of clothes, a box of documents, a cardboard box of ammunition, and all the guns he owned, except for his Glock 19, which was currently residing on his hip.

The final things being loaded were his camping supplies, which were plentiful. He had always enjoyed camping and over the years he had accumulated a variety of sleeping bags, tents, outdoor cooking items and tools. By the time he closed the rear hatch on the Jeep, there was no more room to put anything. The last thing he needed to do was load his mountain bike onto the rear carrier. He tightened the ratchet straps and stepped back to look at the heavily laden vehicle. Seeing the two small fuel cans mounted to the top cargo rack, he decided he should double check those straps as well. One of the cans was only about half full. He had drained that from his Harley Davidson and his Yamaha YZ450F dirt bike that were still sitting in the garage.

Finally satisfied that he had done everything he could do, he went back into the house for one last walk through before leaving. He paused in his bedroom, looking around the room. *It's not like I'm not coming back*, he thought. As an afterthought, he grabbed his favorite pillow from his bed. *I can find a place to stuff this.*

He checked the back door to ensure it was locked and left out the front door, locking the deadbolt. Starting the Jeep, he checked the fuel gauge and the time. The tank was full and it was half past six. The drive from Travelers Rest to Louisa usually took about five and a half hours. He could be at his parents' house by about noon.

The trip was almost exactly due north and would take him through North Carolina, east Tennessee, the western tip of Virginia and finally up the east side of Kentucky. He was concerned about driving through Asheville. He knew about the violence, looting and riots in the big cities. He had seen it himself in Greenville and he had heard some crazy stories coming out of Ashville. He had considered trying to drive around it, but was concerned about the additional fuel it would take to do so. He only had about four additional gallons with him. In the end, he had decided that he would stay on the interstate and make a sprint through the city, trying to minimize his exposure to the urban area.

As Scott exited his neighborhood, he saw a woman come running out the front door of her house, waving her arms. He had seen the woman before, but didn't know her. He returned his eyes to the road and accelerated. He glanced up at the rear-view mirror and saw the woman stop in the street behind him, throwing her arms up in frustration. *Great. It's already started.*

He worked his way out to Route 25 and north out of town. The drive to Interstate 26 was essentially uneventful, although he did see numerous vehicles parked on the side of the interstate, presumably out of gas. At the onramp onto the interstate, a sheriff's deputy had his vehicle blocking the road. Scott rolled down his window as he approached the young man. The deputy wore a tactical vest and was carrying an AR-15.

"Sir," the deputy asked, "where are you headed?"

Scott was immediately angry. *What does it matter where I'm heading? This is still a free country and I'm allowed to drive without explaining myself.* However, that response stayed in his head and he responded. "Just heading to my parents' house, man. Is there a problem with the interstate?"

The deputy glanced up in the direction of I-26. "Well, I guess that depends on your definition of *problem*. Is the road okay? Yes. Are there crazy people on it? Also yes."

"How bad are we talking?" Scott asked, following the man's gaze.

"The deputy looked back at him. "Sir, I don't recommend you drive anywhere. The Governor has issued a 'Shelter in place' order. However, if you're traveling to your *shelter,* I'd be obligated to allow you to pass. Is that what you're doing? Are you traveling to your home, so you can shelter in place?" He didn't smile or wink, but he was clearly transmitting a message.

"That's exactly what I'm doing. I'm traveling to my shelter in place location so I can follow the Governor's order," Scott said seriously.

"Well in that case, sir. I'm going to have to let you pass. However, it's dangerous. Are you armed?"

"Am I breaking any laws?" Scott asked, suspicious of the question.

The deputy sighed. "If you're not, you should be." He didn't wait for a response. He stepped back away from the window, still facing Scott and motioned back toward his patrol car. A man Scott had not noticed before stood up with an AR-15. Scott now realized with a start that the rifle had been pointed at him the whole time. The other deputy raised the gun into the air and waved Scott forward with his other hand.

"Just drive around the back of the car, there's enough room to pass. Don't go around the front, there are spikes in the road there. Have a good day, good luck," the first deputy said, stepping further back from the Jeep.

Scott eased forward and glanced at the other deputy as he passed him. He followed the long curving bridge and soon merged onto the interstate. *I don't think I'm going to worry about the speed limit today.*

Twenty-five minutes later, he transitioned from I-26 onto I-240 as he entered Asheville. He didn't need a GPS or map for this trip. He'd made this drive enough that he knew where he was going. He needed to follow I-240 for about four miles, then he would take a left-hand exit back onto I-26 near downtown Asheville. As Scott entered the half-mile straight stretch leading to his exit, he saw a small crowd of people in the road up ahead. They appeared to be holding signs. *What the...Is this some kind of protest?* He eased back on the throttle, dropping down closer to the speed limit.

As he approached the group, everyone was looking at him. Then he read one of the closer signs.

Toll Road

Pay your tax

"Oh, hell no!" he said out loud and angled toward the exit. There were fewer people there. He slowed and acted like he was going to stop. Two men took up positions to approach his window where they assumed he would stop. One of them was a short white guy with a pistol visible on his hip. The other was a tall black man. He had an aluminum baseball bat resting casually over his right shoulder. Three women and a young man stood blocking the exit with their arms interlaced. Scott couldn't help but notice that one of the young women had her hair dyed a brilliant pink.

Scott lowered his window as he slowed to about five miles an hour approaching the group. The man with the bat popped it off his shoulder and bounced it against his left hand. As his window came down, he could hear the group chanting. "Pay the tax! Pay the tax!"

Scott smiled at the men as they closed the distance to him. Without warning, he turned his head back toward the group blocking the road and slammed his foot down on the gas pedal. The man with the pistol jumped back. The man with the bat took a wild swing at the Jeep as Scott passed him, shattering the left rear glass of the cargo area. The four people in the road scattered. The man wasn't quick enough and Scott heard a distinct thud as he bounced off the front of the Jeep and landed in a jumbled mess just left of Scott's path. Scott felt two mild bumps as first the front tire and then the rear tire rolled over one of the man's legs. He shrieked in agony as Scott hammered the gas and negotiated the lefthand curve back to the north.

His window was still down and Scott heard the distinct *pop pop pop* of gunfire as someone fired a pistol at him. He ducked at the sound, but the shots were wild and missed him. He glanced in his driver side mirror and he could see a group rushing to the fallen man. "Play stupid games, win stupid prizes," he said to himself as he reached eighty miles an hour and rejoined I-26.

He suddenly realized he was sweating. He rolled the window back up and turned the air conditioner to full blast. His heart was racing. "Holy crap," he muttered under his breath. He was abruptly aware of the wind sounds behind him as the air rushed into the broken rear window. He frowned and shook his head slightly. *I'll have to do something about that soon, but not right now*. His thoughts were racing. *I guess maybe I should have gone around the city.*

Doing some mental calculations, he determined that he still had about four hours to go. Glancing down at the fuel gauge, he estimated that he could probably make it without using the gas in the cans, but he'd be empty when he got there. *Maybe it makes more sense to just put the fuel in the tank now so I don't have to worry about it. Maybe. Not right now, though.*

He continued north, eventually crossing over into east Tennessee. He passed the towns of Ervin and Unicoi without incident, although he did see large groups of people out in the cities. He kept driving, as fast as he felt like he could go, often hovering around ninety miles an hour. He knew he had to pass through Johnson City. *I should go around the city*, he thought.

He pulled his cell phone out to check the map. Checking the road first to make sure he didn't have any potential obstacles, he eased of the gas, and clicked on the icon. It opened, but the map wouldn't load. "Dammit!" He tossed the phone in the passenger seat beside his go bag.

He didn't know the area around Johnson City. He didn't even know if there was a reasonable way to bypass it, so he just kept driving. *I'll figure it out when I get closer.* The road was still essentially empty and he was making good time. He saw a blue sign coming up. GAS-EXIT 27

"Crap!" he said out loud, but kept driving. A minute later, he saw a green sign announcing Exit 27 for Okolona Road and 359 North. *I don't know 359 North. I wonder if that goes around the city.* He had to make a decision. *Do I take the exit? Yes.* He started off the exit, but as he started down the ramp, he saw several vehicles blocking the end of the ramp. He hit the brakes and as soon as he got slowed down, he cut the wheel to the left into the grass and climbed back up to the interstate, reentering the roadway just before the beginning of a guard rail.

"Dammit! Dammit! Dammit!" He pounded the steering wheel with each word. He got back on the gas and accelerated again. *It looks like I'm going through the city.* He leaned to the left and withdrew his pistol from the holster, tucking it under his leg. *I'm not stopping.*

27

Well, That Sucked

August 11, 8:00 a.m.

Near Kingsport, Tennessee

As Scott passed Kingsport, Tennessee, he looked out the window on the passenger side. There were several columns of smoke rising from the city. He slowly shook his head. *People have lost their minds.* He pushed the Jeep a little harder, trying to put as much distance between himself and the city as possible. He glanced down at the fuel gauge again. He was burning more gas than normal on this trip because he was driving so much faster than he typically would. He made the decision that as soon as he saw a stretch of road with no structures on it, he was going to stop and add his extra fuel to the vehicle. It didn't take long. Soon after crossing the state line into Virginia, the road turned almost due west just past the small town of Gate City. He saw a sign coming up with the distances to Duffield, Big Stone Gap, and Cumberland Gap. He slowed to a stop on the shoulder and killed the engine. The terrain sloped up to the right into a tangled mess of a forest. The other side of the road was a stunningly beautiful valley with a small pasture rising up beside the road. He assessed the location as safe. He could see anyone approaching for quite a way from either direction.

Throwing the Jeep into park, he jumped out and shoved the pistol back into its holster. He quickly relieved himself on the side of the road before climbing up onto the rear bumper and retrieving the gas cans. He kept scanning left and right as he tried to will the gasoline to defy physics and empty into the filler neck faster. As soon as the second can finished, he secured them back on top of the vehicle and took off. Reaching into his pocket, he retrieved a can of Zyn. Tucking one into his lip, he thought to himself. *Two and a half hours. I wonder if the radio is working.*

He turned on the radio and searched for a station. He found one with a man and a woman having a conversation. *I wonder how they're transmitting.*

> "...country has essentially stopped going to work," the man said.

The woman responded.

> "How can people be expected to go to work when gasoline is twenty-five dollars a gallon and there are roving gangs that are holding people up like it's the old west!"

> "I don't have a solution either," the man responded, sounding more than a little frustrated. "Unfortunately, staying home isn't necessarily safe either. Many cities are reporting an explosion in home invasions. I don't know what people are supposed to do. I guess we'll have to see what law enforcement and the National Guard can do to get things under control."

> "That's a good point," the woman said. "Forty-three governors have now activated their National Guard and the others are expected to follow suit soon."

The station started fading out and eventually static overtook it. Scott scrolled through the dial looking for another station, but was unable to find anything else, so he turned the radio off.

A little over an hour later, he was winding along Route 23 past an area known as Fords Branch. He noticed a road sign on the left side of the road that read 'Smiley Fork Rd'. He only had about seventy-five miles to go to get to his parents' house. This area was making him nervous. While it certainly didn't qualify as an urban area, there seemed to be houses and small businesses all along the road. He didn't like it. A minute later, the road curved in a long consistent turn to the left. Halfway through the curve, Scott saw a tractor trailer facing the road at a ninety-degree angle, facing out on a road that looked too small for the vehicle. Behind the truck, he glanced a sign that said "Foxcroft". It appeared to be the entrance to a gated community. As he passed the vehicle, he saw someone sitting in the driver's seat. *That was weird.* He continued around the curve.

The road had a concrete divider separating the four lanes into two lanes each. On the right side of the road, it was a cliff, evidence that this road had been cut out of solid stone. There was a guard rail and a tall fence designed to catch rockfall from the cliff. As he exited the curve into a straight stretch, he saw another tractor trailer ahead of him. It was moving into position across the road at a ninety-degree angle, blocking the road between the concrete divider and the guard rail.

He locked up the brakes, coming to a stop two hundred yards from the truck. He stared for a moment as the truck adjusted its position, processing what he was seeing. *I need to get out of here.* He executed a three-point turn and headed back up the road going east in the westbound lane. He started back around the curve in time to see the truck he had passed earlier maneuvering into position, blocking his escape. He hit the brakes again. He was trapped. On one side was the cliff. On the other side was the concrete barrier. Beyond the barrier was two more lanes and then The Levisa Fork River. He unzipped the outside pocket on his go bag beside him and pulled out a spare fifteen round magazine for his Glock, stuffing it into his left front pocket. He wished his rifle didn't have a bunch of stuff piled on top of it in the back. He glanced back between the seats, trying to decide how long it would take him to dig it out the gun case. When he looked back up, he saw five men emerge from behind the truck and start walking toward him side by side, spread out across the roadway. Every one of them was carrying a rifle or shotgun.

He cranked the wheel and turned around a second time, heading back in his original direction of travel. He stopped as he saw six more men walking down the road from that direction. They all had long guns too. *Well, that's not good.* He put the Jeep in park and opened the door, drawing his pistol. Standing behind the open door he yelled at the approaching men. "What the hell do you want?"

The men didn't react, they just kept walking, they were about a hundred fifty yards away and closing. He looked behind him. He could see the others, but they were a little farther away still. He drew his pistol and pointed it through the gap between the vehicle and the door. "Stop!" he commanded.

Two of the men raised their rifles and began shooting. The windshield exploded. Scott ducked behind the door as more rifles opened up. A bullet punched through the open door right beside his head and he dove into the front seat. He heard more bullets impacting the engine compartment. "Shit!" he yelled. He looked over at the passenger seat at the backpack and made a decision. He dragged the bag across the center console and bolted toward the concrete barrier, pulling it with him. He vaulted across the low concrete barrier and kept running. He heard multiple rifle shots and the distinct sound of a shotgun. He heard one of the rounds impact the concrete barrier where he had just been. In a second, he was jumping over the guard rail and sliding down the steep embankment toward the river. He slid to a stop against a large tree trunk and threaded his arms through the straps on his pack, being careful not to drop the pistol. He rotated around the tree, placing it between himself and the road above and took aim at the guardrail. The pistol sights were bouncing up and down as he tried to catch his breath. He heard voices. The guard rail was only about ten yards above him. A quick glance behind him revealed that the water's edge was about another twenty yards. He returned his attention to the guard rail.

He heard voices again. "Davey, go over there and get him."

A moment later, a man with a rifle popped over the top of the guard rail a few feet to the left of where Scott had jumped over. Scott adjusted his point of aim and fired twice. The first round struck the man in the upper chest. The second round went high.

The man disappeared from sight. *Crap. They're all gonna be after me now.* Scott looked behind himself again. *It looks like I'm going swimming.* Before the other ten men had a chance to get to him, he secured his pistol in his Safariland GLS holster, ensuring that it locked in place. He then turned and slid down the remainder of the steep embankment, and plunged into the water. As soon as his head went under, his feet struck bottom. It wasn't very deep. He pushed off the bottom and pulled at the water to propel himself forward. He came up for air, looking toward the opposite bank and started swimming. He suddenly became very aware of the pack on his back. He went under again. He felt the pack pull down on him as he was going up, and it pulled up when he was going down.

As his feet impacted the rocky bottom a second time, he decided that this would be his technique. He pushed off the bottom, angling forward. Emerging from the water a second time, he judged the remaining distance to the far bank.

That can't be more than thirty yards. Do it again. He was being pushed downstream at the same time. As he came up for air, he heard shouting behind him and twisted in the current to look over his shoulder. The trees were obscuring him from view -- for now. He had to move fast before someone decided to slide down the hill after him.

The current continued to carry him downstream, but then his foot struck bottom. The water was getting shallower. He started pulling at the water, bouncing awkwardly toward the bank. By the time he stumbled onto the low, muddy edge, he was gasping for air, exhaustion pressing in.

He reached back and grasped the pistol, worried that he might have lost it while fighting the river. It was still there. *A good holster is worth every penny.*

Forcing himself upright, he staggered into the trees to find cover. His legs felt like he was wearing ankle weights, but he kept moving, grabbing branches and trunks to steady himself. Only when he was deep enough in the woods to feel hidden did he allow himself to collapse, dropping into a seated position and leaning back against his pack.

Sucking in a deep breath, he looked up through the branches at the sky. "Well, that sucked."

28

The Cylinder Was Empty

August 11, 8:45 p.m.

Charles and Edna's Farm

Edna was finishing up washing the dishes from dinner. Charles had a dishtowel in each hand, drying a plate. The generator was running. Charles had been running the generator from 7:00 a.m. to 9:00 a.m. and then doing the same thing again in the evening, running it from 7:00 p.m. to 9:00 p.m. It wasn't quite completely dark outside, but in the house, it would have been too dark without the aid of the lights. Both Charles and Edna had adopted the new habit of keeping a flashlight in their pocket at all times. Charles had also placed some old-fashioned kerosene lanterns around the house that they used after they shut the generator down for the night.

Dinner had been pork chops, corn, and broccoli, all from the freezer. Edna was specifically looking through the freezer for food to use, now concerned that she could lose it if they didn't use it soon.

"I'm going to fry up some more pork chops to have with eggs in the morning. We have several packages of them," Edna said.

"Wow," Charles replied with a smile. "This power outage is gonna cause me to gain weight."

"Oh, I don't think that'll be a concern."

Charles placed the plate in the cabinet. "You know, it's Sunday."

"Oh, I know. Are you thinking about how weird it feels to not have gone to church today?"

"Yes. It just feels wrong. I still took the time to pray for Scott today, though," Charles said.

"Yeah, me too. I know we talked about it earlier, but now he's really late. Do you think he's okay?" Charles could hear the concern in her voice.

"I'm sure he's fine, Honey. Maybe he ended up needing to work another day, or maybe it's just taking him longer to get here. I tried calling him earlier, but nothing's working. I'm sure it's crazy out there. He's probably just being extra careful." Charles was trying to sound comforting to his wife, but he was just as worried as she was.

He accepted a Mason jar from her to dry. "I'll stay up late tonight in case he's just running late."

"I'd like that. Would you like me to make you some coffee?"

Charles thought about it for a second. "You know, that actually sounds pretty good. Yes please." He placed the jar in the cabinet.

"After the coffee, do you have anything else you need to get done before I turn the generator off?"

"Hmm, maybe we could watch some Jeopardy," she answered with a smirk.

Charles shook his head. "I'll take that as a no."

"While I make the coffee, go ahead and light the lanterns before you shut it down," Edna replied.

"Sounds good. I'll get started on that now." He hung the dish towels on the oven handle to dry and retrieved a long lighter from a drawer before heading toward the bedroom.

As he disappeared around the corner, there was a knock at the door.

"Now, who could that be?" Edna said out loud, starting for the door.

Charles came back around the corner, trying to get his revolver out of the holster.

"Wait Edna!" he demanded as he finally extracted the little .38 Special.

She froze.

"Let me check it first." He passed his wife, pulled the curtain back on the door, and glanced outside. Relaxing, he returned the gun to his holster. "It's just Jenny."

"Well, don't just stand there, let her in."

Charles huffed, unlocked the door, and opened it.

"I'm sorry to bother you at this hour. Would it be okay if I came in?" she asked meekly.

Edna stepped up beside her husband. "Of course, Jenny. Come in, come in. Is everything alright?"

The couple stepped back from the door, allowing her to enter.

She walked in and stopped by the table. "Um, yes. Everything is okay. I mean I guess it is." She glanced back toward the open door.

Edna noticed a slight discoloration on the left side of Jenny's face. *Was that a bruise?*

Jenny continued. "I, uh, just wanted to tell you how much we appreciated everything you've done to help us."

"It's fine, but why did you need to come over now? It's late. Did something else happ..." Edna was interrupted as the door burst open and Billy rushed in. He had a wooden ball bat and was running straight at Charles. Edna screamed.

Jenny fell backwards against the wall and pulled her knees up to her chest. She put her head down and pressed her hands against her ears as she started to sob.

Charles stepped backwards, grabbing for his revolver with his right hand as Billy swung the bat. Instinctively, Charles threw his left arm up to protect himself from the assault and the bat connected with his forearm with an audible *crack* as the ulna fractured. The impact knocked him to the ground in front of the open door to the pantry. He clutched his broken arm to his chest.

Edna screamed at Billy. "What are you doing?! Stop!" She looked over at Jenny who was now rocking forward and back. Her eyes were squeezed shut and her hands were still over her ears.

Billy took a step to reach Charles and bent over to pull the revolver from the holster. "You won't be needing this anymore."

Charles glared at Billy, cradling his arm.

Standing up, Billy stuffed the gun into the front of his jeans, still holding the bat with the other hand. He turned around to face Edna and pointed the end of the bat at her.

"You! Sit down and shut up!" He kicked a chair in her direction.

"You don't have to do this! We're more than happy to help you. I already told Jenny that. All you had to do was ask," Edna implored.

"And I told *you* to shut up! Now sit down and shut up!" He was fully focused on her now. "You people and all your food! You're just giving us scraps so you can make yourself feel superior! I bet you brag to all your rich friends about how you donate to the poor, don't you?!"

"What are you talking about?!" Edna asked, exasperated.

"You know exactly what I'm talking about! Jenny came over here to tell you we didn't have any food and what did you give her? Huh? You gave her some Mason jars and instant potatoes. You have years of food in here and you couldn't be bothered to share enough to make a difference!" Spittle flew from his mouth as he screamed at her.

"I gave her what she could carry," pleaded Edna. "I told her to come back when she needed more! I don't understand why you're doing this!"

"I'll tell you why I'm doing this! All this food you have in here." He glanced back toward the pantry and was looking down the barrel of shotgun. The end of the barrel looked as big as a golf ball.

Charles was still sitting on the floor, but had grabbed the shotgun from the pantry and now held it in his uninjured right hand and was supporting it in the crook of his injured arm.

Billy heard the *click* of the safety coming off and dove to the floor as the shotgun blast passed over his head. The kitchen window behind him exploded into the night.

Quickly, Charles lay the gun on the floor with the butt against his leg. Working as fast as he could, he reached up, grabbed the slide and pulled it to the rear, ejecting the spent shell. Picking the gun up by the slide with his one good hand, he shook it and the slide went forward, loading the next round. Billy dove on him before he could get it back into position to fire again.

Billy pressed the revolver into Charles' neck. The ball bat was now abandoned on the floor behind him.

"I should kill you right here for that, old man," he said through clenched teeth. His face was crazed and he was breathing hard. His breath smelled of stale cigarette smoke. He reached over and grasped the shotgun, ripping it from Charles's hand. He kept the pistol trained on Charles and stood up. Charles still didn't speak, he just continued to glower at the man.

Edna's chair squeaked on the tile floor as she stood up, focused on the bat. Billy didn't take his eyes off Charles, but spoke to Edna. "Sit back down old woman. I'll blow his head off before you can get there."

Edna obeyed, starting to cry.

"What do I do with you?" he asked out loud. "Oh, I know what I'm going to do." Billy said, grinning. "We're going to go for a little walk. Jenny, come here."

Jenny didn't respond. She was still in the same spot, rocking forward and back, bouncing lightly again against the wall.

"Jenny!" he yelled.

She looked up, tears streaming down her face. "I'm sorry!" she cried, looking at Edna. "I didn't want to! He made me!"

Edna looked at the young woman and understood exactly what had happened. She was scared of her husband.

"Shut up! Shut your mouth, you stupid bitch!" Billy screamed at Jenny. "Now get your ass up and come over here!" He kept the revolver pointed at Charles with his right hand while holding the shotgun in his left.

Jenny slowly began to move.

"Hurry up! Get over here!"

She got to her feet and walked around Edna. Her shoulders were slumped and she was looking at the floor as she walked.

Billy stepped back so he could more easily see both Charles and Edna at the same time. As Jenny made it to him, he offered her the revolver. "Here, you keep this pointed at the old lady. Me and gramps are gonna take a walk. If she tries anything, you shoot her, understand?"

Jenny was shaking her head violently. "No. No. No," she sobbed. "I can't. I can't do that."

Billy grabbed her hand and put it on the revolver. "Here. Take it! Now!"

Jenny snatched her hand back and looked up at Billy. Her eyes were puffy and she screamed back at him. "I can't! Okay? I can't do that!"

"Dammit, woman! Do you want to eat or not? Do what I say!"

"I can't do that Billy! You know I can't do that!" She dropped her face back into her hands and began to sob more loudly.

"Oh, this is just great!" Billy roared. "I guess I just have to do everything! *As usual!*" He tucked the revolver back into his pants again and brought the shotgun up, pointed at Edna's chest. He glanced over at Charles. "Alright, Gramps. Get up!"

Charles looked at the shotgun and then at his crying wife and began to struggle to his feet.

Billy stepped back again until he backed into the stove, keeping distance between himself and Charles. "Now, go the door!"

Charles began to slowly walk to the door.

"You too, lady!" Billy commanded. "Apparently, I can't trust her to keep an eye on you, so I'll just take you with me. You're gonna walk behind your husband and if he tries anything, I'll blow you in half." He made eye contact with Charles. "You got that?"

"I won't try anything," Charles responded. "Come on, Honey. It's okay. Let's just do what he says."

Edna got to her feet and embraced her husband. He winced as the hug jostled his broken arm, but he didn't pull away from her.

"Enough of that lovey-dovey crap!" Billy interrupted. "Let's go! Out the door."

Jenny was now leaning back against the counter, her arms wrapped around her chest in a self-embrace, crying.

Charles and Edna started for the door, Billy following them a few feet behind. As he passed the baseball bat, he reached down and grabbed it, tucking it under his arm. He glanced over at Jenny as he passed her. "You're freakin' pathetic!" he spat at her and then returned his attention to the task of moving the couple out the door.

Charles stopped at the bottom of the steps and offered his good hand to Edna to help her down the steps.

"Oh, that's sooo sweet," Billy shot, sarcastically. "Now turn left. We're going to the barn."

Charles and Edna did as they were told, walking past the still-running generator. When they reached the barn door, Billy demanded that Charles unlock it.

"I can't see it," Charles said.

Edna retrieved the light from her pocket and held it out to her husband. "Hold the light for me Charles. I'll get it for you," Edna offered.

Charles accepted the light and illuminated the combination lock as Edna entered the numbers.

"Give me that light," Billy barked.

Charles held the light out. Billy snatched it from his hand and took a step back. "Now, open the door!"

Charles pulled at the door with his right arm, grunting, and the door slid open a few feet.

"Inside!" Billy demanded.

Charles and Edna stepped into the darkness, the light from the flashlight spilling around them on both sides. Billy followed them in and sat the flashlight on the workbench so that it illuminated Charles's work area. "Now, turn around and face the wall."

Edna's face was a mask of fear.

"Oh, relax lady. I'm not gonna shoot you. Now turn around." They couldn't see the contemptuous look on Billy's face as it was shrouded in darkness with the light behind him now.

Charles and Edna slowly turned around. Edna lightly tucked her right hand behind Charles's upper arm, being careful not to apply any pressure that might cause him more pain.

Quietly, Billy placed the butt of the shotgun on the floor and leaned it against the workbench. He pulled the baseball bat from under his arm and without hesitation, drew back and swung it at Charles' head, connecting with a sickening *thud*. Charles crumpled forward to the floor.

Edna screamed and dropped to the floor grasping at her husband. She looked up at Billy, the light flooding past him. "Why did you do that?!" she screamed, sobbing into her husband's back.

"That's what he gets for trying to shoot me!" Billy spat. "Now get up!"

Edna didn't move. She tried to inspect his head and her hand came away covered in blood. She shrieked again.

"Shut up, woman!" Billy yelled. He dropped the bat and reached down and hauled her up by the arm, pulling her to her feet. She tried to return to her husband, but he clamped down and held her in place. He turned and slung her out the door. She stumbled and fell into the gravel on her hands and knees. Billy retrieved the shotgun and followed her out the door.

She continued to sob, making no effort to get up.

"Holy crap woman. Quit being so dramatic. Now get up!" He pulled her to her feet a second time and started dragging her to the house. When he got to the door, he slung it open and pushed her into the kitchen. He followed her in and shoved her back into the same chair she had been in earlier.

Jenny was still in the same place, leaning against the counter, crying. Billy didn't acknowledge her. He leaned the shotgun back against his shoulder and faced Edna. "Now, this is what's going to happen. First things first, you're going to make us something to eat." Billy sighed. "You're gonna have to stop crying woman so you can listen."

Edna was unable to stop. She was doubled over with her elbows on her thighs, crying into her hands. Billy stepped forward and slapped her hands away from her face. He grabbed her by the chin and raised her face up to look at him.

"There! That's better. Now, as I was saying, you're going to cook me some dinner while I decide what's next. Do you understand?"

She was trying to catch her breath. "You didn't have to do that," she said in a weak voice. "He was all I had."

"Well, he shouldn't have taken a shot at me, so here we are. Now get up and make me something to eat! And wash your damn hands first. I don't need his blood in my dinner."

Edna slowly started to get to her feet. She still couldn't breathe. Every time she tried to take a breath, it hitched in her chest. She slowly shuffled over to the sink and began washing her hands in the dishwater that was still there.

Billy looked over at Jenny. "And you! Go look around our new digs. This place looks pretty good. They've got power and everything. Go check out the bedroom. Let's see where you're gonna to earn your keep tonight."

Jenny just nodded slowly and walked out of the room. She avoided looking anywhere near Edna.

Edna retrieved a hand towel from the front of the oven and dried her hands as she walked to the refrigerator, still crying. She pulled out some bacon and a carton of fresh eggs, placing them on the counter. She started to pull open a drawer and Billy grabbed her wrist. "Let's get one thing out of the way. If you try to grab a kitchen knife or something, I'll use it to chop off a finger." He threw her hand away from him and retreated to the other side of the kitchen, pulling a chair with him. He sat down with his back to the wall and lay the shotgun across his lap, watching her work.

In the barn, Charles opened his eyes to darkness. His head hurt as badly as anything he could remember. His thoughts seemed to tumble through space as he tried to focus. He felt every heartbeat. He tried to push himself over onto his back and a new pain shot through his arm like electricity. He groaned and used just his good arm to push off the ground and roll himself onto his back. It was so dark he couldn't tell if his eyes were actually open or not. Slowly, he raised his head and he saw the open door of the barn. He could see the broken kitchen window where light was spilling out into the night.

Struggling through the pain, he fought his way up onto his feet, using a support column for balance. He stood, leaned back against the column for a moment panting, struggling to maintain his balance. Tentatively, he touched the right side of his head and felt the open wound from the blow. Wiping the blood on his pants, he took a breath. *At least he didn't shoot me.*

He dug into his pocket and pulled out his little flashlight. He placed his fingers over the bulb and turned it on. *I need a weapon.* He let a little light escape from between his fingers and looked around. He saw the bat on the ground. It had a smear of blood on it. *That won't do me any good with one arm.* He moved on to the work bench and sat the light down, covering it partially with a shop towel so it only offered a soft glow, just enough to see. He saw the selection of chains and thought of an idea. He selected a short, lightweight chain and retrieved the bowl of padlocks from the shelf. He sat the bowl on the bench and stopped to catch his breath. Panting, he winced as he pulled one the padlocks out and locked it onto the last link of the chain. He pulled the key out and dropped it absentmindedly onto the bench. *Okay. That might work.*

Charles took a test swing with the chain and pain shot through his injured arm from the movement. *I'm going to need to bind that arm before I do anything.*

He scanned the shop a second time and found his duct tape. Using his teeth to get it started, he pulled off a section and reached across his body, over the injured arm and stuck the end to his shirt. Carefully, he pulled the tape across his torso, pinning his arm against his abdomen, then wrapped it around his back.

Backing up to the bench, he laid the roll down, reached around to the front again, grabbed the tape, and repeated the process until his arm was more or less immobilized. He pulled out enough tape to bring it up to his mouth, tore it with his teeth, and pressed the end to his shirt.

Leaning back against the bench, he dropped the tape onto the bench and reached for the chain again. Standing, he took another test swing. It hurt -- but not nearly as much. His head still throbbed, but he could manage this.

He gave it one more swing. *Yeah, this'll work.*

He retrieved his light, turned it off, and stowed it back in his pocket. He carefully returned to the open door and peered out. He saw movement through the open kitchen window.

Edna! She's okay! He felt a bolt of renewed energy surge through his body. *I can do this.* He carefully picked his way across the driveway, being careful to lift his feet so he didn't kick any gravel that would betray his approach.

He worked his way up to the open door and carefully eased around until he could see into the lit room. He couldn't see Edna from this angle, but he could hear something. He suddenly became aware of the smell of cooking bacon! *That psycho is making her cook for him!* Rage overtook him, fueling his resolve. He squeezed the chain in his hand. *On the count of three. One...two...three!* He reached up and grabbed the storm door, pulling it open and attempting to run as best he could.

Billy jumped up, startled from the sudden appearance of a what appeared to be something out of a horror movie. This figure was running across the kitchen at him with his face covered in blood and screaming like a madman! As Billy jumped up, the shotgun that had been sitting in his lap was launched across the kitchen and landed in the floor, sliding toward the stove.

Charles swung the chain in a wide arc, aiming for Billy's head. But Billy took a step forward and the chain impacted the side of his head, wrapped around the back of his head, and the lock struck him on the other side, just behind his ear. He staggered and took an uncoordinated swing at Charles, but the impact from the blow had him disoriented and he only punched the air. He lunged forward and shoved Charles backwards. They both fell to the floor in a heap. Charles' head struck the floor and light flashed in his vision as pain assaulted him from both his head and his arm. Billy was almost instantly on top of him, raised up onto his knees. He drew his fist back, preparing to punch Charles in the face, but Charles grasped for the revolver in Billy's waist band.

Billy abandoned the punch and grabbed at the gun. Billy was stronger and had two hands versus Charles' one. He wrenched the gun from Charles' hand, turned it, and fired point blank into Charles' chest. Gasping for breath, Billy saw movement in front of him as Edna stood up with the big shotgun, bringing it up toward him.

The little revolver was much easier to maneuver. He quickly raised it and fired twice, striking her in the abdomen. The twelve-gauge clattered to the floor. Edna fell back against the counter and grasped at her bleeding belly. Looking down, she dropped to her knees, waivered, and then fell forward beside her husband. His head was turned toward her and she was looking into his eyes, but he could no longer see her.

Billy jumped to his feet. "Look what you made me do! Look what you made me do! This is your fault!" he bellowed. "This is your fault!"

Jenny came running into the room and stopped when she saw Charles and Edna on the floor, blood spreading across the tile from under their bodies. Her hands shot up to her mouth, but she couldn't make a sound.

Edna slowly reached out and placed her hand on her husband's shoulder. She took a ragged breath and just stared into his eyes.

Billy stormed over to her screaming, but she could no longer hear him. The edges of her vision began to contract. "I'll see you soon..."

Billy stepped over and looked down at the stricken woman. "You made me do this!" He lifted the pistol with one hand and shot her twice more in the back. He kept pulling the trigger. *Click. Click. Click.* The cylinder was empty.

29

Here We Go Again

Pike County, Kentucky

After escaping from the men who were willing to kill him for his stuff, Scott had caught his breath in the woods beside the river, and then started walking away from the water. He immediately came out of the trees onto a set of train tracks that were running parallel to the river. He turned right and started following the tracks. His wet boots squished with every step and he became concerned that he would get blisters. However, the need to put some distance between himself and the area where the men might be looking trumped any concern about his feet and he pushed on. Less than a mile later the tracks ran under a bridge and he could see an open field just past it. He was concerned that if he tried to cross the field, the men might be able to see him if they were still looking. He decided to leave the tracks and find a place to hide and regroup. To his left was a guard rail separating the tracks from an asphalt backroad. He hopped the guardrail and started across the road.

As he crossed the paved road, he saw a dirt road leading back into the woods and decided that it would be his best choice. He jogged down the dirt road about a hundred yards until he saw a reasonably flat area in the woods and darted in, glancing behind himself nervously. He kept walking until he could no longer see the dirt road and collapsed to the forest floor. Squirming out of his pack straps, he pulled his go bag around in front of him. He had a camouflage 4'x6' tarp secured to the bottom. He pulled that off and spread it onto the ground, taking a seat on it. He pulled out his waterproof clothing bag and extracted a microfiber towel and one of his two pairs of clean socks.

The next item was his hygiene kit, which was in a Ziploc bag. He grabbed the travel sized bottle of foot powder from that and started getting out of his boots. A few minutes later, he was in dry socks with freshly powdered feet. His boots were sitting beside him with the insoles pulled out to dry. He took a long drink from his Nalgene bottle and lay back on the tarp. *Well crap. I'm apparently walking the rest of the way.* He tried to calculate how far he had left. Reflexively, he reached for his phone. *It wasn't there. Oh, it's in the Jeep. It probably would've gotten destroyed in the river anyhow.* He sighed. This was a lot.

He looked at his watch. *I think I had a little over an hour to go driving, so I'm probably forty-five to fifty miles from Mom and Dad's.* He had a lot of hiking experience, and he knew that he could get fifteen miles in a day, maybe twenty if he pushed himself. *Let's say, best case, three days.* He sighed again. *This sucks.*

He checked his food. He had two of the freeze-dried meals Paul had made him, spaghetti with sauce and a breakfast scramble. Plus, he had one pack of beef jerky, three energy bars, and one packet of trail mix. One advantage was that Paul's freeze-dried meals had more food in them than the store-bought variety. *I could probably break those into two meals each. I have three energy bars, that's one a day, and*

I'll still have the jerky and trail mix. That's enough. I guess it'll have to be, won't it?

He checked the other items in the bag. He had a Sawyer Mini water filter with its pouch and syringe for flushing it, a bottle of water purification tablets, a fire starter kit in a small Tupperware container, a folding saw, a bottle of insect repellent, some paracord, three bunji cords, and a small garden trowel that he called his "poop scoop." He sat all those items to the side and pulled out a Mora fixed blade knife and a Leatherman. The bottom of the bag had a small, one quart camping-style cookpot with a little stove stand that would allow him to cook over a fire. He had recently added a box of 9mm ammunition and that box had gotten waterlogged in the river. It was one of the few items that hadn't been waterproofed. A few rounds of the ammo spilled out into the bag when he pulled it out. He fished some of them out and used them to top off the magazine in his pocket. He had put the full magazine in his pistol after shooting the man earlier. His mind went back to that encounter. He closed his eyes and took a cleansing breath. *He was going to shoot me. It was him or me.* Then he thought about the group trying to collect 'taxes' in Asheville and repeated the same words he had muttered then. "Play stupid games, win stupid prizes."

The final item in the bottom of the bag was a small fishing kit. It didn't have much in it, but he still opened it to do a quick inventory. There was a little roll of 6-pound test monofilament, several different types of hooks, a few sinkers, and one small bobber. He checked the bottom of the pack to see if he had missed anything. It was empty. He checked the side zipper pockets. One was empty. That's where the spare Glock magazine had been. However, the other side had a Petzl headlamp in a Ziploc bag. It was the Aria 1 RGB model with red, green, and blue options in addition to standard white.

Three additional AAA batteries were taped together in the bottom of the same pocket. *Oh yeah, I forgot about that.*

He looked at the food and decided he was fine for now. He reloaded the pack and slipped his wet socks under the straps on the outside to allow them to dry. He suddenly felt very tired. He thought he should probably wait until dark to start walking. *Maybe I'll just take a quick nap now and head out around dark.* He lay back and closed his eyes.

Scott awoke with a start. Panic briefly pulled at his mind as he tried to figure out where he was. Then it all came back to him in a rush. The ambush, the river crossing, finding this place in the woods. He checked his watch. It was 10:35. *Dang it!* He bolted upright and felt around for his boots. *Crap! I need my headlamp.* He felt for his pack and retrieved the light. Using the red-lens option, he got his boots back on, stowed the tarp, and got ready to move. The boots and pack were still wet, but they weren't as bad as they had been earlier. *Okay, here we go.*

He slipped back out to the pavement, killing the light as soon as he could make out the road in the moonlight. He turned north and started walking. After a few minutes, he realized he was walking too fast. If he didn't back it off a little, he'd wear himself out too quickly. He could see the railroad tracks to his right and beyond that, the river. He knew Route 23 was on the other side of the river, although he couldn't see it. That's the road he'd been on when he was trapped by the... *What were they? Ambushers? Criminals? Bad guys?* He didn't know exactly what to call them. The word *highwaymen* came to mind. Scott shook his head. *No. These were just assholes.*

He had no idea how long this road paralleled 23, but as long as it did, he was going to stay on it. A little after eleven o'clock, he heard gunshots. He stopped and strained to listen, trying to determine the direction they had come from. As he was about to start walking again, he heard two more shots. He was certain these had come from across the river, but in front of him. *Oh, that's just great,* he thought and started walking again. His feet were feeling the results of the impact on the pavement, plus his wet boots had already soaked through his dry socks. This was different than hiking on trails. It was certainly flatter and he didn't have to worry about tripping on a root or rock, but the surface was harder and he found himself trying to soften his steps to lessen the impact. Even with the discomfort, he felt like he was making pretty good time.

The weather felt pretty good. *Maybe it's better to walk at night anyhow. It's not as hot.* He walked for about forty-five minutes when the road dead-ended at someone's house. *I guess I'm walking the tracks again.* He scrambled down the hill to the rail bed and kept going. At first, he tried walking along the tracks, but found that cumbersome. The spacing of the ties forced him to take steps that felt either too long or too short, so he worked his way back down to the edge of the ballast and continued walking.

After another half hour, he felt like he needed a break. He didn't even look for a spot, he just stopped and sat down in the gravel. He instantly felt the relief on his feet. He pulled out his Nalgene bottle and took a big drink. Looking at the bottle, he saw that he was down to about a quarter of the one-liter bottle. He remembered Paul saying that your best canteen is your body, but he still wanted to keep some water in the bottle for his next stop. *I need to start looking for an area with easy river access to go get some more water to filter.*

He recalled a conversation with Paul when Paul had told him that the standard in the infantry was twelve miles in three hours with a forty-five-pound rucksack and rifle. He said that to do that, you needed to walk at a brisk pace. *What's that even mean? A brisk pace.* He thought about his pace so far and checked the time. He had woken up at 10:35, so it was probably around 10:50, maybe 10:55 by the time he had started walking. It was now 12:15. *Almost an hour and a half. That's probably around five miles, at least four.* He shook his head slightly in the dark. If his original estimate of fifty miles was correct, and he had covered five miles so far, then he still had forty-five miles to go. *I can't think about it like that. I need to think of it as fifteen miles a day. That means I only have ten miles to go before I rest. That sounds better.*

He stowed the bottle and stood up to a mild sting in the bottom of his feet and started walking again. The first few steps stung, but as he continued to walk, it got a little better. He debated turning on his headlamp. He had it draped around his neck right now, but he still didn't feel comfortable. Of course, it was after midnight, so it would probably be okay. He considered it again and decided to continue to walk without it for now and see how it goes. There was still some moonlight, although it was not nearly as much as he would have preferred.

As he walked, he devised a plan in his head. *I'll walk for an hour and a half, take a break, then walk another hour and a half. That should be about fifteen miles, more or less. Then I'll find a place to camp for the daylight hours.* His stomach rumbled. *And get something to eat,* he thought.

Several times throughout the night a road or path would run parallel to the tracks and Scott would hop over onto the better surface to walk. He also used his headlamp in a few places. Several times he passed by dark houses that were built along the tracks. He was careful in these areas to be quiet and not use his light for anything. As he passed Betsy Layne on the other side of the river, the tracks curved to the left. There were several houses along the right side of the tracks and a single lane asphalt road along the left side. The road was in rough shape, but it was still better than trying to walk on the tracks. He looked at the houses across the tracks.

Everything was dark. He stopped and observed, listening intently for any sound that might indicate that people were around. He glanced down at his watch. It was 3:45 in the morning and he was utterly exhausted. He had to keep going. He wanted to get away from the houses before searching for a place to set up camp. His feet throbbed, his shoulders ached, and the muscles of his legs were feeling rubbery. He needed water. He had emptied his Nalgene bottle during the last stop. *I wonder if the water is still working in those houses. I bet I could grab some from an outside spigot.* He took a step toward the railroad tracks, then hesitated. *Screw it. It'll only take a minute. If their water is coming from a water tower, they should still have pressure.* He pulled his water bottle out and started across the tracks toward the closest house.

He couldn't see any lights, so he went to the corner of the house and started walking around it, looking for a garden hose. It has gotten darker as the moon had dipped below the horizon. He tripped on a kid's bicycle and went down. He muttered a curse under his breath. Inside the house, a dog sounded a single bark. He froze and waited. *Maybe this was a bad idea.* He saw a flashlight beam pass by a window from inside the house. He got back to his feet and headed back the direction he had come. His heart was racing. He reached the tracks a moment later and carefully picked his way across them back to the road and resumed his march toward home.

"Crap!" he said in a low voice as he pushed on in the darkness. People had been throwing trash out along the sides of the road and as he walked, he saw an empty two-liter soft drink bottle in the ditch. He quickly scooped it up and kept going. At least there was enough light to see the road. Another three hundred yards and the road separated from the tracks, going up into the hills, so he jumped back on the tracks again. They went into a wooded area with no roads or evidence of structures. *This is promising.* He continued until he felt like he was far enough away from the homes that he wouldn't be discovered when the sun came up. He turned his headlamp on, using the red light setting and moved into the wooded area between the tracks and the river, finally settling on a spot that was nearly flat.

He collapsed onto the ground. *Holy crap. I don't know if that was fifteen miles or not, but that sucked.* He extracted himself from his pack straps and pulled out the tarp. The mosquitoes had been aggravating him earlier, so he had applied insect repellent during his last break; now he felt like he needed some more. He spread the tarp out on the ground and sat down. He was soaked with sweat and his feet were throbbing, so he untied his boots and gingerly pulled his feet out. His feet were wet. He was sure it was a mixture of river water and sweat. Carefully, he began massaging his feet. It hurt, but after a couple minutes he felt like it might have helped a little. He slid over to one side of the tarp and stretched out, pulling the pack with him to use as a pillow. He pulled the other side of the tarp over him like a taco and soon fell asleep.

A couple of hours later as the sun was coming up, a pain in Scott's right calf pulled him from his sleep. He immediately tried to stretch out his leg as the cramp pulled at the muscle. "Ow, ow, ow. Oh, come on!" he said out loud. He quickly got to his feet and started stretching. *Apparently, I'm dehydrated.* He continued the stretch until he got the muscle cramp to subside. *Okay, I need food and water. That was horrible.* He slipped on his boots, which were still damp, and grabbed his Nalgene bottle, his Sawyer water filter and the pouch that went with it. There was plenty of light now, so he picked his way over to the water's edge. The water was low, so he had to drop down from the bank about three feet to reach it. Squatting, he held the Sawyer pouch in the water, so it could flow into the pouch. It didn't work. The pouch was flat and there wasn't enough pressure from the flowing water to make it open up.

Frustrated, he pulled the pouch out of the water and remembered the two-liter bottle he had picked up last night. He worked his way back up to his pack and got the bottle from the ground beside where he had been sleeping. He returned to the river and held the bottle under the flowing water. It filled. The Sawyer Mini water filter had the same thread pattern as a standard soft drink bottle, so Scott threaded the filter directly onto the bottle. He opened the top of his Nalgene and held the filter so it would discharge into his bottle. He squeezed the two-liter bottle and clean water started coming out of the filter and filling his bottle. Once he had it about a third full, he laid the bottle/filter combo on the bank, grabbed the Nalgene, and drank it all. He let out a breath as he finished it. "*Aaaah*". A few more cycles with the filter and he had a full water bottle. He refilled the two-liter from the river, capped it, and took it with him.

Back at what he now thought of as his campsite, he used his trowel to dig a small hole for a fire. He wanted to make some breakfast. Looking around the area, he collected a small pile of sticks and dumped them beside the hole. He pulled out his fire starter kit and found the little medicine bottle in it. He opened it and fished out one of the cotton balls that was infused with petroleum jelly. He placed it in the bottom of the hole and lit it with a lighter from the kit. He immediately started feeding small twigs into the flame until he had a small but consistent fire going. He placed his stove stand over the flame and sat the cookpot on it, adding about a cup of the filtered water. He wasn't worried about getting it to a boil, but he did want it good and warm.

Once he saw the bubbles starting to form around the edges of the pot, he dumped in half of the freeze-dried breakfast scramble, stirred it, and placed the lid on it. He lifted the pot from the fire and placed it on the ground beside his tarp. He used the trowel to remove the stove stand and then immediately kicked the dirt back into the hole and stomped it down, smothering the fire instantly and preventing it from smoldering. He didn't want smoke pointing anyone to his hiding spot.

A few minutes later, Scott enjoyed a hot breakfast and drank the rest of the water in his bottle. His mind wandered to the Glock getting dunked in the water yesterday. It was probably fine, but he'd feel better if he at least wiped it down. He cleared the gun and pulled the slide off, removed the recoil spring and barrel, and quickly wiped everything with his T-shirt. He looked inside the frame. He didn't see any water, so he put everything back together, reloaded it and secured it back in its holster. The whole endeavor only took about three or four minutes.

Throughout the rest of the day, he ended up refilling the bottle two more times, trying to hydrate for the upcoming night's walk. He aired out his feet, socks and boots and tried to sleep as much as he could. He considered throwing out a fishing line, but felt like he was too close to houses to risk trying to cook a fish over an open fire. During one of his naps, he tucked one pair of the still-damp socks into his T-shirt. When he woke up, they were nearly completely dry, so he put them back in his shirt, opting to leave them there so his body heat could finish drying them out before he left. Around six in the evening, he added half of the spaghetti to his cookpot with some water and sat it to the side to rehydrate. He opted against the fire this time, reasoning that people were much more likely to be awake now versus this morning at dawn. He hoped there was enough salt in the meal to help stave off the cramps. He saved the energy bar, deciding to eat it during his first stop of the night.

He packed everything up as soon as the sun started dipping toward the ridgeline to the west. The light hadn't quite started to fade, but he was ready to get moving. His feet felt better, he was hydrated and he had taken some Motrin from his hygiene kit. Even though he wouldn't have admitted it, the largest factor was that he was just bored and ready to get moving again. He shouldered his pack and started working his way back up to the railroad tracks. Turning to look down the tracks, he sighed. "Here we go again."

Over the Precipice

30

He Showed Mercy

August 13, 7:00 a.m.

Paul and Sandy's Farm

Paul and Dangle were loading up Paul's pickup truck for the return trip to pick up Charles, Edna, and Scott. Paul had tried to call his parents several times, but the call wouldn't go through. He and Dangle had put all their gear into the back seat, opting to leave the bed of the truck empty for additional cargo on the return trip.

Paul walked back into the house. "Hey, Babe. We're about ready to leave."

Sandy was nervous. "You've already talked to Tom?"

"Yeah. Let's do another radio check with him right now." Paul picked up the radio from the kitchen island. "Copperhead, Copperhead, this is Doc. Radio check, over."

Nothing.

Sandy instantly looked concerned.

"Copperhead, Copperhead, this is Doc. Radio check, over."

The radio squawked back. "Doc, this is Copperhead, I have you Lima Charlie. How me? Over."

Sandy instantly relaxed.

"Copperhead, Doc. I have you same. I'm about to do that thing we talked about, over."

"Good copy Doc. I got you. Over."

"Thanks Copperhead. Doc out."

He held the radio out to her. "Make sure you keep the radio with you at all times, okay?"

"Definitely," she said, grabbing it and clipping it onto her belt.

"McKinley too. Make sure she keeps hers on her. And you both need to keep your pistols on you at all times. Keep your rifles close. I know you and McKinley have your .22s, but if you need a rifle, I want you to grab your AR. They're the same ones we've been practicing with."

"I know, I know," she said. "I'm just so much more comfortable with the .22."

"I know you are, but the 5.56 is a better defensive round than the .22, so if you think you need a rifle, grab the AR and call Tom. He's only a few minutes away."

She huffed. "Please hurry back. I don't like this at all."

"It should be just like last time. I'll run down there, they should be packed up, we'll grab them and come straight home. Scott will be with them, so we'll have plenty of help," Paul said, trying to reassure her.

He gave her a kiss on the cheek. "You got this, Babe."

She rolled her eyes at him. "Yeah, yeah. Just hurry up, okay?"

He winked at her with a lopsided grin. "Yes ma'am."

Paul went to his office and opened the safe, extracting another AR-15. This one was his replica of the Vietnam-era Special Forces XM-177 carbine. It had a fixed carrying handle and was a gray color in contrast to his black AR-15, although functionally, they were essentially the same. He walked out with the little rifle and a camouflage bandoleer with three additional thirty round magazines in it.

Sandy saw him as he headed for the door and realized that it wasn't his normal rifle. "That's the gun you're taking?"

He stopped with his hand on the doorknob. "No. Dad doesn't have an AR. I'm taking this one for him so he'll have it for the trip back. Scott has his own."

"You keep pulling ARs out of that safe like clowns out of a clown car. How many do you actually have?"

Paul smiled. "Sorry, that's classified."

"Get out of here and hurry up!"

He turned and headed out the door, calling over his shoulder. "Love you!"

A couple minutes later, Paul and Dangle were easing down his driveway and an hour after that they were approaching the bridge over the Big Sandy River. Several people were milling around the bridge and one of the men motioned for Paul to stop. Paul just waved and offered a smile, but kept going.

"What was that?" Dangle asked.

"I don't know, but I had no intention of stopping."

"Agreed," Dangle offered. He pulled his phone out. "We had cell service the last time we came through here."

"How about now?"

"Nah," Dangle said, putting the phone away. "Nothing."

"Figures."

They continued to drive. Dangle looked for a radio station at one point, but was unable to find anything. Paul's old truck didn't have the satellite radio like the Durango did.

When they were finally approaching Charles and Edna's house, Paul slowed to make the turn into the driveway and saw an additional car in the driveway. He immediately accelerated and passed the driveway.

He pointed it out to Dangle. "I'm going to go up here, stop on the side of the road, and approach by foot. I want to see what's going on," he said.

"Got it." Dangle didn't need further explanation. He understood. Paul and Dangle had known each other for a long time and had worked together extensively. At times like this, it showed.

They both exited the truck and donned their plate carriers. They also both grabbed their AR-15s. Approaching through the woods, they emerged across the driveway from the house. After observing for movement, they quickly advanced to the side of the house. An old Honda Civic sat in front of Charles' truck. Paul glanced into the bed of the truck. There were household items and clothes he didn't recognize. He moved along the side of the house, closing the distance to the kitchen door. He stopped at the door, his AR at the high ready. Dangle came up behind him and gave him a squeeze on the shoulder. Paul nodded and Dangle reached past Paul, grasped the door, and flung it open. Paul burst through the door with Dangle close on his heels. Paul broke to the right, clearing the kitchen. Dangle broke left, bypassed the table, and locked down on the open door to the pantry.

Jenny screamed from the pantry as Dangle appeared in the doorway. Paul flowed past him toward the entryway that led to the living room and the bedrooms. He could see that the living room was empty, so he broke to the left toward his parents' bedroom. Billy was coming out the door with a shotgun in one hand. Paul stopped and locked down on Billy. His AR-15 was pointed at Billy's chest.

Billy froze.

"Drop the gun!" Paul ordered.

Billy looked down at the shotgun that was not in any position to fire. "Okay. Okay, man. Let's everyone stay calm, Buddy." He offered a smile, attempting to appear friendly.

"Drop it!" Paul repeated.

Dangle passed behind Paul, checking the remainder of the house.

"Okay, man. I'm going to put it down. I'm going to. But how 'bout you lower your gun too. We don't want no accidents here," Billy said, almost nonchalant.

"Not going to happen. Do it now!" Paul raised his voice with this command.

Billy's mind raced as he tried to figure out how to kill this guy. He looked like a soldier, but talked like a cop. *This is a problem.* He leaned forward as if to put the shotgun on the floor gently. Without any warning, he slung it underhanded right at Paul's face and charged him.

Paul used his gun to deflect the shotgun just as Billy impacted into Paul's midsection. Paul allowed the momentum to take him backwards, letting go of his rifle and grasping Billy's clothing. Rolling onto his back, Paul simultaneously brought his leg up, planting his foot into Billy's pelvis and launching him right over top of himself. Paul held on tightly to Billy's shirt and followed him over. Billy landed hard on his back as Paul used the momentum to follow him over. Billy opened his eyes and Paul was on top of him with his pistol in his face. *What the hell just happened?* Billy's eyes went wide.

He looked up at Paul, who appeared completely calm. Dangle came running back into the room. "The house is cl…" He assessed the situation. "Oh, well this is new. Uh, the house is clear. The girl is zip-tied in the pantry."

"Cover him while I stand up," Paul said. "If he makes a move, shoot him in the hip."

"The hip?" Billy screamed. "Why would you do that?"

Paul carefully stood up. He saw a pistol on Billy's belt and used his left hand to take it. It was a 1911. Paul stepped back, putting distance between himself and the man on the floor. "Because," Paul said. "It'll kill you, but it takes a long time." He glanced down at the 1911. It was his father's.

Billy's eyes went wide again. "Okay, okay. Let's not do nothin' crazy, fellas."

"You got him, Dangle?" Paul asked.

Dangle had dropped his AR and it hung loosely from the sling in front of him. He had his Glock 19 trained on Billy. "Oh yeah. Go ahead."

Paul holstered his 9mm pistol and inspected the 1911. It was loaded, with one in the chamber, but the hammer was forward. He cocked the hammer and looked over the sights at Billy.

"Where are my parents?" Paul asked calmly, the 1911 now held firmly in a two-handed grip and pointed right at Billy's face.

"Oh, uh they went out. They uh, they said we could stay here until they got back. You know, just keep an eye on the place. We're helping them out." Billy was sweating, trying to make up this story as fast as he could.

"Dangle, bring the girl in here."

Dangle passed by Billy, staying far enough away that he couldn't reach him. He returned a moment later, guiding Jenny in front of him. Her hands were still bound behind her and she was crying.

Paul didn't take his eyes off Billy, but spoke to Jenny. "Okay, spill it."

Billy turned to look at Jenny and his face contorted into rage. "You better keep your damn mouth shut, bitch!" He didn't see Paul take a step forward.

Paul raised his right foot and stomped down hard on Billy's testicles. Billy screeched in pain and doubled over, rolling onto his side.

Paul calmly stepped back; the big .45 caliber pistol still trained on Billy. "As I was saying, young lady. Where are my parents?"

Jenny appeared to be on the verge of hyperventilating, tears rolling down her face. "It wasn't me! It wasn't me! He did it! No one was supposed to get hurt! He told me no one would get hurt!"

Paul's expression hardened as the implication of her statement registered. Billy was still on his side curled up. Paul took a knee beside him and pressed the barrel of the pistol into the side of his neck. "What did you do?" He made no effort to mask the anger in his voice.

"It was self-defense, man. It was self-defense. I didn't wanna hurt nobody," Billy squeezed out the words, still struggling to recover from the kick.

Paul tucked the 1911 into his waistband at the small of his back and forcefully rolled Billy onto his stomach, extracting a set of plastic zip-tie cuffs from his plate carrier. Everyone who worked for Tri Point Solutions kept a set on their kit. Paul zipped Billy's hands behind his back and wrestled him to his feet.

"Where are they?" Paul growled.

"They're in the barn, man!" Billy said, gasping for air and having trouble standing upright.

Paul looked over at Dangle. "Keep her here. I got this." He had the 1911 in his hand again.

"Roger." Dangle guided Jenny over to a kitchen chair. "Take a seat."

Paul pushed Billy out the door and shoved him down the steps. Billy missed a step and stumbled forward landing hard against his car. Paul grabbed him again and wrestled him across the driveway toward the barn. The door was closed but not locked. Paul planted one leg behind Billy and pulled him backwards by the cuffs, tripping him. Billy landed hard on his butt. "Take a seat," Paul said, mimicking Dangle's earlier command.

Paul kept the pistol on Billy with his right hand and used his left to open the door. He glanced inside. It was dark, but the light spilling in was enough to see two forms in the middle of the floor. Paul felt his emotions rush over him, but he struggled to maintain control. He didn't want to turn his back on Billy or leave him unattended, so he returned, pulled him to his feet, and slung him into the barn. He had to check. He had to see.

Paul backed up until his parents were to his left and Billy was in front of him. He squatted down to check for a pulse on his father. He was cold to the touch. Paul's head began to swim. *Keep it together.* He stood up and stepped over to his mother. He reached to check her, but saw her eyes. They were fixed and open. The world felt like it was tilting and he shot his hand out to the left, bracing against the support beam.

That's when Billy saw his chance. He turned and bolted for the door. The flash of movement pulled Paul back into the moment. He ran to the door, raised the pistol, and put a single 230 grain full metal jacket into the back of Billy's right thigh. Billy went down in a heap. His hands were still secured behind him and his face plowed into the gravel, cutting his chin. He howled in pain.

Paul put his left hand against the door frame of the barn, steadying himself. Dangle appeared at the door. "We good, Doc?"

Paul looked up. "Yeah. I don't need any help."

Dangle looked at Billy, now writhing in the gravel and shrugged. "Okay." He disappeared back into the house.

Paul slowly walked toward Billy. His eyes were starting to blur with the beginning of tears. He swiped them away with his forearm and refocused. When he got to Billy, he squatted down in front of his face. "Where's my brother?"

"You crazy son of a bitch! You shot me!"

Paul stood back up and quickly delivered a kick to Billy's stomach. Billy exhaled with a grunt. "I'm going to get my answers. This can be as painful as you want to make it," Paul said calmly. "Now, where is my brother?" He enunciated every word.

"I don't know what you're talking about! It was just them! There was no one else here!" Billy screamed back.

Paul considered this for a moment, then yelled over at the door. "Hey Dangle!"

Dangle's head popped out. "Yeah?"

"Ask the girl if Scott was here."

"Okay. Give me a sec." He disappeared back into the house, emerging again a few moments later.

"She says they haven't seen him."

"Thanks."

Dangle disappeared back inside and Paul returned his attention to Billy. For a long moment, he just stared at him. Considering what to do. "Why?" Paul asked, still calm.

Billy looked up at him like he was crazy. "What?"

"Why? Why would you kill them. They would have given you whatever you needed."

Billy scoffed. "Yeah right. They didn't want to help us. They were just doing it so they wouldn't feel guilty and they could tell their church people how generous they are!" Billy spat.

Paul shook his head slightly. "You see the problem is that people like you can't believe that people like them exist. You think that because you're a selfish piece of trash, then surely everyone else is too. They were the kindest people I've ever known and you killed them. For what? For some food that they would have given you anyhow?" This time it was Paul that scoffed.

He took a deep breath to compose himself. He detected a hitch in his breath and fought back his emotions. "My parents were good, Christian people. Yes, they believed in mercy and charity, but not because they wanted to tell everyone about it, but because it was part of who they were and *you* took them from me." Paul felt the rage welling in him. He could feel his face flushing red with the anger.

Paul walked around behind Billy and grabbed him by the zipcuffs, pulling him to his knees.

"I can't stand up, man. You shot me in my leg!"

"You don't need to stand up, get to your knees!" Paul shot back.

Billy managed to stay on his knees in the gravel, most of his weight on his left leg. Blood now soaked his right leg. "Man, you need to stop the bleeding! That shit hurts like hell!"

Paul squatted down so that he was face to face with Billy. Billy looked down at the ground, avoiding Paul's gaze.

"Look at me." Paul said in a calm, even tone, but he could hear his own heartbeat in his head.

Billy didn't look up.

Paul reached around the back of Billy's head and grabbed a handful of greasy hair, pulling down and forcing Billy to look up. Billy was terrified.

"Hey man, like you said. You said it. Your parents believed in mercy."

"That's true," Paul said, cocking his head to one side like a dog trying to decipher English.

He held the pistol in front of Billy's face and Billy started to cry. "Come on man, aren't you a Christian too?"

"I am," Paul said and pulled forward with his left hand as he thrust the pistol forward as hard as he could with his right. He drove the barrel into Billy's mouth, splitting his upper lip and shattering his front teeth. Billy moaned and gagged as the barrel impacted the back of his throat. Paul held it there as Billy tried to pull away. Paul leaned in slightly and spoke in a low voice. "And I believe in an eye for an eye."

Billy tried to scream.

Paul clicked off the safety, moved his left hand from behind Billy's head, and pulled the trigger.

The back of Billy's head where Paul's hand had been a second earlier burst as the round exited. Billy's body was thrown back and his back thudded against the gravel. Paul could have dragged his death out. He could have chosen to take days to kill him, but no. He showed mercy.

31

We're Gonna Need Another Trip

August 13, 11:00 a.m.

Charles and Edna's Farm

Dangle gave Paul some time in the barn. He stayed in the house with Jenny. She was a mess, but had given him the entire story. Billy had been incensed that Charles and Edna had food, a generator and farm animals. He'd said over and over how it wasn't fair and that he deserved to have "his fair share." He had forced her to knock on the door to gain entry. She had initially refused, but he had eventually beaten her into submission. She was legitimately convinced that he was going to kill her if she hadn't cooperated.

Paul walked into the kitchen. Dangle was sitting across from Jenny with a jar of sweet tea in his hand. Jenny's hands were free and she had some water. Paul didn't question it. He knew that Dangle didn't consider her a threat. He pulled up a chair, sat down, and looked at her with a sigh.

"What am I going to do with you?" Paul said staring at her.

Jenny just looked down at the glass of water in her hand. "I'm sorry." She practically whispered it.

Paul just shook his head.

"Is he dead?" she asked.

"He is," Paul answered without elaboration.

"Okay," she nodded with a sniffle.

He decided to put her mind at ease. "I'm not going to kill you." He saw her breathe a sigh of relief.

"So, my brother hasn't been here?" he asked.

"No. I swear. We haven't seen him."

Paul nodded slowly. "Okay. I believe you."

"Are you going to let me go?" she asked.

"Do you have anyone else in the area?"

"My mom lives in Mount Sterling," she answered.

Paul nodded again, thinking. "Do you have gas in your car?"

"No, it's almost empty," she said, looking at her hands again.

Paul stood up and walked over to the cabinet, withdrew a Mason jar, and went to the refrigerator for some tea. As he started to pour the glass, he was suddenly overcome with emotion. *This is the last jug of tea that my Mama made.* His back was to Jenny. He didn't want her to see him struggling, so he sat the jug back on the counter and took a long drink, settling his nerves. With a sigh, he turned back around.

"I'll tell you what's going to happen. We're going to put your stuff in your car. I'm going to give you enough gas to get to Mount Sterling. That's about a two-hour drive from here. It's probably not even a hundred miles. My brother and I are moving into this place, so don't think about coming back. If you do, I'll shoot you on sight. I won't discuss it with you, I won't ask you what you need. I'll just shoot you in the face. Am I clear?"

She flinched as if he had smacked her, but slowly nodded. "I understand. I won't come back."

"Okay. Dangle, will you supervise her getting her stuff out of Dad's truck and putting it in her car?"

"Yeah man, you got it." He stood up and placed his jar on the counter.

Paul returned his attention to Jenny. "Obviously all that stuff is not going to fit in that little car, so pick what you want and leave the rest. Do you understand?"

"I understand."

Dangle stood up and ushered her outside to get started.

Paul looked around. There were a few random boxes of things the couple had already brought into the house. He opened a box and it had men's clothing in it -- Billy's stuff. He retrieved a trash bag from under the sink and dumped the box into it. He then took the box into the pantry and filled it with food. He selected some pasta and pasta sauce. He also chose some canned vegetables, soup, and several packages of ramen noodles. He grinned weakly as he loaded the ramen. He knew his parents didn't eat ramen but they always kept some on hand because McKinley liked it. Once the box was nearly full, he filled the remaining space with bottled water.

Carrying the box outside, he placed it in the front seat of the Honda and went to get some fuel for the car. He estimated that the little car probably got around thirty miles to the gallon, so he decided to give her four gallons of gas. As he was returning with the gas, he walked past Billy's body which was still laying in the gravel. He didn't even look down.

As he arrived back at the car, Jenny was putting something in the back seat and saw the box of food. She suddenly turned and hugged Paul. He didn't hug her back. He just stood there with the fuel can and allowed her to embrace him. She released him and looked up at him. "Thank you. You didn't have to do that."

"I know. But it's what my Mama would have done. She was a better person than I could hope to be." He stepped around her and went to the fuel door to add the gas.

It took them about thirty minutes to finish loading her car. Jenny walked to the driver's door and stopped with her hand on the handle. She turned and looked back at Dangle and then at Paul. She then looked out across the driveway at the form of her fallen husband. *I'm a widow now. I'm a widow at twenty-four*. Returning her gaze to Paul, she said "Thank you. And...and...I'm sorry."

Paul gave a barely perceptible nod. She returned it, got in the car, and pulled away.

Paul and Dangle watched her pull out onto 201 and disappear into the distance. Paul turned to Dangle. "I need to bury my parents. I feel like I'm doing something wrong. I feel like I should be calling the authorities and figuring out funeral arrangements and notifying my family." He took another deep breath. "I can't do any of that? I don't know what else I can do."

Dangle nodded. "Are we taking them to your farm?"

"No. No, this was their home. They would have wanted to stay here and I know just the spot. When we were kids, we used to sit around a campfire down by the creek. Mama always liked that spot. I'm going to take the backhoe down there. Do you mind pulling security?"

"You got it man."

Paul retrieved the keys to the tractor and the side by side. He also threw a mattock and a couple of shovels into the cargo area of the side by side. He fired up the tractor and brought it over to the driveway. Lowering the bucket, he scooped up Billy's body. *First, I'm going to take out the trash.* He drove the tractor over to the trail going into the woods, following it to their deer plot. Dangle followed in the side by side, his AR-15 laying across his lap.

Once Paul made it to the clearing in the woods, he tilted the bucket and unceremoniously dumped the body onto the ground. *Coyotes hafta eat too.* He turned the tractor around and headed to the creek.

Once he was there, he picked out the spot and immediately started digging. He was going to dig one grave big enough for them both. *They would want to be together.*

He and Dangle took turns finishing the edges with the shovel and mattock. Finally, they left the tractor in place and returned to the house in the side by side. Paul went inside to his parents' bedroom. The bed was a mess. He was disgusted. In all his years, he had never seen his mother leave the bed unmade. He wanted to burn the sheets that he knew Billy and Jenny had slept in. Passing by the bed, he went to the closet and selected three comforters. Pausing at the nightstand, he grabbed his father's Bible then carried everything out to his truck and backed it up to the barn.

Dangle stopped Paul as he exited the truck and started for the barn door. "Hey, do you want to put them in clean clothes?"

"I can't do it man. I would love that, but there's no way I can change their clothes." Paul said.

"I get it man. What about their wedding rings? Do you want those?"

Paul had to think about that for a minute. "You know what. That would feel like stealing to me. I'm sure Mama's engagement ring is inside. I'll get that for McKinley, but I've never seen them without their wedding rings. I'm not going to bury them without them either. It doesn't seem right."

Dangle just nodded. He stayed there as Paul turned and went into the barn. First, he placed a comforter on the ground next to his mother and gently closed her eyes. He lovingly moved his mother onto her comforter and wrapped her up. He selected some twine from his father's workbench and tied the comforter in place.

He then spread another comforter out for his father. He was notably heavier, but Paul was able to repeat the process for Charles. Paul scooped his mother up into his arms and gently placed her on the tailgate. He then climbed up into the bed and maneuvered her into the bed. Climbing back down, he looked at his father. He wasn't sure he could do it. "Dangle, can you give me a hand?"

Dangle immediately appeared and the two of them transferred Charles' body to the truck with as much care as they could. They arranged him next to his wife.

"I'm going to close the barn up and drive over to the creek. Just jump in with me, so I can drive the tractor back," Paul said to Dangle.

"You got it man." Dangle wanted to help Paul, but the only thing he could think of to do was to just follow his instructions.

Paul slowly drove the truck over and backed it up to the newly prepared grave. He immediately got out. He knew that if he hesitated, he might break down. He grabbed the third comforter and climbed down into the grave, centering it in the newly dug hole.

"How do you want to do this, brother?" Dangle asked, looking down at Paul from the edge.

"Can you lower Mama down to me?"

"Yeah man." He climbed up into the truck bed and moved Edna to the tailgate, then hopped out and carefully picked her up. He knelt at the edge of the hole and passed her small body to Paul.

Paul accepted her, thinking that somehow, she felt too light. He lay her on one side of the comforter, then accepted Dangle's hand to pull him out. The two of them maneuvered Charles' body to the edge of the grave and Paul reentered it. It was more difficult but after a few minutes, he had the couple side by side. He folded the comforter over them as best he could and once again, Dangle helped him out of the hole.

Paul went to the truck and returned with his father's Bible. He looked over at Dangle. "I don't really know what I'm supposed to do here. I want to show them the respect I know they deserve, but at the same time, I need to go protect my family."

Dangle walked over to his friend and pulled him into an embrace. "They understand brother. They understand."

Paul felt the tears welling in his eyes again. Once again, he felt the hitch in his breath. *I need to get through this. What would Dad do?* He pulled away. "Thanks, brother."

Paul opened his father's bible. "I actually know what verse I want." He flipped to the book of John, Chapter fourteen and cleared his throat.

"Let not your heart be troubled: ye believe in God, believe also in me. In my Father's house are many mansions: if it were not so, I would have told you. I go to prepare a place for you."

He closed the Bible and held it against his chest. "Mama, Dad. I know that there is a place for you. As a matter of fact, I'm sure you know that too, because by now, you're already there. You've done your best to teach me and Scott to live a Godly life." He paused for a moment as he thought about what to say next.

Dangle stepped over and put his arm around Paul's shoulder.

Paul continued. "I need to ask for a lot of forgiveness, and I'm sure I'm going to keep needing forgiveness. Things are ugly right now, but I'll always have your example. No one can take that from me. I can't promise that I'll always do the right thing, but I can promise that I'll do my best." He reached down and scooped up a handful of dirt and sprinkled it into the grave. Dangle did the same.

Paul began the Lord's prayer. "Our Father, who art in heaven..." Dangle joined him. As they finished the prayer, Paul said "Amen." Dangle patted him lightly on the shoulder with a squeeze and then turned to walk away, giving him some privacy. Paul took another couple of minutes for his own goodbye and then turned back to Dangle.

"Hey buddy. Can you pull the truck up? I'm going to cover them up." He held the Bible out to Dangle.

Dangle saw that Paul was struggling, so he just took the Bible and jumped in the truck, pulling out of the way and giving Paul plenty of room for the tractor. He then got back out and kept watch around the area while Paul worked.

It didn't take Paul long to cover the grave site with the John Deere. He didn't do anything else. As soon as he was satisfied with his work, he just turned the tractor toward the barn and started back.

A little while later, they were back in the house and both men had washed up. Paul selected one of his father's shirts to wear. He picked up his mother's jewelry box and opened it. Her engagement ring was there, among her other jewelry. He stowed the box in the back seat.

Paul looked at his watch. It was almost six o'clock.

"Hey Dangle, I don't see how we can get out of here tonight. I don't want to be driving in the dark. We need to pack up some stuff and I want to take as many animals as possible, I just don't see how else to do it. I wish I had some way to let Sandy know, but nothing's working." His face lit up as he realized that he had the Tri Point Satellite phone in his go bag.

He turned, ran over to his truck, and fished it out. He held it up to Dangle. "I wonder if this will work!"

"It's worth a try."

Paul entered the PIN and then tried Sandy's cell phone. Dangle saw Paul's face darken as he listened.

"It's not working. The phone seems to be working, but I'm getting an 'All circuits are busy' message. Dang it!" Paul dropped his hand to his side. "I say we just stick to the new plan and try to get out of here as early as possible tomorrow."

"I agree. Let's pack up until it gets dark. We'll need to pull security tonight, and there's only two of us so that's two hours on, two hours off."

"Yeah, I'd like to give it another night anyhow to see if Scott shows up. We'll finish loading in the morning. We can take Dad's truck and his trailer too, so you'll have to drive one of the vehicles."

"Okay. Let's do this."

They worked together to sort through what they needed to take, and started loading Paul's truck. They started with full fuel cans, leaving one out for the generator. Then they added ammunition and Charles' modest firearms collection, before moving on to bulk food, a few select pieces of clothing, and Edna's cast iron. Like Charles' guns, Paul considered the cast iron an heirloom item that should stay in the family. It didn't take long until the truck was nearly full. They pulled it into the barn for the night and locked it up, opting to load Charles' truck and trailer in the morning.

Paul looked at the pile staged in the living room and considered the amount of food left in the house and the bunker. "Well, Paul said, we can put this stuff in Dad's truck, but I want to save the trailer for animals."

"That's a lot," Dangle said.

"Yeah, Paul agreed. "I think we're gonna need another trip."

32

The Nickel Tour

August 13, 1:14 a.m.

Floyd County, Kentucky

Scott was not satisfied with his progress since he had left his hiding spot. It was after one o'clock in the morning. His feet hurt. His back ached. Everything ached. His original plan of walking for five miles at a time, covering fifteen miles per night wasn't looking good. He had a blister on his right heel and it hurt with every step. As he approached the town of New Allen, the tracks curved to the left and then back around the town. He passed a few structures and a dog started barking nearby, so he broke into a trot. This made the blister on his heel protest even more, but he pushed through. He was rethinking his technique of having a separate first aid kit from his go bag. He had lost the first aid kit with the Jeep.

As he pushed past another cluster of houses, he noticed something up ahead. Something big. As he closed the distance, he realized what it was. He was passing under Route 23. This is where the tracks and the road diverged. There was a driveway going up to the left that led toward the road. Scott stopped and evaluated the situation for a moment. He didn't know where the tracks went, but he did know where the road went. Additionally, the tracks had proven to be relatively uneventful and had kept him near a water source. If he took the road, he was much more likely to encounter people. He needed to make a decision. Standing here looking at the bottom of a bridge wasn't going to get him any closer to his parents.

He turned and walked up the driveway. At the top, he angled over to the side of Route 23 and kept walking. He was on the outside of the guardrail. *If I see a car coming, I'll jump into the woods and hide until they pass.*

A little less than two miles later, the terrain opened up at a major interchange where Route 23 passed under Route 80. He didn't like leaving the comfort of having the woods nearby, but he chose to stay on the road and kept going. He was getting exhausted and it was frustrating. He knew he should be able to cover fifteen miles a day, but starting this trip with wet feet and developing a blister was putting a damper on his plans. As he concentrated on just putting one foot in front of the other, he was suddenly aware that something had changed in his environment. He looked up. Headlights were approaching from in front of him and he was in the wide open. He looked behind him. It was easily three hundred yard back to the woods. *There's no way I'll make it before they get here.*

Looking at the concrete divider beside him, he decided to try the only thing he could think of. He hopped over the barrier and lay down against the far side of it. He was panting. The sound of the vehicle continued to get louder as the vehicle approached. Then he heard music. They were blasting music! Scott felt like he was about to be discovered at any moment. *Will they be able to see me when they pass by?* He rolled onto his left side, pushing his pack into the concrete barrier and pulled out the Glock, holding it in front of his chest.

Scott tried to control his breathing. The vehicle was still coming closer...closer...closer. Then it passed. Scott released the breath he didn't realize he had been holding. He stayed in the position, not moving as he listened to the sound of the vehicle recede. Once he felt comfortable enough to do so, he sat up and glanced over the concrete divider. He could see the taillights as they disappeared around the curve to his east. He grasped the concrete and used it to haul himself back up to his feet.

He turned and started walking again, but as soon as he did, he saw another light up ahead. This one wasn't moving. He froze. *What is that?* He couldn't tell. *That's the direction I need to go. I'll check it out when I get closer.* He started walking again, slower than before as he tried to evaluate the situation. He had also begun to limp from the blister. Every step hurt.

A few minutes later, he crossed back to the left side of the road and stopped in front of an air conditioning shop, evaluating the light. It was a church! He could hear a generator going and saw a couple of people moving around in the light of a pull through carport. He eased forward and watched the activity as he approached from the opposite side of the road. As he came up beside the church, he could see the illuminated sign: Allen Baptist Church. He stood still in the dark and watched as someone left, holding something. He could hear voices.

A man and woman walked out. The woman had something in her hands. The man patted her gently on the shoulder. "Are you sure I can't have one of the men walk you home?"

The woman looked over her shoulder at him. "Oh no, I'm fine. Thank you again."

"Yes ma'am. We'll keep you on our prayer list."

The woman walked away. What in the world was going on? It was almost five o'clock in the morning! *They're helping their community*, Scott thought. A wave of relief and recognition washed over him. His church growing up had helped the community during the holidays and times of need. Scott turned and walked across the road, heading directly toward the road leading to the church, his limp was more pronounced as he tried to hurry across the road. By the time he got to the door, the man was gone. He paused at the door and looked in. He couldn't see anyone. He tried the door. It was locked. Hesitantly, he raised his hand to knock on the door, but paused. He withdrew the Glock and held it behind him, then knocked with his left hand. A moment later, a man answered the door.

"Well, hello," the man said warmly.

"Hi," Scott responded, looking past the man for any evidence of a threat.

"Please, step inside so we can talk." The man stepped back to allow Scott room to enter. He stopped just inside the door. The man closed and locked the door. He faced Scott and extended his hand to shake. "Hi, I'm Phillip. I'm the pastor here."

Scott swallowed hard. He still had the Glock in his right hand. "Um, sorry." Scott holstered the gun.

The pastor watched him do it, but didn't seem concerned. Scott accepted the handshake. "I'm Scott."

Then Scott saw two men standing in the doorway to his left. One held a shotgun low and loose. The other had a pistol visible on his belt. His body stiffened. Had he just walked into another ambush?

Pastor Phillip spoke again. "Don't be alarmed. We just have some security right now. I'm sure you understand."

Scott nodded. "Yeah. I actually do understand that."

"Would you like to come into the sanctuary? We have clean water and some snacks. I'm sorry, but we won't have any real food until later." The pastor's tone was warm and almost carefree. It struck Scott as bordering on out of place considering the situation.

"Sure, thank you." Scott took a step forward.

The man with the shotgun stepped forward. "Sir, I'll have to ask you to leave your gun and pack out here. We've had some...issues." He motioned toward the wall where a hunting rifle was propped up and two other packs were visible.

Scott debated the situation. He would be totally at these people's mercy if he did this. What if this wasn't really the pastor? What if this was all an elaborate setup to lure people in to rob them? No, that didn't make sense. If people were coming here for help, they probably don't have anything that would be worth stealing. Of course, the gun was worth stealing.

Scott leaned to the side and looked past Pastor Phillip. He could see numerous children sleeping on the floor on blankets. Beyond that, an older woman was offering a Styrofoam cup to someone sitting in a pew. *This looks legit.*

Scott turned to face the man with the shotgun. "That's fine. I'm going to clear the gun first and put it in my pack, okay?"

"Go ahead," the man said, but Scott saw him raise the barrel slightly, closer to his direction.

Scott dropped the pack first and released the straps. His spare socks fell to the floor. He scooped them up and tucked them into the opening. He then withdrew his pistol, dropped the magazine, and ejected the round in the chamber. He placed the ejected round back into the magazine, and dropped the mag and the gun into the pack before closing it back up.

The man with the holstered pistol stepped up. "I need to check you for other weapons before coming in. I'm sorry. You're welcome here, but we need to take precautions."

"I have two pocketknives on me," Scott replied.

"Would you mind leaving them in your pack too?" The man was polite, but firm.

Scott walked over to the pack and deposited the knives in the outside pocket of his pack, then turned to the man and held his arms out. He felt vulnerable and uncomfortable.

The man gave him a quick pat down while the other watched with the shotgun ready.

"Thank you, sir," the man said. "Again, we apologize, but we're trying to keep everyone safe."

Scott nodded and the pastor ushered him into the sanctuary.

"Do you need some water?" he asked.

"Yes please."

The pastor motioned to one of the women who walked over with a pitcher of water, a Styrofoam cup, and a small bag of chips.

"Thank you, ma'am," he said, accepting the cup and the chips. She filled the cup and he gulped down the water in one long drink.

"Wow, you're thirsty. Would you like some more?" She was a kind looking woman of maybe sixty. She wore a simple cotton dress and Scott noticed she was wearing practical white sneakers, which looked a little out of place with the old-fashioned dress. She reminded him a little of his mother. He felt the pull at his heart. He missed his mother and was greatly looking forward to seeing her.

"Yes, please, ma'am," he said, holding out the cup.

She refilled it and he took a sip, but didn't try to drink the whole cup this time.

"If you need any more, it'll be right over there." She motioned to a folding table that had been set up on one wall.

"Thank you."

The pastor spoke up. "So, you're walking somewhere?"

Scott took another sip of the water. "Yessir. My vehicle was stolen. I'm trying to get home to my parents' house."

The pastor had a look of concern. "I hate to hear that. That's been going on. I've heard it's dramatically worse in the cities. Riots, looting, murder, rape. Everything you can imagine. It's not as bad here, but we haven't escaped it." He was sitting on the edge of the pew, turned to face Scott. He was dressed comfortably in jeans and a t-shirt. *He doesn't look like a preacher, but then again, preachers don't wear dress clothes every day.*

"So, tell me, Scott. What can we do to help you?"

"Well," Scott began, "would you happen to have a first aid kit?"

"We do. Are you hurt? I noticed you're limping."

"Not really, but I do have a bad blister and I'd love some iodine and moleskin." He paused. "If you can spare it."

"I'm sure we can spare some. I'm sorry, but we don't have any nurses or anything here right now. We do have one coming back later today."

"I'm actually a paramedic," Scott said. "I can work on it myself. I just need the supplies."

At this statement, the pastor sat up straighter. "You're a paramedic?"

"Yessir." Scott ripped open the bag of chips and began eating.

"Would you be able to take a look at one of our members?"

"Of course," Scott said. "What's the injury?"

"A young man's been badly beaten. I don't think it's life-threatening but it would be great if you could take a look at him. We were planning on waiting until the nurse came back this afternoon. We've done the best we can, but since you're here..." He trailed off without finishing the sentence.

Scott stood up. "Sure, where is he?" Scott glanced down at himself. He was a mess. "And do you have somewhere I could wash my hands?"

The pastor led Scott to a spacious bathroom that had some buckets of water and soap staged by the sinks. "The water isn't running, but this is all clean water. I'll wait outside. Once you get cleaned up, I'll show you where he is."

Scott took the time to use the bathroom, then he washed his face, arms, and hands before emerging, feeling a little better.

"Right this way." The pastor led Scott to a Sunday School room where a young man was laid out on the floor, on a blanket. His face was badly beaten and his left eye was swollen nearly shut. His lower lip was split and his right hand was bandaged. Scott saw a first aid kit on a chair beside him, but didn't touch it. Instead, he grabbed another chair and pulled it up to the man.

"Hey buddy. What's your name?"

"I'm Kyle," the man said. His speech was slightly distorted as he tried to minimize moving his injured lip as he spoke.

"You wanna tell me what happened?" Scott asked.

"I was taking some food to someone and three guys jumped me for it. I tried to fight back, but I hurt my hand when I took a swing at one of the guys. I don't know what I hit, but I cut my hand." He held his bandaged hand up, displaying it for Scott.

"All right. Well listen, my name's Scott and I'm a paramedic. I'm gonna check you out. Would that be okay."

"Yes please," the man squeaked out.

 Scott got up from the chair and knelt beside the man. "Can you sit up?"

"Mm hmm," the man replied, raising himself into the seated position.

Scott helped the man through a test of his range of motion, including his arms, neck, and injured hand. Everything seemed fine, although Scott didn't have the tools he was accustomed to having. A fully stocked ambulance would have been a welcomed addition.

Scott carefully removed the bandage on the man's hand and inspected the cut. It was an ugly cut, but not serious. Scott still cleaned it and applied some antibiotic ointment from the little first aid kit before applying a fresh bandage.

He checked his split lip and even checked for loose teeth. All the man's injuries were pretty minor and Scott didn't even think the man needed to be convalescing. *He got beat up, it's not that big of a deal.*

After about ten minutes, going through some simple checks, Scott put the man at ease. "Well, Kyle, it looks like you're going to be fine. Try to stay hydrated. Your body needs water to heal, but nothing appears to be serious. You should be fine in a couple days. Have you taken anything?"

"They gave me some Tylenol."

"Good. Good. That's exactly what you should be taking. You should go ahead and get up and start moving around. Take the Tylenol like it says on the bottle, keep that cut clean, and drink plenty of water. It looks like you'll come out of this just fine."

Kyle's demeanor changed almost instantly. He just needed a medical professional to tell him he was going to be fine, and he felt better.

The pastor placed his hand on the young man's shoulder and offered a prayer, asking for God's protection and healing. After the prayer, Scott and Phillip stepped back out into the hallway, leaving Kyle to rest.

"We appreciate you taking a look at Kyle."

"I'm just sorry I couldn't do more," Scott replied.

"No, no. You were great. Thank you."

As the two men walked back toward the sanctuary, Phillip put his hand on Scott's upper arm. "Can we pray together too? What can I pray for in your life?"

Scott felt a surge of emotion. This man didn't know him, but he was here, offering to help him and pray for him and he felt thankful for that. "Actually, I just want my family to be safe, and I'd like to make it home to my parents," Scott offered.

They entered the sanctuary and Phillip guided him to the alter. "Please, join me." The two men knelt and the pastor placed a hand on Scott's shoulder. He prayed on Scott's behalf, asking for protection on his trip, safety for his family, and guidance during these troubling times."

As the two stood back up, Pastor Phillip asked "Where are you trying to get to?"

"My folks are near Louisa, just over the county line in Lawrence County."

The pastor's eyes lit up and he held up a finger. "Hold on a sec." He crossed the room to the speak to the man with the pistol who had frisked Scott earlier. The two men returned together.

"Scott, this is Pete Ferguson. He is going to be going that way with the church van. We have some church members up there who are home bound and we're checking on them."

Scott felt a rush of excitement as he heard the news.

"We checked on them last night and we're going up every three days, so they're going to be driving back up Thursday," the pastor said smiling.

Scott experienced a roller coaster of emotions as soon as Phillip said Thursday. His elation instantly changed to dread. *Thursday? That's the day after tomorrow.* "Uh, that's very kind Phillip, but I'm not sure I want to wait two days."

Phillip looked down at Scott's boot. "You know, it's forty miles to Louisa. Do you really think you can walk forty miles in two days? Just wait here with us. Let's get that foot taken care of and when we drive you up Thursday, you'll still be there faster than if you tried to walk."

Scott didn't initially answer. He thought about the logic. *He's right. I know he's right.* Scott felt helpless. "So, there's no way you'd be going up there any sooner?"

"Sorry man," Pete said. "Gas is a problem. We're only driving the absolute minimum. Thursday is the day. Besides, the pastor here says you're a paramedic. We sure could use your help around here for the next couple days. We can feed you, get your clothes washed, and then get you a ride home. We even have a shower set up. What do ya say?"

The two men were looking back at Scott as he mulled over the proposition. *That would be faster than walking.* He thought about his foot again and then stuck his hand out to Pete. "You've got yourself a medic."

"Great!" Pete cried. He took Scott's hand and slapped him on the upper arm with his left hand. "Welcome aboard. Come on, let me give you the nickel tour."

33

Lookin' for Volunteers

August 14, 6:30 a.m.

Charles and Edna's Farm

Paul and Dangle took turns sleeping during the night while the other stayed on security. Paul tried the Satellite phone when he was on shift, but got the same error message. They had opted to turn the generator off for the night and they used their night vision to keep an eye on things. Plus, the generator provided a constant hum that obscured the sounds around the house. But as the sun was coming up on Wednesday, August 14, they were both moving around, trying to get things done as quickly as possible. Paul was concerned about his family. He was sure they were probably scared and thinking the worse since he didn't make it home yesterday as planned. Now he wanted to get there as soon as possible to let them know he was okay. Of course, then he would also have to tell them that his parents were gone.

Dangle was moving some stuff out to Charles's truck so Paul grabbed the keyring from his father's night stand and went out to the barn. He grabbed a trash bag on his way through the kitchen. After opening the barn door, Paul walked past his pickup to the stall where his father had allowed him to store some things. He looked at the lock. Billy had apparently beaten the lock with something, trying to knock it off. It had visible damage, but it had held. Paul had no doubt that with effort and the tools that were there, Billy would have eventually gotten into the stall. Apparently, he just hadn't put the effort into it yet. He was probably concentrating on the easy stuff first.

Billy had obviously found the little keyring, because it also had the key to Charles's gun locker on it. That's how Billy had gotten to Charles's 1911. When Paul was cleaning up last night, he had found the keys, still hanging in the door of the gun locker. Billy just hadn't figured out that the other key was for this lock.

Paul removed the lock and stepped into the stall. He already knew what he wanted to get from here. On one side, there were several black plastic waterproof cases. Paul went straight to a medium-sized one and picked it up. It had a piece of tape on it with the words "Get Home Clothing" scrawled on the tape. He opened the case and removed the camouflage uniforms and boots, placing them in the trash bag. He left the green army T-shirt and two pairs of socks in the case.

Paul pulled the camouflage tarp off his dirt bike and folded it. He then carried the case and the tarp out to his truck and placed them on the tailgate. He went to his back seat and retrieved a few more items then placed them in the case and closed it.

Paul disappeared out the back door of the barn, carrying the case and tarp, and returned empty handed several minutes later. Next, he pushed the dirt bike out into the main part of the barn beside the truck and gassed it up with the ethanol free gas that had been earmarked for the generator. Paul turned on the fuel, pulled the choke, and mounted the bike. After a few kicks, the old bike sputtered to life. He left it running as he retrieved his tire gauge from his tool box and a twelve-volt air compressor from the shelf in the stall. He checked the air pressure and plugged the air compressor cord into the cigarette lighter in the truck. He added air to the tires until he was satisfied and then stuffed the air compressor into the bed of the truck. Next, he retrieved a one-gallon gas can of the generator fuel and used two heavy duty bunji cords to strap it down onto the rear of the seat. Finally, he pushed the bike out the barn door, closed the choke, hopped on, and disappeared. A few minutes later, he walked back into the barn and returned to the stall. He looked around the stall, selected a few more items that looked useful, and placed them into the remaining space in the truck.

Paul walked over to the wood storage area and selected two short pieces of pressure treated 2x4. He carried them over to his father's workbench and used the cordless drill and some screws to fashion them into a simple cross. He plucked a black marker out of a cup on the bench and wrote his father's name on one side and his mother's name on the other. With a handsaw, he sharpened the bottom of the cross, retrieved a hand sledge and used the side by side to drive back out to the gravesite. He looked across the field, scanning for any evidence that anyone was around and then quickly drove the cross into the ground. He paused with his hand on the cross, then dropped the sledge into the passenger seat and drove back across the field.

When he got back to the barn, he put the sledge back where he found it. On the shelf over his father's workbench, he found a can of spray paint and took that with him, then pulled the truck out of the barn, leaving the door open.

On the outside of the barn door, he used the spray paint to write the words: Scott-Castle. He then joined Dangle, who was walking to Charles's truck.

"Hey buddy, can you help me wrestle the generator into the trailer? I think that's about all I want to put in there because I want to leave room for the animals. I'll get them next."

"Yeah man. Let's do it." Dangle said as he placed another item into the bed of the old Chevy.

They loaded the generator and then Dangle returned to the house to keep working.

Paul was able to get both the goats, all the rabbits, and most of the chickens into the trailer. The goats and rabbits were easy. The rabbits even had their own cages, so Paul just loaded them up. The chickens were another story. Paul had found two old dog kennels in the barn and carried them over to the chicken cage. It would probably have been comical to anyone watching as he chased the chickens around the cage, cornering them one or two at a time and then depositing them in the kennel before returning to do it again. Once he felt like he couldn't stuff anymore chickens into the kennels, he asked Dangle to help him and they loaded them into the trailer.

From the barn, he collected the bags of chicken and rabbit food and used them to stabilize the cages so they wouldn't slide around. He tied the goats to the wall on short leashes. The goats had been his mother's animals. They were really more like pets than livestock. He stopped just long enough to pet Bucky, the male goat.

He looked over at the remaining chickens. There were only a few more. He hated to leave them. *Maybe I could just put them in there loose. I guess that would work.* He returned to the chicken yard and captured the last few chickens, one at a time. He would open the door of the enclosed trailer and toss a chicken in before quickly closing the door again. He repeated this action until he had all the chickens loaded up.

He could imagine his father laughing at him for this unorthodox method.

After securing the door on the trailer, Paul went back to the barn and emerged with another salvaged plastic storage box. He had emptied it, stashing the contents in his locker and locking up the stall. He took the case into the house and loaded it with all the paperwork he could find that he thought might be important if the world ever recovered. In his father's filing cabinet, he found life insurance policies, titles, his parent's marriage certificate, and more. He even found copies of his and Scott's birth certificates. He had a little room left in the box, so he added in the family Bible from the coffee table. It had the family history of births, marriages, and deaths recorded in it. He was also able to fit two photo albums and a couple of framed family pictures from the walls. That was it. It was full. He picked it up and headed through the kitchen with the case.

As he passed by the sink, his mama's wall hanging caught his eye. It was a little sign that said "Everything is better in a Mason Jar." Paul stopped and sat the case on the table. "I can squeeze that in here," he said to himself. He retrieved the keepsake and added it to the case. He loaded the case into the front seat of his truck since no one would be sitting there for the ride back.

Paul rejoined Dangle in the house. "How are we looking?"

"Pretty good, I think. They had a lot of stuff in the bunker. I got what I could, but there's still more down there. I was able to fit the freezer stuff into the coolers, though. There was still some ice left, so I split that between the coolers and loaded them last. I'm glad your dad had the ratchet straps to tie everything down with, this is a lot."

"Yeah, I knew they had a significant amount of supplies. I'm worried about leaving anything. If anyone breaks in while we're gone, they'll clean the place out, but I just don't see how we can get any more in the vehicles," Paul replied.

"Are you sure you can't get anything else in the trailer with the animals?" Dangle asked.

"No, besides some of the birds are running around loose in there and I don't want to open the door until we get home."

"Oh," Dangle replied, surprised. "Okay then."

Once the two men had determined they had packed everything they could, they went around the farm and secured every door. Paul took a piece of plastic from a roll in the barn and stapled it over the broken window of the kitchen, then used his father's cordless drill to screw a piece of plywood over that. When he was done, he stashed the drill and the charger in the bed of his truck, tucking it in so it couldn't bounce out.

The barn was the last thing to be locked up. As Paul closed the door to the barn, Dangle noticed the painting on the door.

"Castle? What's that mean?" Dangle asked.

"I'll tell you about it later. Do you mind driving my truck? I want to drive Dad's."

"Of course, man. No problem. Let's do a radio check before we leave. Obviously, the cell phones are useless," Dangle added.

They completed their radio checks and were soon on their way back to West Virginia. Paul was acutely aware of how much fuel they'd burned on these two trips. To make matters worse, the trucks would burn more than normal for the ride back, considering how heavily laden they were.

The trip to Louisa was uneventful, although they did see pedestrians and bicycles on Route 23, which Paul could never remember seeing before. Several people tried to wave them down, but they kept going. One man even tried to run out in front of Dangle and was nearly hit when he didn't touch the brakes. As they approached the bridge over the Big Sandy, Paul called Dangle on the radio.

"Hey Dangle. Let's be on alert through here. Remember, there were a bunch of people around the bridge when we came through here yesterday. Over."

"Good Copy, Doc. Over."

Paul eased up onto the bridge. He could only see to about the center of the bridge where the intersection was because the bridge is higher in the middle. As he crested the center of the bridge, he slowed to observe the other side. He could see the railroad tracks and beyond that, a defunct Citgo station, but he didn't see any people. *That's weird.*

He continued slowly. There was a low, concrete wall on the right as the bridge transitioned to the West Virginia side and Paul looked to the right to make sure there was no one hiding there. He was driving with his left hand and had his pistol in his right hand. Then he saw the bodies. A man and a woman were splayed out on the ground by the wall, laying in dark stains on the pavement. Paul's heart sped up. He immediately called Dangle to let him know, but kept going. As he turned right onto Broadway, he glanced back in the direction of the bodies and could see pockmarks in the concrete wall, evidence of gunfire. He returned his attention forward and scanned the buildings around him. There was an old do-it-yourself carwash on his left and he saw a white Ford pickup truck sitting in one of the stalls, but he didn't see anyone in the vehicle. He didn't see any other vehicles. It all had a strange feel to it. *Okay, something's going on.* He called Dangle again.

"Dangle, this doesn't feel right." All semblance of radio procedure was gone at this point.

"I'm with ya. Where the hell is everybody?"

Paul reflexively used his left turn signal as he turned left onto Court Street and headed toward U.S. 52. He chuckled lightly under his breath when he realized he had done it. *Old habits, I guess.* As the road straightened out toward U.S. 52, Paul saw two pickups parked in the road, blocking the intersection. He immediately stopped, and put the truck in park. He grabbed his AR-15 from the seat beside him and stepped out, replacing his pistol in its holster. He threw the sling over his neck. Three men stood in front of the trucks and they were all looking at him. One of them waved for him to pull forward.

Paul keyed his radio. "Hey Dangle, pull up here by me and cover me. I'm going to see what these guys want."

"Roger."

Paul waited until Dangle was in position and then motioned back to the man to come toward him. The man cupped his hands and called out. "It's fine, come on up!"

Paul didn't like it. "Meet me in the middle!" he called back.

The man said something to the other two men and then started walking toward Paul. He had what appeared to be a hunting rifle, but it was slung over his shoulder. He looked completely at ease. Paul left the door open and stepped out, looking at both sides of the road before advancing. He spoke into his radio again.

"You got me?"

"I've got my red dot on his chest. If he gets squirrelly, I'll drop him." Dangle had positioned himself discretely so the man didn't realize he had a gun on him.

Paul didn't respond, but started closing the distance to the man. He had his AR held in both hands as he would when patrolling. It was low and relaxed, but he knew he could put it into action quickly if needed. He looked past the man at the other two. One of them was leaned against one of the trucks, smoking and watching. The other wasn't even paying any attention to him. He was looking down the road with a set of binoculars.

When Paul got to within about twenty yards of the man, he stopped. The other man followed suit and then spoke. "You're a little jumpy, ain't ya, friend?"

"It's a jumpy time. What's going on up there?" Paul said, motioning to the makeshift road block with his chin.

The man pointed over his shoulder with his thumb. "Me and the boys are protectin' the place. We've had some trouble."

"Yeah, I saw the bodies by the bridge."

The man stiffened. "What do you mean? There's bodies by the bridge? Didn't they stop you when you came through?"

"I hate to tell you this, but there's a man and woman over there. They looked dead. I saw chips in the concrete, so I thought they'd been shot, but I didn't stop."

The man suddenly spun on his heels and called out to his friends. "Morty, you need to go check on your cousin. This guy says there's bodies at the bridge!"

When the man turned back toward Paul, he was suddenly nervous. He reached across his body and grabbed the sling of his rifle to pull the gun from his shoulder. Paul spoke up. "Now, buddy. Let's not lose our cool here. I didn't hurt your friends; I just saw them when I came across the bridge."

The man glanced down at the gun in Paul's hands and realized his mistake. He had put himself at a disadvantage. "I assumed they had already checked you out. We're only letting locals through, so I figured you were from around here. That's why I just walked up to you like this. Apparently, I shouldn't have assumed."

He glanced over his shoulder as one of the trucks fired up behind him. "We had some people running through tryin' to steal everything that wasn't tied down last night so we decided we're going to control traffic in and out of town."

Paul judged the man's speech and body language. He appeared to be telling the truth and was genuinely concerned about the people at the bridge. The truck sped past them with one of the men in it, swerving out into the grass briefly as it headed toward the bridge.

"Listen, I'm not here to steal anything, and I'm not here to hurt you. I'm going to put my gun away too, so you're more comfortable and we can talk, okay?"

"Uh, yeah. Okay," the man replied, a mild waiver in his voice.

Paul left the rifle slung around his neck but pushed it to the side, and let go of it. He saw the man relax somewhat. Paul pressed the button on radio. "We're good here."

Dangle's response was quick and succinct. "Copy."

"I'm Paul." He offered his hand to the man.

"Ronan," the man replied. "Ronan Spurlock." He looked Paul in the eye as he shook hand his hand.

"Nice to meet you Ronan. You any relation to Jim Spurlock in Huntington? He's a buddy of mine."

"Nah, my family's from up in Raleigh County."

"It was worth a shot," Paul said, trying to put the man at ease. He was trying to avoid a violent confrontation. "Can you tell me what happened here?"

"Oh, uh, well, like I said. Me and the boys are tryin' to help out. The cops kinda got their hands full right now, so we're controlling this side and we had some folks on the bridge too. There wasn't any shootin' today. We woulda heard it, so I don't know what happened to them."

Paul listened, trying to piece the situation together in his head. "I saw what looked like bullet strikes on the concrete by the bridge, so I thought that was what killed the folks."

"Nah," Ronan responded. "That was from last night. If they had trouble today, they didn't have any way to call us. The cell phones ain't workin'. If they're dead, somebody did it without shootin'." He paused as he looked in the general direction of the bridge. "Morty's gonna be a mess. That woman's his cousin and the man's her husband." He took a deep breath. "They're good folks...or they were."

Paul noticed Ronan's gaze fall on the loaded truck beds. "If you ain't stealin', what's all that?"

Paul didn't turn to look. He stayed focused on the man in front of him. "That's from my parent's house. I had stuff stored there and we've been moving stuff to my house." Paul didn't see the need to get into the details.

The man didn't look convinced. "Why did you have so much stuff stored at your parents' house?"

Paul knew what the man was doing. He was trying to poke holes in Paul's answer to see if he was lying. Paul decided to give him just enough to make him happy. He had no doubt he could beat this man to the draw if he tried anything, but Paul had assessed him as someone just trying to be a good citizen and didn't want this to turn into a shootout.

"I was in the army for a long time. While I was gone, my dad let me use his barn for storage. Now that things are going crazy, I wanted my stuff at my house, so we're moving it," Paul said in a matter-of-fact tone.

"Is that a fact? I was in the army. What was your MOS?"

"I retired as a 180 Alpha."

The man narrowed his eyes suspiciously. "That's not an MOS."

Paul smiled. He had run into this before. Over the years, he had encountered soldiers who didn't realize that Warrant Officers had an MOS with three numbers. Most Military Occupational Specialties only had two numbers. "Well, I started off as an 11 Bravo, then I went to selection and became an 18 Charlie, Special Forces Engineer. Later I changed my MOS again to 18 Fox, but eventually, I went to the Warrant Officer Course and became a 180 Alpha. That's a Special Forces Warrant Officer."

The guy completely relaxed, then grinned. "Oh, I thought you was bullshittin' me at first. I was an 11 Bravo too. I never heard of a 180 Alpha. So, you're a no shit Green Beret?"

"Retired," Paul said, mirroring his body language and grin. "Who were you with?"

"I just did four years. I was with the 82nd.

"No kiddin? Me too, I was in the third of the '05 before I went to selection." With that statement, he knew the man believed him. Paul had used the slang for the 3rd Battalion of the 505th Parachute Infantry Regiment of the 82nd Airborne Division.

The man reached his hand out for another handshake. "First of the '04," the man said. His grin spread into a toothy smile. "Well, nice to meet you. Hey, I didn't catch your last name."

"Michaels. Paul Michaels."

"And where do you live now?"

"I'm over in Lincoln County. Not far. We don't want to bother y'all any more than we have. I need to get home to my family." Paul was trying to wrap up the conversation so he could get moving now that he was convinced that the roadblock wasn't going to turn into a firefight.

"Alright man. Listen, if you ever hafta come back this way, ask for me at the checkpoint. Ronan Spurlock," he said, repeating his name.

"Thanks, Ronan. Hey listen, do y'all not have radios? You could talk back and forth between your checkpoints."

"Nah, we've been asking around tryin' to find some, but so far no luck."

Paul thought about this for a second before he continued. "Okay, well listen, if you want to lock down the town, you really ought to try to put some folks on the roads coming into town along the tracks in both directions."

"Yeah, we know, we're still looking for volunteers."

"Ah, gotcha. Okay Ronan. Well listen man, it was good talking to you. I wish you the best. You probably need to check on your friends. I'm sorry I didn't stop to check on them, but it felt like an ambush to me."

"Nah man. I get it. I do need to go check on Morty, though. He's been over there a few minutes."

The two men shook hands a third time as a goodbye.

With one of the trucks now gone from the roadblock, they were able to just drive through it. They were on high alert the rest of the way home, but only saw a few people in their yards. It took them an hour to get to the entrance to Paul's driveway. He stopped and keyed his radio. "Household 6, Household 6, this is Doc, over."

Sandy's voice came over the radio. "Where the hell have you been?" She didn't sound happy.

"I'm pulling in now, over." Paul replied calmly.

"Hurry up!"

Paul pulled up the driveway and drove all the way to the house. Sandy was standing outside with the radio in her hand. By the time he got the door open, she was standing there. He started to explain. "Hey Babe. Sorry we..."

As soon as his feet hit the ground, she hit him in the chest with the heel of her fist. "I was worried sick!" she yelled. "I thought you were dead!" She collapsed into his arms and began to sob.

Paul wrapped his arms around his wife. He didn't try to explain anything yet. He just held her. He wasn't looking forward to the upcoming conversation.

34

Screw This. I'm Outta Here

August 15, 7:23 a.m.

Floyd County, Kentucky

Scott had already been up for nearly two hours. He kept looking at his watch. The last two days had been a mixture of relief and torture. He had gotten to rest and heal. He had gotten his clothes washed and was able to keep busy helping with the minor medical concerns he had been presented with. However, the whole time, he knew he wasn't getting any closer to getting back to his childhood home and reuniting with his parents.

Yesterday afternoon, he had been introduced to Emma Richardson, a registered nurse and member of the congregation here. He had worked with her to treat two men, one woman, and three children. Most of that had been today. However, he didn't really feel like it had been necessary. Besides the man that had been beaten up, the most serious thing they had taken care of was a laceration on the arm of a nine-year-old boy. In normal times, the injury probably would have warranted four or five stitches. However, they didn't have access to sutures, so they had closed him up with Steri-Strips and treated the site with topical antibiotic ointment and sterile gauze. Scott felt like most of the things

367

they had seen could have been taken care of without a medical professional.

Luckily, the work had acted as a distraction for him and helped pass the time. Without it, he would have been constantly staring at the nearest clock, willing it to go faster. That's what he was doing now. The church was offering a modest breakfast at eight o'clock and after breakfast, they would be driving to Louisa, dropping him off at his parents' house on the way.

Yesterday, someone had provided him with a pair of house shoes. Scott had gotten out of his boots, showered in an outdoor camp shower, treated his blister, and worn the house shoes until this morning. One of the families had a functioning washer and dryer and had even washed his clothes for him. Everything was packed up. His Nalgene bottle was full and he had two rinsed out Coke bottles of water stashed with it. He still had some of his food left, but the church had provided him with some Beanee Weenees, Vienna Sausages, and a small Ziplock with a couple of pieces of deer jerky. He had a plastic spoon tucked into his pack for the beans.

He checked his watch for what felt like the twentieth time this morning and sat down on a pew. He looked down at his feet. His boots and socks were dry and the blister, which was feeling much better, was protected with some moleskin. He couldn't sit still anymore. He got up and offered to help with the food, hoping it would get the breakfast started earlier.

At 7:55, the pastor got everyone's attention. "If you'll all bow your heads, I'd like to ask for the blessing over the food." The church went completely silent except for a child that could be heard crying somewhere else in the church.

"Dear Heavenly Father, Lord, we come to you today and ask that you would be with us and provide us protection and strength. We ask that you watch over our ministry team as they travel to help those in need and guide their hands that they might bring comfort to those who require it. We offer thanks for the hands that prepared this food and ask your blessing over this meal. We ask that this food would nourish our bodies to do your will. These things we ask in your name. Amen." The whole room joined him in a nearly synchronized "Amen" at the end of the prayer.

The line immediately began forming at the table and Scott saw Pete was near the front of the line. *I might as well eat too. Not eating ain't gonna make this go any faster.* He walked over and got in line. After getting his plate, Scott found Pete and sat down beside him. Trying not to sound impatient, Scott asked "So, Pete. What time are you wanting to head out?"

Pete finished chewing and took a sip of coffee before responding. "I think we should be ready to go about 8:30. Are you ready?"

"Yessir. Just say the word. Do you need me to help you load anything up?"

"No," Pete said. "The van is loaded. We need to get you your gun, though."

Scott had been ready to ask about his pistol. "Thanks. I really appreciate your hospitality and I can't tell you how thankful I am for the ride." He returned his attention to his plate and quickly finished his meal of three pancakes and two sausage links as Pastor Phillip walked up.

"I guess you'll be leaving us this morning," he said, offering his hand for a handshake.

"Yessir, pastor. Thanks for all the help."

Pastor Phillip offered a genuine smile. "Thank you as well Scott. We'll keep you on our prayer list."

Forty-five minutes later, Scott checked his watch as they turned off Route 23 onto 201. It was nine o'clock. Scott looked out the window at a Marathon Gas station as they passed it. He knew the gas station was ten miles from his parents' home. It was a single-story brick structure with a blue steel roof. The glass doors were broken out and Scott could see movement inside. He tapped his Glock on his hip with his elbow. It was reassuring to have his gun back.

As the rural landscape passed by, Scott was mentally counting down the ten miles. When he saw the county line, he knew he was nearly home. The green sign read "Lawrence County" and Scott felt a knot in his stomach. *Almost there.*

"It's right up here," he said, leaning forward and pointing to the upcoming driveway.

Pete slowed the van and engaged his turn signal.

"Go ahead and pull in. That's their house," Scott said, noticing that he didn't see his dad's truck. He retrieved his backpack and extended his hand toward Pete. "Thanks again, Pete."

Pete took the proffered hand with a nod. "Be safe, Brother Scott."

Scott stepped out of the van and closed the door. Pete immediately turned around and drove away.

Scott walked up to the door and tried the doorknob. It was locked. He knocked. Nothing. He knocked again, louder this time. Still nothing. *Well, the truck isn't here. Maybe they've gone somewhere.* He turned and walked over to his mother's flowerbed and retrieved the fake rock with the spare door key in it. As he raised back up, he looked across the driveway at the barn and saw the words painted on the barn door: "Scott-Castle." *What the...?*

After removing the key, he replaced the rock and went to the house, letting himself in and dropping the key into his pocket. "Mom?" he called out. "Dad?" He was met with silence.

Then he noticed the floor. The tiles were clean, but he could see brown stains in the grout around the tiles. *What is that?* The stains formed an irregular pattern around the tiles. He squatted down to look at the stain. *Is that blood? I can't tell.* He stood back up, dropped his pack onto the kitchen table and walked into the living room. He froze. There were boxes and bags stacked up in the living room. *What the hell is going on here?*

He looked in his parents' bedroom. The bed was stripped and the bare mattress sat unadorned except for some bare pillows. Scott tried to figure out what was going on. *Well, they were talking about going to Paul's. Maybe they did.* Scott noticed a pair of his father's sunglasses on the nightstand. They were oversized safety glasses that could be worn over prescription glasses. *Hey, that's better than nothing.* He grabbed the glasses, put them on top of his head, and left the room.

He returned to the kitchen and then began to notice that things were missing -- he hadn't noticed as he walked through the first time. His attention had been on the stain. His eyes returned to the stain again. *That could be blood. I'm just not sure.* He turned to the pantry and opened the door. It was essentially empty. There were small kitchen appliances on the counter, but the shelves, which were normally full, now only held a few items. *They must have taken the food and went to Paul's.*

As he stood there, looking at the empty shelves, he suddenly remembered the barn door. He turned and walked back outside, closing and locking the door behind him. He walked across the driveway to the barn and stood in front of the door, just staring at it. *Castle?* He thought about it for a moment, then it came rushing to him. *Oh! The Castle!* Charles had built a treehouse for him and Paul when they were kids. They had always referred to it as The Castle. The tree house was long gone now, but Scott knew exactly where it had stood for so many years. He took off across the field, angling toward the site.

The tree was in the woods, several yards back from the edge of the field. When the treehouse was still standing, you couldn't even see it from the field in the summertime when the leaves were on. If you didn't know it was there, you could easily walk right past it. Scott, however, knew it well. He cut into the woods and worked his way through the underbrush to the tree. Something was there with a tarp over it. He pulled the tarp back and stared at Paul's old dirt bike. A smile spread across his lips. *Ha! I know exactly what to do with this!* Then he noticed the black box tucked behind the front tire. *And what is this?*

He squatted down and pulled the hard plastic case to him. After opening the four large lever-style clasps, he popped the box open and immediately started laughing. "Paul! I'd recognize your handiwork anywhere!" he said out loud.

Reaching into the box, he extracted the upper and lower receivers of a gray colored AR-15 style rifle. It was too large to fit in the box assembled, so Paul had separated the two halves. Scott lined up the upper and lower receivers and pressed the pins into place, reassembling the XM177 Carbine. Under it was a camouflage bandoleer with three magazines and a fourth magazine laying loose in the box on a brown army T-shirt. He retrieved the loose mag, slapped it into the magazine well, and pulled the charging handle, chambering a round. He double checked the safety, threaded his arm through the sling, and slung the rifle across his back diagonally. He then slung the bandoleer across his body as well. *Four magazines, thirty rounds each, that's one hundred twenty rounds. Not bad.*

He dove back into the case. The only remaining items were some socks and T-shirts. *I wish I would have had these extra socks a few days ago.* He stuffed the socks into his pants pockets and tied the T-shirts to the handlebars to carry them back. He folded up the tarp and tucked it into the case before closing and latching it.

Scott checked the fuel petcock and turned the fuel on. He pulled the choke and threw his leg over the bike. A couple of kicks of the starter and the old bike fired up. Scott grinned broadly. He dropped it into first gear and eased it out of the woods. As soon as he broke out into the field, he reached down and closed the choke then took off. He opened it up a little, testing the throttle and getting used to the feel of the bike. It was definitely different from his. This Honda was only a 250cc four stroke. Scott's bike back in South Carolina was a 450cc four stroke. However, it worked and it would be much better than walking. He rode it back to the house and parked it on the back side of the house where it couldn't be seen from the road.

Scott liked that this bike had a kickstand. His bike was a motocross style bike with no kickstand, but Paul's bike was a trail bike, so it had one.

Retrieving the key from his pocket, he reentered the house and looked around again. It felt weird to be here by himself.

He opened the refrigerator. It was still cool, but not as cold as if it were running. *This was running not too long ago.* He saw a partial jug of tea and grabbed it, quickly closing the door to maintain what coolness was left. He poured a jar of tea and returned to the pantry to look around again.

Hmm. Let's see what we've got to work with here. There were two cans of ready to eat soup, two packages of ramen noodles, an unopened box of Nutri-Grain breakfast bars, and ten bottles of water. *Not bad, not bad.* He nodded his head as he inventoried the items.

Now he had to decide what he was going to do. He knew that under normal conditions it was about a two-hour drive to Paul's. He wasn't sure how long that would be on a dirt bike. He suspected maybe closer to three. He thought about the knobby tires on the bike. *That asphalt is gonna eat those tires up. Oh well.* It was August, so he knew he had plenty of daylight to get there, but he also wanted to allow time for problems. He checked his watch again and decided to look around and have lunch, then decide if he was going to leave this afternoon or stay the night.

He tried to think of the route that went through Fort Gay along the backroads to Paul's place. He wasn't sure that he could navigate it. In the past, when he had driven to Paul's he had always taken the interstate and gotten off onto Route 10, which went almost all the way to Paul's. He suddenly missed the ability to look up maps on his phone. He had some paper maps, but they'd all been lost with his Jeep. *Maybe Dad has maps in his filing cabinet.*

Scott headed to the filing cabinet and opened it up. He could immediately tell that someone had gone through it and taken stuff, but everything else still seemed to be orderly. *If someone had broken in and done this, they wouldn't have taken such care with this cabinet.* He dug through both drawers of the cabinet, but at the end of the search, he still didn't have a map. *I guess I'm taking the interstate.*

Returning to the kitchen, he decided on an early lunch. The breakfast at the church had been appreciated, but small. He checked the gas stove. The gas came on, but the electric ignitor didn't work. He retrieved the lighter from his fire-starting kit. Looking at his mother's pots and pans, he noticed that most of her cast iron was gone. He selected a saucepan, then retrieved a can of vegetable beef soup and a package of ramen from the pantry. He put the soup and the noodles in the pan and added a little water from his supply. Using his lighter, he lit the stove and began heating the soup. After a few minutes, this resulted in a hearty meal that was filling and satisfying. He finished off the tea with his meal.

Leaning back in his chair, he looked around, his eyes settling on the refrigerator again. He walked over and opened the door to the freezer, peering in. It was empty. He quickly closed it. Then he did the same with the refrigerator. It had condiments and other various items, but not much. *They cleaned out the refrigerator too.* He looked at the remaining items. This stuff is going to ruin. He retrieved a trash bag and carefully removed the remaining items from the refrigerator, placing them in the bag. He then carried the bag out to the road and deposited it in the receptacle they used for the trash collector.

Walking back into the house, he opened the refrigerator and the freezer and left them open to air out. *When we come back, I don't want this to be a science experiment in here.* Then he had another thought. *What if the power comes back on and the doors are open?* He squatted down beside the fridge and fished his hand behind it, unplugging it. He repeated the process for the empty upright freezer in the pantry.

He walked back out into the living room again. He was considering spending the night, but the place felt strange. It was empty and he was alone. "Screw this. I'm outta here."

35

Freakin' Deer

August 15, 1:30 p.m.

Charles and Edna's Farm

Scott Michaels sat at his parents' kitchen table developing a plan. He had his supplies sitting on the table in front of him. He had his backpack, plus food, water, and the rifle Paul had left him. Counting his Nalgene bottle, he had thirteen bottles of water, so he opened one of the repurposed Coke bottles and sipped on it as he worked out his plan. It was going to be a tight fit to get it all in his pack – and heavy. He wasn't overly concerned about leaving any water that wouldn't fit, though. He still had his filter.

He was trying to picture what it would take to get to Paul's place. He would need to get out to Route 23 and take that north to the interstate. Then he'd be running down the interstate on a freakin' 250cc dirt bike for something like twelve miles. *What was Paul's exit? I think that's exit eleven.* Then he'd be on Route 10 for a while and he couldn't remember how far that was. When he was driving his Jeep, it always seemed like it took forever. His brother lived out in the dang sticks. *That has to be something like fifteen or twenty miles. Dang. At least I have some extra fuel.*

Then he looked over at the rifle. *Should I try to hide that in my pack? Would it even fit? If I need it, I won't be able to get to it. Maybe I just strap it to the side of my pack, so it's easy to get to. Crap, I don't know.* He got up from the table and paced around the kitchen, trying to create the best plan. *I wish I remembered the back way.* He flopped back down in the chair with a thud and leaned back.

He looked at his watch. It was half past one. He needed to make a decision. He stood up and started placing the food in his go bag. He was barely able to zip it up when he was done, but he got everything packed into it. Everything except the rifle. He used the compression straps on the side to secure the gun to the pack. He ran one of the straps through the top carrying handle to make sure it wouldn't slide down while he was riding. He tried the pack on, checking the weight. It wasn't too bad. The canned food and water were heavy, but overall, it wasn't all that bad, and he wasn't abandoning any water. He turned and looked around the kitchen. *Let's do this.*

He fished the house key out of his pocket as he exited the house. He locked the door and hid the key back in the fake rock. Walking around to the bike, he got it started, waiting a moment for the engine to warm up. He took a deep breath, dropped the safety glasses down over his eyes, and took off.

The first leg of the trip was on Route 201 up to Route 32. He was very familiar with this area. He constantly checked behind him to see if there were any vehicles, but the road was empty every time he looked. He made it to Route 32 and turned right. Twice as he rode down Route 32, someone came out of their house, running out toward the road, waving at him to stop. He just kept going, riding as fast as he felt he could safely go. It didn't take long to get out to Route 23, which would take him to the interstate. However, to Scott, it had felt like an hour.

Shortly after turning onto Route 23, Scott started down the stretch of road right before the fancy Exxon station. He could see that the intersection was blocked with multiple cars and he could see men walking around. He wasn't playing this game. He turned around and immediately pulled off the road into the entrance of the Best Western. He turned back south along an access road that led to the power line right of way and followed the powerlines to the west.

Scott saw a four-wheeler trail to the right and worked his way up onto the trail. It led northwest and eventually turned north, paralleling Route 23. He followed the trail until it up dumped out onto Route 3, which was the crossroad that led back to the roadblock. He turned left, away from the roadblock and then right onto the first road he came to. He read the road sign: Mt Pleasant Rd. He wasn't sure where this one went, but he did know that he wasn't going back toward the roadblock, so he kept going. The road curved to the right, back toward the intersection. Scott didn't like that, so when he saw another turn off on his left, he took it. A half mile later, it emptied out onto Route 23 again. Scott smiled. He was beyond the roadblock. He turned left and ran through the gears, quickly getting back up to speed in fifth gear.

It was a long way to Interstate 64, but the road was open and empty. Scott took advantage of the open road to push the bike. It didn't have a speedometer, but he felt like he was probably doing forty-five to fifty miles an hour. It took him about twenty-five minutes, but when the entrance to the interstate came into view, he breathed a sigh of relief. Then he looked to his left and he felt like his heart skipped a beat. In the Park-And-Ride just before the exit, there must have been forty people. He saw someone pointing at him as he approached. He increased his speed. About ten people began running toward the road. He judged the distance. It would be close, but he wasn't sure he would make it past them before they made it into his path.

He sat up straight and let go of the throttle, maintaining his steering with his left hand as the bike started to decelerate. With his right hand, he drew his pistol and pointed it in the general direction of the mob. They didn't seem to notice. He adjusted the gun to the right, in front of the group and fired a shot into the median. Collectively, the group flinched and ducked. All but two turned and ran back toward the parking area. Two younger looking men stopped, but didn't run.

The bike was losing speed. Scott stomped it down into fourth gear without using the clutch. He looked forward toward the on-ramp. He thought he could make it. He let go of the handlebar and passed the pistol to his left hand. Grasping the throttle again with his right, he accelerated again. The two men continued to watch him, but neither advanced nor retreated. As Scott passed them, he glanced over at them and the one closest to him held his middle finger up in Scott's direction. Scott just shook his head.

He continued onto the on-ramp and merged onto the interstate, still in fourth gear. He looked around. Everything appeared to be clear. His heart was racing and he wanted to get the gun back into its holster. He passed it back to his right hand and quickly shoved it back into the holster. *I wish I would have thought to rig the holster to the handlebars. Oh, well. Too late now.* He accelerated again and crossed the bridge into West Virginia. *Okay. Eleven miles to the exit.*

Fortunately for Scott, no one seemed to be interested in the interstate, at least not this part. He passed a sign showing that his exit was three more miles. As the road curved left, he saw that he was about to pass under an overpass. Movement caught his eye on the road above. There were a several people on the road above. It looked like at least five or six. They all seemed to be focused on him. He felt his anxiety spike. *Great. Now what?* He stayed on the throttle. *Three more miles.* He went under the bridge. As he was emerging from the other side, a gallon jug of water just missed him and exploded on the road beside him. "What the hell?!" he yelled, nearly losing control of the bike. "What the hell is wrong with these people?!"

He regained full control of the bike, his heart thumping so hard, he was sure it could have been heard if not for the sound of the motorcycle. *People are going crazy.* He stayed in the left lane, away from the woods on the right side of the road and ducked down, trying to improve his aerodynamics. As he approached the exit, he expected to see people up on the bridge, but it appeared to be empty. Halfway down the ramp, he rolled to a stop. He realized he was still breathing hard as a result of the last attempt on his life. *Why the hell would they use a water jug? Maybe they were trying to wreck me without completely destroying the bike, so they could steal it.* He shook his head. If he had wrecked at fifty miles an hour, it would have been catastrophic.

He took a few deep breaths and then looked around again. He could see pretty far in both directions. *Maybe I should go ahead and put the extra gas in the tank.* He had faced this same dilemma when he still had his Jeep. As quickly as he considered it, he dismissed it. *I need to keep moving.* He took off for the final leg of the journey, Route 10 South to Salt Rock.

Scott didn't know what to expect on Route 10, but he certainly didn't expect to see a man and woman riding a horse down the road. However, that's what he encountered about a mile and a half from the interstate. He came up behind them as they turned from Green Valley Road onto Route 10. He slowed down. *Should I pass them? Should I speak to them?* He decided to ease past them and see what happened. He slowed down into third gear and closed the distance. The woman on the back was wearing a backpack and turned to look at him as he approached. He waved at her and smiled, just to see what kind of a response he got. She didn't smile back. However, she *did* wave. He eased up beside them, keeping some distance. He didn't want to spook the horse. It didn't even react. It was probably accustomed to four wheelers or side by sides on whatever farm they came from. The man on the horse eased back on the reins and brought his horse to a stop. Scott decided to go with it. He hit the kill switch on the bike and the engine died.

"How y'all doin'?"

Scott now saw that the man had a rifle draped across his chest. It was a short bolt action with a scope on it. "We're doing fine. Can I help you with somethin'?" the man asked, eying Scott suspiciously from beneath a worn-out ball cap.

"No, I just hadn't seen anyone else on the road, so I thought I'd be neighborly," Scott said, feeling a little silly as he said it. *Neighborly?* It was all he could think of at the time.

"Uh, okay. Well, if you don't need anything, we'll be going," the man said curtly.

"Before you go, can I ask, have you seen any trouble on this road?" Scott asked.

The woman chuckled. "There's trouble. Your best bet is to get off the road with that bike. If you got gas, somebody's gonna want it."

Scott nodded his head. "That's what I needed to know, thank you. Safe travels."

"You too, young man," the man said and bumped the horse with his heels. The horse obeyed and started down the road again.

Scott kicked the starter. The bike started, but immediately began sputtering. "Crap!" He reached down and rotated the fuel petcock to the reserve setting. The engine leveled out and he took off. *I need to find a place to get off the road and refuel.* He scanned the road on both sides, looking for a place where he could pull into the woods. Almost immediately, he saw a road that went up the hill to the left with no visible structures. He made a quick decision and swerved left up the hill. The road leveled off and went into some woods. *This is as good a place as any.*

He stopped the bike and removed the gallon of gas, dumping it into the bike as quickly as he could. He resecured the empty can on the rear fender, spun the bike around and coasted back down the hill. As he approached the bottom, he popped the clutch, and the bike took off. Turning left, he was on his way again, passing an Exxon station on the right-hand side that had a large "NO GAS" sign taped to a pillar by the pumps.

As he continued south, he felt like there was an ambush waiting around every turn. It made him think of a saying his grandfather used to use. "He's as nervous as a long-tailed cat in a room full of rocking chairs." He just needed to make it a few more miles. He was almost there. He was close enough at this point that he could walk it pretty easily, but he had no intention of doing that. *Just stay focused. Stay alert.* He scanned the sides of the road. There were people out, but they just looked at him as if he were an attraction at the fair. He started up a hill and recognized it. He remembered this hill because there was an unusual near one-hundred-eighty-degree curve on it. Then he saw the sharp turn, confirming that he was remembering it correctly. The road was in very good condition here. The state had apparently widened the road in the curve since the last time he had driven through here. As he crested the hill, he noticed the sign showing the name of the cross road: Doss Hill Rd.

He also knew that meant there a perfect ambush position coming up because the road had a very sharp blind curve to the right. *Just keep going. You're almost there.* He eased into the curve and saw something in the road. His brain tried to process what he was seeing. It was a board, a 2"x 4". Then he saw the nails sticking out of the board. He hit both brakes as he swerved left around the board. He registered the guard rail coming at him and leaned back to the right, bringing the bike back into the right-hand lane as he passed the trap. He opened the throttle. *I've gotta get out of here.* Ahead, the road curved back to the left again and Scott looked over his left shoulder back toward the trap. Two men were now standing in the road, watching him ride away. *Damn! Where did they come from?*

He returned his attention to the road and continued down the hill. There was a similar curve at the bottom of the hill and now, Scott was as jumpy as he'd ever been. He pulled the clutch, then hit the kill switch. He let the bike coast, trying to be stealthy. The road was a steep enough grade that he was able to maintain most of his speed as he coasted. He veered to the left and stopped beside the road about fifty yards before the curve. He pulled his backpack off and unlaced the strap holding his rifle in place. He had chambered it before leaving his parents' house. He double checked the safety, pressed the rifle into his shoulder, and started walking. He eased around the curve looking over the sights. Nothing. It was clear. He let out a breath and turned back toward the bike.

He decided that for the rest of the trip, which wasn't far, he'd keep the carbine handy. He left it draped over his neck. It was a little inconvenient, but not as inconvenient as needing a gun and not being able to get to it. He restarted the bike and took off, still easing into the curve, he couldn't help it. He was expecting someone at any moment. A moment later, he was in fifth gear again, screaming down another big straight stretch. He saw a small store on the right and glanced the name as he passed it, Morrison's Market. He remembered that too. All this was looking familiar. *I'm close.* He saw a church on the right. There was a hand written sign taped to the non-functioning electronic sign that read "Fran's Food Pantry-Saturday 9:00 a.m."

He returned his attention to the road. *I think its about another five or six miles.* He concentrated on his riding. Scott was an experienced motorcyclist, both on road and off, but he wasn't accustomed to riding while constantly watching for ambushes.

He came down the hill into the little town of Salt Rock and his heart rate went up again. What would he find in the town? To his surprise, he saw a four-wheeler. Then another. He saw a side by side parked at the little gas station. *What in the world?* He didn't understand the difference, but he was going to take advantage of it and hurry up. He did remember this. He knew that the turn to Paul's place was two miles from Salt Rock. He was almost there. *Stay on the gas. Pay attention to the sides of the road and GO!*

Then, he saw it. He saw the turn! His stomach felt like it was turning in flips. He eased off the gas and turned left. It wasn't much of a road, just a little asphalt road barely wider than a vehicle, but Scott was thrilled to be on it. *Maybe four minutes, I'll be there.* He kept going. As he rounded the last curve before Paul's drive way, Scott saw movement out of the corner of his eye to his left. Something was coming at him, and fast! He instinctively ducked his head and hit both brakes, stopping abruptly. Two whitetail deer bounded across the road in front of him. He stared for a short moment, then burst into laughter. It was a genuine, roaring laughter. He shook his head, shifted back down into first, and eased out on the clutch. He was still laughing a minute later as he turned left and started up Paul's driveway. He shook his head again as his laughter finally began to subside. "Freakin' deer."

36

We've Got Work to Do

August 15, 5:25 p.m.

Winchester, Kentucky

Today was to be the last day of the contract for Tri Point Solutions at the Winchester job. The client had reported what Mack and Rotor had seen coming: they couldn't access their funds to continue the contract. Mack had the conversation with the client. They had parted on good terms, but Mack knew they would never see the last payment for the contract.

At 6:00 that morning Loki and Joker took over the site for the last day. Mack would be dropped off at 5:30 that evening to pick up the Suburban and they would be done with this job. Over the last several days, the TPS teams had heard gunfire multiple times in the area, and they'd had some minor issues, but for the most part, the job had been pretty standard. Often, just having visible security was enough to reduce problems. They were all aware of the problems they were having in the larger cities like Lexington and Louisville. There was rampant looting and the gangs were out in force. They were taking advantage of the situation to settle scores with other gangs, steal, and generally do whatever they wanted.

However, Winchester was a smaller city and the activity had not been as bad here. There were reports of home invasions and looting, but not nearly on the scale of the larger cities. The Winchester Police Department had stopped by twice to check on the site. They were aware that TPS was on site and armed, and had made an appearance. They had shared information about what was going on, and pointed out that they were doing some general patrolling. However, for the most part, they were essentially unavailable. The 911 service had crashed prior to the power going out, so even with working phones, there was no way to call for help. The point of the interaction had been clear: You guys are on your own.

At 5:25 p.m., Loki saw a vehicle approaching the front gate and walked casually in that direction. It was Rotor's personal vehicle, a Subaru Outback. As they reached the gate, Loki unlocked it to allow them to enter. He stepped back, pulling the gate with him and Rotor pulled in. That's when two more vehicles, a beat-up Ford Ranger, and a newer Toyota Tacoma turned into the entrance road and accelerated toward them. Loki saw the vehicles approaching and started to quickly close the gate, but realized he wasn't going to get it closed in time. He jumped back as the first truck glanced off the partially closed gate, throwing the gate open. Loki immediately drew his pistol and ran for the company Suburban.

The Ranger veered to the right, narrowly missing a collision with the rear of Rotor's Subaru, and skidded to a halt. The Toyota passed between the two vehicles, veered to the right as well, and stopped in the open parking lot between the Ranger and the building. Two men burst from each truck. The driver of the Ranger had a pistol in his hand and the passenger exited with an AR-15. Mack burst from the Subaru at the same time, ducking as he ran around the front of the car, putting the engine block between himself and the little Ford. He already had his Glock 19 in his hand. The driver fired his pistol rapidly at Mack as he ran, but missed. Two rounds struck the side of the SUV and three more went high. By this point, the two men from the Toyota were out of their vehicle as well. Each one had a rifle. The passenger had a lever action rifle and the driver came out with an AK-47.

The passenger of the Ranger had stopped at the rear of the truck and had his rifle on the side of the bed, shooting over the tailgate. He was dumping rounds into the Subaru. By this point, Rotor had joined Mack behind the engine block and although they were pinned down, the two shooters couldn't get a clear shot on them either. The men in the Toyota, however, had a better angle. The man with the AK took a shot at Mack and the round struck the fender right in front of him. Mack dropped to a knee and pivoted toward the man, firing three times. The man crumpled and his rifle clanked to the pavement.

It was at this point that Loki emerged from the rear of the Suburban. He was wearing his plate carrier and ballistic helmet and had his AR-15 presented in front of him. He placed his red dot on the passenger of the Ford and walked slowly and smoothly toward him firing between each step. The first round went over the man's shoulder, but as the man turned to face this new threat, the second round caught him in the left collarbone. He spun from the impact, but held onto his rifle. He tried to turn back toward Loki, but Loki was still firing. The second round hit him in the side of the ribcage. Loki stopped beside the engine block of the Suburban and kneeled to avoid exposing himself to the men in the Toyota and continued to fire.

The man with the AR-15 dropped the rifle just as another round struck him in the abdomen. He fell to his knees, trying to grasp at the wound with his right hand. His left hand hung uselessly beside him, immobilized by the shattered collarbone. The final round entered his face, just above the left side of his mouth and he thudded to the ground. Loki turned to face the remaining threats. From his position, he could see Mack and Rotor's backs. They were still behind the Subaru, but he couldn't see the either of the two remaining intruders from his position.

He could hear the man with the pistol, though. He had retreated to the front of the Ranger, shooting down the driver's side with his 9mm. The man with the lever gun was quiet at the moment, reloading behind the Toyota.

Mack turned to Rotor. "We're exposed out here, head back to the Suburban, I'll cover you!"

Rotor leaned out and put two well aimed shots into the Toyota, keeping the man from leaning out, then turned and ran past the driver side of the Suburban. As soon as he broke from cover, Mack sent a few more rounds toward the Toyota to maintain the suppression. Rotor continued past the vehicle to the rear and out of sight. As he rounded the back of the vehicle, he looked inside and saw another AR-15. He grabbed it, and pulled a magazine from the plate carrier laying in the back of the vehicle. He slammed the magazine home and chambered a round.

The man at the Ford placed another magazine in his Taurus 9mm and called out to his companion. "Come on, man! Do something with that rifle!"

Lever action guy moved around to the front of the Toyota and peered around the driver side, with the building behind him. From his position, he could see the Suburban, but couldn't quite see Mack, who was still at the Subaru. He looked over his sights at the big Chevy, but couldn't see tell if anyone was behind the vehicle because of the tinted windows. *Maybe if I shoot the windows out, I can see where the hell those guys are.* He adjusted his aim toward the rear of the vehicle and fired. He cycled the lever and fired again.

He didn't see the door behind him slowly opening. Joker had been conducting the final check of the building before leaving and had reacted when he heard the shooting. He had been on the back side of the building and on the third floor. As soon as he heard the shooting, he started running toward the fight. Unfortunately, he had to stop numerous times to use the key card to pass through doors, plus he had to run down two flights of stairs. It had taken him the better part of two minute to get here. A lot can happen in two minutes.

Joker carefully pulled the door open until he saw the back of the man who was shooting at his teammates. He raised his pistol. The man was about twenty yards away. Suddenly, the man turned and ducked back in front of the vehicle to cycle his gun. He now had his back to the front bumper of the vehicle and was facing the building. That's when he saw Joker. His eyes went wide and he attempted to reacted to the formerly unseen threat, but it was too late.

Joker fired two shots in quick succession. Both shots hit the man in the middle of the chest and he simply dropped down onto his butt, still holding the rifle. He had a look of disbelief on his face. However, it was only temporary. As he died, his head fell forward until his chin rested on his chest. The Marlin 30-30 just flopped over onto his lap as if he had intentionally placed it there.

The man in front of the Ranger heard the shots and turned see Joker in the doorway. He raised his pistol and immediately fired five rounds in Joker's direction as fast as he could pull the trigger. It was nearly forty yards away, and the man's shots were fast and wild. They harmlessly impacted the concrete block wall near the door. However, they did force Joker to duck back inside the block structure for cover.

As this was going on, Loki had advanced to the rear of the Subaru and was on the ground, using the rear wheel for cover. He was peering under the car, but couldn't see much at first. Then he saw a flash of movement as the man shifted his position to shoot at the building. Loki used the ground to brace his gun and fired a single round, striking the man in the left ankle.

The man shrieked as he hit the ground, falling forward and out of his protected position in front of the Ford, landing hard on his right side. As he hit the ground, Mack stood up from behind the engine block of the now sputtering Subaru and fired three times into the chest of the fallen man.

Then, everything was quiet. Joker reemerged from the building, pistol up and scanning. He moved forward and checked the two men at the Toyota, confirming that they were both dead. He slung the AK and tucked the 30-30 under his arm. Loki emerged from the rear of the car and moved toward the fallen man that had been shooting the AR-15. He kicked it away and checked the body as Mack checked the last man. They were all dead.

Mack reached down and grabbed the Taurus, which was lying beside the man's hand. Loki picked up the AR-15.

The rush of adrenaline was starting to wear off and Mack let out a long breath as he thought about what was going to come out of this.

Loki glanced into the back of the Ford. "This thing's full of fuel cans!" He reached into the back and checked a couple of them. "Empty fuel cans!"

Joker called from the Toyota. "This one too."

Mack shook his head. "These clowns died over some gas." He leaned into the cab of the truck and plucked an ID card from the cup holder. Holding it up to inspect it, he announced. "This guy works here. He must have known about the fuel storage." He shook his head again, looking down at the man on the ground. "Idiot." He flung the ID card back into the cab of the truck.

The three men started back toward the Suburban. Loki was looking out toward the road, checking for any other potential threats. "Hey, Mack. I'm going to go secure that gate so we can do what we need to do."

"Okay man. Thanks," Mack responded.

"I'll go with him," Joker said.

Loki and Joker trotted off toward the gate.

Mack reached the Suburban and walked around to the rear. "Hey Rotor, that was some crazy..."

Mack saw Rotor on the ground in a puddle of blood. He instantly reacted and dove on him, placing pressure on the gaping wound in the right side of Rotor's neck. "Man down! Rotor's down! Get the aid bag!" Mack screamed.

Joker came running back while Loki ran to lock the gate. They didn't need anyone else rolling up on them while they were treating a casualty. Joker ran around Mack and Rotor on the ground and dove into the back of the Suburban. He dropped the 30-30 and snatched the aid bag up in one movement, pulling it back out and dropping to the ground beside Rotor. He unzipped the aid bag and opened it up. It was a clamshell design, so opening it up provided instant access to the different compartments. He ripped the Velcro open on the red compartment, which held the trauma supplies.

Rotor was coughing up blood. *He's still alive, we have to stop the bleeding and get him stabilized!* Mack was still holding pressure on the wound as blood seeped through his fingers. The blood that Rotor was coughing up ran down his cheek and intermingled with the blood from the wound. Joker pulled out some S-packed sterile gauze and ripped the top off.

"On three, I need you to move your hand so I can pack the wound!" He was nearly yelling, even though Mack was only a foot away from him.

"One, two, THREE!"

Mack withdrew his hand and Joker began stuffing the end of the gauze into the hole left by the 30-30 bullet. The gauze was soaking through as fast as he could pack it. Without stopping what he was doing, he said "Quick! Get me another one of these!"

Mack started to reach for the bag as Loki arrived. "Mack, stop! Your hands are covered with blood. I got this." Loki grabbed the next packet of gauze and ripped it open, exposing the gauze so it was ready to be applied to the wound. He held it out for Joker.

Joker grabbed the end of the gauze and continued to pack the wound. "We have to get him stabilized. Mack, check the pickup trucks and see if they're still running! We'll use one of them to get him to the hospital!"

Mack leaned down and put his hand on top of Joker's as Joker continued to try to get the gauze into the wound. Joker flipped Mack's hand away. "What are you doing?! I gotta control the bleeding!"

Mack put his hand back on Joker's again and spoke in a calm, even tone. "The bleeding has stopped, buddy."

"What are you talking about?!" Joker nearly screamed. He glanced up at Mack who was looking back at him. Mack had a look on his face that seemed inappropriately calm to Joker. He repeated his question. "What are you talking about?!"

Mack motioned toward Rotor's face with his chin. Joker turned and looked at Rotor. His eyes were closed, but his mouth hung open. Loki had his fingers on the other side of Rotor's neck, checking for a pulse. Loki looked at Joker and slowly shook his head. "He's gone, man."

"Damn it!" Joker screamed, letting go of the gauze. Without warning, he jumped up and took off running toward the Toyota with the dead man in front of it.

"Joker!" Mack called out to him.

Joker ran to the front of the truck and in one swift move kicked the dead man in the face. His head bounced up and back down, then the body slowly fell to the right and he landed on his side. Joker drew back his foot and kicked him in the face a second time, just as Mack arrived at his side. Mack put his bloody hand on Joker's shoulder.

Joker was breathing hard. He wanted to rip this man's body apart with his bare hands.

Mack gave Joker's upper arm a light squeeze. "Come on Buddy. Let's go. We've got work to do."

Over the Precipice

37

The Collective, Part III

August 15, 1:15 p.m., Earlier that day

Washington, D.C.

Nancy Pelosi came rushing out of her office, startling her secretary, Maria Sanchez. Maria jumped to her feet, surprised.

"Maria, Maria. Listen, um, I'm going to be going on a trip. I'm expecting Adam, um, Representative Schiff. Has he called?"

"No ma'am. The standard lines are still malfunctioning. Is your secure line not working?"

"It is, but he's not answering. I don't know..." Her face was flushed and she was clearly distraught.

"Look, we are, um, evacuating, so he needs to be at the airport absolutely no later than three o'clock. He should be on his way here. When he gets here, tell him to be at the airport by three. No...tell him two thirty. Do you understand? No later than two thirty! And tell him to charge his sat phone!"

"I understand, Ms. Pelosi. Do you have instructions for me?"

"Oh, I hadn't even thought about you. Uh, yes. I'm sorry. After you deliver the message, just report to the security desk. They should have a vehicle to take you home."

Maria offered her standard perfect smile. "I will ma'am, thank you."

Nancy turned without saying anything else and headed for the door. She had one of her large handbags with her. Maria considered asking her if she could assist, but decided against it. *No, she doesn't give a crap about me. I'm not going to worry about her. At least not anymore.* She settled back into her chair.

Maria let the mask of professionalism fall away since there was no one there to see it. She was worried about getting home. The crime on the streets of Washington was completely out of control. She hoped the security office really was still offering rides to the staff. They had picked her up today. If they hadn't, she wouldn't be here right now. She tried the phone on her desk again. It still wasn't working. *How had this happened? How could our enemies have targeted us so effectively?* At least she still had power at work. Her home had no electricity or water. They had offered the "essential" staff the opportunity to shower here at work, but she hadn't taken advantage of it. It just felt wrong.

She pulled out her cell phone and checked it. It was charged, but not connected to the network. She decided to distract herself with one of the games that didn't require internet. A few minutes later as she was engrossed in a game of solitaire, she heard footstep approaching. She quickly put the phone face down on her desk. Adam Schiff burst through the door.

"I need to see Nancy right now!" He didn't wait for Maria to announce him or open the door. He trotted past her and snatched the door open to Nancy's office. Seeing it empty, he spun on his heels to face Maria.

"Where is she?" he demanded.

"I'm sorry sir, but she's not here." Maria said, not bothering to stand up.

"I can see that she's not here. I asked you where she was!"

Maria smiled. "Sir, she was going home. She said that she needed to pack for a trip. I'm assuming it's the same trip that you'll be going on?"

"That's none of your concern! When is she leaving? Why hasn't she called?" He fired the questions at her back-to-back.

"Yessir. She said to tell you to pack whatever you needed and to be at the airport at exactly nine o'clock tonight. She hasn't called because she said the satellite communications have been compromised and that you shouldn't turn on your satellite phone for any reason. Apparently, it's some kind of security breach. Something about the Chinese tracking the phones. I didn't really understand. It was all really too complicated for me, or maybe I just don't have a high enough security clearance. I don't know, I'm sorry." She looked genuinely apologetic.

"Typical," he said disdainfully. His brow was furrowed as he glared at Maria. He was furious that she hadn't stood up to talk to him, but now was not the time. Without another word, he spun on his heels. He needed to get home to get his things. He only had seven hours before he needed to be at the transport. It was normally about a forty-five-minute drive to his home in Potomac. However, considering the state of things outside, it might take him twice that to get there. He still had time, but he needed to get going.

Maria Sanchez watched Representative Schiff disappear out the door. She opened her purse and removed her lipstick. She used the camera function on her phone to see herself and applied the lipstick, trying not to smile as she did it. She carefully replaced the lipstick back into her purse and stood up to leave. As she was about to walk out the door, she stopped and turned back to her desk. She had no intention of coming back. It was time to take care of herself for a change.

As she walked down the hall, her stylish heels clicking with every step, she imagined Adam Schiff arriving to an empty airport later that night and she couldn't suppress her smile. She glanced behind her to make sure there was no one close enough to hear her and said, "Checkmate, asshole."

Two hours later, the pilot spoke to Nancy in the cabin of the private jet. "Ma'am, I'm sorry but we can't wait any longer."

Nancy looked at the other passengers on the luxurious aircraft. There was one empty seat. "Hold on," she said, pulling out her secure satellite phone from her handbag. "I'm going to call one more time."

She dialed the number for the fifth time and she got the same recorded message indicating that the system was unable to locate the other phone. She huffed as she dropped it back into her expensive handbag and turned to the pilot. "Fine. Let's go."

She returned to her oversized seat in the front row as the pilots closed the door and a ground crew removed the mobile steps to allow the aircraft to depart. Nancy settled into the supple leather seat, fuming. She buckled her seat belt as the flight attendant pushed a loaded cart down the aisle.

The attendant was an early twenty-something black girl and she was *stunning*. She had green eyes and makeup that was so perfect it looked like it had been professionally done. Her neat uniform included a skirt that was just short enough to be sexy, but not so short as to be impractical. She smiled, showing her perfect teeth and leaned slightly toward Nancy as she spoke. "Would you care for something before takeoff?" she asked. Nancy glanced down and noticed that her blouse was cut to share just enough cleavage to get some additional attention.

I know why she got this job, Nancy thought. "Vodka, make it a double."

The young woman gracefully removed a glass and poured the drink, maybe adding just a little more than a double. "And for you, sir?" she asked, continuing to offer drinks to the other passengers. After serving five of the nine passengers, the captain made an announcement that they were cleared for take-off. The young lady made a quick statement that she would continue distributing drinks immediately after they were airborne then took her own seat, securing the cart in a compartment made just for that purpose.

As soon as they were in the air, Nancy retrieved the phone again. She hit the first number on the speed dial. A woman's voice answered. "Hello?"

"Tell him it's Nancy," she said without formality.

"One moment please."

A few moments later, The Chairman answered the phone. "Are you in the air?"

"Yes, but Adam never showed." The annoyance was apparent in her voice.

"That's fine," he replied. He didn't even seem bothered. "We have a long flight. Just get comfortable."

The flight to the Lihue Airport on the island of Kauai, Hawaii would take about eleven hours. The preparations were in place for the American members of the collective to weather the storm that was ravaging the mainland. Steel Global Group had been paid well for the custom-built accommodations that were to house the senior members, some of the secondary members, and a robust support staff. The Collective members from other countries had quarters there as well, but were not planning on retreating to them until they had a need to do so.

From the Lihue Airport, it would be a short drive into the mountains at the edge of the Lihue-Koloa Forest Reserve. The project had had been under construction for several years and was nearly finished, but all the living quarters were complete, furnished, and stocked with the finest of everything. They had bribed local officials to bypass the licensing and permitting requirements to siphon power from the nearby Mahipapa biomass facility. There was no need for that paper trail. The electrical needs of the compound were augmented by a sizable solar array that took advantage of the sunny location.

Water was supplied by an onsite water collection network, backed up by water provided from the Halenanahu Reservoir. In addition to the Lihue Airport, they would also have access to the miniscule Haiku grass airstrip that was reserved for short takeoff and landing aircraft, commonly referred to as STOL aircraft. The Retreat, as it was called, also had its own helipad that could be utilized if they didn't want to be bothered with more public facilities.

Communications had been a major undertaking, since private, secure communications were paramount to The Collective's activities. There were multiple backups, but the most costly had been running underground fiberoptic cables over a mile and a half and utilizing the local radio station's towers and infrastructure. This was in addition to the redundant satellite communications onsite. The communications room was manned by at least two people, twenty-four hours a day.

There were three private aircraft on their way to Kauai. They would arrive at different times in a pattern that shouldn't garner any unwanted attention. Nancy's husband would be on the one leaving from the west coast. She glanced down at her empty glass. *When did I finish that?* She turned and made eye contact with the young woman and held her glass up. The woman didn't bring the tray, but appeared with the bottle and another napkin, refreshing the drink.

Nancy knew the jetlag was going to be dramatic, so she opened her purse and withdrew a pill bottle. She had asked Maria to reverse the lid so it was easier to remove. *Maria. I think I'm actually going to miss her. She never made a mistake.* It wasn't long before Nancy was sleeping.

The next day, the five senior members who were present, gathered in The Chairman's private dining room. No secondary members were invited. Once the servants had retreated and closed the doors, The Chairman began the meeting.

"I trust you've all found your accommodations to be acceptable." Everyone around the table nodded.

Someone softly muttered, "Very nice."

Someone else said, "It's beautiful here."

He nodded then continued. "I've spoken with the other senior members who aren't here. Most of them will be making appearances from time to time, but for now, they send their regards. I don't want to rehash the entire hour-long meeting, so I'm just giving you the important takeaways. Obviously, we have time to discuss things in depth, but now is not the time for that."

"You all know that the current trajectory of things in the United States was not our original intention. However, we're adaptable. We always have been, which is why we've been so successful." He paused and looked over at Nancy.

"It also doesn't hurt that we always stack the deck in our favor," he added with a wry smile. This elicited a collective soft chuckle from the group. Nancy just offered a slight nod.

He continued. "Our analysis is that we can still make this work. One very positive aspect of all this is that we've effectively stopped Donald Trump. There is no reasonable way to expect an election in November, so we don't have to worry about Harris screwing it up anymore."

The laughter from the group was more pronounced this time.

"So, from that aspect, I consider this to be a significant success. The immediate plan is to relax. We'll continue our other global efforts to harvest money from the population and we'll wait this out for a while. If you get tired of this tropical paradise," he raised his hands to his sides, motioning around him," we have our additional retreat in Switzerland. Of course, that option is reserved for the senior members. We're not made of money."

This time, the group burst out into full blown laughter. The Chairman was laughing as well. He was enjoying this. Plus, he was in a good mood because he already knew about the surprise he had in store for the group later. "Obviously I'm kidding. Our latest haul from our various USAID projects has us set up for as long as we need." He waited a moment for the group to return their attention to him. "I'm sure you all know that we still have plenty of operatives on the mainland, tending to matters. However, the recent attacks on the powerplants seem to have done most of the work for us. I can assure you we have everything under control that needs to be controlled." He offered a smile that looked genuine to Nancy. Of course he was an accomplished liar, so it was hard to tell. He had spent years lying in front of the camera and was a master manipulator.

"For the time being, I want you all to enjoy yourselves. This evening I've already arranged for some young entertainment to join us. There will be plenty of girls for everyone." He paused as a smile crept onto his face. "And boys."

The faces around the table lit up. A couple of the men leaned in, whispering to one another conspiratorially and laughing.

"Until then, you have your valets if you need anything. We can enjoy ourselves in the lap of luxury while the mainland burns." He retrieved his wine glass from the table in front of him and raised it as if to toast. "And I say…" He broke out into a full-fledged smile this time.

"Let it burn."

38

We're In This for the Long Haul

August 15, 6:30 p.m.

Paul and Sandy's Farm

Paul reacted to the motion detector going off. Someone had just crossed the bridge onto his property. Paul had his pistol on his belt, but his rifle and body armor were staged by the door. He told Sandy and McKinley to wait in the house as he threw the plate carrier over his head and secured it in place. He snatched up his rifle and opened the door to go out. However, he immediately heard the sound of a dirt bike and grinned. He still went out to make sure it was his bike, but he suspected it was Scott arriving. Paul trotted to the corner of the house. Just as he got there, Scott topped the driveway and turned toward his house.

Paul stepped out so Scott could see him and raised a hand in a wave. Scott motored over to him and killed the engine. He dropped the kickstand on the bike and stepped off. Paul met him and the two men embraced in a hug.

"Good to see you, little brother," Paul said with a smile. That was a running joke with the two of them. Paul was older, but Scott was almost two inches taller and outweighed Paul.

"Good to see you too, *big* brother," Scott replied with a grin, slapping Paul on the shoulder.

"Come on in the house, I'm sure that was a helluva trip."

"Dude, you don't know the half of it," Scott replied, shaking his head.

The two headed in and Sandy and McKinley both ran up to Scott and hugged him. Scott looked around. "Where's Mom and Dad?"

"Come on in, man," Paul began, his expression changing from one of joy at seeing his brother safe to one of sorrow, knowing the news he had to deliver. He turned and started toward the table to sit down.

Scott didn't move. Paul turned back around to face his brother.

Scott spoke first. "They're dead, aren't they?"

Paul slowly nodded his head, barely enough to notice. "Yeah, brother." He paused, waiting for Scott's reaction, but Scott just looked down.

"I found them a nice spot down by the old fire ring by the creek."

Scott nodded slowly, before looking back up. His eyes were wet, but tears weren't flowing. "I saw the stain in the kitchen. I've been wondering ever since. What happened?"

"The neighbor boy killed them for their food."

Scott's face instantly flushed red. Paul saw both of Scott's hands close into fists. "That little punk with the cat? Well, we need to go find him...and kill him."

"I already took care of it," Paul said flatly.

"What?" McKinley asked. "What do you mean you took care of it?"

Paul had told Sandy the whole story, but he had only told McKinley that her grandparents had been killed. He'd left out the rest.

Paul turned to face his daughter. "Honey, you hafta understand the world we're living in now. There are people who will be more than happy to kill you for what you have. There's no way to call the police. We're on our own. There're a lot of people out there who have followed the rules in the past just because they didn't want to face the consequences of getting caught. With those repercussions taken off the table, those same people are going to do whatever they want." He glanced back as Scott before continuing.

"That guy down there was a bad person. He killed them because killing was easier to him than asking for help, or offering to work in exchange for food. He would have killed again. I'm sure of that. He needed to be put down. I just did what needed to be done."

McKinley just stood there staring at her father. She didn't know what to say. She knew he had killed people in combat before, but that almost didn't seem real to her. It was a long time ago, in another country. This was right here, and it had just happened. Her father hadn't been acting any differently, other than being sad for the loss of his parents. She was struggling to process all this.

"But...but...how?" she asked timidly.

"I'm not going to get into that. He's not going to hurt anyone else ever again. That's what matters," Paul said. He didn't know what to do here. Should he hug her, try to offer comfort?

He didn't think so. Her expression looked like a cross between shock and fear.

"Good," Scott interjected, breaking the silence. "I wish we could resuscitate him and kill him again."

"Uncle Scotty!" McKinley cried.

"What?" Scott asked. "I'm not going to sugarcoat it. He got what he deserved."

"Come on, brother. Let's get you off your feet. You look like you could use a beer."

"No," Scott said. "I look like I could use a whiskey."

Paul threw his arm over his brother's shoulder and led him to the kitchen.

"I think that could be arranged."

Paul leaned his gun against the wall and peeled off the body armor. He then reached for the gun that Scott still had slung. Scott passed it over and Paul put it next to the other one.

Scott slid out of the backpack and dropped it onto the floor as Paul retrieved two glasses from the cabinet and added ice to both. "I have a bottle I save for special occasions. I think we should use it to toast Mom and Dad."

"Mom wouldn't approve," Scott replied, accepting the glass of ice.

"Oh, I think she'd understand," Paul said. He didn't smile. He didn't cry. He and his brother were going to find their own ways to deal with their loss. He went to the cabinet and came back with a bottle of WhistlePig Farmstock Rye whiskey.

"I'm normally more of a bourbon guy," Paul said, pouring some of the liquor into Scott's glass. "This is rye whiskey, but it's out of this world." He poured his own glass, corked the bottle, and placed it on the table.

Scott smelled the liquor, but didn't say anything. Paul sat down beside him.

"I'm glad you're here, brother."

"Thanks, man." He sighed and held his glass up.

Paul raised his glass and touched Scott's lightly and they both took a sip.

Sandy and McKinley came over and joined them at the table. Sandy sat across from Paul and McKinley sat across from Scott. Scott looked over at McKinley and offered the glass to her. "You want some?"

Sandy put her hand on Scott's arm. "You don't have to be the uncle that's always a bad influence, you know."

Scott offered a slight smile. "What? It's not like the cops are gonna show up and arrest us for contributing to the delinquency of a minor."

McKinley cut in. "Dad has let me try whiskey before. No thank you. It tasted like gasoline."

This got a chuckle from the adults.

An electronic tone interrupted them and Paul quickly got up and walked over to the kitchen counter where the satellite phone was plugged in.

"Hello?"

Scott looked over at Sandy. "What is that?"

"Satellite phone," Sandy said. "It belongs to the security company that he works for."

"Ah," Scott said, taking another sip.

"Okay," Paul said into the phone. "Yeah, thanks for letting me know. Give me a call if there's anything I can do." There was a pause as he listened to the person on the other end of the phone call. "Yeah man. Thanks." He ended the call and turned back toward his family who were all looking at him. He walked back to the table.

"Well," Sandy said as a question. "What was that about?"

Paul sat back down at the table. "The team got hit at Winchester." He had a solemn look on his face.

Sandy leaned forward in her seat. "Is everyone okay?"

Paul sighed before replying. "No. Rotor didn't make it."

Sandy's hand shot up and covered her mouth. McKinley didn't say anything.

Scott put his hand on his brother's shoulder. "You good, bro?"

Paul was trying to process the situation. He and his brother were dealing with the loss of their parents and he gets a call about the death of his friend and teammate. "Yeah. He was a good dude."

"What in the hell is happening in this world, man? Mack said that the guys were trying to steal gas. They hit them at shift change. They think because that's when the gate would be unlocked." Paul shook his head.

"Did they get them at least?" Scott asked. He didn't know Rotor or Mack.

"Yeah, there was four of them. They killed them all."

This time it was McKinley who reacted. She gasped as her father said it.

"I don't understand all the killing," she said, standing up. "I'm going to my room." She turned and left the table.

Paul looked over at Sandy.

"I got this," Sandy said, following McKinley.

"Doc, Doc, this is Dangle. Over." Paul's radio came to life.

Paul walked over to his plate carrier and pulled the radio from the pouch. He took a deep breath before answering. "Go for Doc."

"Hey Doc, me and Copperhead are coming in."

"Good Copy Dangle. Over."

"Dangle out."

When Paul turned back toward him, Scott asked, "Who's Copperhead?"

"Oh, that's my neighbor, Tom. His radio callsign is Copperhead. I've mentioned him to you, but you've never met him. Really good dude. He and Dangle are our only real support network around here, well, besides David."

"Cousin David?" Scott asked.

"Yeah, but I haven't heard from him since things went dark."

"I hope he's okay," Scott said. He looked like he was thinking.

"I'm sure he's fine. He's tough. Plus, as much as he camps, I know he has some supplies stashed away. We've talked about it. One thing I know he keeps is fuel. He has a stand-alone fifty-gallon fuel tank and he keeps some diesel on hand too, for his skid steer, but I don't know how much."

"Yeah, but he's got Ashley and Grace to take care of too," Scott added, referring to David's wife and twelve-year-old daughter."

"That's exactly why I'm sure he'll be fine. He'd move heaven and hell for those two."

The motion detector went off again, but this time it made a different tone than when Scott arrived earlier. Scott looked toward the source of the sound.

Paul didn't wait for the question. "I have solar powered motion detectors around the property. Each one makes a different tone, so I know which one it is. That's the tone for the trail coming over the mountain. Dangle has been over there helping Tom out with a defensive position overlooking his property."

"Oh," Scott said. "I guess with all that's going on, that makes sense." He thought about that statement as he said it. A couple of months ago, if someone said they were preparing defensive positions for their property, they would have sounded like a nutjob. Somehow, now it sounded appropriate.

Paul grabbed the two rifles. "Let's go meet them," he said, extending the XM177 to Scott. They walked outside and Scott followed Paul around toward the back of the house. The other two men came pulling up in Tom's side by side.

"I thought you might have walked to save the fuel," Scott said as the two men exited the vehicle.

"Well, we would have, but I wanted to bring you some concrete blocks." He motioned to the rear of the machine.

Paul walked over and looked into the bed of the side by side. Several concrete blocks were secured in place with two ratchet straps.

"Are these extra? Do you have enough?" Paul asked.

"Yeah, these have been in the barn for years. My dad bought them forever ago for some project and I guess they were extra. We've been using them for miscellaneous projects here and there, but I know you said you wanted to add an overwatch position to your driveway, so I thought you could use them."

"Thanks man, I appreciate that. Oh," Paul said, looking back toward Scott, "this is my brother, Scott."

Tom stepped forward and extended his hand. "Nice to meet you. I've heard a lot about you. I'm Tom."

Scott accepted the handshake. "Nice to meet you man. Scotty."

Tom looked over at Paul. "I guess we're gonna need another callsign, ain't we?" He motioned toward Scott with his head.

"I guess we will."

Scott already knew Dangle. "Good to see you again."

"You too, man."

"Hey guys, let's head into the house, I want to fill everyone in on what's going on," Paul said, heading toward the front porch.

When the four men got back into the house, Sandy and McKinley were back in the kitchen. Sandy was pouring some sweet tea for McKinley.

"I'm glad you two are in here. I need to talk to everyone."

The table had six chairs, so everyone took a seat. The ice in McKinley's tea was clinking as she sat down.

Paul grabbed his drink from the table and finished the last little bit as everyone settled into their chairs. "I wanted to take a sec and make sure everyone's on the same page. Here's the way I see it: we need to plan to take care of ourselves for the foreseeable future. I think everyone understands just how serious this is. This power outage is countrywide and from the reports on satellite radio, it's catastrophic at the national level. Yes, we have generator power here, for now, but we need to be prepared to lose it."

McKinley tried to interrupt. "But Dad, if we don't..."

He stopped her. "Hold on, Honey. I need you to listen and understand, okay?" Paul knew this talk was probably more for McKinley than for anyone else. He hoped if she saw all the adults taking it seriously, she would be more likely to do the same.

She nodded and he continued.

"Everyone here is a prepper to some extent, but this is a whole new level of disaster. We've seen next to no response from the government, either local or national, so we have to assume that, at least for now, we're on our own. I'm going to work under the assumption that the federal government is trying to fix this and hopefully trying to track down the terrorists to prevent additional attacks, although I haven't heard any details on that. So, for now, we need to work together to figure things out. I have an inventory of most of my supplies, but it's certainly not an indefinite supply. We have our garden, but now I wish it were three times as big."

"I have mine too," Tom interjected.

"Yes, and Tom has his too. But you also have four mouths to feed over there yourself."

Tom nodded in acknowledgment.

Paul looked across the table. "Dangle, I think you ought to consider consolidating over here with us. I don't need an answer now, but just think about it. We can discuss it later." He turned his gaze to his brother.

"Scotty, I'll show you my security plan. You and I are going to need to stay vigilant, but we still have to get the work done around here at the same time."

"You got it," Scott answered.

"And Tom, you have your own place to take care of, so I'll help you with your plan as well. The bottom line is that help isn't coming any time soon. What we have is what we have." He looked toward his wife and daughter as he continued. "This is going to be hard work, but it *can* be done."

"Now, I'm still in communication with Mack and the boys." He suddenly realized that he hadn't informed Dangle of Rotor's death. That was going to have to be a conversation for later today.

"They're having a rough time down there in Kentucky too. Hell, everyone's having a rough time *everywhere*. We just need to plan to take care of our own and we need to do so with the understanding that we're in this for the long haul."

EPILOGUE

August 15, 8:30 p.m.

South of Kenova, Wayne County, West Virginia

Zamir looked around the abandoned cabin at his men and smiled. His entire world had transformed over the last few days. He had gone from leading the sixteen-man group that launched the opening attacks on America to the leader of a five-man group, one of many, that was about to start terrorizing its citizens. At first, it had felt like a demotion, but after the last few days, he realized that he felt free, even empowered. He felt as if the weight of a great responsibility had been lifted from his shoulders. He had accomplished his task. He was successful. Surely back home, they were singing his praises as a hero. The thought of it made him swell with pride.

He had been granted permission to make his own decisions, choose his own targets. He thought about the orders again: *Go into the population, kill the people.* He was ready to do that. The supplies they had brought with them would last a few more days, but it was time to start venturing out to kill and take what they wanted. He would follow the orders.

Zamir felt that Commander Assaf must have had great confidence in him to accomplish this mission without oversight. He had no idea that he was little more than another pawn. Commander Assaf had used him to complete a set of tasks. Those tasks were now complete. The commander had sent him and his men into the population to create havoc and terror because he assumed that eventually, it would get them killed. Zamir and everyone who had worked for him were all expendable. They were no more than disposable tools of the organization, and they had exceeded their usefulness. He

419

never had any intent on bringing them home. Instead, he gave them a mission that felt like a reward, but the unspoken truth was that it would eliminate his disposable force. Zamir was quite skilled in manipulating others. He was less adept at recognizing when Commander Assaf was manipulating him.

Commander Assaf had stressed the importance of destroying the John E. Amos Power Plant. He had led Zamir to belief that it was critical to the overall success of destroying America. It's not that it wasn't useful, but it hadn't even been in the top ten most important targets that had been hit that day. Teams had hit targets all over the country. Most had been successful. Others had achieved only partial success, and a few had failed altogether, but the impact had been significant enough to meet the desired end state: America was spiraling into darkness and despair.

Now, five days after the attack on the power plant, they were about to continue the efforts of sowing fear amongst the infidels. Zamir looked at the paper map spread in front of him. He had identified a few specific locations he wanted to hit, but he also viewed the entire surrounding area as a resource for supplies and targets. He had decided to try to avoid the larger cities for numerous reasons. They would be more difficult to hide in, they would likely already be imploding, and the resources would most likely be used up faster than in the rural areas. That made the urban locations a good option for raids or ambushes, but he wasn't going to try to stay in one. He not only needed to kill civilians, but he needed to be able maintain his own force. Zamir assessed that the rural areas were more likely to provide him with what he needed for a protracted guerrilla war, and he was looking forward to it.

APPENDIX

Gear in the Precipice Series

This list is not all inclusive, but I thought it might be fun to add it. There are things in the list from Book 1 and Book 2. If you like this, please leave us a note on The Precipice Series' Facebook page. Thanks!   -Charlie Mike

Firearms

- CZ P10C & CZ P10S (9mm)

- Glock 19 (9mm)

- Smith & Wesson 9 Shield (9mm)

- Smith & Wesson Model 638 (.38 Special)

- Smith & Wesson 380 Shield EZ (.380 ACP)

- Browning A-Bolt Hunter (.270)

- Marlin Model 336 (30-30)

- Remington 870 (12 gauge)

- AAC Micro 7, Remington Model 7 (.300 Blackout)

- Ruger American Predator (6.5 Creedmoor)

- Bergara Divide (6.5 PRC)

- MK13 Mod 5 (.300 Winchester Magnum)

- M24 Sniper Rifle (.308 Winchester)

- XM177 Special Forces carbine (5.56mm)

- MK12 Special Purpose Rifle (5.56mm)

- Ruger American (5.56mm)

- Ruger 10/22 (.22 long rifle)

- Ruger Precision Rifle Rimfire (.22 long rifle)

- POF USA Rebel (.22 long rifle)

- Tactical Solutions Owyhee takedown (.22 long rifle)

Firearms components and accessories

- Ruger BX-25 magazine (.22 long rifle)

- Aero Precision (Misc AR-15 components)

- Ballistic Advantage AR-15 barrels

- Noveske AR-15 barrels

- Dead Air Mask suppressor (.22 caliber)

- Surefire SOCOM300 SPS suppressor (.30 caliber)

- Surefire SOCOM556-RC3 suppressor (5.56mm)

- SilencerCo Spectre 9 suppressor (9mm)

- CCI Standard Velocity 40 grain ammo (.22 long rifle)

- Vortex Razor red dot sight

- Paul's leather holster: Craft Holsters model 141R

Other

- Mechanix tactical gloves

- Wheeler Engineering Professional Reticle Leveling System

www.ingramcontent.com/pod-product-compliance
Lightning Source LLC
Chambersburg PA
CBHW061542190726
48289CB00004B/1140